"The Nomad's Mission *is an exciting beginning to an epic saga of space exploration. Morrisey and his crew of daring, corrupt rogues will hold you breathless as they loot the wrecks of spaceships—until they find the one that could change everything in the galaxy."*

—Nancy Kress

"The Fields of Long-Forgotten Battles series by Robert J. Szmidt shows a truly remarkable imagination, and is told with charm and originality. I highly recommend it."

—Mike Resnick

"A fast-paced tale of a piratical salvage crew who find more than they expected when they discover an ancient Alien artifact. An engaging story."

—Jack Campbell

"Robert J. Szmidt writes on a vast canvas. His stories are ambitious space opera that will capture your imagination."

—Kevin J. Anderson

"With the right tech, it's easy to be a god. But as Robert J. Szmidt points out in this impressive novel, to be a god for the right reasons, sometimes you have to spend a few years in Hell, first."

—David Weber

I0591243

ESCAPE FROM PARADISE

THE FIELDS OF LONG-FORGOTTEN BATTLES
BOOK 2

ROBERT J. SZMIDT

WFP
WordFire Press

EBook ISBN: 978-1-68057-338-1
Trade Paperback ISBN: 978-1-68057-337-4

Cover design by Janet McDonald
Cover artwork images by Adobe Stock
Kevin J. Anderson, Art Director
Published by
WordFire Press, LLC
PO Box 1840
Monument CO 80132

Kevin J. Anderson & Rebecca Moesta, Publishers
WordFire Press eBook Edition 2022
WordFire Press Trade Paperback Edition 2022
WordFire Press Hardcover Edition 2022
Printed in the USA

Join our WordFire Press Readers Group for
sneak previews, updates, new projects, and giveaways.
Sign up at wordfirepress.com

DEDICATION

I dedicate this work to the memory of
Forrest J Ackerman,
whom I've met and called my friend
and
Mike Resnick, whose stories I've devoured
and who mentored me when I created this series.
May the Force be with you both.

PROLOGUE

THE VALIS 11 SYSTEM, ZEBRA SECTOR

09/18/2354

"How many stars are there in our Galaxy?" Commodore Garyan Zachs asked out of the blue.

The six recruits went dumbstruck. When just moments ago their new commander had been telling them about the Recon Corps' operations, and the upcoming missions, they'd been grinning like crazy. Now, you could virtually hear their jaws slamming shut.

"Four hundred and seventy-six billion," answered Danthony Reyes after a moment's hesitation. Sitting at the far-right end of the second row, this slim, short blond with an oblong face was the youngest conscript.

Zachs closed his slanting eyes with irritation. That was ABC of astronomy; everyone should know it, even a dimwit—not to mention a cadet of the Orbital Fleet Academy whose job was to reel off this sort of information in the dead of night after having been violently shaken awake. Unfortunately, there wasn't a single cadet in the small briefing room. Commodore Zachs faced mere run-of-the-mill civilians, lured from the space boonies by the promise of adventure. Only six of them, although he repeatedly requested for nine new operators.

Back in the day … he thought.

Back in the day, only the chosen ones found their way to the Inner Rim lying beyond the Inner Territories. Only best of the best could operate unmanned probes, which were sent outside of the Known Universe.

Today, when deep recon no longer meant contact with the unknown, the discovery and cataloging of new planetary systems fell on the shoulders of dweebs such as these boys—and a girl, Commodore Zachs corrected himself internally, glancing toward a skinny (much too skinny for his liking) female born and raised in one of the outlying orbital stations—whom he now was conveying to Valis 11, the outermost outpost of the Federation. And no wonder; during three hundred and thirty-two years of exploration conducted in the Orion Arm, no trace of advanced alien civilization was ever found. Thus, so far, nothing suggested that somewhere out there, among the hundreds of billions of stars, Humankind would eventually find intelligent extraterrestrial life.

Commodore Zachs smiled thinly. It wasn't quite true that the Universe was devoid of Aliens. He knew one—albeit unrepresentative—exception. The Xan 4 System with its two fighting races. The excitement he felt while watching the first messages from Beta was still vivid in his memory. Back then, he believed that he witnessed the birth of a new epoch; that he made history —not of the Corps, but of Humankind. Today, he felt only the bitterness of defeat, which wasn't even sweetened by a well-deserved promotion to commodore.

After long and close observation, the Aliens turned out to be very primitive creatures, in his opinion unworthy of being called civilized. As for the Admiralty … Well, the Admiralty acted as usual in such cases. They put a lid of secrecy on everything so that nobody except the handful of scientists and soldiers who had been assigned to the Two Suns project could find out about the breakthrough, which wasn't such a huge success as initially thought, although in the grand scheme of things the Corps benefited from it.

Manyfold budget increase, almost one hundred new probes and four extra deep recon bases in the Inner Rim simply had to accelerate the pace of exploration. And, in fact, within just six years, the Federation borders were shifted by a record-breaking eight hundred parsecs, albeit—despite the hard work of hundreds of crews and the exploration of more than twelve thousand further planetary systems—Xan 4 remained a glorious exception and, worse still, nothing indicated that this was going to change any time soon.

"Four hundred and seventy-six billion," repeated Zachs, turning his attention toward the recruits again. "In the second half of the twentieth century, it was thought that the Milky Way comprised about a hundred billion stars, but then, as the technology developed, this number began to grow rapidly. At the beginning of the twenty-first century, it was commonly assumed that there could be twice as many stars; fifty years later this number was doubled again. Today, we know with absolute certainty that at least four hundred and seventy-six billion stars circle the massive black holes forming the heart of our Galaxy."

He paused for a moment to activate the holo. "For simplicity, let's assume that there's half a trillion."

The lights in the briefing room dimmed, and a hypnotic lambent-light whirl appeared over the commodore's head.

"Milky Way … If we spent only a second to investigate each system, we'd need almost sixteen thousand years to fully explore all its arms. If we had as much as an hour to do it, we'd reach the last star in fifty-seven million years. The blink of an eye, isn't it?" he said jokingly, but the keyed-up recruits didn't notice that their commander tried to break the tension.

Only now did he realize that it must be the first such a far expedition into space for most of these young people.

"Unfortunately, the truth is much more complicated than even the most accurate estimates. Although the Corps now has more than three hundred modern, long-range probes, each mission lasts not seconds, not hours, but days, sometimes weeks. At this rate—unless we change drastically the methods which for now include combing systems one after another, sector by sector—we won't have colonized the place where the Orion Arm joins the Perseus Arm by the end of the millennium. Who will tell me why these star clusters are so important?"

Everyone raised their hands; after all, it was another no-brainer. This time Commodore Zachs chose the only girl of the bunch.

"Danaomi?"

"For whatever reason, wormholes connect stars within a particular arm of the Galaxy."

"That's right. The only known way to the neighboring Perseus Arm runs through this junction."

"And what about subspace travel?" the girl asked hesitantly.

Zachs sighed. Another thing he wouldn't have had to mention if he had been dealing with professionals.

"Subspace drive has three basic limitations. Firstly, technology: the most powerful reactors allow you to make jumps within the maximum range of one and a half parsecs. Secondly, time: spaceships of this type are much slower; wormholes make it possible to cover the distance of one light-year in less than fifteen minutes whereas with subspace travel we're talking two standard days. Thirdly, precision: for reasons unknown, we aren't able to predict the exact exit point. In addition, the farther we jump, the bigger surprise we're in for. Therefore, we use subspace drive only in local traffic, between systems very close together. You wouldn't want to find yourself a dozen billion clicks away from your destination, especially with a core overload. Or go straight into the scattered disk, not to mention the central star. And such incidents are reported several times a year."

He nodded sadly, recalling the fate of FSS *Magellan*, one of the first victims of the new technology. After the maximum range jump, it left subspace almost on the border of the local star's photosphere. The great research vessel evaporated in a split second, and High Command learned about its annihilation from the later analyses of the gravitational field.

"Let's face it. Until we reach the cluster of stars in the junction area, we can't even dream of traveling to other arms of the Galaxy—"

"Then why not take a chance and send a probe out there?" Zahartur Gavrylenko cut in. He was the only uniform among the six recruits: a police sergeant from a shabby mining colony, which name was practically unpronounceable. "This way we could get some answers without waiting for—"

Commodore Zachs raised his finger, thus cooling the recruit's enthusiasm.

"Do you think, kiddo, that nobody else came up with this idea?"

Disoriented Gavrylenko went silent; the others exchanged uncertain glances, and then looked to Zachs. Seconds passed until the uneasy silence was broken by Danaomi Ritter.

"The Corps has already sent probes to the junction?" In her voice, Commodore Zachs detected astonishment and even a pinch of disbelief.

"Yes. We sent a probe to one of the junction's globular clusters," he confirmed.

The New Russian, having reacted the way he did, stood out from the rest.

Chances are, he won't turn out to be a dumb tool in his superiors' hands, Zachs thought. *Maybe he'll even show some initiative, just like the officers who I used to work with once.*

"Forty-eight years ago—after a few decades of continuous failures on that front—the Corps Command finally convinced the Admiralty to take action. Hence, a super-long-range mission," he added, settling more comfortably into the cocoon of his chair.

"The probe was sent to a globular cluster located in the heart of the junction. The logic of our line of reasoning led to a conclusion that it's the only way from the Perseus Arm to the Galactic Center. If there is intelligent life in the Milky Way, then we'll find its traces right over there. High Command designated a special team with sixteen best operators, including me."

Zachs paused abruptly, as if he'd come to realize that the introductory lecture had gone awry; however, his hesitation didn't last long.

What the hell, he thought. *Maybe I'll inspire them. Maybe they won't skimp on performance.*

"Back then, we mapped the unexplored regions of deep space in a bit different manner than we do now. There were no van Vogt meters, which enable us to measure space warps. For that reason, our probe—on reaching yet another system—sent drones to all newly discovered gravitational wells to see where they were leading. When the drones returned, we put the data on the holomap and moved on to the next destination.

"It took three years and eight months to find the way to the junction. We made three hundred and ninety-four jumps, of which two hundred and sixty-eight were ineffectual. Sometimes, we had to go back eight or even ten wormholes to get on the right track again. But in the end, we came out on top." Commodore Zachs paused, then lowered his head.

"And what did you discover?" someone in the first row asked after a moment of awkward silence.

Zachs sighed heavily.

"Nothing. Nothing at all. Neither along the way nor in the junction, even though we were combing the globular cluster for almost six months, exploring every wormhole that we found there. All we came across were dead planets circling the most ordinary stars. We saw nothing new; nothing we hadn't seen before in the thousands of systems of the Orion Arm. Something snapped inside us.

"We must have realized, just then and there, that we wouldn't find intelligent extraterrestrial life. When the mission came to an end, we left the probe in the junction, along with a plaque informing of our existence, and returned to routine flights closer to the Known Universe. Another thirty-eight years—"

"Forty-four," Gavrylenko interrupted him. "If the mission began forty-eight years ago."

Zachs snapped out of his reverie.

It was a close call, he thought. *Luckily, I didn't blurt out the secret of Beta to these whippersnappers.*

"Yes, of course. I got distracted. Well, let's get back to the subject ... Tomorrow, I'll start instructing you in the procedures. Then, after you've passed all your tests, you'll be assigned—"

He paused again when a ruby icon appeared on the display of his console. It blinked steadily, informing him of an incoming call. Someone from Gamma, the terraformed planet circled by the Corps' station, was trying to reach him by means of audio-visual quantum transmission. It must have been urgent; otherwise, the mining colony's authorities would have never allowed such an overload, especially since their reactors weren't very efficient.

"Excuse me a moment," he muttered, activating the force field around his workstation and simultaneously turning on the holoprojector. A ghostly face of an olive-skinned, elderly bearded man with a hooked nose and deep-set eyes appeared on the opalescent wall. "Hello, Administrator Rami—"

"We have a problem with the monitoring station at the jump zone!" bellowed the administrator before his interlocutor finished the greeting formula. And instantly added, "Two hours ago we were notified of an increase in the activity of one of the gravitational wells—well number five, specifically— suggesting the arrival of a hyperspace vessel. A few moments later, the incoming data confirmed the jump had been made, and—"

His voice trailed away. Apparently, he needed to collect his thoughts. "And this is where things get weird. Five seconds later, we were alerted of another jump—in the opposite direction this time—and finally, the station went silent for good."

"It doesn't even ping?" Zachs began before he realized what he'd really heard.

Well number five led to a system still outside the Federation borders, so only the Corps' probes could use it. However, none of them was able to perform the maneuver just described by the administrator. The equipment needed at least six minutes before it could jump again.

"Can you check what's going on, Commodore?" Ramirez exploited Zachs's hesitation. Each second increased communication cost. "Your ship is now halfway between Gamma and the jump zone. It'll take you forty-eight hours to get there, five times less than any of our vessels."

Commodore Zachs swore under his breath.

The monitoring station failure caused a serious problem for the colonists, not to mention the Corps' base. All wormhole exits were located in a very narrow zone, only one-fourth of an astronomical unit from the central star's photosphere, precisely in the plane of the Milky Way's ecliptic. In short, if the average person could discern this anomaly, they would see a swarm of gigantic snakes, squirming behind the star, traveling across the boundless void of space. Appearances to the contrary, the Milky Way was not monolithic. Single stars, clusters, nebulae, all the elements of the whirl, which was a hundred and seventeen thousand light-years wide, swept through the void with various speeds, sometimes varying by thousands of clicks per second, so it was no wonder that the gravitational wells, which were connecting them, remained in motion too. It wasn't unheard of for them to tear and disappear—when excessively stretched—although this was extremely rare. Only two such cases had occurred over the past two centuries. Once, a red giant intercepted a sweeping by anomaly, divided it, and created a "transfer point" as it was described in the unofficial reports of the scientific department. Researchers kept observing the system in question to see if further star motion would lead to the merging of the bisected hyperspace tunnel.

No monitoring station meant no departures from the system. The traffic on Valis 11 wasn't the heaviest—only two of the six discovered anomalies led to the Federation territories—but the jump zone handled several, and sometimes as many as a dozen, freighters per day. Plus courier ships, teledrones, and personal vessels owned by people working in the Gamma and Kappa mines. Also, there were the Corps' probes, which used the other four wells. Forty-eight hours of intra-systemic flight—FSS *Walternest Rutheford* needed as much to reach the jump zone—would save the miners three, or maybe even four, days of demurrage. The repair vessels were really slow, especially in comparison with a mighty warship.

Another reason why Commodore Zachs was willing to help the colonists was the fact that it must have been one of the returning probes that damaged the monitoring station. For nothing that didn't belong to the Recon Corps emerged from the wells leading outside of the Federation borders.

"We'll take care of it," promised Zachs. He'd just noticed the administrator's twitching eyelid. Ramirez had also started to sweat profoundly. "If the station failure is our fault, we'll make all repairs at the Corps' expense. If the corporation's equipment has failed for some other reason, we'll settle up as usual."

Ramirez nodded quickly and terminated the connection without saying goodbye. Every second of this communication deprived his colony of valuable megawatts of energy. Zachs checked the time. They talked for almost a minute.

Miners won't be happy to see another blackout, he thought.

"Good news, everyone ..." he said, deactivating the force field. "Our flight will take a little longer than I initially thought. We're going back to the jump zone to provide technical assistance to the colony. Before we reach the base, we'll have the opportunity to practice the standard emergency and rescue procedures, which are a must when it comes to the final exam. You pass it, and you receive your basic access codes."

———

"That's odd ..." Zachs muttered, staring at the streams of data flowing across his holoscreen. "Check it again," he told the noncoms sitting at the circular workstations to his right. They were responsible for the communications and the sensors.

"Yes sir!" the answer came almost immediately. This was not

the time or place for discussion, although both the commodore and his subordinates were well aware of the fact that re-scanning would bring nothing new.

FSS *Walternest Rutheford* reached the jump zone earlier than scheduled, after less than forty-two hours of flight. Getting so close to the star required force fields set at maximum power. The *Minotaur*-class cruiser had no problem with that. Just as any other large warship, its shield generators had immense reserves even when the main reactor had been working at full capacity for hours; and that was exactly the case, because Zachs wanted to get down there as soon as possible and look into things.

Unfortunately, the Corps didn't have any recordings from the moment of the crash—for it must have been a crash, going by the slowly dispersing debris cloud—because at the time of the incident Gamma, the orbital station, and the seven transports which were now headed for the jump zone, were on the other side of the central star, much farther out than the cruiser. Thus, the sensor readings and previously intercepted quantum transmissions were the only evidence, which in Zachs's opinion didn't explain anything.

He repeatedly read a concise message, containing information about the activity of well number five. Then, there was an even shorter confirmation of the completed jump; and five seconds later, the sensors received another signal, indicating that the same object entered hyperspace. And that was it.

It just didn't add up.

Firstly, nobody expected the return of any of the eighteen probes exploring the neighboring sectors of space on that particular day. Secondly, all the equipment located outside of the Federation borders sent a feedback signal when the check was carried out. Thirdly, only one black box, namely that of the destroyed monitoring station, was found at the jump zone, and the data that were downloaded from it didn't help to explain the mysterious collision.

StarMin, which was exploiting the natural resources of Valis 11, was a typical profit-oriented corporation which was determined to economize at all hazards. Especially here, in the Inner Rim, where nobody had any regard for rules and people. In a civilized system, such an old monitoring station would have been scrapped long ago, but here it was expected to work for many years yet—if not for this unfortunate incident.

Of the three recorders prescribed by the rulebook, only one worked and it wasn't that great. Someone had disconnected its video module, probably to minimize the antique's CPU's load. Zachs wasn't particularly surprised when the information extracted from the black box by his technicians suggested that the meddling had taken place a few years ago. For corporations, quantum transmission was the most important; colonists could remotely control the extra-systemic traffic only in this way. The inability to determine the course of events in case of a potential accident was the least of anyone's problems. Whoever heard of the station's disintegration as the result of a collision with an object leaving hyperspace?

Commodore Zachs didn't recall such an incident, and he'd been on active duty in the Outer Territories for several decades. But—as his deputy once had said—there's a first time for everything. And as bad luck would have it, this unusual incident happened right here, right now.

However, Zachs established one thing beyond all doubt. The accident hadn't come about due to a defective probe. Thus, the Corps wouldn't have to indemnify the miners, but, on the contrary, they would receive a tidy sum from the administration of the colony for conducting a rescue operation and lending the equipment to replace the destroyed monitoring station until StarMin brought some junk to the Inner Rim.

Despite all, Zachs felt disquieted. He'd done the scanning and conducted a meticulous investigation, but he still didn't know what destroyed the station. Available data and subsequent analyses of the dispersing debris showed that several dozen hours earlier, an object emerging from hyperspace had collided head-on with the monitoring station. And that was the strangest thing about this.

Everyone living on a planet would say there was nothing untoward about it: after all, the huge monitoring station—a cylinder with a diameter of two hundred and forty feet—floated in front of the gravitational well's exit. It was as if someone put a graviplane right in front of a multilane tunnel of a transcontinental flyway. Something left hyperspace at just the wrong angle, didn't slow down in time, didn't make a turn when needed … Bullshit. In space, distances were so big that using planetary measures made no sense. The monitoring station floated in front of the gravitational well's exit, true, but half a light-second away from it. One hundred and fifty thousand clicks away from the place where the spaceships left hyperspace. In addition, its thrusters always set it in such a position that it ruled out a collision course with any of the arriving vessels. And even if they'd failed this time, the odds that a one-thousand-foot-wide object spewed from a tunnel with a diameter of one to three thousand miles would bash into the monitoring station were worse than winning Galotto three times in a row. This shouldn't have happened, unless …

Unless whatever came to Valis 11 was supposed to destroy the monitoring station!

The nature of the space warps indicated that a very small object had been involved, something with only one-eighth of the average probe's mass.

What could it be? What object, so little, could come from outer space? Commodore Zachs wondered as his displays came to life again.

Just as he predicted, the data filling his holoscreens remained the same. Whatever the trespasser was, it vanished without a trace. Each located piece of the debris came from the monitoring station. *Rutheford*'s mass sensors couldn't be wrong.

Slowly, Zachs stroked his smoothly shaved jaw. Had he just witnessed some large-scale illegal operation? He'd heard about private probes being sent to—yet unknown—parts of the Orion Arm. That way, the richest companies had tried to outrun competition in the resources race. Up until the civil war, they'd been able to legally acquire exploitation rights in systems explored by them; but then that policy underwent drastic changes and sixteen years ago, unexpectedly, the last gateway allowing for the big business to exploit the resources which were still waiting to be discovered had been closed. Zachs didn't know what had brought about this move, but he sensed that corporations hadn't given up so easily and were still doing their thing, albeit on the quiet.

Never before had he encountered illegal exploration, but in this instance he didn't rule out the possibility that the monitoring station had been destroyed by people who'd wished to conceal their return to the Federation territory. Actually, with every passing moment he grew more confident that this was the case.

If my instincts are right, he thought, *well number five will be activated again, and soon, and some corporation's research ship will try to enter Valis 11 to immediately make another jump to another system, most likely uninhabited, but lying on this side of the border. Two, three such jumps, and the blockade-breaker vessel will dissolve into thin air —or rather vacuum—and the scientists and data onboard will go to the corporate headquarters, of course after changing spaceships a few times.*

Zachs was sure of one thing: no space warps suggested that any of the five wells was activated after the incident; none of the van Vogt meters in the Gamma observatories, the Corps' base, and his cruiser had noticed even the slightest twitch in the gravitational field.

However, the commodore's theory had one serious flaw ... The last alert transmitted by the station, the one about the return jump, which the trespasser made less than five seconds after the arrival.

Zachs was certain that even the Fleet didn't have the technology which would enable so quick consecutive jumps, even though the military had best of the best working for them—and if anyone beat them to it, it was the mining industry research centers' personnel. Which brought us back to the corporations.

Six minutes. That's how long it took to return to hyperspace.

Zachs couldn't—and wouldn't—believe that the eggheads being on the payroll of some corporation or other had made such a breakthrough. Reducing that time by half seemed real; in the briefing room, the commodore had heard people divagating on the subject of whether it was worth investing in technologies which would allow similar performance. But accelerating this process seventy times over?

No, that's pure science fiction, he decided.

"Commodore Zachs!" A voice snapped him out of his reverie. It was Warrant Officer Honved, who oversaw the scanners on this watch. "The equipment registered increased activity of well number five."

So, I had it right! Zachs was pleased with himself.

The bastards who'd destroyed the station were coming back just now, sure of their ground. If they'd made a thorough reconnaissance—and Zachs couldn't imagine anyone who risked billions of credits flying blind in this situation—they must have known the freighter flight schedule and been aware of the fact that the colonists would need three standard days to do overhauls and regain full control of the gravitational wells. They couldn't have foreseen, however, that one of the Corps' cruisers would happen to be in close proximity to the jump zone.

"Red alert," Zachs said calmly.

He knew it wouldn't take much convincing to get his co-commander to agree that they should assure the malefactors a most hearty welcome. The crew could use some distraction, and, who knew, High Command might appreciate such a stance and maybe even reward them with something more than just a pat on the back.

"The space warp is getting bigger," the warrant officer reported. "The readings suggest that it's not just one object, but a few, and quite large at that."

It was a disturbing piece of news.

"How large?" asked Zachs.

"At least *Sword*-class." Honved was visibly upset.

Sword was the base model of the Fleet's corvette. From bow to stern, it was five hundred and seventy feet long, not counting the propeller nozzles behind its stern ruff. It still wasn't much compared to the full-size cruiser, but …

"If the readings keep increasing at this rate, we can expect craft the size of a third-generation destroyer." He turned toward the military commander after he'd analyzed the latest data provided by the warrant officer.

"Or a big freighter," Captain Attanasio piped in before falling heavily onto his chair.

Judging by the smell, he was in the mess hall when the alarm had gone off. Now, he didn't ask any questions; he'd assessed the situation before he reached the bridge. However, he didn't seem worried. He placed unwavering faith in the deterrent power of an almost twelve-hundred-foot-long warship, and he pinned even more of his hopes on the most advanced weapons systems. *Rutheford*'s firepower was comparable to that of some previous-generation battleships. Only a madman would want to engage in combat with such a might.

"Thirty seconds to the emerging of the first object from hyperspace!" Honved reported in accordance with regulations, although this information was on all displays.

"Okay, let's rock it!" Zachs said, nodding toward the battle stations.

Attanasio looked at him in astonishment.

"You want to kick their ass right after they enter the system?"

"No," replied Zachs. "But I don't think a little show of force will hurt. These bastards destroyed the monitoring station to conceal their return to the Federation territory. If they don't comply with our commands—"

"Yes, I know, three warning shots to the stomach, and then we start negotiations," Attanasio muttered, rubbing his fingers over the virtual keyboard. He typed a few commands and suddenly froze. "And if they are—" He paused significantly, casting a nervous glance at the navigational commander.

Commodore Zachs winced. He'd pushed aside the thought of Aliens early on. The very idea was preposterous. Now, however

—seconds before encountering the enemy—he felt a twinge of uncertainty. He realized that blockade breakers hadn't had to return to the Federation territory by way of Valis 11.

They could have easily slipped through one of the neigh-boring dead and unguarded systems, where they would have disappeared without a trace. So why had they decided on a place with—besides a large mining colony—the significant Corps' base?

"Ten seconds," reported Honved, breaking the commodore's train of thought. Attanasio managed to enter the last activation code before the final countdown began. "Three, two, one!"

Contrary to popular belief, there's nothing spectacular about emerging from hyperspace. One moment you look at the bottomless, black void and the next you see a peacefully flying object against the background of distant stars. Where there was nothing a millionth—even a billionth—of a second ago, the space suddenly "swelled up" (that's what it looked like, although the human eye was unable to see it) and when the bubble burst, a vessel leaving hyperspace appeared in its place, with no accompanying flashes of light, explosions, or discharges. Only supersensitive sensors were able to capture this phenomenon, but the subsequent holoimages didn't enrapture the observer. The first showed vacuum, the second a bulge, and the third a newcomer to three-dimensional space in its full glory. In addition, sensors registered gravitational vibrations, which propagated wave—likely around the jump point. Their intensity depended on an object's mass, but even the strongest could only be measured by van Vogt meters.

And this was exactly what happened now. However, Zachs, Attanasio, and the rest of the bridge crew held their breath as the tactical screen showed a bizarre object unlike any spacecraft built in the Federation shipyards.

Thanks to the drones spaced around the jump zone, Commodore Zachs could see several projections of the weird vessel. At first glance, it resembled an asteroid with a hyperdrive attached. Its hull was bulb-like, its plating—smooth, but ununiformly ridged—in the front part was covered by two rows of almost identical, oblate, concentric domes, and many smaller bubbles. Openwork structure topped off with a cube and several nozzles protruded from the narrower end. Objects number two and three, which appeared at one-second intervals, looked practically the same. *Rutheford*'s computers detected only minor differences in the plating and the distribution of the domes.

"Aliens?" Zachs and his crew whispered in unison.

The commodore shifted his gaze to Attanasio. The military commander sat stiffly upright, his mouth wide open, his finger within a hair's breadth of touching the pale red button of the virtual keyboard.

"Wai—" Zachs began, but didn't finish.

The alien flotilla leader opened fire.

From that distance, even a blind man would have hit a stationary target the size of a Federation cruiser. However, the warship, with its larboard to the gravitational wells' exits, was protected by force fields and only this saved it from immediate destruction.

But it was just the beginning of the scuffle. The second alien craft was already taking a firing position, and the third was performing a turning maneuver.

Attanasio snapped out of his lethargy just before the computers darkened all the screens so that the people on the bridge would not be blinded by the glow of laser-blasted shields. His finger jabbed at the red button. FSS *Walternest Rutheford* wasn't going to give up without a fight.

A swarm of rockets flitted toward the enemy, one volley after another fired automatically from all the rotary launchers, but the laser guns' batteries were still silent. An almost forty-two-hour flight at full capacity depleted most of the energy reserves, so rebuilding its stocks to regain combat readiness required time. Unfortunately, the *Rutheford*'s crew did not have it. They couldn't redirect energy from the shields either. The starboard deflectors had to work at full power to hold back the lethal radiation of the nearby star.

The Aliens destroyed most of the maneuvering missiles before they managed to reach their craft's deflectors, but concentrating the fire on more than four hundred additional targets gave the cruiser crew a brief respite. Too short, however, for the co-commanders to develop a new strategy.

A few seconds later, flashes of explosions mantled the rounded bow of the attacking craft, which—unfortunately—did not bring the expected results. The deflective field of the alien craft had absorbed the energy of thirty-seven five-pound kinetic rods sped up to 0.01 of the speed of light, no problem whatsoever. The weapon designed to disarm the largest warships proved completely ineffective against the shields of a new, alien enemy.

The deflectors of the bizarre craft glowed only after *Rutheford*'s turbolaser bow batteries finally opened fire. However, even consecutive series of invisible to the human eye millisecond rays, which could have run right through fifty-foot-thick blocks of plasteel, failed in the face of alien technology, albeit after the last volley the force field flickered for a while, and that could mean that it was starting to give out.

Unfortunately, *Rutheford*'s crew did not live to see it. The second aggressor opened fire shortly before the midship turbolaser batteries joined battle. The cruiser shivered as if it had hit some invisible obstacle. Alarms sounded, but they were quickly silenced by the technicians' hands.

"Shield Bb7 down!" reported a panicky petty officer, supervising the defense systems.

Section B7. A larboard stern. The central part of it. The bastards didn't shoot in a haphazard way! They knew exactly where to concentrate their fire. And they succeeded. *Rutheford*'s lights and computer displays flickered, and then dimmed for a moment as the systems switched to emergency mode.

Zachs didn't listen to the alerts, which were coming in from all directions. He already knew that he'd lost the battle—despite the fact that the stern battery was still in use, and rockets kept flying. The enemy took out their drive, cut off the midship and the bow from the main reactor. They lost ability to maneuver and could only dream of escape. The shields crumbled second by second and it was clear that they wouldn't withstand such fire much longer, especially in the situation when the third alien craft was looking to enter into combat any moment now.

Another impact; longer and heavier this time. If it hadn't been for the cocoon harnesses, the technicians would have fallen off their chairs.

"Ba7, Bb6, and Bb2 are gone. Bb4 at fifteen percent."

The opponent couldn't care less about *Rutheford*'s continued kinetic bombardment. The Aliens knew that even a hundred simultaneous hits wouldn't deactivate their shields. So they focused on the turbolaser battery shields and the bared stern, which held twin reactors.

"Get the base on the fucking line! Right fucking now!" Commodore Zachs growled at Honved, all jittery.

FSS *Walternest Rutheford*, the pride of the Recon Corps, turned into a cloud of white-hot plasma before the warrant officer managed to carry out his command.

PART ONE
INVASION

ONE

THE ANZIO SYSTEM, ZEBRA SECTOR

09/21/2354

Grand Admiral Farland leaned back in his armchair, standing on the one and only dais behind the oval conference table. Of the remaining twelve seats, just one was still free. At the other consoles, he saw the illuminated faces of his senior officers, forming the staff of the Third Metasector. Nine of them were present in the flesh, two participated in this meeting by means of quantum links. Their motionless holograms shimmered in the gloom under the dome ceiling of the briefing room.

Farland made no attempt to hide his anxiety. He gritted his teeth as if he wanted to crush the words he couldn't utter yet. Nebulae of red and blue veins adorned his slightly sagging, ruddy cheeks. His eyes flashed with anger. If looks could kill ...

When there was a quiet hiss of the sliding door behind him, he started, but didn't turn his head. The other officers followed his lead and pretended they ignored the latecomer. Only those who sat opposite the entrance watched curiously the athletic strider. In the dimness, it was hard to see any more details, but everyone in the room knew the man well enough to feel bad about what was to happen. Farland was already looking at the victim, stopped gritting his teeth, and clenched his jaw with such force his muscles twitched at his temples.

When I open my mouth—and it's going to happen at any moment now—Vice Admiral Duarte will regret everything, even the fact that he was born into this world.

The grand admiral was going to play it cool; he waited until the latecomer took his seat and activated his terminal. Farland intended to teach everyone a lesson, not only the head of the intelligence section.

However, when the light coming off the livening display illuminated Duarte, the tide of invectives didn't pour out of the metasector commander's mouth. For his subordinate precluded it, informing drily:

"Gentlemen, we're under attack, again."

Everyone moved nervously.

Farland, surprised at the turn of events, swallowed the invectives he had at the ready, which—judging by the look on his face—wasn't easy or pleasant. However, not being a wuss, he quickly got a grip on himself.

"Report, Vice Admiral!" he said before the murmurs ceased.

"Yes sir!" Duarte leaned over the virtual keyboard.

A moment later, the holoprojector mounted behind the conference table came to life, and the metasector's map appeared—with not just two, but three icons flashing red at the top.

"The Vandal System, Belt V, three light-years away from the Federation's border," the vice admiral began, and zoomed in, narrowing the field of vision to the selected space quadrant and then the aforementioned planetary system.

Finally, he focused on its three central stars and the jump zone, located almost in the plane of the system's ecliptic. "Twenty-three standard minutes ago, four enemy vessels entered our space. We've established that one of them most likely participated in the attack on Valkyrie 7—"

"Most likely?" the grand admiral interrupted him.

"Nobody can be one hundred percent positive that it was the very same craft—equally well, it could've been a similar vessel—

anyway, the dome arrangement and the shape of the plating are more than ninety-nine percent identical to the Valkyrie 7 records."

"I see. Carry on."

Duarte coughed before he spoke. He was starting to get nervous.

"The enemy showed up fifty-one hours after the local monitoring station had been destroyed. The Third Fleet strike force, stationed on Vandal, set off for the jump zone right after the first incident, but it's flying with minimal thrust, in accordance with the High Command's guidelines. At the moment, it is ..." Duarte checked the readings. "About thirty-five light-minutes from the enemy."

The holoprojector pulled back to the wide shot. The triple star system at which the jump zone was located receded, as did the bulb-like craft, and the officers saw a tactical formation consisting of a third-generation battleship, which resembled an airship, two cruisers, which looked like its miniature scale models, and sixteen spherical *Sword*-class destroyers.

"This time, the clones-of-bitches walked into a supernova," one of the officers said. The rest grunted their approval, and some even chuckled.

"I wouldn't be so sure."

The hubbub of voices ceased instantly. All eyes turned toward the hologram of not such a young man with a flat face devoid of any expression.

"What do you mean by that, Colonel Rutta?" the grand admiral asked.

"Thorough analyses of the material recorded during previous battles suggest caution when it comes to pronouncing on these matters."

"Could you be more specific, Colonel?"

The fact that the metasector commander spoke almost gently surprised everyone. Farland never handled his subordinates with kid gloves; if anything, he treated them in a very harsh or patronizing way, often abusing his power and exceeding his authority. Especially when put under pressure. No wonder that every officer in the briefing room was astounded when Grand Admiral Farland showed a total lack of aggression toward the low-ranker. They all looked more closely at the colonel nobody'd ever laid eyes on before, who—if you believed computers—was now thirteen light-years away from Anzio aboard a craft having no name and carrying only tactical markings. The latter also seemed very strange.

"Of course, Grand Admiral," said Rutta, undaunted. "Gentlemen, as you don't know me yet, let me say a few words by way of introduction. For the last couple of years, I've been investigating …" He hesitated. "The problem which—although only indirectly—we are dealing with now.

"For this reason, Grand Admiral Farland commissioned my team to analyze the transmissions from Valkyrie 7 and Valis 11. In both cases, the attack was carried out by a squadron of three vessels of unknown class. Their size conforms to that of our second-generation cruisers, but in terms of weaponry and shields, they are as good as the most modern battleships, and maybe even better."

He fell silent, but his words already provoked an impetuous reaction.

"Shut the fuck up!" Farland lashed out. He didn't have to repeat himself; it was dead quiet under the plasteel dome in an instant. "Please, continue."

"Thank you, Grand Admiral. Could you put on the holo showing *Rutheford*'s battle at the jump zone?" he addressed Vice Admiral Duarte.

"Of course."

The current hologram disappeared, replaced by a similar image—already familiar to everyone present in the briefing room. A cylindrical cruiser against the star's disc, and bulb-like ships flying one after another. Rutta took over control of the equipment, made a few adjustments, and soon they could see only the vessels involved in the battle. Then, he sped up the recording and stopped it only when the first shots were fired.

"Before we concern ourselves with the details, I'd like to point out one thing. I know that some of you tried to analyze each of the three previous battles. You became acquainted with the general sequence of events, and—" Seeing his colleagues' agitation, he added quickly, "And you assumed that there had been two separate incidents on Valis 11. One, the Aliens' attack on our cruiser at the jump zone; and two, their subsequent attack on the Corps' base and the colony."

He had to wait a moment until there was silence again.

"The problem is, nobody thought to approach it in a comprehensive manner. This is not criticism; unlike me, you didn't have access to all the reports. Some of the recordings relating to the battle with the Aliens are classified, so you couldn't see them; others, less important in your opinion, you simply missed out due to lack of time.

"But I have enough resources, both human and hardware, and so I'm able to look at the matter comprehensively. Needless to say, I came to some very interesting conclusions."

A murmur of excitement rose from the audience, but then, very quickly, silence fell with no reproof on Farland's part.

"Specifics, Colonel," the grand admiral said.

"Yes sir. I'll try to be brief." Rutta started the holopresentation, zooming in on the alien formation's image. "First and foremost, the enemy has better shields than we do."

"Better shields, my ass," snapped the shortest staff officer.

"I know it seems pretty obvious," Rutta smiled, "but I'll bet nobody can tell me why their force fields are so powerful."

Protracted silence proved him right.

Rutta typed another command. The hologram now showed only one enemy craft. Once again, they saw the rocket and laser barrage, which destroyed most of the targets in a split second, and then the surviving kinetic rods hit the front shields of the bulb-like hull before their eyes. Now, everything was happening in slow motion, plus the regular hologram was supplemented with computer graphics.

The alien craft's shields bulged and thickened in places just before the rods hit them. It was a very smooth process, as though the alien defense systems were not made up of separate generators, surrounding the craft with separate force fields, but formed one great shield, which could be strengthened in any place practically without weakening the rest of the force field. This was demonstrated by subsequent replays of the moment captured by a legion of sensors.

All watched it in silence. The discussion, which flamed up after the presentation, was cut off by the grand admiral.

"The floor's yours, Colonel."

"Thank you, sir. Here's another thing." Rutta took up the opportunity immediately. "I can say with complete certainty that the enemy uses absorption fields, not desorption fields, as had been assumed until very recently. Yes, I know," he added to calm the flurry. "We're familiar with this technology, although our top scientists believe that absorbing such huge amounts of energy is not and will not be physically possible.

"But you can take my word for it—whatever our scientists say, such shields exist and the Aliens use them. The readings from all three battlefields confirm it. The enemy's technology is almost completely based on energy absorption. The only way to deactivate such shields is overloading them, but to do that, you would need an unimaginable amount of energy delivered in a very short time.

"I don't think all *Rutheford*'s turbolaser batteries would have been able to take down the alien shield. According to our—very conservative, I may add—calculations, every alien ship can face our fourth-generation battleship and easily win such a duel. And why? Because it's not only about energy shields, but also about weaponry. Ours is inferior to the Aliens', it's as simple as that."

This time there was no oohing and aahing. The staff officers sat as if petrified and watched in silence successive graphs and simulations demonstrating the Aliens' technological and military supremacy on Valkyrie 7 and Valis 11.

Each time the enemy used only laser guns against the Federation ships. However, these laser guns were nothing like human-made turbolasers. In sixty seconds, *Rutheford*'s three-emitter turbobatteries could fire three five-gigawatt, one-microsecond volleys. This was their maximum rate of fire. And the problem wasn't the risk of overheating optical systems, but the lack of power. The gigantic cells which stored the energy only allowed for three volleys at a time, and their refilling took exactly one minute—provided the reactor didn't power the main drive at the same time, because the ion generators' demand made almost two minutes out of one.

Thus, the Fleet commanders tended to strike a powerful blow to begin with, which more often than not meant a three-microsecond volley or three successive microsecond ones, and then they fired a volley every twenty seconds, each time immediately after refilling the cells to one-third of their capacity. However, this tactic left commanders no leeway and, to be honest, it only worked in situations where one side had superior firepower.

It took Rutta just a few minutes to demonstrate that the strategy of the civil war—when almost all battles took place in the Lagrangian points—could be counterproductive in the face of the Aliens. With such an overwhelming advantage the enemy had, stationary or drifting warships were too-easy targets.

While the issue of maneuvering during the battle could have been solved provisionally with the help of solid-fuel auxiliary engines, the real problem was how to put up full desorption shields, which couldn't be avoided. Plus, continuous energy consumption necessary to sustain the force fields and replenish them after each hit also had a bad effect on the cell charging time —as *Rutheford*'s crew found out in the worst way possible.

The Aliens didn't seem to have such problems. Their numerous single-laser guns, despite their relatively high-power output, maintained their rate of fire. However, the pulse duration seemed to be the most serious problem, especially when it came to stationary targets.

Rutta's team discovered that—while attacking the Corps' station (which had very powerful reactors and layered deflectors designed to protect it against a massive kinetic or laser attack)—the enemy managed to take down the shields firing twelve-gigawatt, seven-microsecond volleys every dozen seconds, which with more than twenty battle stations located on a knobby bow gave the impression of a relentless cannonade.

The station simply couldn't withstand such a barrage.

Three minutes were enough for the Aliens to exhaust the deflectors, which protected the section connecting the generator's dome with the station's main body. After that, a couple of precise impacts sufficed to cut the gigantic structure in half and deprive the defenders of the most powerful source of energy. As the auxiliary reactors, overloaded to a point where it wasn't possible to squeeze another watt out of them, couldn't replace the main reactor—eighteen seconds later, there was nothing left of the pride of the Inner Rim, except for a sphere of rapidly cooling plasma and a debris cloud.

When Rutta finished, there was not one person in the briefing room who doubted the obliteration of the Vandal's strike force.

"Any suggestions?" Farland asked.

Duarte raised his hand.

"I think we should advise Admiral Khumalo of the danger threatening his squadron," he said.

"Any other ideas?" By way of reply, the officers shook their heads and quietly grunted their approval of the vice admiral's suggestion. "I see. I'm all for it too. Let's talk to *Silvana*'s commander."

The alien ship's hologram disappeared; only the Fleet's logo glowed in the dim light of the briefing room for a moment, and then the image suddenly brightened. An obese black man flickered to being in front of everyone's eyes. His face had an almost circular affect, and his eyes were so narrow that they were practically two slits.

"Hello, Grand Admiral, hello, gentlemen." The commander of the Third Fleet's strike force spoke in a husky voice as if he had a stuffy nose.

"We need to talk." Farland, as always, cut to the chase. "In private, if you don't mind."

Having said that, he immediately disappeared behind an iridescent force field, and the hologram darkened simultaneously. A short while later the remaining officers noticed that Rutta—or rather his avatar—also withdrew. Apparently, the colonel joined the conversation.

"Who the hell is this … what's-his-name …?" Duarte asked a supercilious woman sitting next to him.

"I have no clue," replied Admiral Schwartz, who was the head of the navigational section. Then she added, "I've never even heard of him."

"Anybody?" Duarte wasn't one to give up easily.

Silence answered him. One of the officers shrugged his shoulders helplessly.

That's strange, thought the vice admiral.

During the meeting, he'd tried to check who the man giving them a lecture was in the Admiralty's database, but he'd found no information about the last years of the colonel's service. The tactical number adorning his console hadn't been listed, which meant that the ship carrying him aboard wasn't one of the craft officially allocated to this metasector.

Rutta returned a second before the force field surrounding the grand admiral dissipated. However, Admiral Khumalo remained absent. Judging by Farland's expression, something went wrong.

"Gentlemen, you're dismissed. The next meeting's scheduled for seventeen twenty-six standard time, that is in exactly three hours," Grand Admiral Farland said, rising from his seat before anyone could ask him a question.

They all saw that he was pissed off. He gathered his things together quickly and left the room, not even glancing back. Thus, everyone looked eagerly at Rutta for an explanation.

"Colonel," Duarte said irritably. "Can you tell us what's going on?"

"You've got no clue, do you?"

"In my line of work, I prefer to rely on facts rather than guesswork," the vice admiral replied evasively.

"Khumalo refused to withdraw his ships," the stunned officers heard before Rutta's avatar disappeared again. "In three standard hours' time, he's going to attack the enemy."

TWO

THE BATTLE of Vandal began forty minutes later than originally planned. Admiral Khumalo—contrary to what the staff officers said about him—was not a complete idiot. He realized that he'd undertaken a difficult, or even impossible, task which was no less than a suicide attempt. However, there was a method to his madness.

Vandal's colonies were the most populous places in the Inner Rim. In local rare-earth-element mines, there worked more than twenty-six thousand people, who inhabited three planets and an orbital station, being also the largest and most efficient processing plant of helium-3 sourced from Gamma, the only gas giant of this system. The station had its own sub- and hyper-space drive, but it needed time to fully activate either one.

Thus, every minute gained thanks to the slowing down of the enemy could save not only the lives of hundreds, perhaps even thousands of people, but also salvage production facilities and raw material, which could prove indispensable to Humankind at the next stages of the war with the Aliens—for nobody doubted anymore that there would be a full-size conflict.

However, this wasn't the only reason why Admiral Berkofi Khumalo decided to fight despite a very small chance of survival for his strike force and crew. Another, no less important factor—especially from the High Command's point of view—was the need for checking to what degree alien ships exceed man-made equipment.

Having familiarized himself with Rutta's team's research results, which included thorough analyses of all previous battles, Khumalo undertook to explore the potential of the bizarre, bulb-like craft.

The admiral's plan, frequently consulted with the metasector headquarters, assumed that all forces would seek to damage or —if possible—destroy one of the four alien vessels that had entered the Vandal system.

At the cost of the lives of five hundred and twenty soldiers, sailors, and officers alike, Humankind could gain knowledge that would save millions, if not billions, of people, both civilian and military. At least this was what the slant-eyed Black man argued in a long conversation with Farland and Rutta, who finally succumbed to his arguments and agreed to help develop the most effective strategy for the upcoming battle. Admiral Khumalo also ordered to reduce *Silvana*'s and the rest of the strike force's cruising speed to the absolute minimum necessary to save a few percent of power and give Colonel Rutta another fifteen minutes to refine the plans.

The battle of Vandal started exactly at eighteen oh six standard time. An hour earlier, the strike force made a sharp turn and accelerated as if it was about to skirt around the incoming enemy and escape from the battlefield. The trick was supposed to make the Aliens go off the course which led straight to the inhabited planets. The enemy fell for that, and course-corrected.

Rutta was pleased—now he had tangible grounds for believing that the enemy, although so far undefeated—also made mistakes. Regardless of the outcome of the battle, Gamma's orbital station's crew had just gained an extra hour or two to coordinate the evacuation and make a subspace jump. That should be enough.

Unfortunately, Admiral Khumalo's situation was far worse.

———

The plan was simple. In the first phase of the battle, all ships would launch kinetic rods in the direction of just one enemy craft—even if the Aliens deployed their forces so that all their "liners" could take part in the battle (the Admiralty recommended the name "a liner" for an alien bulb-like vessel, because they always flew one after another). However, twenty nuclear torpedoes would be hidden among the swarm of kinetic rods. Rutta's staff officers decided that this was the most effective way of masking the bombardment with the kind of weapon generally used to attack spaceships with already deactivated shields. This time, however, nuclear torpedoes were supposed to ultimately overstrain the force shields weakened by the avalanche of kinetic rods and lasers.

The battleship's and cruisers' turbolaser batteries would open fire when the opponent concentrated on destroying the incoming rods. It was agreed that one three-microsecond volley was going to be used in order to intensify the barrage. Rutta and the two admirals hoped that six three-emitter, seven-gigawatt battleship's turbobatteries and just as many six-gigawatt cruisers' batteries would overpower the enemy's force field, or at least weaken it so that the nuclear torpedoes and—preceding them by fractions of a second—kinetic rods could finish the job. Especially that the latter would be eight times more numerous than during the clash with *Rutheford*.

These few seconds of the battle would be crucial—not for the people taking part in it, because they were doomed no matter what, but for the rest of the Fleet, as the analysis of the effects of this massive fire would allow the High Command to develop a successful strategy, and perhaps even win the next skirmish.

Everything that unfolded in the Vandal system was watched by the High Command thanks to thirty-six drones, which the strike force had launched several minutes before the battle began, just before making a turn toward the pursuing opponent. Those small devices packed with dozens of scanners and sensors broadcasted a broadband signal to three communication stations, drifting in a safe distance of fifteen light-seconds from the battlefield. Images and data reached the headquarters with a little delay, preventing them from interfering with the course of action, but no one cared. Such far-reaching precautions helped to maintain the key transmission, and this was the most important thing now.

The Aliens, as expected, changed their formation when Admiral Khumalo's ships appeared on their approach vector. Nothing in a hurry, though; they did it slowly and smoothly, as if AIs, not living beings, were at the controls of these ships. Two minutes before establishing contact, the alien vessels—which were flying in a linear formation—began to decelerate rapidly. The Federation's ships, larboard to the enemy, held a tight formation around the battleship. In this position, all turbolaser batteries of larger vessels could open fire simultaneously. Spherical destroyers, on the other hand, were spinning to be able to use the full potential of the kinetic launchers as soon as possible.

The officers gathered in the briefing room held their breath, seeing that the alien formation was approaching the point beyond which the strike force could open fire. Five seconds before the bows of the bulb-like craft crossed the red line, showing an effective striking distance on the holoscreen, the shields of the Federation ships flashed blinding white. The human eye could not distinguish the microsecond impulses, and the command center computers needed a tenth of a second to locate, process, and mark all targeting vectors; for this reason, the lines connecting both formations and relevant data were displayed after the officers saw the fallout through the polarized lenses of their tactical goggles.

The Aliens concentrated on destroying the smallest vessels of the strike force, leaving the battleship and both cruisers alone. The force fields protecting the spherical bows of the destroyers were unable to neutralize such massive amounts of energy—all at once there were six holes in the wall formation. When the last of the smallest ships turned into glowing plasma, the liners flocked to the cruisers as if they wanted to leave the battleship for dessert.

Khumalo could not hear the officers shouting; he was saving every watt of energy and his quantum communicator was also off, but even if they had been right next to him, he wouldn't have been persuaded to act faster. He waited for several—long as eternity—seconds before he gave his orders to the surviving crews: make the last turn and open fire.

Rutta gasped when he saw the swarm of red icons and, quickly replacing them, vectors swirling toward the chosen liner. Dense data strings appeared on the displays in front of him. However, he couldn't take his eyes off the gigantic hologram where the battle drew nearer and nearer to its decisive moment.

The battleship and the cruisers gave the alien craft a mighty volley. More than seven hundred kinetic rods and all nuclear torpedoes were flitting toward the target, and another three hundred kinetic rods would be launched before the turbolasers kicked into action.

Which is going to happen in three seconds, two, one ... Rutta thought, counting silently. Before he finished, the powerful batteries came to life. He couldn't see their rays because the pulse duration was unbelievably short. Within three microseconds, the light traveled only—or as much as—nine hundred clicks, and the distance between both formations was a hundred times greater. Eight-second flight if you took into consideration the sum of the speeds of ships on both sides.

The Aliens employed no evasive maneuvers, as if they didn't care that they were flying straight at thousands of missiles. As if they were sure they would deal with them without any problem. Their defense systems, like on Valis 11, began to eliminate targets with great precision and efficiency, even though three new rods replaced each destroyed one. Khumalo had one more ace up his sleeve, the multi-rods, which he used to the best of his abilities. The timing of the attack couldn't have been better. When the first wave of standard, single rods evaporated, two things happened: laser rays penetrated the front shields of the liner, and incoming missiles of the second wave fired their charges, increasing the number of targets tenfold. Thanks to this clever move, torpedoes —hidden in a huge mass of kinetic rods—gained the additional chance of breaking through the enemy fire.

The alien defense systems were unable to deal with such assault fire, even though three of the four liners had joined the battle. Multi-rods carried ten two-pound wolfram rods, guaranteeing quadruple attack force. And in the next half a second, more than three hundred missiles hit home.

The force fields, weakened by turbolasers, flared up. If it hadn't been for the band limiters, the people gathered in the briefing room could have been blinded by the sudden flash of light. However, even the best polarizers weren't fast enough. Before Rutta regained the ability to see, at least three seconds passed.

One of the officers must have had better sight, or he hadn't been looking directly at the hologram. The colonel didn't care which; what mattered was that the swarthy General of Special Forces groaned with disappointment before Rutta opened his eyes again. None of the nuclear torpedoes hit the target. Rutta would learn why much later, studying the reports.

At this point, he didn't have time to analyze the details. He squinted at the virtual battlefield. The Aliens had broken through the cannonade, turning one of the cruisers into a debris cloud. The vectors of now parallel formations resembled the double helix of DNA. The firefight continued, but it was very unequal. All the alien ships' lasers were focused on the other cruiser which withstood barely a second before going supernova.

Rutta closed his eyes again—he didn't want to see what would happen to the old battleship. He didn't want to think what would happen to the inhabited star systems either. If such massive fire hadn't been able to destroy or even stop the alien ships, the Fleet, scattered across many belts, had no chance of winning this war.

All available data would be analyzed by his subordinates in

the shortest possible time, but he could already advise the grand admiral of one thing: if people in the Inner Rim were to live, they should be evacuated immediately. He saw no other choice.

Anyone wishing to stop a squadron like the one currently flying deeper and deeper into Vandal would need to have a much stronger strike force. The very thought gave Rutta the shivers. The Federation didn't have enough equipment in the Inner Rim to protect even a portion of the border between its own territory and the uninhabited part of the Orion Arm.

THREE

THAT NIGHT, none of the command staff slept well. The night shifters—officers and noncoms alike—continued to labor over the reports from Vandal; they looked at them more than dozens of times, broke them down into sequences, then single frames, compiled data and summed up the results. To be thorough, four analyst teams were formed, working simultaneously. It wasn't just them who didn't get a wink of sleep. Even at this time of night, the station's crew crowded in clubs, canteens, and dimly lit cabins, watching those fragments of the battle that were made publicly available, and talking quietly of the strike force's destruction.

The grand admiral was no exception. He was sitting in the very heart of a gigantic station, separated from the crew by armored walls of the military command section, and watching the looped holo over and over again. He was most interested in the seconds between the first shot and the annihilation of the battleship.

The longer Farland stared at these images the more depressed he became. The bitterness of defeat quickly turned into sadness, and this in turn gave way to despair that sprouted overwhelming feelings of helplessness. For the first time in his life, Theodoreginald Farland—a man of success, moving up the Fleet ranks with the proverbial speed of light—felt ... insignificant. So what if he had several hundred warships and tens of thousands of people under his command if he wasn't able to stop an Aliens' attack?

When he couldn't take it anymore, he resorted to alcohol just like most of his subordinates. The only difference was that under the console he kept a bottle of really old whiskey from the Central Systems. A gift from his father on the occasion of his commissioning. It was distilled properly, on a planet with an oxygen-rich atmosphere, in real oak barrels imported from Earth. What it was distilled from, he couldn't—and didn't want to—know. It was enough that this whiskey tasted exquisitely and knocked him down hard, without condemning him to the special form of torture known as a hangover.

He took a cone-shaped decanter and removed its umbrella-like stopper. An ancient craftsman had tried to form the glass-ware into a futuristic spaceship. And almost succeeded. The grand admiral picked one of the glasses seated in the lining of the drink cabinet, looked at it against the light, huffed at it, and finally wiped a tiny spot. The glass was equipped with a microscopic antigrav, so he didn't have to worry about the lack of a flat surface on the console—it hung a couple of inches above the shining metal and lowered slightly only when Farland filled it with some amber liquid, but even then it stayed seemingly afloat.

After the fortieth replay, and the third round of whiskey, an orange icon flashed on his side display. Farland didn't notice it at first, but when the blinking caught his attention, he immediately tore his eyes away from the myriads of missiles, put the recording on pause, and activated the comlink. However, he enabled the sound only.

"Farland," he growled, and held his breath.

"Grand Admiral, this is Lieutenant Wagner from the communications section." The duty officer sounded normal; his voice was flat, devoid of any tension. *Hopefully, the news isn't bad at all,*

Theodoreginald thought. *Hopefully, the Aliens didn't attack again.* "I've just received an interstellar request to open a quantum link. Colonel Rutta wants to talk to you, sir."

Farland breathed deeply. Not yet, but … He might hear of the next damaged probe any moment now. Over the past forty-eight hours, another six monitoring stations in the farthest recesses of the Inner Rim had fell silent.

"Put him through," he said, instinctively reaching to his uniform collar.

After a moment's hesitation, Theodoreginald gave up buttoning his uniform. He'd known Franciscollin for years, so he didn't have to pretend to be a dull, devoid of all feelings, star-studded clone-of-a-bitch.

Where just moments ago were the alien shields covered with plasmic spheres appeared a bridge with a chair and the colonel sitting in it. Even though the lights at the command post were dimmed, and no people to be seen, Rutta immediately activated the force field, separating his console from the rest of the bridge.

Taken aback by the way his friend looked, he began uncertainly, "Grand Admiral—"

"Come on," Farland interrupted him. "Nobody can see or hear us. There's no need for this."

Franciscollin made a wry face. Time spent in the military changed him into a stickler—whenever he saw a superior, he recognized the proper manner of address out of respect. Even if he'd known them since childhood. He was surprised to see Grand Admiral Farland, the commander of the whole metasector, in a nonchalantly open-necked uniform and with a glass in his hand. On the other hand, just a moment ago he'd knocked down a stiff drink too—hoping that he would free himself of the burden. Except he did it in solitude, taking care not to have any witnesses of his weakness.

"But—"

"Come on," Farland repeated, waving his hand dismissively. "We've known each other since … since … since time immemorial."

"For sixty-five years," Rutta said.

"Yes. A very long time. This whiskey is almost as old as our acquaint—as our friendship." The grand admiral, already tipsy, lifted his glass to a silent toast.

The colonel just nodded.

"I've just received the final report," he said as Farland tossed off a shot of whiskey. "That's why I wanted to talk to you right after leaving hyperspace."

"This report ... it doesn't add anything new, does it?"

"We're not dealing with a worst-case scenario, true," Rutta admitted, "but it's not too good either."

"My boys have come to a similar conclusion—" The grand admiral glanced at the displays, checking yet another of the constantly incoming documents, then helped himself to one more shot of whiskey. "Go on."

"Spectrum analyses show that it was this close to destroying their shields."

"How close?"

"Nineteen percent."

"Only nineteen?" This information electrified Farland. He put his glass over the console. It looked much worse in the trans-missions from Vandal. "If these nukes—"

Rutta cut in, "Unfortunately, the bastards traced them unmis-takably, as if they were afraid of them. When it got really hot, they concentrated their barrage fire on the torpedoes in order to destroy them before the detonation as far as possible. Hence such a high hit rate when it comes to our kinetic rods."

"As if the Aliens were afraid of the torpedoes, you say ..." the grand admiral mused.

"That's how it looks," Rutta confirmed. "I don't know why yet, but it can be a very valuable tip for the future."

Farland nodded. That had to mean something. But what? Such torpedoes were usually used to depressurize ship plating. Khumalo had sent them in the second wave, just after the hail of kinetic rods, hoping that these weapons supported by the turbolasers would have overpowered the liner's force field. The Aliens, however, had gone the vole. They'd been willing to sacrifice their shields so as not to let a single nuclear torpedo near them. Intrigued, the grand admiral typed several commands, instructing the system to analyze the data concerning one specific moment of the battle. The results were in line with his expectations. From a tactical point of view, the Aliens were better off destroying more rods than torpedoes. The total force of the kinetic attack was more than double compared to the destroyed nuclear torpedoes. This was probably the only illogical behavior of the enemy observed during all the attacks.

"Maybe their nuclear weapons are much more powerful than ours?" he thought aloud.

"I doubt it," Rutta countered. "A warhead this size can't accommodate a teraton nuke."

"That's true."

Rutta leaned toward the holocamera.

"The tactics used by the Aliens shows that they know a lot about us. They strike precisely at the most critical parts of our ships, plus they don't give a damn about weapons that can't hurt them. It's almost like they know all the specifics. Meaning, they also know the warheads' force."

"So why—"

"I don't know. I don't know yet, but this discovery can turn our situation. On Vandal we were really close to success ..."

"Success?" the grand admiral snorted. "What kind of success? For all the gods' and godlings' sake! We lost more than five hundred men and nineteen warships. Just like that, in a heartbeat. And for what? To check the performance of some ... some ..."

"You're wrong," Rutta protested. "Learning what the maximum performance of the liners' force fields is, we have achieved our objective. And Khumalo knew what he'd signed up for," the colonel added. "If the Admiralty don't ignore our reports, his sacrifice will save—"

Farland raised his hand as if he wanted to silence him.

"Before we talk about the new orders, I'd like to ask you

something. Tell me honestly, just between us, what you'd do in my position."

"I'd order an emergency evacuation of the compromised systems and begin—"

"Wait!" the grand admiral interrupted him. "Suppose retreat is not an option."

"What do you mean, not an option?" The colonel was surprised.

"Suppose the Admiralty don't want to surrender even the tiniest piece of the Inner Rim."

"It's just plain stupid."

"I know, but … consider it anyway. Purely hypothetically, of course."

"Hypothetically, my ass! Be straight with me. Xiao told you—"

"Not Xiao." The grand admiral shook his head with resignation. "It's a direct order from the Council. We've got to stop the enemy at all costs. 'Not one step backwards,' Chancellor Modo said."

Rutta paused for a long moment. He checked something on the displays of his console, typed further commands, and studied the incoming data again. Finally, he raised his head.

"I'm sorry," he said, "but I don't see any other way out."

Farland replied with a crooked smile.

"Okay, let's try a different approach," he suggested, activating the holoprojector. An enormous map of the Inner Rim appeared between them. "I'll sketch out the plan and you'll tell me what you think. Whether there's something wrong with it. Can you do that?"

"No problem."

"Let's start with the basics …"

A few gestures and icons flashed around some of the stars. First green, then blue, and in the end red, most numerous. "These are our colonies, industrial installations, and the ships at the metasector headquarters. We keep watch over a hundred and thirty-six colonized systems and almost two thousand ones which aren't worth exploiting.

"To sum it up: we're still protecting one hundred and eighty —" He did some mental arithmetic, subtracting lost outposts. "One hundred and eighty-one planetary colonies and three hundred and twenty-six orbital installations, of which two hundred and ninety-one don't have propulsion allowing them to make a jump. According to the latest records our metasector is inhabited by six billion, one hundred and fifteen million, three hundred and sixty-five thousand, eight hundred and sixteen civilians. Not counting those who lived in the colonies we've already lost.

"These territories are to be defended by eighteen battleships and one hundred and seventy-five cruisers, over half of which are older generations. Also, we have more than three thousand destroyers, frigates, and corvettes. The bulk of landing craft and patrol ships at our disposal don't count in the slightest, because they're useless in space battles with the Aliens."

"I'm well aware of all of this," Rutta assured the grand admiral with a tone of urgency.

Farland was silent, but only for a moment.

"Let's create nine strike teams of similar firepower. Each will comprise two battleships, eighteen cruisers, and three hundred smaller warships, depending on their class and armament. I'm going to form them into three task groups and deploy them as follows—"

The grand admiral touched another virtual key and the red icons started to gather in Belt S.

"Why don't you send them closer?" Rutta asked.

"Redeployment of such a large force with logistical and tactical backup will take us about three standard weeks. At the same time, we'll lose all remaining inhabited systems from Belt V and about one-third from Belt U."

"I see."

"If your calculations are accurate, and I've got no reason to doubt it, two strike teams should deal with four enemy ships. To neutralize the alien liner's shields, I'll need to carry out a coordinated attack of one battleship, four cruisers, and a hundred, maybe a hundred and fifty, destroyers, but I'm not going to take any unnecessary risks. Therefore, each task group will consist of three task forces. Two will fight with the Aliens, the third will be on standby in case something goes wrong."

"Did you evaluate the effectiveness using the rates from Vandal?" the colonel asked, because in his opinion the calculations were off somehow.

"No." Farland smiled triumphantly.

"No?"

"Not only you've been busy, my friend. I thought hard about how Khumalo wanted to break the defense of these clones-of-bitches, and I found one very big mistake in his tactics. Look."

The first moments of the battle of Vandal reappeared on their displays. This time, however, the Fleet's attack looked different. The destroyers were in the second line, behind the battleship and cruisers so that the Aliens couldn't fire at them directly. This maneuver gave their crews time to launch extra hundreds of kinetic rods. The Aliens had to focus on defense, concentrating their fire on the myriads of incoming missiles, and the Federations' warships survived almost unscathed until they could open fire themselves.

Rutta checked the readings hastily.

"You've increased the effectiveness up to ninety-four percent," he said, making no attempt to conceal his satisfaction.

"Now think what we would have been able to do if we'd put up two of my strike teams against these four liners," the grand admiral said. "And fired two hundred nuclear torpedoes instead of twenty," he added, entering new data.

Another, even more impressive simulation showed the hypothetical clash of four latest-generation battleships and thirty-six cruisers with the backup of kinetic rods fired from more than five hundred destroyers, corvettes, and frigates. The onslaught smashed first the alien shields, and then the liners. This time the battle ended with complete destruction of the enemy, although the Federation's losses were significant too. Two battleships evaporated, the other two were badly damaged. As many as seven cruisers also were history, and another fifteen needed major overhauls, but—interestingly enough—almost all escort vessels survived.

The colonel, focusing on the foreground, didn't notice their massive retreat. Farland had everything figured out. The destroyers and the rest of the smaller vessels made subspace jumps immediately after firing the last missiles, so that the liners would have nothing to shoot at when they went past the main formation again.

"Any comments?" the grand admiral asked smugly.

"Only one," Rutta said calmly. "What will you do if they don't fight back?"

"Why wouldn't they?"

"They are not fools, and they've proven it more than once."

"That's true, but—"

"No buts, Theo. If you redeploy in such a way, you'll have two options. Or, you'll have to leave your strike teams in Belt S to react to further attacks with a delay. If my math's correct, your strike teams will appear in the attacked systems about six hours after the Aliens. Taking the fight to them won't be easy. If you block the jump zone, they will do their bit in front of your eyes and then disappear into subspace."

"We don't know if they have the technology to—"

"We're talking about beings who have equipment we can only dream about. Do you really think they haven't discovered subspace travel?"

Farland glanced at him furiously, but finally, he nodded.

"You're right," he said angrily. "We can't rule out this possibility, so I'm going for option number two. We'll follow them."

"To get them, you'll have to go at full throttle. For a day, maybe even two. And this will have a negative impact on the effectiveness of subsequent actions. You'll lose about thirty percent of the shield power."

"The remaining seventy percent will still be enough to beat the Aliens."

"Yes, but at the cost of more than double losses," Rutta said, initiating a simulation. "And we just can't afford it."

The grand admiral watched the unfavorable version of events with his eyelids half-closed.

"Any other comments?" he asked.

The colonel nodded.

"It would be more advisable to deploy these strike teams on the most valuable of the compromised systems and wait for the enemy there, but this in turn generates other problems. The Aliens may ignore the systems defended by the Third Fleet and storm into our space, unhampered ..."

"I'm beginning to understand why the Inner Territories' headquarters so eagerly complied with my request for their best analyst," said the grand admiral, reaching for his glass.

"You'd have me agree with everything you say?"

"No, my friend. This is not a drill, it's a war, and my mistakes can have catastrophic consequences. That's why I'm asking you for help, not the sycophants. Just speak your mind, would you? Nobody likes being criticized, but I'll get over it."

He poured himself another glass. "And if I don't, props or no props, you'll have nothing to worry about. I'll have you posthumously rehabilitated, like all other pesky advisors."

They both laughed.

"What else can go wrong?" Farland asked.

Rutta entered some additional data to run a new simulation. This time ten bulb-like ships appeared opposite the strike teams.

The grand admiral straightened up and watched the holoprojection with an intent gaze. When it finished twenty seconds later—and after there was nothing left of his strike teams but the clouds of debris—he started adding extra teams furiously and ran simulations until all of them pitched into the fray. Success, finally, but at what cost!

"Just one battle will strip you of all the battleships and almost three-quarters of the cruisers," Rutta concluded, as the computers spit out rough estimates. "You can't afford it."

"Even if this Pyrrhic victory will mean the end of alien invasion?" Farland asked.

The colonel looked at him with pity.

"Do you really think that these ten liners are all they have?"

The grand admiral shook his head slowly, as if with disbelief. "Are they just scouts?" he croaked, remembering the reports about further monitoring stations that had been lost.

"Yes, my friend. In my opinion, we haven't seen the real invasion fleet yet."

"What's your advice?"

"I've already told you."

"If we withdraw from the Inner Rim, we'll take this war to the Inner Territories," Farland said.

"Yes," Rutta admitted. "But by implementing my plan, we'll gain time. The Admiralty will be able to redeploy the remaining fleets. Maybe it'll even get down to building the fifth-generation ships, which we've been hearing about for several years now."

"What about the Council's order?" the grand admiral asked.

Here's where the rub came. They could convince the Admiralty, sooner rather than later, but politicians weren't soldiers—they would remain unswayed by even the strongest arguments. For them, the ships and crews were just numbers in the statistics. The only exception was an election campaign, when politicians begged citizens for votes, but it was still sixteen years away.

"I'm sending you some documents." The colonel looked his friend in the eye. "Read them carefully and convene a briefing at oh seven hundred standard time. By then, I should already be on site."

FOUR

THIS TIME there were ten people gathered around the elliptical table—Farland, Rutta, plus eight commanders of the Third Fleet's sections. Starting at the top, these were: Admiral Gerdagmar Schwartz, the navigational section chief, and Admiral Anselmodesto Bonaventura, the logistics section chief. Then General Adambrose Wexler, the operations section chief, General Toshikochiyo Kaneda, the armaments section chief, and General Achilleon Rulescu, the communications section chief, who were all sitting to the right of Bonaventura. Spindly Rear Admiral Standriej Lee, incessantly scribbling in his virtual notebook, was in command of the shipyards and mobile repair and renovation units. Colonel Modestiepan Korolenko, sitting shoulder to shoulder with Lee, represented the security section. The seat next to Rutta was occupied by Vice Admiral Allandreas Duarte, the Third Fleet's intelligence section chief.

"Less than fifteen minutes ago, I spoke to Earth again," Farland said, breaking the tension. "Unfortunately, the Council upheld their earlier decision, so we have no choice but to undertake all necessary and possible measures to stop the invaders."

He raised his hand to calm the subordinates, and when they finally fell silent, he added, "Colonel Rutta will outline the plan we worked on last night. I'd like to hear your opinions, but"—he raised his hand again—"after the presentation, not earlier."

Everyone nodded and looked at Colonel Rutta expectantly.

"Ladies and gentlemen," he started. It wasn't his intention to drag the briefing out. "The Council's order puts us in an extremely difficult situation. We all know that an open battle with the Aliens will lead to rapid extermination, not only of this sector but also of the whole Third Fleet. To put it bluntly: if we follow Order 3-79/54, we'll lose the war. That's why the grand admiral and I have decided to use a certain stratagem—"

"Am I hearing correctly?" Schwartz interrupted him. "Is this about circumventing direct orders given by the Supreme Council of the Federation? It would be an act of betrayal!"

"You're hearing it wrong, Admiral!" Farland roared, and he smashed his fist down on the table.

"Colonel Rutta was clearly—" The young, not even sixty-year-old brunette, with an olive complexion and a prominent nose on her slender face, wasn't going to give up.

Theo had warned his friend that Schwartz might be the most cantankerous, being one of the latest-generation senior officers who'd been waiting too long now for a chance to prove their worth, especially on a battlefield. In Rutta's opinion, she was ready to fight to the last man, unless someone told her to plant her tight, round bubble ass on board one of the ships. And he itched to make it happen.

"Silence!" the grand admiral lashed out again. "This is a serious discussion, not shooting the breeze in the canteen! Behave as befits the Fleet's officer!"

Gerdagmar's cheeks burned, but she didn't say a word. She sat proudly as an offended princess might, showing that it wasn't over yet.

"We will carry out the Council's order," Rutta professed. "However, we'll do it in such a way as not to lose all the ships and crews.

"To get back to the main point … If Grand Admiral Farland is right—and I'm two hundred percent sure that he is—then the recent attacks on our border systems are just the beginning of an invasion on a much broader scale."

They did not grumble at his words; every officer in their right mind had already concluded the same thing.

"The action we've seen so far, involving a few liners, is a classic combat reconnaissance. We don't know how much time we have left, but one thing is for sure: if we want to stop the Aliens' march, we've got to change our strategy, totally and utterly."

This time they nodded; it was obvious to them too.

"Let's sum up some basic facts ... Firstly, the enemy did a thorough reconnaissance. They know where to strike, and are doing it with surgical precision, which may suggest they have agents on this side of the border."

This stirred everyone up, especially the security and intelligence section chiefs. Rutta paid them no heed.

"Secondly, the Aliens have shields and weapons that we can only dream about. To have a fighting chance of winning with their liner squadron, we would have to send a dozen, maybe even several dozen, of our heaviest warships with adequate escorts. Still, the simulations show that our losses would be enormous. Unless we used everything that's stationed in the Inner Rim."

Schwartz nodded excitedly. This idea suited her to a T: a gigantic battle, one that the whole Galaxy would remember for centuries.

"But I'm not sure it's the wisest solution," added the colonel.

"Why?" Duarte asked. He didn't mean to say anything at all, it just slipped out of his mouth. A moment later he hunched forward as if he was gearing himself up for Farland's wrath.

Calmly, Rutta replied, "Because it can be exactly what the enemy wants. If we concentrate the Third Fleet in one of the systems nearby, we'll be an easy target for the armada which is lurking somewhere out there."

He gestured at myriads of stars beyond the imaginary line marking the Federation's border. "Twenty or thirty liners would be enough ..." He paused to emphasize the next sentence. "And yet there may well be a hundred of them."

Rutta achieved the desired effect. He'd built the tension and then gave them time to think. Now he could get down to specifics.

"We have no idea how big the Aliens' fleet is, that's true, but only a madman could believe that their military power is restricted to those ten ships. The most recent attack was preceded by reconnaissance. If you'd read the reports, you'd have noticed that the enemy knows what tactics to use with us. It was no coincidence that *Rutheford*'s weakest points were targeted straight off.

"I doubt that the Aliens—who know our defense capabilities and are aware of our determination—believe they can defeat the Federation with just ten warships. Even having such technological advantage, they would lose this war, because sooner or later the Federation would redeploy a large part of the remaining four fleets here, and that would be a real game changer.

"Taking this into account, we began to wonder what the enemy had in mind when they attacked Valkyrie 7, Valis 11, and Vandal. There's probably more than just one answer to that question, but we figure that the Aliens' actions were meant to provoke us to concentrate the Third Fleet so that it would be easier to destroy it with one decisive assault. It goes without saying how such an unprecedented defeat would affect the morale of the people inhabiting other metasectors. That would be the end of the Federation."

Everyone agreed with the colonel. Even Schwartz nodded.

Rutta continued, "That's why we should change our approach. From now on, our main goal will be to hinder or halt the enemy's progress. The Federation needs time to gather all the strength and implement new armaments programs without losing much of its Fleet."

"Are you talking about the fifth-generation warships?" General Wexler asked.

"Among other things," Rutta said, before the grand admiral

opened his mouth. "Let's not veer away from the subject," he added quickly.

"Here's what we suggest. The Third Fleet will be regrouped into nine strike teams, each of them comprising three smaller flotillas. Within the next two weeks we'll deploy them in Belt T. Here, here, and here." Some red icons flashed on the holographic map of the metasector. "This will enable us to respond to a crisis situation as quickly as possible."

"Does that mean we'll give up Belts V and U?" There was pure indignation in Schwartz's voice.

"Yes." Once again, Rutta was faster than the grand admiral, but this time he looked at him pleadingly. Now was the right time to enter into a dialogue with these people. Farland also understood this; his head moved in an almost imperceptible nod when he allowed his subordinate a little more freedom.

"You have my permission to ask single questions. However, I don't want this discussion to descend into chaos!" he said.

"In that case, let me ask what about, and I'm quoting, 'not one step backwards'?" Gerdagmar smiled triumphantly.

Got'ya, she thought.

"One thing does not exclude the other, Admiral Schwartz," Rutta replied with such calmness as if he was giving her instructions how to reach the nearest maglev station.

"We're going to redeploy our ships from deeper zones to the Inner Rim, which isn't stepping backwards." He smiled maliciously. "Besides—contrary to popular belief—the Council members are no idiots, and Highest Admiral Xiao has already approved all main aims and objectives of our plan and also agreed to conduct mediation. Even if he meets with resistance, the new directives will arrive long after the redeployment is completed."

"Nevertheless ..." Schwartz began.

"That would be question number two," Farland restrained her immediately. "Let's close the book on this matter. Please continue, Colonel."

"Yes sir. Before I get down to details, I'd like to draw everyone's attention to the one aspect of the invasion that we haven't discussed until now."

The section chiefs looked at him expectantly.

"Since the appearance of their first liner, we have received no message from the enemy. I don't know if it's just me, but they're behaving as if in their eyes we were—" Rutta fell silent. It seemed that he was looking for the right word, but in reality, he knew what he wanted to say perfectly well, he just preferred someone else would do it.

"Vermin," Colonel Korolenko said finally.

"Yes." Rutta smiled at the security section chief. "They're treating us like vermin. As if we were worthless, not able to communicate with them. As if we were a plague that needs to be eradicated.

"You've all seen the messages from Valkyrie, Valis, and Vandal. After *Rutheford*'s destruction, the Aliens remained at the jump zone until they annihilated all our drones. Then they went deeper into the planetary system and started firing at the Recon Corps' station and colony installations. On Valkyrie, it was the same; the enemy didn't leave the system until they wiped out all our installations in space and on the surface.

"The latest report said that they'd also launched some sort of long-range cruise missiles targeting our ships with no sub- and hyperspace propulsion as well as the relay stations located in the farthest parts of the system. Based on this, we can expect that the alien squadron which has defeated Admiral Khumalo's task force will soon organize a similar purge on Vandal."

"Everything seems to indicate that," Duarte agreed. "We're closely monitoring the alien crafts' progress, so we know that seven hours ago they split up and set their course for the most important installations in the system."

"Do you have any news about the helium-3 orbital mine?" Rutta asked.

"The first evacuations came immediately after the attack. The station will be ready to jump in four and a half hours." Duarte consulted the report. "Long before the alien liner arrives on Gamma. But that's probably the only good news."

Rutta ignored the last sentence.

"From what we can see, it's obvious that the Aliens' aim is not to conquer our space but to exterminate Humankind. If so, let's use this knowledge to our advantage. Why not give them something to do for months, maybe even years?"

He glanced at Admiral Bonaventura, the squat logistics section chief, and Rear Admiral Lee, who was the antithesis of the former. There was no realization in their eyes. The colonel nodded his head sagely—just a few hours ago he would have been as perplexed as they were now.

"How do you want to do that?" General Wexler cut in.

"In a very simple way," Rutta replied. "Since they're bent on erasing us from the Galaxy's map, we'll provide so many targets that they'll need weeks to deal with each system. Even if they come in greater numbers, they'll get stuck in the Inner Rim for months."

"You've just said that their combat intelligence worked us out," Duarte pointed out. "If they have such a detailed knowledge of our warships, they should also be aware of which systems we've colonized so far."

"They should," the colonel admitted. "But if you look at the pattern of their reconnaissance devices—"

"Are you talking about these strange probes that fly into our space and disappear after a few seconds? The ones that destroy the monitoring stations of our jump points?" Colonel Korolenko inquired.

"Yes, them. They're scouts. They leave hyperspace for a few seconds, record all the signals, and disappear before we can respond. If a target seems promising, an alien squadron arrives a couple days later. Please note, however, that these probes appear not only in the inhabited systems. Of the seventeen reported incursions, only five systems were colonized."

"If they are as smart as we think, they'll quickly see through our stratagem," General Rulescu butted in, momentarily damp-ening the enthusiasm around the table.

"Why do you think so?" Farland asked.

"Well, it's obvious," the chief of communications section said. "All they've got to do is analyze the radio signals that we've emitted recently."

Rutta bit his lip. The skinny Black man, who didn't look like someone who spent all day long in front of a computer console, was undoubtedly right. Although …

"Yes and no," Colonel Korolenko said. Of all the people in the briefing room, he knew most about tapping. "This part of the metasector was colonized just a few years ago, and as you all know, the radio waves travel at the speed of light, so they can't have gotten too far. If we set traps in Belt T and farther, the enemy won't be deceived. Signals from that part of the meta-sector will reach the Frontier in ten years or more."

"But from Belts V and U, they could have already reached the nearest star systems," General Rulescu insisted.

"So what?" Duarte snorted. "The Aliens are much farther."

"What makes you think that?" General Wexler asked.

"They need about fifty hours to send combat craft," the vice admiral explained. "Hyperspace allows you to travel a light-year in fifteen minutes. It's not a question of technology, it's simple quantum physics," he added as an afterthought.

"So, their base may be located twenty-five parsecs from the Federation's current boundary. In Belts plus twelve, fifteen, or eighteen."

"Who says that they need so much time?" Schwartz snapped. "They may well be lurking in Belt plus one or plus two."

"I doubt it," Duarte responded. "Such location wouldn't be a good idea. Listen to this, my theory is more likely. It doesn't have to be about maximum distance. Ten jumps from the border—" He did some calculations. "That means more than seven thousand probable locations. And with each belt, this number is increased by hundreds of systems. One neutron in a tokamak."

"Come on," Schwartz snapped. "Give me people and equipment and I'll find the Aliens in a week."

"Maybe you would," Duarte admitted. "But at the cost of sending hundreds of patrol ships or other small reconnaissance craft. Not to mention the fact that the Aliens could have already locked jump points in Belt plus five, let's say. I would do it," he added, seeing that the ambitious head of the navigational section was opening her mouth again. "In this case, we'd lose a lot of ships and crews, and we wouldn't get anything in return."

Schwartz squinted her almond-shaped eyes threateningly and blurted, "You can't wage war and not suffer losses!"

"So very true," Farland said. "You've just volunteered, am I right? Your bravery and courage will show our pilots the way. You've won me over to the extent that I'm willing to grant you the permission."

She shot him a withering look, which would have disheartened him if only he'd cared.

"It's not what you meant, Admiral Schwartz?" he added, seeing that she went a bit pale. "Then I'm sorry, I took you for someone who values the lives of their subordinates and stands strong in the face of danger."

"There are probes," she said through clenched teeth.

"There are," General Wexler admitted. "But not as many as you might think. After the Valis 11 base was destroyed, we lost communications with one-third of the equipment, and most of the probes from other stations were reversed immediately after the alarm, so—"

"Still, it's worth the trouble," Rutta interrupted him, glancing at the dais. "We need to talk to the Recon Corps. Their probes can comb farther belts when we do what we've got to do closer to the border."

"Duly noted," Farland muttered.

In the meantime, Schwartz smirked at the intelligence section chief. She had to settle for a micro-victory, offered by Rutta who didn't want her to disturb him any further.

"Well, back to the point," he said, capturing everyone's attention again. "Our plan is to send transport craft to all systems in Belts T to R. Their task will be to deploy satellites in the orbits of the planets and create fictitious footholds on the surface of every celestial body. In short, these systems must seemingly teem with life—"

"Great idea!" Duarte said. "It could work."

"Oh, I don't know," Admiral Bonaventura mused. Then, encouraged by the grand admiral, he added, "What about scanners detecting life forms? Such an advanced civilization must have them, right?"

Once again, they all looked at Rutta.

"We'll have to populate these systems," the colonel said after a long moment of reflection.

"What do you mean?"

"The Fleet has thousands of auxiliary ships. We'll deploy all of them; that is, everything we don't need to engage the enemy in defensive and aggressive actions. Let these people and their equipment enrich the background."

"And I am the one who willingly condemns subordinates to death?" Schwartz snorted.

"In this case, they can die of boredom at best," replied Rutta. "As soon as the alien liners arrive in the system, an evacuation order will be issued immediately. Our boys will simulate a panic escape and after pulling the enemy deeper into the systems, they'll make a subspace jump. Upon returning to their bases, they'll be sent to farther belts."

"Wait a minute." Rear Admiral Lee, who'd been silent until now, looked around gloomily.

"Yes?" Rutta turned to the spindly chief of repairers.

"Who's going to handle the evacuation if nearly all transporters are assigned to this operation?"

The colonel wasn't able to answer this question right away. The rest were also reluctant to open their mouths. Finally, Theodoreginald broke the silence.

"That's just a technicality which needs fine-tuning."

Lee, who didn't look any more cheerful, said, "Then you

should hurry, because the Aliens may appear on Warsaw 74 and Winder 9 any week now."

These two systems were the largest colonies in Belt S. One hundred and thirteen million people inhabited the oxygen-rich planet on Warsaw 74, and another seventeen million were dispersed throughout the colonies on four globes encircling the red giant called Winder 9. Evacuating so many people from the front line would require a lot of effort and plenty of equipment, and the latter was too scarce to handle both operations at the same time.

A deathly silence reigned in the briefing room. Rutta was skimming through his notes while trying to come up with a way to reconcile fire with water. Finally, the solution dawned on him.

"We can do this if we change our approach a bit," he said.

"To what? Evacuating the civilians, or building false targets?" Farland asked.

"The former. We are going to move people the whole way to the Inner Territories, which means that the transporters will have to make a dozen or so jumps in each direction."

"Correct. This needs to be done right. Nobody wants to repeat the same operation with cumulative populations."

"I know, but the situation calls for more desperate measures."

"Meaning?"

"Let's evacuate people only to Belt Q. There we have several large orbital stations which we can convert to transit points. If the Second Fleet arranges further transportation, everything will run smoothly."

"Milowicz would have to work in our metasector," Schwartz said.

"I have nothing against it," Farland professed.

"Me neither," Wexler echoed.

Korolenko was third, followed by Duarte. Gerdagmar didn't wait until the others declared themselves; she just let it go. Allowing another fleet to conduct operations in one's metasector was unprecedented. It wasn't something the Admiralty might approve of—however, Rutta was right: desperate times required desperate measures.

When the colonel glanced at his superior, Farland promised, "I've got it."

Admiral Bonaventura, who for some time had been paying more attention to the displays than the discussion, raised his head suddenly.

"I have an idea," he said. "Related to the subject. I might just know how to compensate for losses caused by giving up some of the transporters."

"We're all ears," Farland said.

"Since the issue of shifting the border no longer exists, we could make use of all the private equipment that's been collected to build new colonies."

"Go on."

"Almost two thousand megaprinters are sitting in the magazines of the corporations which have been granted new exploration licenses. So, we can create not only the impression of systems teeming with life, but also entire fictitious colonies."

"That sounds expensive."

"Not at all!" The logistics section chief was indignant. "We're sending our ships there anyway, so transporting the megaprinters won't cost us a thing. And when placed on the surface, this equipment will take care of building material by itself. The installations don't need to be functional, so it's enough to put up some buildings only. Our boys will cram some old electronics into them, thus creating a pretty successful mirage of real colonies."

"Excellent," Farland commended him. "And when the work is done, the printers can be moved to other systems."

"Without the slightest difficulty." Bonaventura turned to Lee, who was sitting beside him. "Standriej will help us."

"That can be arranged," said the chief of repairers. "Unless you try to fight with the Aliens at the same time," he stipulated after a moment's thought. "Then, judging by the simulations that I've seen here, I'll have my hands full with the shipyard work."

"The corporations won't like it," Korolenko said wryly. "I bet they've already sent freighters to move these printers to the other Rim. Capital doesn't tolerate losses."

"Any suggestions?" Rutta asked, knowing that the esdee was right. The corporations wouldn't give a shit about the war effort and the Aliens' attacks as long as the latter didn't threaten the Central Systems, but then, of course, it would be too late.

"We could confiscate their equipment," General Wexler suggested. "By decree of the Admiralty, or even the Council."

"The Council would rather shoot you dead than abridge the privileges of those who fund their election campaigns," General Kaneda said bitterly. He knew what he was talking about, because as a very young man—long before he joined the Fleet—he'd tried to bring down the system. This information was still in his personnel file.

"How about ..." Bonaventura said uncertainly, as if his idea scared him. "We could tell the corporations that their equipment is irrecoverable. Because it was sent to Vandal just before the Aliens' attack and—"

"That's a good one," Duarte laughed. "However, the corporations won't be easily outsmarted. For instance, how do you want to explain the fact that the Fleet happens to have identical but non-inventoried equipment?"

Two staff officers spoke at the same time. A quarrel was brewing, but Rutta wasn't having any of it. One look at the dais was enough.

Farland reacted immediately, "Shut your black holes! We'll start moving the equipment to designated systems as soon as the time frame is agreed. Legal issues, leave them with me. Is that all?"

He looked at Rutta.

"If you don't mind, I'd like to make a suggestion," Kaneda said hurriedly, seeing that the grand admiral was about to end the briefing. "How about we mine the jump points in randomly selected systems?"

General Wexler gave him a stink eye. Nobody in the Fleet

liked mines, especially those who served on warships. In their view, it was one of the vilest types of weaponry—sordid and foul. However, this wasn't about people but the Aliens, whose goal was to annihilate Humankind.

"I'm all for it," Schwartz said before the chief of operations section had a chance to speak.

"Me too," Rutta backed her up, surprising not only Wexler. That was it, he realized. Nuclear mines, which the Aliens will encounter unexpectedly right after they leave hyperspace. "But we've got to play it smart."

"What do you suggest, Colonel Rutta?"

"We'll mine the jump points, but only after an alien probe visits the system."

"I see." The armaments section chief grinned. "Those clones-of-bitches will be in for a surprise."

You've no idea, the colonel thought before he realized that such a trap could only be set once. It meant he still had to work on his plan.

"One more thing," Farland said. "The evacuees can't know the real reason for leaving the Inner Rim."

"Why not?" Schwartz queried, and several officers supported her.

"The Council wishes so," the grand admiral explained. "Panic is the last thing we can afford."

"What are we supposed to tell our people?"

Farland and Rutta exchanged a quick, meaningful look.

"The official version. That one of the stars in Belt Zero is going supernova. It's a very unstable but surprisingly fast process. Science has no explanation yet."

"And who's going to believe it?" Lee snorted.

"Someone will spill the beans anyway," Wexler added.

"For now, few people know about the invasion," Farland said calmly. "Let's keep it that way. Personnel seconded to this operation will consist of officers and sailors, so far stationed in the farther belts and having no idea what's going on. Those who know the whole truth will be delegated only in exceptional cases, for instance when there's risk of coming into contact with the Aliens."

"You want us to lie to our people?!" Schwartz bridled at the very suggestion.

"There's no other way." The colonel spread his arms helplessly. "This is the lesser of two evils. Our scientific department says that panic caused by the Aliens' attack could be catastrophic."

"And how are you going to curb the colonists who managed to escape from Valkyrie, Valis, and Vandal?" asked Lee.

"As we speak, all of them are being gathered in separate sectors, specially designed for this purpose and cut off from the rest of the Federation. They're going to remain there until the situation becomes clear," the grand admiral replied.

"Besides—as you probably know—by the order of the Admiralty, on the very first day of the attack quantum communications censorship was implemented and commercial traffic was discontinued in the Inner Rim. It seems that—at least temporarily—these incidents are a secret. Let's hope it stays this way."

PART TWO
DAY ONE

FIVE

THE ULIETTA SYSTEM, ZEBRA SECTOR

10/23/2354

"We'll emerge from hyperspace in three, two, one …"

The computers came back to life, the panoramic screens of the control room suddenly full of images depicting the nearby star and its planetary system. FSS *Djangonzalo Cervantes'* crew would have to rely solely on the sensor readings for another six minutes. Visuals were to be back when the massive cruiser did an about-face and the central star disappeared behind its stern.

Immediately, the first reports sprang up on the command post screens. They were soon followed by more data. The vast majority were calmingly green; orange could be seen only here and there, but that was to be expected. The ship's shields worked with maximum capacity, and some generators were experiencing local overloads. Not something that could jeopardize the mission.

Henryan looked through the alerts without focusing too much on them. That was technicians' job. Fairly routine procedures which they'd gone through hundreds of times since joining the Fleet. He saw them around him in the dim light of the large bridge. They were working in quiet concentration, like machines. He didn't notice any signs of anxiety or nervousness.

They'd keep a cool head until they saw red on the displays in front of them—

"Damn," Henryan swore under his breath, seeing a flickering ruby dot in the upper right-hand corner of his display. With a tingle at the base of his skull, he opened a brief report sent from the navigational section. Nothing was wrong with his ship, but besides the cruiser, there were colonist arks as well as more than sixty transporters in the convoy. Failure or loss of any of these vessels would mean serious problems. This mission had received the highest priority—though why, Henryan had yet to find.

He didn't even know why he'd been given orders to hand over the command of the evacuation operations to another officer, but he hadn't challenged them, and despite the protests of the despairing colonists, he'd immediately left Uganda 6.

In Belt S he'd joined a newly formed convoy—or rather a motley array of colony ships, transporters, and warships, hastily withdrawn from other squadrons in this part of the Belt—and after receiving further directives, he'd made a jump to Ulietta. As he hadn't had time to organize a proper briefing then, now he was worried that one of the accompanying civilian vessels started to fall apart, jeopardizing the entire operation.

He read the first sentence and felt overwhelming relief. The report was not about the convoy, but about one of the Ulietta's planets.

"What do you think, Commodore Hines?" he asked, turning to the cruiser's co-commander, a young Latino with deep-set black eyes and an aquiline nose. When on the bridge, within earshot of their subordinates, they always addressed each other in accordance with regulations.

Javiernesto was flipping through the Fleet's astroatlas files to check previous entries. When he was done, he shook his head decisively.

"I've never heard of such a classification error," he said. "It's just impo—"

"We're on the intercept course." Darski's next words were drowned by a message from the navigator's post.

The side screens filled with star-studded blackness of space and the front one showed the Galactic Center, on which background gleamed eighteen globes of the Ulietta system. From this distance, they didn't differ from the stars in any way, but luckily, the computer marked them with special tags.

"Delta's scan," barked Hines.

"Aye aye, sir."

They were heading toward the ecliptic plane of the system, so at this moment, Delta could be seen at the top of the domed screen. They had to crane their necks to detect it. Soon, however, a tiny white spot began to grow, and a few seconds later, it obscured the view, taking up most of the gigantic holoscreen.

The majestic blue and white sphere looked like the truest oxygen-rich planet. At first glance, it wasn't much different from Earth, partially hidden beneath the dense veil of clouds, covered with russet outlines of continents and sapphire oceans—including intrinsic polar ice caps.

"It's impossible," Hines repeated, shifting his gaze to Darski.

According to the astronavigational atlas, they should have been looking at a radiation-scorched, devoid of atmosphere piece of rock with not even one ice crystal, not to mention a living bacterium. At least this was what the long-range recon analysts had stated while classifying the globe, and what later had been approved by the Astronavigational Committee. Exactly the same information was to be found in all the documents of Etoile Blanc Corporation, which had an exclusive license to exploit Ulietta's resources.

"Has it been terraformed?" Henryan asked incredulously after he'd shaken off his initial shock.

It was the first oxygen-rich planet he'd seen with his own eyes. In all the Known Universe, which comprised five metasectors, there were only thirty-seven globes having their own atmosphere, and only twenty-nine of them were oxygen-rich; that is, Earthlike to the extent that people could live on them after introducing some changes in the ecosphere, more commonly referred to as terraforming.

"No," Hines disagreed. "Over four years, you can make significant changes to the composition of the atmosphere and begin to vanquish the biosphere, but it's certainly not possible to change a piece of stone-dead rock into a copy of Earth, bustling with life. Just look at the readings ..."

Henryan glanced at his display. Ninety-two percent of standard gravity, temperatures ranging from minus eighty-three degrees at the poles to plus forty-four in the equatorial zone, the axial tilt of forty-two degrees, the composition of the atmosphere slightly different from the Earth's, although—as per spectrum analysis—in the troposphere there were still gases presenting danger to humans. However, they occurred in such small amounts that people could spend on the surface a standard day without using breathing apparatus. With specialized equipment, life on Delta would be a fairy tale.

"I don't want to make any assumptions, but I think I know why there was such a rush to leave Uganda 6," Darski said. "Apparently, we've found someone's private paradise."

The fact that some corporation could afford such a gigantic scam was beyond him, and yet he was looking at the evidence. If it hadn't been for the alien invasion, the existence of this planet would have been known only to a narrow circle of insiders ...

A flashing yellow light brought him out from his reverie. Right after leaving hyperspace, Henryan reported that the convoy had reached its destination, and now he received a reply. Although the quantum message didn't come from the metasector's High Command as he'd expected, but from the Admiralty. It came directly from the Central Systems, without going through the proper channels.

He didn't accept the communication straight away. For a brief moment, he held his finger over the flashing yellow key, as if he was afraid that with just one brush of the virtual surface, he would lay out trouble for himself. He'd just wriggled out of a penal colony and even worse shit on Xan 4. *My rehabilitation is all well and good*, Darski thought, glancing suspiciously at the blue and white globe before him. *But ... am I not the perfect scapegoat for these clones-of-bitches in ridiculous hats?*

Even the thought of gruff Dr. Godbless didn't cheer him up. Someone in the Admiralty knew exactly what they were doing when they sent him here.

Henryan lowered his finger. The flashing icon was replaced by a message box, which contents turned his hitherto knowledge about this system upside down.

SIX

THE SHUTTLE SHUDDERED AGAIN. This heavy-duty multitasking craft designed for short-haul flights worked perfectly in the vacuum of space, but after entering the thick atmosphere of Delta, it started having problems. Henryan wasn't sure whether this was the case due to both pilots' lack of experience, or bollixed aerodynamics of the bulgy vessel. In any case, another jolt forced him deeper into the cocoon of his chair.

"What are you guys doing?" Darski snapped over the intercom.

"It's not our fault, Captain," the pilot answered, sounding a bit robotic. "Turbulence is a normal occurrence in such thick atmosphere."

Turbulence? You're calling this turbulence?! Darski wanted to yell, but he felt nauseated by the perpetual shake and continual swing. He swallowed hard and then shifted his gaze to Lieutenant Hondo, who had served as his assistant since being assigned to *Cervantes* at the beginning of the evacuation.

"Let's roll, Toranosukenjiro!" he hissed through clenched teeth.

"Again? The third time?" A very slim, freckled, redheaded

vicenarian groaned. "You already know these numbers by heart, Captain."

"I need to keep my mind occupied. When I have nothing to do, I think about what's in my stomach too much. Thanks to those scoundrels ..." He nodded in the direction of the cockpit behind the bulkhead.

Hondo nodded. Unlike most of the soldiers, he didn't wear a helmet. In the light panels' glow, his cropped hair was the color of copper. This, and the freckles, made the lieutenant look like one of Henryan's distant ancestors on his mother's side. Even Toranosukenjiro's face was similar to those in the old family holos: oval, with a pointed chin and very high but not too prominent cheekbones.

"The alien probe appeared in the Ulietta's jump zone seven hours and twelve minutes ago," Hondo said in a bored voice. "That means we still have about forty-one hours to complete the operation."

"Come on!" Henryan growled, feeling that the hull and the seats attached to it were starting to vibrate again.

"Within the allotted time, our transporters and the requisitioned arks will get to the transit area of Belt Q twice, going back and forth, which means we'll be able to pick up one hundred and eighty-two thousand people—"

"Out of the three hundred and twenty-five thousand colonists inhabiting the system," Darski cut in.

"Yes. Out of three hundred and twenty-five thousand, six hundred and seventeen," Hondo specified.

"Anyway, it's only fifty-six percent of the Ulietta's population."

"As many as fifty-six percent, Captain," Toranosukenjiro corrected him. "After all, evacuating these people isn't even our priority."

"Son," Henryan looked him in the eye, "saving them is and always will be my priority."

"But the Admiralty clearly—" Hondo fell silent when his superior shot him a withering look.

"I know what the orders are, Lieutenant, and believe me, I don't intend to break them. But you've got to understand one thing: the evacuation of half the population will be my personal defeat … what am I saying? … it'll be a personal tragedy. It's more than one hundred thousand of potential victims, can't you see that?" He kept his eyes trained on the lieutenant until he nodded. "That's why I'm going to focus on this aspect of our mission."

"What about the rod-ship?" the lieutenant asked in a slightly shaky voice.

"What about it? Stowing is in progress. It won't stop until the very last minute. The miners and mine management know best what to do. By interfering, we'll only worsen the situation."

"Right."

"Really?" Henryan smiled wryly.

"Yes. It's the same in the Fleet. Let's take maneuvers. Everything's going swimmingly until some star-studded clone-of-a-bitch starts to interfere."

"Oh, yes." The captain's smile widened. "That's why we should focus on what really matters. Rescuing these people."

"But how do we do it? Since numbers don't lie?" Hondo lifted his reader. "As per your orders, I took the maximum value of each factor into account. The Admiralty had planned to evacuate forty percent of the Delta's population, including its moons. Thanks to your tips, I managed to raise this number by another sixteen percent. It's a lot—"

"Perhaps," Henryan admitted. "But still not enough for me."

"That's all we can do." Judging by the sound of his voice, the lieutenant believed it.

Darski leaned forward as far as the cocoon harness let him.

"In the next two days you will understand that when you're determined enough, you've got the power to change statistics."

Hondo didn't reply. After another jolt, accompanied by loud scraping, the soldiers heard the voice of the co-pilot. "Attention, the craft is now making its final approach to Delta."

SEVEN

THE SHUTTLE HOVERED RIGHT NEXT to the landing pad. Its pilot positioned it so that the rear platform was above the plasteel grille, which had the shape of a circle with a diameter of one hundred and fifty feet. This large military vessel was too heavy to be supported by the structure crowning the top of the twenty-one-hundred-foot-tall tower of the colony's administration building, housing the Board offices.

Henryan disembarked first, followed by the rest of the crew. Everyone, Hondo included, was wearing a fully equipped space suit, even though not one person from the delegation awaiting them on the other side of the landing pad used any visible breathing aids. The same was true for the service staff. They bustled around the pad without breathing apparatus. Feeling a sudden blast of air behind his back, Henryan glanced over his shoulder. The shuttle had disappeared behind the edge of the landing pad, right after the last soldier set foot on the grille, in order to join the rest of the squadron in a nearby spaceport.

Darski strode toward the jetbridge leading to a glazed air lock from which a modest welcoming committee emerged, consisting of three men and a very attractive brunette.

Dressed in a simple but very tight burgundy dress, the

woman was the head of the delegation. The clinging fabric, apparently non-synthetic, emphasized her curves in a way rarely seen on orbital stations and spaceships. Her tanned arms were completely bared, as were her legs, exposed up to above her knees. As for the face, Darski switched his focus to it when he was halfway there. She seemed very young, couldn't have been more than forty, and her looks … She must have been a local beauty, especially with that thick makeup. Obligatory shadows on her cheeks and a wide strip of black from one temple to the other, bringing out her eyes. The bald spot on top of her head, in keeping with the latest fashion trends, was masked by a thick hairy material reminiscent of fur.

The men who accompanied her weren't so impressive. One was ruddy and fat, the other two could have been brothers if they had not—

Henryan froze in mid-stride. Something was trickling down the visor of his helmet. When he looked at his space suit, he noticed many glittering, fast vaporizing droplets. He lifted his head and simultaneously reached for the computer on his wrist, but stopped his finger just above the key that activated the personal force field. Something big and gray seemed to be drifting across the Delta's blue skies. Was it … dripping? Darski smeared one of the droplets on his visor and put his fingertip to the scanner.

"It's just the rain," he heard, a second before the computer had finished analyzing the liquid.

H_2O with small quantities of other, fortunately harmless elements. Henryan glowered at the smiling hosts, super embarrassed. Even before he introduced himself, he'd made a spatial goof of himself, who didn't know that on oxygen-rich planets atmospheric moisture condensation is a normal process.

He straightened up hastily, glancing at the soldiers standing behind him; most of them also stared at the sky or tried to catch the droplets. At least they didn't notice his blunder.

"Welcome to Delta, Captain," the brunette said, genuinely amused. "My name's Ninadine Truffaut. I'm an Etoile Blanc third-level manager. The gentlemen who accompany me are ... Jeantoine Lescaud, our chief of police." She pointed to one of the square-shouldered, bald as a coot, big guys who seemed to be twins from a distance. "Xavieric Dupree, acting director of the mine." Henryan bowed his head, responding to a similar gesture. "And this is our invaluable Dr. Jerryan Pallance—"

"I've got to see the colony's CEO. At once!" Darski interrupted her unceremoniously because he'd already understood that none of them represented the actual Board. Faced with some petty officials, he was truly indignant. Every minute of delay meant leaving more colonists on Delta.

"Unfortunately, Mr. Mountavon is not available." The brunette still had a smile on her face, though she must have felt offended by his rude reaction.

"Then please take me immediately to the person in charge."

"I'm trying to explain that—"

"Don't bother. I think it would be best if you just showed me the way to the Board offices. There's no time for idle chatter."

Hondo cleared his throat meaningfully.

"What's going on?" Darski glanced at the lieutenant over his shoulder.

"You're looking at the colony's management." Toranosukenjiro smiled apologetically, tapping his finger on the holopad.

Darski bit his lip. *Another blooper,* he thought. *This mission is far too important to screw it up like this. The colonists have to obey me implicitly if I'm to make the plan work.*

And the worst was still ahead of him.

EIGHT

THE COMMUNICATIONS CENTER was located a few stories below, under the executive suites, on the one hundred and ninety-seventh story of the Tower. Surprisingly, the incident on the landing pad allowed Darski to save time. Since there were only small-timers in the colony, he didn't have to fawn on the financial sharks and could get on with it. That's why he'd made his way straight to where he was supposed to appear after talking to the CEO.

The barges, which were to take the Delta's inhabitants aboard and deliver them to the transporters and arks, were expected within thirty minutes. By that time, at least five thousand colonists would have passed through the spaceport checkpoints, currently being intercepted and manned by Henryan's subordinates. The captain knew that it wouldn't be easy to persuade men and women of Delta to leave their possessions at such short notice and run away. Especially since they had to relinquish one of the few places in the Known Universe that really deserved to be called Paradise. Even if they'd spent only a third part of their lives on it, for two-thirds toiling in the mines located on Delta's moons.

And what did he have to offer them? On the one hand—

rescue, but on the other … Months or even years of misery on distant orbital stations or on low-category planets, somewhere on the outskirts of the Universe. The smartest colonists would figure it out very quickly, so the only question was, "How many people will they turn around?" If Darski had been a cynical person, he might have wished there were many of them. Leaving the malcontents behind wouldn't have weighed on his conscience too heavily since it would have been them who refused to evacuate and brought their fate on themselves.

The problem was, Henryan could not—and would not—condemn anyone to certain death. Not after what he'd seen on the recordings from a dozen or so already destroyed colonies. Not after what he had experienced in Draccos's penal colony.

As Etoile Blanc Corporation did business in all the metasectors, many colonists would probably find new homes in the newly discovered worlds in the Outer Rim. The rest would go back to the old way of life, known to them before they traveled to the Ulietta system several years ago. Eventually, the former and the latter would come to terms with this necessary change and with time, they might even forget about the lost Paradise. Darski kept telling himself this was true, although he didn't feel assured. He knew people all too well. However, he couldn't show weakness. Not now.

Entering the communications center, he started to bark out orders.

"Corporal White, please secure the posts."

Two noncoms dragged both technicians from their seats and took their places; a couple of gendarmes, armed to the teeth, put the kicking and cursing men against the wall. Nobody paid any attention to the protests of the four officials. Henryan had decided to proceed this way during the flight. Of course, he could have done it differently, but time was of great importance.

"Lieutenant, recordings!"

Toranosukenjiro handed a crystal to White, then another data storage device to the staff sergeant sitting next to him.

"Cameras!"

"Aye aye, sir!" Hondo said as several spherical objects hovered in front of Henryan's face.

Darski lifted his hand to silence the still grumbling chief of police and Ninadine, who was supporting him bravely. The logo of the Third Fleet appeared on all the displays of the communications center. A few moments later, the screens got dark, and when they brightened again, Darski's face was on them. This, and the enraged officials in the background. It was also a part of the plan.

"Three, two, one!" White counted down, holding up successive fingers.

"Citizens of Ulietta, my name is Captain Henryan Darski, co-commander of FSS *Djangonzalo Cervantes*. By the order of the Admiralty of the Combined Fleets, we're taking control of your system. In less than forty hours one of the nearby stars will go supernova. The unimaginable force of this explosion will render sterile many systems, Ulietta included."

At this point, in the upper right-hand corner of the screens appeared a clock counting down the time to the expected arrival of the alien liners.

"Due to the inevitable annihilation of this part of the sector, the Admiralty have decreed the state of emergency on Ulietta and the immediate evacuation of the entire colony. In a moment, a special bulletin will be sent to your comlinks, describing the evacuation procedures in more detail. Along with it, each of you will receive a number entitling you to a seat on a shuttle which will take you to the transporters and arks. Follow the instructions, and no harm will come to you."

Henryan nodded toward the soldier at the second console. The staff sergeant had already put the crystal into the reader, so now he just had to activate the transmitter.

"The Third Fleet will make every effort to provide safe passage to each of you. However, I'm warning you that all attempts to get onto our barges out of turn, as well as refusal to board them, will be punished by depriving such an individual of their number and moving them to the end of the waiting line.

"I'd also like to inform you that none of my subordinates can change your status, so all attempts to bribe them will come to naught. If someone offers you a speedup, report it immediately to the local police or our officers, because you have most certainly become the victim of a scammer."

Hondo, who stood beyond the cameras' field of view, waved his hand, telling White to turn the recorder off.

But Darski didn't stop talking. He just straightened up, as if he were moving on to more important matters.

"To expedite the evacuation, we'll temporarily requisition all private and corporate extra-systemic vessels. The owners of these ships are to go immediately to the landing pad number nine of the spaceport, where they will receive further instructions. This also applies to the vessels currently en route and at rallying points in the jump zones. Anyone trying to avoid requisition or escape from the system will be treated as a traitor and severely punished as such—"

"Captain," White interrupted him.

"Can't you see that I'm delivering an address here?" Darski snapped.

"I can, sir, but you told me to report if someone tried to run away on their own accord."

"Visuals!" Darski said.

Some of the screens showed the edge of the local star's photosphere and its jump zone with the escorts, left there by the convoy to distract the enemy from the evacuees. Seeing the cruiser and twelve destroyers, the Aliens would first set off in pursuit, and only then would they return to Delta—their attempt to destroy the Fleet's vessels a failure because the commanders of all the ships had been ordered to make subspace jumps as soon as things started to slip out of control. Thanks to a similar maneuver, Khumalo had bought his people some extra time, and now each minute thus obtained would allow the embarkation of further refugees. However, no one on Delta could know about it.

That's why the sensors weren't aimed at the gravitational wells and warships. In the middle of the displays, those gathered in the communications center saw a small streamer. The ninety-foot-long, needle-shaped hull ended with a ruff, separating the utility section from the reactor and nozzles. A vessel like many others, neither new nor too old. Something anyone could afford, even a small business owner, who didn't have to work on the bottom rungs of the corporate ladder.

"To the pilot of a civilian vessel approaching the jump point. This is Captain Henryan Darski, the co-commander of FSS *Djangonzalo Cervantes*. Please identify yourself."

There was a moment of complete silence, then the transmitter came to life.

"It's Zulu Echo Kilo Foxtrot seven nine one, what do you want?"

"How many people are there on board your vessel, Zulu Echo Kilo Foxtrot seven nine one?"

"And what's that to you?"

"If you don't have a full set of passengers aboard, you have to return to the nearest boarding zone immediately."

"You don't say! I'm traveling with my family on board my own streamer. All the seats are occupied."

Darski looked at one of the noncoms.

"Check it."

"Yes sir!" The staff sergeant leaned over the displays. A few seconds later, he reported, "The *Cervantes'* scanners have detected two spectra peculiar to living organisms. This reading's been confirmed by the duty officer of FSS *Deighton*."

"Did you hear it, Zulu Echo Kilo Foxtrot seven nine one?" Henryan looked at the screen again, and when there was no reply, he repeated his call in a louder voice.

Again, there was no answer, but the streamer's engine nozzles began emitting brighter light. The tiny spacecraft accelerated as it changed its course, turning to the nearest gravitational well.

"You have to break off the approach and reverse immediately. If you don't do this within fifteen seconds, we will open fire on your vessel."

This time Darski got through.

"By what right, I wonder," the pilot said mockingly.

"Under the provisions of the state of emergency decreed in this system," Henryan explained calmly. "We'll find you guilty of attempted murder of at least four people, because your vessel could carry as many additional passengers."

"Bullshit."

"Eight seconds," White said.

"Suck my dick!" the runaway yelled. "I'm not afraid of you!"

"Break off the approach, this is your final warning!" Darski raised his voice.

"Fuck you!"

The captain nodded and Corporal White typed a command. Two seconds later, the little ship exploded, struck by a laser beam invisible to the human eye.

"Murderer!" Truffaut cried out. She managed to take two steps toward Darski before one of the gendarmes stopped her.

The other officials and the technicians, forcibly dragged away from their consoles, stared incredulously at the flotsam.

Henryan looked into the holocameras' lenses again.

"To all vessels within the Ulietta system. If you don't have a full set of passengers on board, return to Delta immediately. From now on, we'll shoot without warning at anyone who tries to violate the order. End of transmission."

He stood motionless until the corporal signaled to him that the cameras were off. Only then did he let the air out of his lungs and looked at Hondo.

"What do you think?"

"It went better than I thought." The lieutenant didn't take his eyes off the holopad. "The vast majority of vessels going toward the jump zone have already changed their course."

"Great."

"'Great'?! What are you, because you can't be human, that's for sure!" Truffaut flipped out again. "Why are you acting as if nothing happened? You've just killed two innocent people. Civilians trying to save their lives. Would these four seats really make such a big difference?"

Henryan turned to her slowly, casually. She was dumbfounded when she saw a wide smile on his face; with her mouth dropped open, he could have counted all her teeth if he'd wanted.

"Can you name a type of a six-seat streamer, which has a quantum communicator on board?" he asked in an indifferent tone.

Ninadine goggled at him. She understood neither his reaction nor question.

"Well, there's a clever clone-of-a-bitch for you ..." Lescaud muttered, then chortled.

As an experienced cop, he knew the truth before the civilians did. Ninadine turned to him violently as if he had stabbed her in the back.

"What?"

"It was all just a hoax, boss," he said, shaking his head in disbelief. "A show. Nobody shot anyone."

"These six seats wouldn't change a thing," Darski admitted. "But we'll cram a few hundred, maybe even a thousand people on board all the vessels which are returning to Delta as we speak. Plus, those yachts and ferries will go there and back at least twice before—before the cataclysm occurs."

"Well-engineered," the chief of police said. "Even I fell for it."

Truffaut stood between them, disoriented. She kept her eyes trained on the officers occupying the communications center and you could almost see the cogs in her brain moving. It took her a moment or two, but eventually she understood what had just happened.

NINE

THE NEXT THIRTY minutes were critical to the success of the operation. For that reason, Henryan had refused to use a guest suite, located a few stories above, on the same level as the executive living quarters. He wasn't persuaded even by the prospect of taking a proper shower and changing his clothes. He preferred to focus all of his attention on the evacuation, and revise the plans as needed.

The address was being broadcast continually on repeat, over and over again, at all frequencies and across all channels. The system showed that nearly two hundred and fifty thousand people had received the bulletin and gotten to know their number in the line.

So far, so good ... Darski thought. The only question was whether the earlier demonstration of strength had been sufficient and if the colonists would rush to the spaceport.

The barges sent from the first four transporters had already entered the atmosphere. In less than twenty minutes, the first one would touch down at the nearest landing pad. Henryan could see it through the window of the communications center: a large pool of poro-concrete, encroaching into the northern boundaries of the colony. From the south and the east, the mining town's buildings were stormed by sea waves; from the west, there was a thick wall of green pressed against them.

However, Darski's head was just not in the game to admire the breathtaking views; so far, the sense of mission had been winning with his sensitivity to Nature's beauty and curiosity about the Universe. But he promised himself he'd find a moment to explore this incredible planet. He would dip his hand in turquoise waters, immerse in emerald primeval forests, and do whatever else this place offered people like him—for such an opportunity might not present itself again.

But first he had to take care of the colonists, making sure that the operation, planned down to the last detail, was running smoothly. And, most importantly, come up with an idea how to increase the survival rate.

This could be difficult, he thought. *Toranosukenjiro was right when he said—*

"You've got to see it, Captain." Hondo's voice snapped Henryan out of his thoughts.

"Send the visuals to the main screen," Henryan said, turning his back to the panoramic window.

Now, when the welcoming committee disappeared from the communications center—as did the gendarmes—except them both, there were only two civilian technicians left, who knew the modified manifold colony's system better than any soldier.

Darski stood in the middle of the room, just like before when he was recording the address, and craned his neck to see the images better. They changed every few seconds, showing more and more places, mostly wide arterial thoroughfares, and the conchae of maglev stations. There were swirling crowds of people everywhere. Lots of men and women stormed the entrances to the platforms in the hope that they'd leave the rest behind, but even more humans walked along all the traffic lanes of the roads which were leading to the spaceport.

"What's the situation like at the checkpoints?" Henryan asked his subordinate.

The lieutenant didn't answer, but referred him to the side displays with numerous charts and a counter at the top of each screen. Three and a half thousand people had already been checked in. When Darski was inspecting other readings, this number increased by another seventy-two.

Good, he thought. At this rate, not even one barge will be pushed into demurrage and the transporters should leave Ulietta in five hours. Then, they'll go straight to the transit systems located at a distance of about six parsecs. The flight, docking to orbital stations, leaving the refugees, and flying back will take another seventeen hours, provided everything goes according to plan …

That means we'd see them again in twenty-two hours. So, there's going to be time for only two jumps. If we wanted to make the third jump, we'd be short of as little or as much as five hours. And we're talking about the ships that will be the first to leave. The rest will takeoff even later and … Henryan deliberated some more and finally, he concluded that mathematical principles couldn't be bent like space.

He glanced at the counter once again; the number was approaching three hundred thousand, and the counter was still spinning like crazy.

If I don't figure something out, and quickly, one hundred and forty thousand people will remain on Delta and die …

The captain had no doubt about it, even though the Aliens had never attacked an oxygen-rich planet before. And in such environment—unlike on globes devoid of all atmosphere—you could also survive after the destruction of the infrastructure. For some reason, and contrary to the admirals' opinions reflected in the orders concerning this mission, it was Darski's strong belief that the enemy would spring a murderous surprise on the inhabitants of Delta.

The alien invasion was not a work of chance. Carefully planned and scrupulously executed, it had been purging consecutive systems of even the smallest traces of human existence. So why would this incredible planet, being a Paradise for people, be an exception?

What can I do to save more colonists without breaking the Admiralty orders? Henryan wondered, watching the transmissions from the drones and surveillance cameras, and observing the men and women flocking to the spaceport. Unfortunately, nothing came to his mind, and he knew full well that he was running out of time.

"Lieutenant, have you sent the report to the metasector's High Command?"

"Yes. Seven minutes ago," Hondo said.

"Great. Tell Ms. Truffaut that I want to talk to her before leaving for the mine. We can meet in the suite I was assigned."

TEN

DARSKI STOPPED IN THE DOORWAY. Frankly speaking, when he heard "a suite" he instantly saw a windowless cubbyhole in his mind's eye. One of the rooms in which he'd stayed while serving on FSS *Lem* and visiting some colonies as an assistant to Admiral Duster. This hall—as he called it for want of a better word—was twenty times bigger than his cabin; it could fit the entire bridge of a cruiser in it and there'd still be plenty of space. A man accustomed to cramped spaceships could have been struck by agoraphobia there.

Ninadine noticed his confusion. Continuing to upload the driver software to his holopad, she responded with a crooked smile.

"The interface is really intuitive," she said, clearly deriving satisfaction from his bewilderment. "Here's how to change the polarization of the window." She moved her finger over the virtual screen, darkening the huge, glass outer wall. "This is a color equalizer, with a twenty-point memory ..."

Every movement of her finger meant a color change of the surrounding walls and even some of the furniture. "You can also program your own settings if none of the default ones are satisfactory," she added, continuing to grin mockingly. "There's a bathroom and a wardrobe." She pointed at the wall to the left. "And here's your bedroom." She turned right. "This knob regulates the speed of story rotation ..."

Henryan felt a slight vibration under his feet as the woman made a circle over the holopad with her finger.

"If you're more of a traditionalist, Captain, you can go for the stationary option," she said. "The fastest mode allows you to move the story at the pace of the sun. You'll see it from the moment it rises until it disappears below the horizon, provided the weather holds."

"And if a neighbor sets different parameters?" Darski asked.

"There is only one priority suite on each story," she explained. "Other rooms are occupied by middle-level managers."

"Such as yourself?" he blurted out.

She gave him a baleful look and nodded reluctantly. What was she supposed to do? She'd reached barely the third rung of the corporate ladder, and they both knew that.

"Yes. Such as myself."

"I didn't mean to offend you," he said, trying to salvage the situation. "In the army, hierarchy is everything. Maybe even more so than in corporations."

"Here, in the Inner Rim, level three means a lot more than in the Central Systems, which I am living proof of," she said, raising her head proudly.

Henryan decided to change the subject. He didn't want to upset her more than he already had. He needed her. She might be an invaluable source of information.

"Back there, on the landing pad, I made you mad on purpose," he lied, hoping to make amends. "I wanted your anger to look convincing. I didn't mean to hurt your feelings."

For a moment, she just stared at him. Listlessly, as if he was a colleague talking about production results.

"That's what I thought, Captain," she said eventually, nodding at a heavy sofa upholstered with the most realistic imitation of genuine leather, standing six feet from the panoramic window.

He followed her and sat on surprisingly soft cushions. She took a seat on one of the armchairs.

Ninadine was still wearing the same tight dress, only its color changed from burgundy to deep blue. Prior to arriving at the suite, she'd also gotten rid of her furry headgear.

"What would you like to drink?" she asked as the row of bottles and decanters emerged from the cabinet between them.

Henryan looked at the impressive bar. He was unfamiliar with most of the brands and felt tempted, of course, but he didn't give in.

"I'm on duty. Soon off to the mine—"

Truffaut laughed. "It won't be you at the helm."

"That's true, but I'd rather my subordinates didn't smell alcohol on my breath."

"In that case, I recommend this rum." She reached for the crystallite decanter. "Valisian. It's completely odorless, but it retains its natural flavor. And it packs a punch too," she added, pouring amber liquid (being the same shade of brown as her eyes) into two glasses. Just a finger each.

"In that case—" Henryan wanted to lean forward to take the drink, but she'd beaten him to it. Before he did anything, she put the glass to his nose. "Thank you," he mumbled, surprised by her gesture, and sniffed.

He didn't smell anything; it could have been water for all he knew. Then, he took a sip and smacked his lips. Pure delight to the palate. It was superior liquor, one bottle probably worth more than a captain's monthly pay. If the reason behind his visit to Delta had been different, he would have indulged himself, but as things stood ...

Darski put his glass on the table.

"Since we broke the ice, Captain, I'd like to ask you something," Ninadine said in a much more relaxed tone of voice. It must have had something to do with her taking a big gulp of rum just a second before.

"I'm listening." Henryan sat up. He felt confident that in a moment she would disclose the reasons behind the show she'd put on.

"Your priority is to load the rod-ship, I figure. However, what interests me is how many people you're going to evacuate from Delta. Just be honest with me, Captain."

Darski stiffened.

"I don't understand. What do you mean: how many? All of them, of course."

She smiled, took another sip, treating it as a bracer perhaps, and, finally, put the glass down on the table.

"I'm not an idiot, Captain," she said passionately. "There are only five people in their thirties who got promoted to level three in this corporation. As you might guess, I'm one of them."

"I never took you for a foolish person," he countered, warily.

"So please treat me like an equal, at least in terms of intellectual abilities."

"Absolutely."

"And don't patronize me," she added, reaching for the decanter again.

"I'm trying to be polite."

"I asked for honesty, not politeness." She refilled her glass, this time pouring a more generous dose of rum, then she waved the bottle before his eyes.

Henryan firmly refused.

"I was as frank with you as one can be," he assured her as she drained the glass in one swift movement. "My intention is to save all the colonists living on Delta."

"And how many of them do you have a real chance of saving? Or let me rephrase that … What losses is the Admiralty prepared to accept? I'm sure you have it in writing."

He thought he knew what Ninadine was getting at, but he wasn't sure as to her purpose. That's why he decided to play for time.

"Why do you want to know that, Ms. Truffaut?"

She looked him straight in the eye. Urgently, aggressively

even. He felt uncomfortable, much more uncomfortable than the first time she had given him that look when greeting him. But now, she said nothing—just bent her right elbow and activated the implant. All the rage these days, like her makeup and outfit. A virtual screen of her personal comlink appeared over her right forearm. She fumbled at it, then showed him one of the incoming messages, in fact just a part of it. The very last one. The number she'd been assigned by the Admiralty.

Henryan got a tingly feeling in his neck. Six green opalescent figures, and the first one was three.

"Is that enough of a reason?"

Darski nodded. If she had all her marbles, and it looked like she did, she'd already realized that the sudden promotion from a few days back was in fact a death sentence.

"Well ..." he said, collecting his thoughts. Eventually, he decided there was no point in concealing the truth. "Fifty-six percent. That's the limit set by the Admiralty."

"Fifty-six percent?" she repeated, disbelief in her voice. "It means one hundred and eighty thousand people—"

"Yes. Approximately," Darski admitted, reaching for his glass. Suddenly, he didn't care whether his subordinates would smell alcohol on his breath, or even notice that he was tipsy. "But I'm going to do all I can to save more colonists."

"How many more?" she asked, her voice cracking. "Ten thousand, twenty?"

Henryan was silent. *Even if I did my damnedest*, he thought, and somehow managed to bring back the transporters for the second time, I won't be able to bundle enough people with lower designated numbers and take her too.

"When I was summoned to the CEO's office three days ago, I was overjoyed. I'd been hoping to be promoted to a chief legal officer for quite some time, but to my surprise, the offer on the table turned out to be something different.

"Mr. Betancourt suggested I'd take up the temporary position of the colony's manager. Only for a week. He claimed that Head Office had called in the members of the Board and most of the senior level managers to the Central Systems because of the big changes ahead, and he decided to give me a chance to prove my worth. One in a million, he said."

She took a swig of rum. "Now I can see that he exaggerated a bit," she added, nodding at the screen and the still visible number.

"I'm so sorry—" Henryan began, but she didn't let him finish.

"No, don't interrupt me, Captain!" She gestured to him with her left hand, covering her mouth with the palm of the right one. Apparently, she overdid it on rum. "I don't need your compassion. You just made me realize that I was only a pawn in their game …"

Her eyes welled up. "Back there, on the landing pad, you were pissed when I introduced the others. Please don't deny, Captain, I can read human faces and emotions behind them. That's what I've been paid for, among other things, over the last twelve years."

"You've got me." Darski spread his arms. "I was really pressed for time, and on seeing you guys I started to suspect that the CEO had sent some minnows, because greeting the Fleet's captain was beneath his dignity."

"You're not far off. If Betancourt had been present, you'd have been welcomed by one of his numerous assistants."

"*Nihil novi sub sole*," Darski muttered, raising his glass.

"A military man, who knows dead languages?" Her surprise was so great that for a moment she forgot all about the doom hanging over her head, and looked at him curiously.

"A general is just as good as the troops under his command make him," he replied with another, though slightly newer, archaicism.

This time, she didn't get it.

"Communing with some soldiers, you can come away with an opposite impression … *Ad rem*, however," she added quickly. "What are the chances I'll get out of here legally?"

"Very little," he said.

"Seriously? Can't you change the order in which the colonists will embark the arks?"

Henryan shook his head, his eyes full of sadness.

Such is the truth, he thought. *Only the Admiralty can change the assigned number. And in her case, the request will certainly not be granted.*

He shared his thoughts with Ninadine, who accepted his words in silence. She sat with her head down, staring at her own knees, for a long time.

"And is there any not so legit way?" Darski heard her strangled voice.

He knew how much it cost her to ask this question.

"No," he cut her off, guessing what she was thinking about. "Trust me. None of my subordinates, no matter what they promised, is able to smuggle you aboard. Besides, esdees monitor all the checkpoints. And you know how they are."

"But I don't want to die," Truffaut whispered.

"Then please help me. I still have thirty-something hours to find a solution which will save not only you but also more than one hundred thousand other people."

ELEVEN

THE ANZIO SYSTEM, ZEBRA SECTOR

10/23/2354

Rutta was preparing for another meeting, probably the hundredth since arriving at the headquarters of High Command in this metasector. The grand admiral always summoned his staff officers when he got a report stating the arrival of the Aliens, and there were more and more of them with each day. The colonel had been right to think that only a fool would attack the Federation with ten ships. Even if they were as powerful as the almost indestructible alien liners.

It took Humankind a month to lose control over more than a hundred uninhabited planetary systems in Belts V and U as well as more than sixteen colonized systems. Five more were being attacked right now.

The comprehensive analyses of quantum transmissions from the conflict-affected areas showed the Admiralty of the Combined Fleets that the enemy had at least twenty-five warships operational in the Inner Rim. And this, in Rutta's view, wasn't a final estimate. The Aliens had to have some reserves at their disposal which they hadn't disclosed yet, probably waiting for fiercer resistance.

Still, in the part of space until recently occupied by the Federation, as many as eighteen liners had operated two standard days ago. More than ever since the beginning of the invasion. And the successive attacks on the monitoring stations suggested that within the next twenty-four hours, alien squadrons would also appear on Ubik 5 and Ulster 12. Both were large mining and transit centers, against which the enemy could throw at least eight liners altogether. This meant that on this side of the border, there would soon be more enemy vessels than had been identified so far. Thus, Rutta felt confident that any day now, he'd be able to support his persistently promoted thesis, which for the time being was rejected by some staff officers. However, he was not at all happy about it.

The Third Fleet was conceding ground faster than anticipated. The enemy was getting closer and closer to Belt S, and not in the section that the Federation's computers had indicated as most likely. Plus, creating fictitious targets on the new vector wasn't going as it should have. Admittedly, almost eight hundred pseudo-colonies had been built on ninety-six planets and one hundred and thirteen moons in sixty-five star systems altogether, but not even a third were on the current route of conquest, as the Aliens had changed tactics after two weeks of attacks and gave up purging the whole width of the Orion Arm, instead deciding to hammer their way into the human space as deep as possible.

This move had been countered. The Third Fleet's High Command had transferred its engineering troops from the least vulnerable areas of Belt S and farther to the new vector of attack, but even that hadn't boded well—the suffered losses were very high, and nothing could change that. When it had become apparent there was no time to create a new buffer, panic had broken out in the Admiralty. Farland had feared the new orders would command the Third Fleet to commence offensive operations—no one was ready for this, especially since Rutta's simulations left no illusions.

If it came to battle, the Third Fleet, even backed up by the neighboring metasector's troops, would be decimated at best and at worst annihilated. Such an unprecedented defeat would leave the Inner Rim exposed to enemy fire, lower the morale of soldiers and officers serving in the remaining fleets of the Federation, and—probably worst of all—open the door to the Inner Territories, beyond which the Central Systems were located.

Farland hadn't kept it from Xiao in the last quantum transmission. On the contrary, he'd tried to talk some sense into the highest admiral, but he couldn't know if this brought the desired result. One thing was certain, though: the Council were starting to lose patience. If the situation didn't change in the coming days (and there was nothing to indicate that), Chancellor Modo would crack and make the worst possible decision. A decision that would seem rational and reasonable but in reality would bring about the downfall of the Federation.

Doing up the buttons of his uniform, Rutta wondered what else could be done to slow down the enemy's progress. Despite many hours spent in the Fleet's archives and long discussions with other staff officers, he failed to come up with anything that would guarantee a fundamental change of the situation. The strategy he'd proposed a month ago still seemed to be the only sensible solution.

And that was exactly what he was going to say in the meeting which was to start in fifteen minutes.

———

It wasn't yet another standard briefing. When Rutta stepped into the room, he noticed that there was practically no one at the conference table. Only Farland occupied his seat on the dais.

"Did I miss something?" the colonel asked in astonishment.

Theo shook his head apathetically.

"I canceled the meeting a few minutes ago," he said, even his tone disconcerting.

Rutta glanced at his holopad, but didn't see any new messages.

"How strange," he mumbled. "The memo didn't go through."

"Sit down!" Farland growled.

The colonel did as he was told, looking curiously at his superior and friend at the same time. By now, the door had been secured; a moment later, the dome glowed as if someone had gilded it. Farland had surrounded the whole room with a cocoon of force field, and this meant—

Suddenly, a movement caught Rutta's eye. Opposite him, in places usually occupied by staff officers, two spectral figures appeared. He felt a tingling sensation in his neck as he recognized them. He was facing the ebony physiognomy of the Fleet's chief commander, the Highest Admiral Tadam Xiao, and that of rawboned, emaciated Chancellor Gerdanielle Modo. This was a meeting at the highest level, where he had no right to be. And yet, they both looked at him serenely as if there was nothing extraordinary in his presence.

The colonel glanced toward Farland, but the grand admiral was welcoming his guests, and he did it with so much energy that no one would have believed he'd been apathetic just a short while ago. Years of experience in the ranks allowed him to mask his feelings in the face of those who his career depended on. Rutta instantly regretted that he wasn't able to control himself in equal measure. Xiao and Modo must have already noticed his sour expression.

When Theo ended his short speech, Rutta stood up to add a few words, but he didn't manage to utter a single syllable. Chancellor Modo silenced him immediately.

"Every minute of this transmission costs us millions of credits, gentlemen, so let us get straight to the point," she said loftily. Her distinctive voice was legendary among the Fleet's officers serving in the farthest metasectors, where she was heard least often. "The Council and the Admiralty are unanimous."

Both Rutta and Farland stiffened. Their worst nightmare was about to come true; they were sure of it.

Modo, however, paid no attention to them. "The Aliens'

march has to be slowed down because we need a minimum of fourteen months to prepare a new defense line. You will give us that much time even if it means the Third Fleet's destruction."

Rutta narrowed his eyes. This was to be expected, but … One sentence sounded less strongly than it could have. They were told to slow the invader down, not to stop them.

"Sacrificing my people and ships won't discourage the enemy," Farland remarked. Somehow, he managed to keep his tone firm even though he felt tightness in his throat.

"We won't order a frontal attack," Xiao said, confirming the colonel's assumptions. "We are not crazy. Your report, and the simulations attached to it"—he turned to Rutta—"made everyone aware of how disastrous the defeat of the Third Fleet would be for the Humankind. Still, as Chancellor Modo rightly pointed out, we have no choice. If the Federation is to survive, you must stop the enemy in the Outer Territories until we have completed the construction of the fifth-generation warships."

Farland and Rutta exchanged astonished glances. That was news to them.

"Single battleships, even as powerful as the ones I had a chance to see projects of last year, won't tip the scales back in our favor." The grand admiral expressed their doubts. "You would need to build the entire fleet of them."

The legendary fifth-generation warships, on the table for nearly a decade, had been long bogged down in the wheels of the government bureaucracy machine, and the world was slowly beginning to forget about them. Rutta tried to calculate how fast the project could be implemented and how long it would take the Federation to build a few dozen of such vessels, because only that number of them would make a significant difference in this war. Whichever way he looked, it added to the same: a few years at least. Even if all the ordnance factories and shipyards in the other metasectors were put to work.

"Contrary to popular belief, we have never abandoned this project," Modo said. "It is well underway. What we have already got are the reactors, weapons systems, millions of metric tons of parts from which our shipyards are assembling state-of-the-art warships. What we have not got is the time. That is why we need you. Buy us a little over a year. At any price."

Farland stirred uneasily. It would have been interesting to know what had shocked him more: the information about the ongoing work, or another reminder that the Third Fleet might be expendable.

"We'll do our best, Chancellor," he said half-heartedly, certainly without such enthusiasm she'd been hoping for.

"You'll need to do better than that," Xiao admonished him. "The Aliens will reach the Inner Territories in about four months. If they take our mines and yards, all the efforts will go to waste."

"Colonel, your plan was brilliant in its simplicity," Modo added, haughtily acknowledging Rutta. "Unfortunately, it turned out to be not enough."

"This is war, Chancellor," Farland protested. "It can't be planned in advance, especially since we know so little about the enemy. That's why the Aliens can still surprise us."

"I blame neither of you, gentlemen," Modo said. "I am just stating the facts."

"We'd responded immediately," Rutta began to make excuses. "We'd moved all our forces to the most endangered areas. I think we'll be able to slow down the enemy in the coming weeks."

"And I think," Xiao cut in, "it's high time you took the bull by the horns. By mere multiplication of targets, we won't achieve much. Especially when the Aliens see through our strategy, and in the opinion of the Council's analysts, this is what we should expect."

"I see." Farland didn't even try to argue.

It wasn't a suggestion but an order. Just one of a long list they'll receive in writing after this conversation.

"How are things on Ulietta?" Modo changed the subject unexpectedly.

The grand admiral scowled and looked at Rutta who was as surprised as himself.

"Colonel?" he asked meaningfully.

"We're in the process of evacuating this system's inhabitants. The last report came in three hours ago. So far, everything's been going according to plan. No delays as of yet. One hundred and fifty-one out of one hundred and seventy-two rotary holds have already docked into the rod-ship."

"Great. Who's overseeing the operation?" Xiao asked.

"The colonel's subordinate, Captain Henryan Darski," Farland replied.

The chief commander turned to Rutta. "That Darski?"

"I'm not sure I understand …"

"Are we talking about the same man who you'd gotten out of the penal colony?" Xiao clarified.

"Yes sir. He's a real professional, sir. He's been completely rehabilitated too," Rutta replied, feeling thirsty at the sudden dryness of his throat.

"Yes, I know. And I can see why you've commissioned him, instead of someone else, although I must admit that in the case of Ulietta I'd rather have on the spot an officer with a less over-sized ego and not so wild imagination," Xiao said.

"I can vouch for him," Rutta blurted out before he could even think about it.

"Let us focus on what is really important here, gentlemen," said Modo, who seemed a little confused by the chief commander's words. "If you take care of this, Colonel Rutta, you will not have to worry about your well-deserved promotion. All rotary holds must dock into the rod-ship, even if it has to remain in the system until the Aliens come, and make a subspace jump at the last moment. Even if the protracted loading forces you to leave the most of colonists behind. Understood?"

"Yes ma'am. I will take care of it personally," Farland assured her.

"Great."

"And one more thing," Xiao said. "The Admiralty granted your request: you will get support from the other fleets, with full blessing of the Council. Also, all new plans and orders have already been sent to the Communications Headquarters of the metasector."

"Do not disappoint us, gentlemen," Chancellor Modo adjourned the meeting.

Both holograms disappeared simultaneously, leaving Farland and Rutta in deathly silence.

"Fourteen months ..." Rutta said absentmindedly.

"Yes ..." The grand admiral also had a blank look on his face. "This Darski thing ... What was that about?" he asked after a long pause.

"I don't have the slightest idea," Rutta answered honestly.

TWELVE

10/23/2354

Traversing the distance of two hundred and seventy thousand clicks that separated the spaceport from the landing pad on the largest of the three moons orbiting Delta took the shuttle less than twenty minutes. Darski set foot on the hollowed globe sooner than the miners starting their next shift, even though he took off some time after them.

A small military shuttle overtook a convoy of fusiform corporate transporters which were carrying more than two thousand miners each in their commodious multi-story compartments. For the next eight hours, those people would be operating heavy equipment, such as boom-type roadheaders, to extract helon ore; then, the output would go into extremely large containers called "corves" which later would be launched into low-moon orbit, where a gigantic rod-ship was already waiting. One of the biggest bulk carriers that Humankind had ever manufactured.

The shuttle overtook this monstrous ship during the final descent. Henryan watched it with awe. Against the backdrop of the moon, lit by Ulietta's sun, he saw an almost three-mile-long cylindrical structure with a six-hundred-foot-wide deflector dish on one end and four gargantuan nozzles and a ball of a reactor on the other. The entire space between the propulsion and the umbrella-shaped bow were filled by rotary holds. At the moment, there were more than a hundred and fifty of them; another twenty would reach the orbit before the arrival of the Aliens.

If everything went according to plan, the bulk carrier would take one hundred and seventy-two million metric tons of ore from Ulietta, helon being the rarest—and most tenacious—metal found in the Galaxy. One hundred and seventy-two million metric tons, that is more than all the shipyards and processing plants of the Federation had used over the last two years.

"If ..." This one word covered the whole drama of the situation. Since the bulk carrier was to be fully laden several thousand people would have to sacrifice their lives—just as many as worked one shift in the mine. The Admiralty doubted that all of them would give up their lives for the benefit of Humankind willingly, so Darski received clear guidelines how to suppress the mutiny. Guidelines he couldn't disagree more with, by the way.

He'd been told to make these people remain at their posts until the very last moment. He'd even gotten clearance to shoot the most recalcitrant miners if other coercive measures failed. Three companies of uniformed esdees were to assist him in this work—they would appear on Ulietta in a few hours to fill strategic positions in the mine and, if necessary, smother any sedition.

Darski was beginning to regret that he hadn't declined the offer. But if he'd said "no" to Rutta, someone else would have been sent in his place. Someone much more ruthless. An officer who would have executed any order. If the miners were to have a chance of survival, then it was him who had to complete this mission and find a way ... a method thanks to which on the one hand, helon ore would remain in Humankind's hands, greatly increasing its chances of winning the war with the Aliens, and, on the other hand, the miners' lives would be saved. Of course, Henryan knew it wouldn't be easy. And time was running out.

THIRTEEN

IN HERE, gravity was so low that the rover, in which one of the corporation managers was chauffeuring him around, spent more time above the moon's surface than on it. And this fact had nothing to do with the driver's recklessness—Iandreas Drechsler was a staid, stout Hindu in his eighties, one of the mine's six deputy technical directors. That was simply how driving in 0.4 G looked like. Luckily, the force that allowed them to glide (and the flight sometimes lasted even ten seconds or more) was also the best shock absorber when it came to the inevitable contact with the ground. The six-wheeled rover fell on the rocky surface as softly as a cloud.

"Another mile and we'll be there!" the driver called out when the metal wheels left the rocky surface yet again.

Henryan nodded, though he realized that the other man couldn't see it. The colonists used such archaic equipment, so different from anything he was accustomed to, that after landing on this moon he felt as if he'd gone back in time to the days before the hyperspace drive was invented. The space suit he'd put on to inspect both the aboveground and underground installations weighed more than a hundred and fifty pounds, and the bulbous helmet, although very large, had an exceptionally small visor and was practically devoid of virtual support, so Henryan had to rely on his own perception. He couldn't even use his holopad, because whoever designed this model of suits didn't think of a suitable hookup.

The miners stayed in touch with one another and their supervisors thanks to radio communicators, and a straightforward CPU was enough to handle the life support system of their vacuum suits. No one needed sophisticated high-tech gear; simplicity and reliability were most important here. In that order, as Drechsler had stressed when after leaving the main dome they'd headed for the first of seven installations which Darski meant to visit.

Three hours later they were approaching the penultimate point of interest: the ejectors.

The rover left a long ravine, which floor had been leveled to create a makeshift road, and came to a halt at the foot of a steep embankment surrounding one of the craters, excavated in the surface when another celestial body had collided with the moon millions, perhaps even billions, of years ago. At the height of thirty, maybe forty feet, where the rock was almost vertical, Henryan saw the outlet of a rectangular tunnel. A long chute of iridescent plasteel ran out from it. Supported by dozens of pillars, the installation crossed a boulder-covered flatland and at a distance of about a mile curved gently to aim at the black sky.

"This is the pride of our mine, one of the most powerful ejectors ever manufactured," Drechsler explained. Glancing at his watch, he added, "And ... now!"

A large container adorned with the corporate logo noiselessly emerged from the inside of the tunnel. Rushing just above the electromagnetic chute, it was accelerating continually; it reached the arc in the blink of an eye, left the rail, and, finally, sprang out into the boundless blackness. Darski watched the plasteel container for a few seconds until it blended with the darkness of space.

"The next one will be launched in four hundred seconds," Drechsler said. "This rate allows us to send nine loads per hour, each weighing more than ten thousand metric tons. And we have five similar installations here. Please look—" He pointed to a container over their heads, which must have been launched from another electromagnetic railgun, because this was what in its essencean ejector was.

Darski didn't answer, in this very moment trying to figure out whether at this pace the miners would be able to meet the Admiralty's demands. It seemed that loading would end in about thirty-six hours—ballparking, of course. By that time, the Aliens would have already traveled halfway the distance from the jump zone, even if the rest of the squadron had been able to pull them away from their original target, which was by no means certain.

They moved on, heading for the structure looming another mile away. The elevator leading inside one of the dozens of zonal control rooms was on the other side of the ejector.

"Can you speed up this process?" Henryan asked when they were driving under the chute.

"No," Drechsler said without a second thought.

His voice sounded strangely metallic, and it was hard to understand him through the static and interference. A few moments later Drechsler slammed on the brakes in a narrow strip of shadow cast by the ejector.

"What are you doing?" Darski huffed.

As if to calm him down, the driver raised his hand.

"We are in a dead zone, Captain," he said. "The field generated by the ejector won't allow for either listening in to our conversation or recording it. We can speak freely here. Ninadine had asked me to be completely honest with you."

Henryan looked him straight in the eye, or rather at this part of the foggy visor where they should have been. Truffaut had promised to help him and apparently, she'd meant it. But why this conspiracy? Did corporations have their own security department?

"What do you think our chances are?" he asked hesitantly.

"Of completing the task?"

"Yes."

There was a long moment of silence. Drechsler didn't even move when another container flew over their heads.

"Not too great," he said finally.

"Why?"

"We've been working at this pace for more than two hundred hours, and the equipment is on its last legs."

"Are you afraid of failure?"

"It's a wonder that we haven't lost any ejectors yet. They are designed to launch one container every ten minutes. And we've not only exceeded the time limit, but also have been loading a thousand metric tons more than we should, which is ten percent above permissible levels. And this won't hold forever." He raised his chin toward the chute above their heads.

Darski glanced up, reflexively. The poro-concrete was covered with a cobweb of cracks. Here and there, dust was flowing. You could see it clearly, because in such low gravity it took long minutes for the particles to drop to the surface of the moon.

"What's the probability that these installations won't hold for another thirty-six hours?"

"I talked to the chief engineer before your arrival. In his opinion, there's seventy-five percent chance that one of the lines will fail within the next twenty-four hours."

Seventy-five percent? Henryan thought. *That's not good, not good at all …*

"How much time will you need to repair it?"

"I don't know, but—"

"Please remember that I'm not an engineer," Henryan interrupted him. "So spare me the details. How long did such repairs take in the past?"

"The problem is none of our ejectors ever broke," Drechsler said.

"What?" Darski shifted in his seat. "Then how—"

"Easy, Captain," Drechsler cut in. "I'm not done yet. We're not afraid of equipment failure, we deal with things like this regularly. For three days in a row now, we've experienced over a dozen minor malfunctions. The real problem is that—" He pointed his finger at the cloud of dust, falling as if in slow motion. "Our ejectors have never worked so long and under such heavy load. These depots have been filled for the past five years," he added by way of explanation. "And the biggest single shipment which I recall was seven million metric tons. All done without haste, without making norms more stringent."

"I see."

It made sense even to such a nonexpert like Henryan.

"So now you know …" Drechsler watched the sinking dust with a look of sadness in his eyes. "And it's getting worse with every hour," he added almost as an afterthought.

"What will happen if one of the pillars collapses?" Henryan asked.

"What will happen?" Drechsler laughed. "It depends. If we lose the prop after the container has been launched, we'll just turn the ejector off, print the required element and fill the gap."

"How long will it take?"

"A day at least. Optimistically speaking, that is. The cambering itself can take up to eight hours, then a trial launch … And it's always possible that things will go sideways."

"Then what?" Henryan asked, though he had a premonition of what he would hear next.

"Nothing." Drechsler shrugged. "Game over. An unbalanced container will demolish a length of the chute. Dozens of pillars and hundreds of yards of rail."

Neither of them spoke for a long moment.

That would have reduced the effective shipping tonnage capacity by one-fifth, Henryan thought, and did some calculations in his head. *About a hundred thousand metric tons per every hour of loading, and this multiplied by twenty-four hours, maybe more—*

"Will reducing the load to the permissible level change anything?" he came up with a suggestion.

Drechsler nodded.

"Yes. Definitely. But I'm not allowed to make such a decision. None of us is."

"I'll take full accountability," Darski said.

"Will you put it in writing for me?"

"Absolutely. Upon my return, I'll discuss this with the chief engineer first and then with my superiors. Don't worry, I'm going to tell them what I've seen here without mentioning your role.

"We don't know exactly how much time we have left, so maybe, just maybe, we'll have one or two hours to spare and that would compensate for the losses, although if another ejector breaks down, we'll lose much more than one and a half million metric tons."

"I'll get in touch with some people too. Within an hour, we'll implement the new system," Drechsler promised.

"What's the holdup?"

"Hundreds of pieces of equipment are going to need reprogramming, plus it will be necessary to create a new timetable for the tug crews, who handle reloading in orbit."

"Pardon?"

"Reloading in orbit," Drechsler repeated.

"As I said before, launching ore into space isn't exactly my cup of tea. What I do is I deal with laser weapons and blow everything to smithereens, more like. I'm not familiar with the mining procedures."

"It's just that we know all of it backward and forward, so I thought you'd been told what's what."

"All I know is that I have to supervise the loading of this rodship and protect it until the jump is made. Even at the cost of my subordinates' lives."

"I understand and I don't envy you your job. From what I heard—"

"Can we just get to the point?" Darski interrupted him unceremoniously. He was all edgy, knowing that it was him who would have to pass the dismal news to High Command.

"Yes sir. The containers launched from the ejectors go to low orbit, where they are intercepted by tugs and connected to the air locks of the freely orbiting holds. We pump the helon ore ..."

He hesitated. "It's just a common term, because it's really about pressure pom—"

"I don't have to know all the details."

"Yes. Of course. Where was I?"

"Pumping the helon ore."

"Exactly. The ore goes into the holds, then the drones bring empty containers over special magnetic traps, or so-called landing pads. From there, we transport them back to the depots, fill them up and once again send to space."

"So you don't actually load the containers into the rod-ship hold?"

"And what would be the point of it? Have you any idea how many containers would be necessary to carry a hundred and seventy-two million metric tons of helon ore? Even Etoile Blanc Corporation doesn't have so many of them."

"Interesting," Darski muttered. "Very interesting ..."

FOURTEEN

ON THE WAY BACK, his comlink became red-hot. The reports from the moon were coming in one after another—Drechsler did very well, just as the chief engineer. The latter was quite eager to do accurate analyses. Fifteen minutes after the shuttle had taken off, he'd told his technicians to scan all the pillars. Their findings were to be expected within the next two hours, but even the preliminary reports clearly showed that Darski had been right. Six of the ten pillars tested so far had major structural defects.

Keeping an open comlink, Henryan spoke to Truffaut too. He asked her to organize a meeting in a narrow circle of trusted people right after his return. Not being sure if the crazy idea he'd had while talking to Drechsler had a chance of success, even though it took shape after he'd questioned several other engineers, he decided to discuss it with some people who had not only sufficient expertise but also the means to implement his plan if it made sense. He didn't mention any of it to Drechsler because the corporate communications system was reliable only within the magnetic field of the ejectors, and the idea brewing in his head was one of the craziest sorts. Furthermore, it meant losses during the loading so there was a strong possibility that the employees loyal to the Board—those who the deputy technical director was talking about before—would forfeit the initiative.

Ninadine responded a moment before the shuttle landed, informing Henryan that everything was ready. The official cover for the meeting with her, Dupree, Pallance, and another man, whose identity Darski didn't know yet, was a formal dinner in honor of their "savior," as he was christened.

Hopefully, they don't mean it with a capital S, Henryan thought. He looked through the translucent plasteel to watch the blue waters of the ocean and the fast-approaching pastel smudge of the colony. Beyond that an emerald thicket was extending as far as the mountains looming in the horizon.

For some reason, Truffaut laughed when he'd said he'd like to walk through these woods …

FIFTEEN

SINCE HE'D BEEN INVITED to a formal event, Henryan breezed into his suite to take a shower and put on his parade dress uniform. Such at least was the official story for the benefit of the hosts, in case they had the courage to ask why the captain was late. The truth was, Darski wanted to sink into the lap of luxury. A glass, or even two, of Valisian rum and a long, hot shower in actual water. Humankind would lose this planet in just thirty hours or so; Henryan thought it only fair that he should use the offered comforts, especially that he'd spent most of his life in cramped cabins in artificial gravity.

Refreshed and relaxed, he stepped into Ninadine's much smaller quarters fifteen minutes late. He could tell at a glance that third-level managers weren't particularly pampered by Etoile Blanc Corporation, though Truffaut's apartment was five times bigger than his cabin on *Cervantes*. In no respect, though, could it compete with the luxuries offered to him on Delta. The furniture, equipment, everything looked meager. Even the palette of available colors was limited, not to mention the window taking up only half of the outer wall.

All the invited guests were already seated at a large table. Henryan greeted the three men, starting with the doctor and ending with a stranger: a young athletic blond, whose attire differed from the standard outfit of a colonist. It was … somewhat archaic. Darski was curious why this man had joined them, because surely there must have been a good reason for his presence.

"Captain, will you allow me to introduce the head of the scientific department, Professor Olivernest Fitz, our grand huntsman and the best cook that can be found in this part of the Inner Rim …"

"Nice to meet you." Henryan shook the professor's hand, which was strong and toilworn, so unlike the soft hands of the eggheads he'd known on Xan 4. But it didn't escape his notice that the identity of the big guy didn't clarify anything.

"I've taken the liberty of asking Ollie to serve real meat. It's kind of our corporate tradition," Ninadine babbled, leading the guest of honor to his seat. "I hope you don't mind?"

"I like meat," Darski confessed, dropping onto a chair. Seemingly very simple, it was equipped with an antigrav. It never ceased to amaze him what sumptuosity these people lived in. "Contrary to popular belief, we eat decently up there," he pointed to the ceiling.

"But I suppose your meat comes mostly from cultivators," Professor Fitz said in a quasi-friendly, yet chilling voice.

"I assure you that our poultry, fish, and beef can compete with any of their natural equivalents," Henryan snapped back, smiling venomously.

"Please wait until you finish the meal," Ninadine said, giving him a small box.

He looked at the tiny plastic cube with curiosity. He wasn't expecting any gifts. "What's this?"

"Enzyme regulators. In case your organism doesn't tolerate our venison. You know, the animals brought to Delta have been genetically modified so they can breathe freely here. The terraforming isn't over yet, you understand …"

He understood; Truffaut handled the situation very well. It

was more than likely that he would get an upset stomach after eating something he'd never tasted before.

Fortunately, he could give her something in return because he didn't come empty-handed. Having noticed how greedily she'd poured herself a glass of expensive rum when she'd been showing him the suite, he brought half of the most eye-catching bottles from the drink cabinet. It turned out to be a very good idea. As he was putting them on the table, everyone was watching the bottles admiringly.

"I think we can skip the official part of this meeting, if such was planned, and go straight to the point," Henryan suggested, when Ninadine—acting the hostess—was placing pieces of rust-colored meat, potato purée, and vegetables that looked like imported from Earth, all looking extremely appetizing, on their plates. "Before we do, however, I'd like to ask one thing. Where's the chief of police? Had his duties prevented him from joining us?"

"Jeantoine is in orbit now," Truffaut explained, and Henryan sensed a glimmer of jealousy in her voice.

"He got a first-class ticket for the largest ark," Dupree added, seeing that the captain didn't quite understand.

"Lucky devil," Darski mumbled. "Well, then we'll start without him."

Everyone gave a grunt of satisfaction. They were curious what he'd come up with, especially since they didn't stand much of a chance in the evacuation. The corporation needed them to keep order in the mine until the very last minute. If Darski had been a bureaucrat, they would have lived in blissful ignorance. And then, when the Aliens entered Ulietta, it would be too late.

Does natural meat really taste so good? he wondered. *Or maybe it owes its palatability to Olivernest's exceptional culinary skills?* Just the same, he praised Professor Fitz, admitting that he hadn't had anything like it in ages. That was his only digression in the conversation; then, he stuck closely to the subject. Speaking at lightning speed, he was putting successive bits of food to his mouth once in a while.

"Visiting the mine today, I learned that the loading of the rod-ship was slightly more complicated than it seemed. From what I gather, the orbit the containers are being sent to is too low for such a large freighter. That's why the ore is reloaded to the disconnected rotary holds, which then are towed and attached to the rod-ship. Please forgive me if I'm putting it in layman's terms. I'm a soldier, not a miner, so everything's been explained to me like I was a four-year-old."

"Don't worry, Captain, it's common knowledge here," wheezed Dr. Pallance, who also had little or nothing to do with the mining industry.

"When I'd gotten the grasp on the process, I had an idea. As you probably know, the Admiralty won't give us any extra time, which is understandable, and I haven't got resources to evacuate all the colonists—"

"Captain," the doctor said, "just lay it out there. We know."

Darski froze.

"Excuse me?"

"I and my colleagues know what the situation really looks like," Dr. Pallance said calmly. "It was my call."

"What does it look like in your opinion?"

"There is no supernova. You're evacuating us because of the alien invasion."

"How do you—"

"Didn't Ninadine explain what my real role was? I work for the Admiralty. I'm in charge of the local rehabilitation center for veterans."

Darski looked at the obese physician with astonishment, as if he'd socked him one right in the eye. That was the first Henryan had heard of a rehabilitation center for veterans of the Combined Fleets. If such an institution had been located on Delta, he would have received relevant instructions. Yet, he was absolutely sure that his orders didn't mention either this man or his patients.

"What are you talking about? There is no—"

"There's no need to dwell on this," Dr. Pallance cut in.

"You shouldn't have …" Darski began, but instead of finishing, he just put his knife and fork down. He could feel the other guests' piercing stares.

This fatty put me in such an awkward position ... now, when everything was starting to go my way ...

"You're right," Dr. Pallance spoke up after a moment's silence. "But believe me, your secret would be out anyway. It's not some shithole, it's a top-notch colony. We have equipment here on Delta which would enable Professor Fitz to easily demonstrate that there's no supernova within a hundred-light-year radius."

The chief of the scientific department nodded.

"An hour ago, my subordinates requested access to our radio telescope," he said in a neutral tone, though his eyes were glowing. "Jerryan was the witness."

"I thought it was the most reasonable course of action," Dr. Pallance said hastily. "Olivernest settled their hash, saying that he'd checked everything himself."

Henryan swallowed the last fiber of meat.

"This information was confidential. Have you any idea what punishment—"

"Would you rather deal with the miners' revolt?" Dupree asked before the doctor opened his mouth. "If the information had spread through the colony, most people would have headed home."

Darski looked at him.

"If it had been up to me, I'd have told you the truth, but I'm a soldier, I swore an oath—"

"We don't nurse a grievance against you, Captain," Ninadine assured him. "We can see how hard you're trying. Don't worry, none of us will breathe a word. We really want to help."

"We all know what will become of us if your operation fails," said the newly minted director of the mine. "So please, just forget the whole thing. Let's get back to the main point."

"Believe me, I really don't want to leave anyone behind," Darski said. Natural or synthetic, he'd forgotten all about the flavory meat. "But I don't have free rein. My superiors made themselves clear. This rod-ship has absolute priority. It must be loaded regardless of the cost and losses."

"We realize that, Captain. Really. Please tell us what you've come up with and we'll do our best to help you," Professor Fitz said.

"Okay ..."

Henryan pulled himself together. The cat was already out of the bag anyway. "The Admiralty is of the opinion that if I evacuate one hundred and eighty thousand people, the operation will be considered a success."

They murmured, just as he'd expected.

"For them," Darski continued, "you're only numbers in the columns of reports, but not for me. That's why I'm contriving ways of getting the remaining hundred and forty thousand people out of here. And I think I've got one at last ... What would you say if we used the containers to this purpose?"

Olivernest and Jerryan looked at the director of the mine, who apparently didn't understand what Darski was getting at.

Having realized that, he added, "Each of them is docked to a special air lock in space, and its load is then blown into the hold by means of compressors. Anyway, this is what the deputy technical director had told me.

"The air locks are located on the outer walls of the rotary holds. If we could dock the containers to them permanently, we would create dozens, if not hundreds, of pseudohabitats.

"This would enable the evacuees to reach the transit stations in spartan conditions."

Dupree smiled and creased his brow in a deep frown. He was trying to crack the technical side of the problem. Henryan kept his fingers crossed; he wasn't even sure that such use of the containers would be possible at all. The devil was in the detail, and the captain—in his excessive optimism—could have overlooked something obvious, something Dupree would point out and reproach him for.

"I think that it can be done," Dupree said eventually. "We could bung up the front air lock to avoid accidental 'blowing' of the chamber right after docking, and also adjust the compressors in such a way that there will be a nice supply of air."

"How big?" Dr. Pallance asked.

"Let me think …"

Dupree put his knife and fork down to calculate something on his personal holopad. It took a while, so the others finished eating the meal. Certainly, the last on this planet. Perhaps the last one in their lives. Even Darski reached for his fork, though this time the roast didn't seem just as tasty to him.

Xavieric looked up from his holopad.

"We can accommodate about eleven thousand people in a chamber that size, but they'd run out of air before reaching Belt Q with its transit stations. Even on the assumption that everyone will have their own space suits and full oxygen tanks," he added.

"Do you have so much personal equipment here?" Henryan was surprised.

"This is a mining colony. Everyone who works in the mine has at least two assigned suits," Ninadine explained. "Besides, the depots are chockablock. The corporate regulations require that tanks are replaced every two years, and suits have a three-season warranty. It's a trick to pump some money back out of the miners."

"So how many people can we place in one container to be on the safe side?" Darski asked.

"Eight thousand adults," Dupree replied, glancing at his holopad.

"That's a lot, but …" Henryan closed his eyes for a moment. "We'll need almost twenty containers to accommodate everyone. Can you convert that many?"

Dupree seemed dejected.

"Technically …" he started, but changed his mind. "I guess so. This is a unique situation, so there should be plenty of volunteers. The workshops are not working because we finished mining yesterday. No one needs more ore, when we can't even take what we have with us."

"I'd rather know for sure," Darski said.

"Then you have to give me thirty minutes," the director replied and stood up. "I'll run this idea by my technicians. However, in my opinion it's possible."

"In space too, I hope?" Henryan asked.

Dupree seemed surprised by his question.

"In space? How do you mean?"

"In low orbit."

"Why the hell should we do anything in orbit? It'll be much easier and faster to make modifications in our workshops."

"Let's just say it's a *sine qua non*," Darski said. "Will you be able to convert these containers in space?"

Dupree flumped down onto the chair.

"I seriously doubt that. We don't have enough equipment to work in open space. We've never needed it."

"Damn it!" Henryan was very disappointed.

"Why is this a problem?" the doctor asked.

Darski was silent for a moment, wondering how much he could give away, but quickly came to the conclusion that since the officials had already heard about the Aliens, they were all in the same boat and they shouldn't have any secrets between them. Mutual trust was a must in their situation.

"As the ejectors are falling apart, I've forced the chief engineer to reduce the load of all the chutes. That means we kissed the loading schedule goodbye."

"With the Admiralty's blessing, I hope?" Truffaut chimed in.

"No," Henryan shook his head. "Not yet. But they'll have to approve sooner or later. We're on the verge of disaster here."

"Okay, but what exactly is our problem?" Dr. Pallance asked.

"You see … The Admiralty won't accept further losses and will never allow us to launch empty containers. That's why we ought to use those that are already in space."

The director of the mine couldn't believe his ears. "Two hundred thousand metric tons of helon are more important than the lives of almost one hundred and fifty thousand people?"

Darski sighed heavily. "I'm afraid helon is more valuable to the Council than all of us put together."

They brooded over this for a long moment. They'd already seen the light at the end of the tunnel, even felt a sense of relief at the thought of saving their lives.

"I don't believe it, I just don't believe it," Dupree kept muttering under his breath, which made Jerryan snap.

"Captain Darski knows what he's talking about!"

"It's simple," Henryan said, spreading his arms. "These numbers of yours? They weren't assigned to you by lot, oh no; they were determined by cold calculation. Only those indispensable to the Federation have the right to be evacuated. The rest is just an unnecessary burden on the budget, especially at the present stage of war. Don't look at me like that. If I subscribed to this point of view, I'd be on board *Cervantes* now."

"Instead of catastrophizing, we should focus on solving the problem," suggested Professor Fitz.

"But what can we do?" Dupree asked, sliding his gaze over the remaining officials.

"Get to work and prepare as many containers as we can in space?"

"Given current capabilities, we'll manage to convert four, maybe five of them."

"It means forty thousand survivors more."

"True."

"What I think is that—" Darski began, but he paused in mid-sentence when his comlink vibrated. One glance at the display was enough. "I'm sorry, I need to take this," he said, excusing himself.

"Is something wrong?" Truffaut seemed alarmed.

"My superiors have finished reading my latest report," Henryan said shortly.

SIXTEEN

THE ANZIO SYSTEM, ZEBRA SECTOR

10/23/2354

Rutta returned straight to his cabin. He was still torn—on the one hand, he was flattered by what Xiao and the chancellor had said, but on the other, anxious, even fearful about the yoke put on his neck in the same short conversation. The Admiralty and the Council expected him to submit another breakthrough plan, and he had a blank mind. As if to make matters worse, he didn't believe it would pass. Humankind seemed to be running low on options. In the colonel's view, the only solution was to face enemy squadrons head-on. But this might have disastrous consequences, and not just for the crews of the Federation's warships. If the Third Fleet sent one of the newly formed strike teams and suffered an abysmal defeat, the morale of the soldiers and sailors —already low—would deteriorate, reaching an unacceptable level.

Historically, such defeats seldom ended well. Mass desertions, dereliction of duty, and eventually final dissolution of the army. And Rutta couldn't let that happen. Not now, when the light appeared at the end of the tunnel. Even two lights, if you factor in the Admiralty's consent to deploy other fleets' detachments in the Third Metasector. In two or three months, new bases would be created, and hundreds of new warships would appear in the farthest reaches of the Inner Territories. The message from the Admiralty contained very detailed plans and schedules. Xiao agreed to almost all of Farland's demands. The only exception was keeping the largest vessels of the First Fleet in reserve. Even though the civil war had ended more than a hundred years ago, the Central Systems were still paralyzed by fear of another secession. Pity, since the fourth-generation battle-ships could alter the balance of power significantly.

Fourteen months, Rutta thought, taking off his mess jacket. *Less than the blink of an eye in comparison to the age of the Universe, more than eternity from the perspective of those on the front line.*

Being in a generous mood, he poured himself three fingers of whiskey and then plopped down on the chair at his console, hoping that alcohol would soothe his frayed nerves and open his eyes to the aspects he hadn't seen as yet.

Drinking helped him sometimes—unless, of course, he overindulged. Tipsiness didn't murder gray matter, but rather stimulated it, allowing to look at an issue from just the right angle and put things into perspective.

Hopefully, this will be the case today, the colonel thought.

He woke his computer from a sleep mode. The virtual screens lit up almost immediately, showing previously opened documents, charts, and simulations. On one of the side displays, Rutta saw his mail folder. It was brimming. Over the last thirty minutes he'd received seventeen messages, including fourteen analyses of recent attacks, two notifications of further moni-toring stations falling silent, and—

He narrowed his eyes, incredulous at who the sender of the last message was. Dr. Annelly Godbless. The goddess of bad taste and mistress of witty repartee. The concise subject suggested that the body of the message would raise his blood pressure:

How could you, you clones-of-bitches?!

Rutta took a large sip of whiskey and activated the recording. To his surprise, the message was text-based. He needed a moment to realize how much a video-based transmission from the neighboring sector would have cost. The scientific department's funds weren't such as the military's, so the eggheads were used to archaic methods of communication. *And glory be* —Rutta thought, immersing himself in Annelly's message.

I am back, you old bastard, and galacticunt, a black hole stuffed from behind, you won't believe it, you turd, but I lost my tongue. For the first time in my life, I was actually speechless. You had thwarted six years of my team's work! Six years, you schlub in a ridiculous hat, may you shit yourself today with the stars that they've pinned to your collar. How dared you allow such blasphemy? I won't let it go, no way! I have already filed a complaint with the Admiralty. This time, you won't get away with it, you and that lackey of yours. The clowns in ridiculous jackets will sort you out. They have more stars than you, and that's what matters to you, you half-assed clones-of-bitches.

Disrespectfully yours,

Dr. A. Godbless,

Xan 4.

Xan 4 … Somehow, the harridan had gotten funds to complete her research, but why did she have to inform him about this fact? And what blasphemy was she referring to? He looked at the message more closely. The word "blasphemy" was in fact a hyperlink redirecting to the attachment. Well … Rutta drained his glass and activated the link.

———

Farland received the transmission, without even checking who was trying to reach him. He, too, was sick of everything, even though things hadn't gone as badly as he feared.

"What is it?" he growled, not taking his eyes off the documents.

"I think I know what Xiao was about," Rutta said cheerfully.

The grand admiral looked at him with a puzzled expression. The smile on Franciscollin's face seemed unreal to him, almost fake.

"Pardon?"

"After the meeting, you were curious why the highest admiral asked after Darski? I think I know."

"And the answer is so funny?"

"See for yourself."

Rutta disappeared from the display, and a miniature image appeared over the holoprojector's pad.

Above the river crossing some plain, there was a figure of a man in an NCO uniform, rising to the sky. Theo didn't recognize his face, nor did he understand the melodious rumble coming from the speakers.

"What's that?" he asked in a voice filled with marvel.

"Wait …" Rutta fumbled with his comlink. "Now, listen."

The mechanical voice of the translator came from the speakers.

"My name is Henryan Darski, I am a human, an intelligent being belonging to another highly developed race, inhabiting distant star systems. I came to you in peace, but when I've seen your actions, *I am become death, the destroyer of worlds.* I have powers your scientists haven't yet dreamed of. I tame the suns, I annihilate the planets, I bring whole races to ruin. I will defeat your armies with a single flick of my finger, I will make barren the fields you sow with a single breath, I will crush all the circles that you have built since the beginning of time with a single look. I will do it without hesitation if you don't obey my orders! Hear, therefore, what my will is …

"You will depart to the other side of the Adal Vin, and you will stay there forever. From now on, the longest river of Suhurta will be an impassable border for you and for the Warriors of the Bone. You have my word that no Suhur touches the southern bank with their claws if you don't allow them. I will burn to ashes every warrior who opposes me, and I won't leave a single bone of him that could end up in the clan's totem. If you don't listen to me, I will ban you from Suhurta for good, and then I will lead the countless clans to the fertile plains of Gurdu'dihan so that they can turn them into desert. Go away immediately, and you will be spared."

After this rant, the river was struck by laser beams, which must have been fired from a camouflaged graviplane or satellite.

"Who's that homebred Oppenheimer's clone from a cheap holo?" Farland asked.

"This, my friend, is—unknown to you Captain, then Sergeant —Henryan Darski. On Beta, one of the planets on Xan 4."

"I don't quite understand what this recording is about."

"Do you know what I was doing for the last six years?" Rutta asked.

"Yes. You were supervising a planetary study, specifically concerning two highly primitive alien races with not even zero in the Kardashev scale."

"Something like that. We were called off in a very interesting moment. The Gurds, those more advanced, were about to exterminate the remnants of the Suhurs, whom we named 'savages' not without reason. Emergency was declared a few days before the final battle, which was supposed to take place right there."

Theo listened to Darski's speech once again.

"I still don't get it. How did you come into possession of this recording?"

"I found it in my inbox after I got back from the meeting. It had been sent today from Xan 4. The eggheads somehow managed to persuade the authorities to continue the study, but —" He paused for a moment. "Upon their return, it turned out that the Beta dwellers have a new god. Our priceless sergeant."

"Clone-of-a-bitch," the grand admiral muttered, and played the recording for the third time.

"Dr. Godbless, the harridan I've mentioned …"

"The one calling us clowns in ridiculous jackets and hats?"

"The very same. She wrote to me. Wrote, can you imagine?" he repeated, grinning. "In a terse note, she informed me that the recording had been sent to the Admiralty too. Xiao got it first because Godbless wasted some time looking for my new address."

"Wonderful, just wonderful. I must be the only admiral who has the true god under his command, a god worshipped by two completely different alien races, no less. But ... if this Darski screws things up on Ulietta, then I swear, I personally will castrate him in front of all his believers."

"I don't think we have anything to worry about," the colonel said. "This guy knows what's he doing."

"So I see." Farland leaned back in his chair, unable to tear his eyes from the alien planet and the specter of Captain Darski.

SEVENTEEN
THE ANZIO SYSTEM, ZEBRA SECTOR

10/23/2354

"No!"

"Sir—"

"I said no! Who gave you the right to make such a decision without consulting the High Command?"

Darski swallowed. He never thought that the colonel would be so angry. The documents he'd sent him last night clearly showed that no reaction would have catastrophic consequences. The chief engineer of the mine, when pressed by Henryan, had requested the on-site inspection of all the chutes. Having analyzed the data, he'd come to the conclusion that further overloading would lead to an inevitable disaster within the next twenty-four hours.

"I was ordered to make sure that the loading of the rod-ship would go without a hitch," Henryan said, pretending he was calm. "I identified the hazards for my mission and took measures to prevent the worst."

"No, Captain, you still don't get it." Rutta's face was alternately white and red, as if he was about to have a stroke. "I vouched for you, and you … you …"

"Please understand, sir," Henryan tried once more. "You've

seen the documents prepared by the mine's management. They leave no doubt. We were hours away from the tragedy. If I hadn't ordered to reduce the load, we might be talking about a fiasco on an unprecedented scale right now—"

"The one and a half million metric tons which we'll leave on Ulietta is a fiasco on an unprecedented scale," Rutta interrupted him. "The Admiralty will have you shot. Instantaneously. And me too, for company. You've no idea how important helon is."

"Please enlighten me."

"This is highly confidential information," the colonel grunted.

There was an awkward silence.

"I'll take the blame for ev—" Darski paused in mid-sentence, severely reprimanded.

"No, you won't take the blame for anything, but you will contact the management of the mine immediately and tell them to stick to the original schedule."

Henryan shook his head.

"If I do this, the rod-ship will leave Ulietta without even more metric tons of cargo."

"You can't know that!" Rutta cried, but less vehemently this time. He was beginning to understand that his subordinate had done the right thing after all. But would the Admiralty treat this unruliness the same way? "And even if you do, it wasn't up to you to make that decision. You should have waited for the High Command's approval."

"Sir, do you really believe that the metasector's staff would have been able to form judgement and come to an agreement fast enough?"

It was a good point. Although the war with the Aliens was on, even important orders had to wait for approval up to twenty-four hours. And the more important the directive, the longer the wait. In this particular case, no one at High Command would have been prepared to risk their career, so the matter would have been handed over to the Admiralty, and—

Darski was right: there was a better chance of a disaster than a unanimous and fast decision made by Farland and Co. But ... at least it would have gone through the proper channels, and neither of them would be accountable for the utter and miserable failure.

"It's not about us," Henryan said as if he could read his superior's mind. "It's about a higher purpose. You said it yourself."

"Don't you tell me about higher purposes, Darski! We're officers, not some white-collar corporate schmucks. The chain of command was invented for good reason. So that Xan 4 doesn't repeat itself."

"Xan 4? What are you talking about, sir? I just wanted to make the right call and minimize losses."

"Minimize losses? Who are you? Certainly not a god."

"I don't understand—"

"Really, oh destroyer of worlds taming the suns?" Rutta snapped, airing his grievances.

Darski felt his neck stiffen.

"Where did you—" He choked on the third word.

"Dr. Godbless returned to Xan 4. She informed the Admiralty about everything. Do you understand why we are in deepest shit ever? Highest Admiral Xiao personally inquired about you. He told me to take care of this operation personally, and I vouched for you, fool that I am."

Henryan lost his composure. He was confident that the High Command would take his decision to lessen the weight of the containers well. The disaster risk was too big, every person in their right mind sooner or later would give him credit for his actions. That was what he'd expected. But when he heard that the Admiralty knew all about Xan 4, he realized his latest measures might be considered another example of his antics. And that would change the perception of the whole matter significantly.

"Is that all?" the colonel asked.

"With your permission, I'd like to bring up the subject of the evacuation," Henryan said warily.

"I'm listening."

"I think I've found a way to save more colonists."

"So go and save them, what's it to me?" Rutta snapped angrily.

"But ..." Henryan licked his lips. "But it will require another, really minor tweak to the original schedule."

Rutta took a deep breath as if he was about to lash out again. His face darkened slightly, but he managed to regain his composure.

"Can you be more specific?" he growled.

"Yes sir. I've already did the maths." Darski sent him a file.

One look at it was enough for the colonel to blow up.

EIGHTEEN

THE ULIETTA SYSTEM, ZEBRA SECTOR

10/23/2354

It was a short distance from the communications center to Truffaut's apartment, all in all less than three minutes. Henryan needed six, because he had to calm down first. Rutta's final decision distressed him. He'd hoped that the chief engineer's vivid report would bring home to them the scale of the problem. He'd imagined they would accept some material losses if it meant saving nearly one hundred and fifty thousand people. However, the colonel dashed his hopes. No, just no and that was that. The colonists' lives mattered little, or nothing, in the end.

And since even such a level-headed officer like Rutta says no ... I have to find another solution, Henryan thought as he walked down the corridor toward Ninadine's place.

His grim silenced everyone sitting at the table.

"From what I can see, your superiors aren't exactly happy with your plan," Dr. Pallance said.

Darski didn't reply. He was thinking. A new idea had just dawned on him.

"Have you been relieved of command?" Professor Fitz asked.

Henryan shook his head.

"Not yet."

He couldn't know for sure that the colonel wouldn't inform him of his dismissal in the next conversation. For someone else it might have been good news, but for him it would have been a total failure. He'd have had one hundred and fifty thousand victims on his conscience, even though technically, none of this would have been his fault.

"We have to concentrate our efforts on converting the containers in space," Dupree said authoritatively. "I've come to the conclusion that if we keep modifications to a minimum, we'll be able to prepare up to six such pseudohabitats."

"Maybe it won't be necessary," Henryan said quietly.

Everyone looked at him expectantly.

However, Darski was silent. Leaning over the table, he reached for the nearest bottle and poured himself half a glass of the amber liquid. He didn't drink all of it in one gulp, but he took a deep swig. Eventually, he asked a question that had bothered him for some time. "Is it really not possible to further shorten the charging time of the ejectors?"

Dupree shook his head resolutely.

"No. It takes four hundred seconds to accumulate the minimum amount of energy needed to launch a full container."

"What would happen if we launched them, let's say, every three hundred and ninety-five seconds?"

The director of the mine looked at Henryan with a mixture of pity and disdain.

"The impulse wouldn't be strong enough for the load to reach the orbit. Don't forget that power grows exponentially in electromagnetic railgun. Plus, under normal conditions we used six-hundred-second intervals."

"I know, but I'd like you to check if it's possible to save a few seconds, perhaps three or four."

"What good would that do?"

"Please count it again," Darski encouraged him.

It dawned on him just a moment ago. He wasn't even sure if saving a few seconds would help, but he thought, since they were clutching at straws, this idea might be worth considering.

"A three-second difference means we'll have sent two extra containers by zero hour," Professor Fitz said before Dupree finished his calculations. "With five active ejectors, it'll give us ten extra habitats."

"And another four or even five we can assemble in space," Truffaut added excitedly.

Dupree turned his comlink off again and looked at the captain.

"If we save as little as two seconds, the containers won't reach the orbit, but …" He grinned. "But our tugs will intercept them. It's going to be a wild ride, at the upper limit of the equipment performance, nevertheless effectual."

"Great!" Darski exclaimed. Alcohol might have had something to do with his undue enthusiasm.

Professor Fitz quickly cooled their ardor.

"That'll give us just one extra container."

"You're wrong, Professor." Dupree reached for a bottle of the oldest whiskey. "Our containers won't be filled with ore, so we'll need to accumulate energy only for two hundred seventy-six seconds." He laughed out loud. "You are a genius, Captain," he added with unadulterated admiration.

"Oh, I don't know about that," Henryan said smugly.

Everyone laughed, realizing that they'd finally found a solution to the most urgent problem.

"What about the Admiralty?" Ninadine asked, sobering in an instant.

"If anyone on the Board finds out that the launching can be done faster, the extra containers will be full of helon," Dupree said immediately.

"Unfortunately, that's the sad truth. The Board—or Captain Darski's superiors for that matter—won't let such an opportunity go to waste," Professor Fitz said.

"So … what are you going to do?" Dr. Pallance addressed Darski directly.

"I think—" Henryan hesitated. "I think I'll fail to mention this detail in my reports."

"There's still our CEOs," Truffaut said.

"And their toadies," the doctor added peevishly.

"How does this look from a technical point of view?" Professor Fitz asked, turning to the director of the mine.

Dupree seemed deep in thought. He was one of those men who put their money where their mouth was. That's why he preferred to think three times before speaking.

Great virtue, Henryan thought, *waiting to hear the definite opinion of the only expert in the room.*

"There is a way," Dupree said suddenly. "All snitches should find themselves on Delta at the same time. If they don't watch every move we make, we can try and tweak the software."

"What are their names?" Henryan asked.

Dupree recited the names of the five supervisors he'd suspected of being the eyes and ears of the CEOs.

Darski entered them to the *Cervantes'* database and smiled triumphantly.

"It's just as I thought. Their assigned numbers are a hundred thousand something." Again, he moved his finger over the holopad's virtual keyboard. "Done. In two hours, they're going to receive an urgent invitation to the spaceport."

The current shift would end in exactly two and a half hours. Thirty minutes later, they'd start to carry out the operation.

"Does it mean they'll be evacuated out of turn?" Ninadine asked, bringing Henryan out of his reverie.

"No. As I've already said, I'm not in a position to change your numbers, but I can make the waiting lines longer. At this moment, numbers from seventy thousand up are boarding the ark. Those from a hundred thousand up will get on board the transporters the second time around, but they don't know that. And when the snitches get stuck in the spaceport ... Actually," he added after a moment, "I could send everyone who has a chance of boarding. It'll render most of the informers harmless."

"This way, you'd make our job easier," Dupree said. "The next shift workers have exclusive access to number seven maglev line. If this line stays unblocked, we'll be able to transfer seventy-five percent of the colonists."

Ninadine supported him, "Closing the last few stations before the terminals will keep people from the street far from the tunnel."

"That's what we'll do." Henryan made a note on his holopad.

"And how will you explain the haste?" Professor Fitz asked.

"I got information about labor unrest. Those who had no chance of evacuation planned to block routes leading to the spaceport. I had to take measures to ensure safe passage to people with lower numbers.

"Gathering the evacuees in one place will also take care of another problem. You don't know it yet, but High Command have sent three companies of esdees to help restore order on Delta if the colonists oppose the idea of leaving them to their fate. I'd rather keep the esdees busy, stop them from prying into our affairs on the moon. And controlling a raging crowd must be something they dream about at night."

"Some of them can watch the station," Truffaut said.

"All's well and good," the professor admitted, "but what about surveillance?"

"Right. Let's not forget about surveillance," Dupree said.

"What are you two talking about?" Darski asked.

"Each computer in the colony is connected to the internal network. Special trackers monitor all the objects and operations the Board is interested in. In our case, it means everything concerning the ejectors. Reporting takes place every two hours; data are sent to our servers in the communications center and then they travel by means of quantum links to their final destination."

"This might give us some trouble," Henryan said, aggrieved.

Ninadine was clearly disappointed. "Yes, it's an insuperable obstacle."

"Unless the reactor goes on the blink," Professor Fitz said casually.

"Reactors don't break down just like that," the director of the mine huffed.

"What capacity does your reactor have?" Darski asked suddenly, realizing that he hadn't seen telltale domes protecting devices which release unimaginable amounts of nuclear energy thanks to cold fusion. "And where is it?"

"This beast generates twelve terawatts," Truffaut said proudly. "You haven't noticed it because it's hidden underwater. It lies half a mile from the shore, against the continental slope, at the depth of one thousand feet."

"I see." Henryan entered the data to his holopad. "How many units?"

"Seven."

"Great. How long does a complete shutdown of this monster take?"

"At least twenty-four hours," Dupree replied. "But within one hour, the capacity drops to just ten percent. However, we don't have a security clearance that would allow—"

Henryan interrupted him. "I have the power to do it. When we finish here, I'll order my subordinates to take control over this facility and turn off all its units."

"On what grounds?"

"From what we know, the Aliens are destroying all human facilities they manage to locate. Let's just say I want to save a few billions of credits that your corporation would lose otherwise. All I have to do is hide the reactor from the enemy." He sneered. "The CEOs will lick my boots."

Professor Fitz seemed impressed. "Clever."

"Not really," Ninadine said. "The Tower has three independent geothermal power sources."

"That shouldn't be a problem," Henryan professed. "What capacity do these sources have?"

"I'm not sure … A few megawatts maybe."

"Eight." Dupree came up with an exact number after checking his holopad.

"Please correct me if I'm wrong, but that's not enough to

send a quantum message beyond this system." Smiling broadly, Darski lifted his glass as if to make a toast.

"You're not wrong, Captain."

"It's going to be a mess," Dr. Pallance said irritably. According to the arrangements, he was supposed to accompany the evacuees.

"A man can die but once," Dupree summed it up.

The others, who hadn't been listed on the flight manifest either, grunted their approval.

"It'll mean turning power off in many districts of the colony," Dr. Pallance pointed out. "The colonists may panic. They'll have a lot of time to think and talk and can try to storm the spaceport. In case of riots, the crowds will get out of control."

"It won't come to that," the head of the scientific department said suddenly, raising his voice a bit.

"Oh, yeah?" Dupree looked at him dubiously.

"Yes. Let's forget about everything else and just do our job."

"While the informers breathe down our necks and report everything to the Board?" Dupree huffed. "Don't be ridiculous!"

"I'm far from it." Professor Fitz managed to keep his countenance. As the others looked at him expectantly, he elaborated, "Instead of two seconds, let's save just one.

"At the moment, we're launching nine containers per hour. And this won't change. Those responsible for checking the reports shouldn't notice such a slight difference. They won't see it as a risk, but in case anyone asks, we'll say that the gauges have gone haywire. It's completely normal that the equipment is out of adjustment after two hundred hours of uninterrupted operation."

The others nodded at his every word. They'd gotten carried away, had gone too far in the calculations, and realized it only now.

"This way," Professor Fitz continued, "we'll save two hundred and seventy seconds, that is exactly what we need."

Dupree checked something, and then nodded gravely.

"What about the CEOs' toadies?" Ninadine asked.

"We could, even should, get rid of them first," Professor Fitz said calmly, then took a tiny sip of cognac.

"Okay, since all's clear, let me ask you something ..." Dr. Pallance's tone sent chills down everyone's spine.

"What again?" Dupree had a vexed look.

"How do you intend to pack one hundred and fifty thousand people into these containers, in space no less, if you'll send them to orbit only after saving those two hundred and seventy seconds, that is more or less at the same time when the Aliens show up on Ulietta?"

Powder me in sugar and call me a donut, Darski moaned inwardly. Until now, he'd thought that rescuing Suhurs was the most complicated mission he'd ever undertaken. This conversation made him realize how wrong he was.

Ninadine went pale, Dupree raised his brows in astonishment, Professor Fitz put his head in his hands, and only Henryan didn't move a muscle.

"Can't we launch them with people inside?" he asked.

They reacted just as he'd expected, explaining to him all at once why such a thing is not possible. Dr. Pallance was the loudest, even though he'd been the last one to join their group—before he began to reveal the Admiralty's secrets—because no one else would have been able to assess their crazy ideas in terms of safety of the evacuees.

"With forces up to thirty g, we'll kill them faster and more efficiently than the enemy," he said emphatically.

"In that case, there's nothing else left for us to do than to turn off the reactor," Darski pronounced.

"You're at it again, aren't you?" Professor Fitz sighed.

"No. We're going to turn it off with the knowledge and consent of all parties. We'll warn the colonists too, not to create panic among them. In, let's say, eight hours. Before that, we need to think of a way how to transfer people *en masse* to the moon's orbit."

"That'll require loading up to five thousand colonists per hour," said the director of the mine.

"Is that even possible?" Dr. Pallance asked.

"We have transporters at our disposal. Under normal circumstances, they bring miners to the mine, delivering twice as many passengers, but a one-way flight takes about forty minutes. If these vessels start to shuttle, we should be able to do it."

"There are our shuttles too," Darski observed.

"So what?" Dr. Pallance grimaced. "They're carrying those with lower numbers."

"In five hours, we'll wave goodbye to the last ark—" Darski paused in mid-sentence. Numbers. Sequence. "Instead of waiting, we could ... Why don't we send those with one hundred thousand numbers and up to the pseudohabitats?" he suggested, grinning at their surprised expressions.

"But ... what about us?" Ninadine asked, thinking not of those gathered in her apartment. What she had in mind were the colonists holding numbers up to two and three hundred thousand.

"You'll board the regular transporters, which are going to return in ten hours or so," Henryan explained.

"They'll never fall for that," Dr. Pallance said.

"Why? No one except my subordinates and the four of you knows what this evacuation is supposed to look like. Besides, the lucky devils will realize what's going on when it's too late."

"And if someone refuses to board the pseudohabitat?" Dupree seemed full of doubts. "After returning to the colony, they'll raise a stink and—"

"Don't be such a buzzkill!" Henryan interrupted him. "'Refusal to board according to the assigned number will result in moving an individual to the end of the waiting line'," he quoted. "Paragraph three of the Admiralty's message. I don't think many people will want to take such a risk. Anyway, all of them will end up in the mine to wait there for the first free seat."

———

For the next thirty minutes, they were working out the details until they dotted the *i*'s and crossed the *t*'s, and each phase of the operation was planned. Beforehand, however, they had to tackle many problems. The biggest issue related to oxygen and how to provide a sufficient amount of it to the habitats. The colonists would spend more than a day in them, waiting for the rod-ship's takeoff, and that meant the first evacuees would need a lot more air than those transported to orbit in the last round. Having consulted his chief technician, Dupree pronounced that the only way was to halve each container and later, put together a single habitat with duplicate compressors. According to their calculations, two oxygen tanks would do. Then Professor Fitz suggested that they shouldn't divide all the containers into halves, but rather cut some of them in one-third, so that the assembled habitat would be bigger and able to accommodate twelve instead of eight thousand people. This idea was also accepted unanimously by the director of the mine and other participants of the meeting.

Darski tuned out when the members of the new Board began to discuss the technical details of the preplanned actions; he sat leaning back in his chair and sipping at his rum while listening in on the conversation, which unfolded without the benefit of his expertise. Eventually, when all the obstacles were overcome or bypassed, Ninadine's guests started getting up to leave.

Dr. Pallance was the first to exit. His graviplane was already waiting on the landing pad, because for him that long day—and a day on Delta lasted more than twenty-nine standard hours—hadn't ended yet. The evacuation of the medical facility he was in charge of also presented many problems. Jerryan shook hands with the hostess, nodded to his colleagues, and stopped for a moment by Darski's side.

"There's something I'd like to talk to you about, but not here," he said. "At the hospital, if possible."

"I may not have the time, I'm afraid," Henryan replied, slightly surprised. What the man had done made him sick to his stomach.

"It won't take longer than fifteen minutes. I just want to show you something."

"I'll try, but I can't promise anything," Henryan said, before turning to Dupree, who had to return to his duties too.

The director of the mine played a key role in their little conspiracy. The technical side of things required a lot of work, both conceptual thinking and manual labor, so none of them envied him the prospect of staying up all night. Full of understanding, they didn't mind his taking three of the seven bottles brought by the captain. The engineers, who Dupree needed to put to work, would certainly take a kind view to their task if they were able to wet their whistle, especially with something costing more than their many months' wages.

That left the three of them: Captain Darski, Professor Fitz and Ms. Truffaut.

"I best be heading off too," Henryan said to Ninadine. "But before I go, I'd like to ask about something that's been nagging me since my arrival."

"Go ahead. I won't hold anything back."

"How in the world did you cook up the records of the Admiralty and deceive the probe of the Recon Corps?" Darski blurted out.

If he'd been sober, he'd never have asked this, but alcohol took its toll and emboldened him.

"Let me …" Olivernest said, noticing that Truffaut had trouble collecting her thoughts. Turning to Darski, he explained, "It's simpler than you think, but first things first.

"Our probe had reached this system a few months before the Recon Corps. Two moons of Delta turned out to be so rich in helon ore deposits that Etoile Blanc began to act immediately. The corporation was prepared to pay any money for the exploration license. Such an investment could set the corporation up not for just years or decades, but for generations. There was one big problem, however. None of the systems with an oxygen-rich planet has been awarded through bidding. Ever. All of them are appropriated by the Council. No exceptions.

"Of course, Etoile Blanc wanted to get their hands on Delta's helon, so they started operating outside the law. We bribed the commander of the nearest Corps' base and asked him to stop their probe one jump away from Ulietta. There, our technicians uploaded the concocted data. After the official discovery and registration of the new star system, we were awarded an exploration license entitling us to exploit all the deposits."

Professor Fitz paused for a moment to pour himself some more cognac. "Unfortunately, not everything went smoothly. The venal soldiers began to splash out credits right, left, and center, the security department got involved, and three years after the colonization of Ulietta, an official investigation was opened up."

He took another sip, smacked his lips and finally, added: "Then, we put everything at stake. Our lawyers presented the Council with an offer. Either the authorities leave us alone, or we announce how much helon we have in our depots and how big our deposits are."

"What a sorry excuse for a blackmail," Henryan laughed. "I'd have kicked those lawyers out."

"Would you?" Professor Fitz put his glass down. "Have you ever heard of 'a bumper crop'?"

"It does ring a bell …"

"A bumper crop is when some fruit or corn is too plentiful."

"Plenty is no plague."

"So they say, but some people have shot themselves in the head because of it."

"Unbelievable." Henryan smiled wanly.

"And yet. Why don't you read about it in your spare time? Anyway, to put it short … If you have more crops than you expected—twice as much, let's say—your business expenses double, and what I mean here is harvesting, transporting, and storing. Besides, wholesale prices go down because the competition never sleeps.

"So, we have doubled the amount of product, which resulted in increased costs, but the revenue doesn't grow, because even if we manage to sell everything—for a current, lower price—we'll get as much money as for a regular crop at best.

"That's why in the old days, coffee growers dumped a large part of the harvested beans into the sea. Although it doesn't seem logical, they were protecting themselves against losses that way."

"Mmm …" Henryan listened carefully, but didn't quite understand what all of this had to do with their situation. Perhaps because he'd drunk too much.

"So much helon was in our possession that its price could drop sharply on all metasectors' markets. And as you probably know, the members of the Council aren't exactly poor, they mainly invest in strategic resources such as—"

"—helon?"

"You bet. So, we suggested that they should drop the case, and in return we promised that we'd release only as much helon as necessary to keep prices at a solid level. If my memory serves me right, it used to be the same with oil on Earth."

"Perhaps."

"The Council, as we'd expected, met us halfway. We didn't lose our license and could further exploit this system's resources for another ninety-nine years. However, we had to agree to certain conditions.

"Aside from the maximum sales amount, and the bribes of course, we let the Admiralty build a military compound here. Also, we're expected to officially announce in thirty-five years since the deal that we have fully terraformed Delta, thereby renouncing all our rights in favor of the Council. When, in three decades, the Fleet's astroatlas would be updated, it's going to be a win-win situation."

"Corporations …" Henryan muttered with disgust.

"The Admiralty is no better," Professor Fitz pointed out rightly.

"Touché, if you know what I mean by that."

"I do." Olivernest raised his glass, nearly empty by now. "No offense, Captain. I'm not your enemy."

Ninadine, who'd been silent until this very moment, looked at Darski with a glimmer of amusement in her eyes.

"You have no idea why I invited Olivernest to this meeting, do you?"

"I presumed it had something to do with his extensive knowledge of the subject," Henryan said. "And his exceptional culinary skills?" he added immediately, his mouth watering again at the mere thought of the roast.

"That too." She waved her hand dismissively. "The real reason, however, has more to do with what you said before ... Something about the walk through our woods."

Both she and Professor Fitz laughed for no apparent reason.

"Did I put my foot in it?" Henryan asked when they calmed down a bit.

"Do terms 'fauna' and 'flora' mean anything to you?" inquired the head of the scientific department. He kept smiling.

"Yes. Fauna, as widely known, is the Satyr's wife, and my brother-in-law's cousin goes by the name of Florachel ..." Darski replied with a grin.

"Ha-ha ..." Professor Fitz laughed before he continued with seriousness, "Now pay attention to what I say. On Delta, Nature took another fork in the road. What we humans call plants, here is predatory and motile, and the creatures we call animals are its food."

PART THREE
DAY TWO

NINETEEN
THE ANZIO SYSTEM, ZEBRA SECTOR

10/24/2354

Rutta stood at the wall of the command center, looking at the stars. The six-foot-thick plasteel was crystal clear, so at times he had an impression that he was outside, right in space as cold as his thoughts. The galactic disc was stretching across his field of vision, inclining from the vertical. Somewhere over there, a few hundred light-years away, a desperate struggle against time took place. In a myriad of the void-suspended sparkles, seeming to be not celestial bodies in their own right from such a distance, but gentle mist, there were also suns which witnessed huge human drama. Can it be that the Aliens are bombarding the planetary system of this bluish star I am looking at right now? Colonel Rutta didn't know the answer, but neither did he want to lose his illusions by consulting computers. Let the Universe remain pure and peaceful for a moment at least, he decided.

The twin suns of the Anzio system were on the opposite side of the orbital station he called home now. It was completely different from the one on which he'd spent the last six years in the capacity of the Xan 4 science team's supervisor. Military facilities were constructed according to very specific standards, disregarding the costs as well as the residents' comfort. And with artificial gravity, the designers were limited only by their own imagination.

However, in case of this particular orbital station, either the architects hadn't been most brilliant, or the Fleet hadn't had very high expectations. The headquarters was housed in a gigantic, 120-story plasteel cylinder, under which the spherical shield of the reactor and several propulsion units were located, allowing this monstrous structure to make hyper- and subspace jumps.

For the time being, Farland and his subordinates could rest easy. It was nearly one hundred fifty parsecs—equaling twenty-one jumps—from the war zone, or rather the evacuation zone. Unfortunately, these numbers were going to decrease weekly. If High Command didn't come up with some ingenious plan, Humankind would have no choice but to face the merciless enemy in an open battle.

The colonel looked at the nearby planet. Its side, facing the center of the system, was brightly lit by the yellow dwarfs which had been devouring each other for millennia. Thanks to their mutual illumination, it seemed solid beige in color, as if it were an orb cast in plastic, not a real globe. But Rutta didn't care about such things, his interests lying in the warships that were placed in Beta's orbit, just like the station itself. Among those, there were numerous rotund battleships and graceful cruisers of the Second Fleet there. Some smaller support vessels could be found on the Alpha's, Gamma's, and Delta's orbital moorings.

Farland's ships were currently deployed at the other end of the Inner Rim—as far away as possible, however, from the systems reached by the enemy's probes, especially that these were arriving in growing numbers. Just like the liners following them. The Fleet was losing contact with more and more monitoring stations every hour. If this fast pace continued and the Aliens didn't change the direction of attack, they would conquer the Inner Rim within two or three months.

Again, Rutta looked at the distant stars and the irregular galactic disc behind them. A head-on confrontation seemed inevitable …

"You won't see it from here." The colonel started when a familiar voice cut through his thoughts. "I know, because I once tried to locate Belt U."

"I'm not looking for the farthest reaches of the Inner Rim," Rutta lied, not even knowing why he was doing it. "I'm just wondering ..."

"Any new ideas?" Farland pricked up his ears, stopping at the command post.

"No," Franciscollin replied, and sighed heavily.

"Then it's time to get ready for battle." The grand admiral fell into a reflective mood. "At least now we have something to fight with." He pointed at the powerful warships of the Second Fleet. Sparse giants of the fourth-generation stood out among other kinds of vessels. "By the way ... How's your god?"

"You don't want to know," Rutta muttered.

"What has he done again?"

"On the one hand, he saved our asses, but on the other ..."

"Just tell me what he's devised!"

"He ordered the miners to reduce the load," Rutta informed his superior. "Arbitrarily, without going through the proper channels."

"What?!" Farland lost his tongue. "But why? No, wait, don't answer that. First tell me how many metric tons we're going to be short of?"

"One million six hundred thousand, in round figures," the colonel said. "Provided the Aliens won't appear earlier than we suppose."

Farland roared, "This clone-of-a-bitch had no right! I'll court-martial him! Recall Darski immediately. Who else do we have in Belt T?" He fumbled for his holopad. "How about sending Wernier there? He's reliable at least."

"There's no need for that," Rutta said, not taking his eyes off the galactic disc.

"What do you mean, there's no need?!" The grand admiral's voice hit the highest notes. "Xiao will rip our heads off when he finds out."

"The Admiralty already know," Rutta offered calmly.

"Have you been talking with them behind my back?" Farland was indignant.

The colonel sighed even heavier than before. "The Etoile Blanc's people are monitoring the situation," he explained. "It was them who sent the report to the Council. They did it as soon as they'd received news from Ulietta."

"Galacticunt ..."

"Xiao's just asked us for our opinion. He'd also like to make sure no error has crept in. As we speak, the duty officer is working on Darski's reports. In a moment, I'm going to sign my statement, in which I'm taking full responsibility for the implemented change."

"Why?"

"Because it's all legit. If Darski hadn't acted on his own initiative, we would have lost ten times as much ore. My subordinates thoroughly checked each and every one of the analyses done by the mine's chief engineer. The ejectors were really breaking up. We were just hours from a complete disaster. I included it in my statement too."

"Do you think Xiao will believe you?"

"Judging by his facial expression and the names he called me during our recent conversation?" Rutta paused and shook his head. "I can be sure of one thing, though: The highest admiral will come to terms with the facts ... eventually. I treated Darski just as Xiao treated me before I understood that the captain had no other choice. Highest Admiral Xiao isn't an idiot, he knows perfectly well that the loss of a dozen million metric tons of ore would mean not only your ..." He corrected himself quickly, "Not only our resignation."

"I hope you're right," Farland muttered, turning off his holopad. "Even though, I won't sleep a wink tonight. I'm so afraid."

"Do you want to know what I'm afraid of?" There was real fear in Franciscollin's eyes. "That the Aliens are watching us and waiting for our forces to be concentrated in one place."

"I'm also haunted by the thought that they'll hit the Combined Fleets with all their might and smash us into dust ..." Farland folded his arms behind his back and rose to his full height. "I'd do it if I were in their place, you'd do it too, surely. But let's face it: we can't run away forever. Constant withdrawal is a form of prolongated suicide."

Rutta made no comment on this. He lowered his head and pondered deeply. When he finally spoke, he muttered something incomprehensible. In the meantime, Farland also fell into thought—considering Darski's insubordination, however, rather than his friend's exaggerated cautiousness—and ignored the colonel's strange behavior, until suddenly he repeated, "Prolongate, you say ..."

"We're just delaying the inevitable," the grand admiral explained.

When Rutta raised his eyes, there was a look of long-lost enthusiasm on his face. "Thanks, Theo, now I know how to convince the Admiralty."

"I don't understand ..."

"You will, don't worry!" Rutta saluted snappily and did an about-face. "Let me just change my statement."

TWENTY

THE ULIETTA SYSTEM, ZEBRA SECTOR

10/24/2354

"You won't believe it, Captain," Hondo said with a big smile on his face and gave Henryan a reader.

Darski looked at him sharply. He hadn't slept much last night, so everything annoyed him now, especially his subordinates in high spirits. Immediately upon returning to his apartment, he'd injected himself with one, and then another dose of alconeutralizer to stop the buzzing in his head. This sudden sobriety, however, had had some negative effects too. All the fears and concerns, pushed into the deepest layers of consciousness by alcohol, had returned.

The Admiralty might, against reason, order reverting to the old schedule, in which case the intricate plan to convert containers into habitats would end with a spectacular failure, if not a total disaster. A great deal of effort had gone into working out all the details, but the engineers improvised too much. Although Dupree sent progress reports every hour, there were still far more unknowns than certainties. To be blunt, the whole thing smelt of amateurishness, and everyone knew that incompetence led to no good. On the other hand, some said that a makeshift solution lasted the longest.

Henryan, still bridling at the lieutenant's good mood, glanced at the reader and chuckled involuntarily before handing the device back to Hondo.

"Surprise, surprise," he said.

"Eighty-six," confirmed his assistant. "And that's just the beginning."

"I hope you're right, Toranosukenjiro. And now show me the schedule for today's meetings."

A moment later Darski held the same reader in his hands, reviewing a short list. It had only a few points, but he very much doubted that he would be able to find any time for himself. He was expected to respond to crisis situations quickly and effectively, and it didn't take much imagination to know that this day wouldn't be different from the last.

"Is that all?" Henryan asked, approving the schedule.

"Dr. Pallance has been calling for over an hour." Hondo showed him the list of incoming calls. The doctor's name appeared six times on it.

"It's just what I need right now ..." Darski muttered, still remembering last night's unpleasant exchange of words.

"Shall I put you through?" the lieutenant asked uncertainly.

"No!" Whatever the doctor had come up with, it could wait. "Anything else?"

"A guy named Fitz left a private message for you."

"Let me see it."

The message was short. The head of the scientific department reported that he was at the captain's disposal, waiting in his apartment for a sign. *The bastard's tempting me,* thought Henryan.

"If that's all ..." He hesitated, but made up his mind quickly. He formulated his answer in writing before adding aloud: "Cancel the welcome meeting with the security chief ... or no, tell Javiernesto to move his ass and go and meet him, it'll be better this way. Also, ask Ms. Truffaut to come to the landing pad in seven minutes max. I'm going to be available only to her, the director of the mine, and the staff members. Otherwise, hold my calls for the next hour. Understood?"

Darski left the room before his assistant's hand touched his forehead in a salute.

———

She waited for him by the elevator, breathless and sweaty as if someone had forced her to run. Darski mumbled a curse; he'd completely forgotten how convincing Toranosukenjiro could be.

"What's going on?" Ninadine asked as soon as he approached her.

"Sorry about my assistant," Henryan said. He preferred to smooth things over before getting to the matter at hand. "We, the military, are kind of specific. Sometimes I forget that I'm dealing with civilians here."

"So … nothing bad happened?" The woman breathed a sigh of relief as Darski pressed the button to summon the elevator.

"I've just got some new information from the jump zone. The pilots of private vessels indeed turned for help to the colonists from Belt S, and the latter sent an entire fleet of civilian ships."

"How big is this fleet?" Truffaut asked, ignoring the hiss of the opening door.

"I'll explain everything on the way. I'm really in a hurry." He let her go in first.

"Of course." Ninadine took one of the seats, probably out of habit as they weren't traveling very far.

"My assistant's going to keep you up to date," Darski said and pressed the button. "For now, however, more than eighty vessels of varying sizes have entered the system but there are more and more of them with every minute."

"It's still a drop in the ocean …"

"You always see the glass as half empty, and I—as half full."

When the elevator came to a smooth halt and the door opened, they saw the glazed waiting room which Henryan had mistakenly assumed to be an air lock. Together, they moved toward the sliding door and the platform behind it; there, a small graviplane adorned with the corporate logo was already waiting for them.

"I'd like you to take this information to the mine. But in my— half full, that is optimistic—version, it's possible that we'll expedite another few thousand people this way. I think such good news will boost the miners' morale."

"Okay, I'll contact them right away," Truffaut promised as he was getting into Professor Fitz's graviplane, leaving her behind on the landing pad.

TWENTY-ONE

"HOW'S YOUR STOMACH?" the head of the scientific department asked when they took off.

"All right," Henryan said, not wanting to spoil the pleasant atmosphere.

Even though he'd used enzyme regulators, he hadn't slept well. The night had been marked by code brown; proper meds saved the day. Darski's stomach simply hadn't been able to handle local venison. He wasn't eager to admit it, however, because he'd have killed for another bite of Delta's dainty. Next to the roast, officers' rations tasted like cardboard.

"That's great!" Professor Fitz seemed glad to hear it. "In my opinion, it wasn't a very good idea and I told Ninadine so. Too risky. Our corporate guests had always had more trouble than fun whenever they'd indulged their appetite."

"Soldiers are tougher than bureaucrats," Henryan said jokingly, and then changed the subject. He wished he could forget all about his last night's diarrhea. "What are you going to show me, Professor?"

Olivernest smiled mysteriously and replied, "Delta's crown of creation."

"What you said yesterday about reversing the roles of fauna

and flora on this planet mightily piqued my curiosity," Darski stated. "What was at the top of Delta's food chain before you showed up, Professor?"

Professor Fitz sincerely laughed out loud.

"I wish your preconceptions were true," he said as they flew over the wall surrounding the peninsula that had been appropriated by the colonists. "Unfortunately, even with all our technology, people are really low in the food chain here."

"How's that?" Henryan wondered.

"Please remember that on Earth plants were much more resilient than animals. And here? I can't even begin to describe it."

"Try nonetheless," Darski said, intrigued.

"As I've already mentioned, Delta's ecosystem differs radically from other oxygen-rich planets discovered in the Known Universe. From what I know, we've always encountered the traditional division of roles so far. Plants are food for animals.

"Here, evolution took a different path, by no means unprecedented. On Earth, there also were many animal species that a layman could take for plants. Cnidarians, for example. Some of them have only one form: a polyp. Take corals …" Seeing that the captain winced slightly at the unknown names, Olivernest reached for the graviplane's console. They flew on autopilot and with practically no traffic, he didn't have to worry about the controls.

"Look," he said. A display rose before Henryan's eyes, showing some magnificent underwater landscape. "This is Earth's coral reef. You might think you're looking at plants, but —contrary to appearances—these fanciful forms are primitive animals."

"Really? I'd never in my life say that an animal can look like this …"

"That's all right, Captain. Today, this knowledge is available only to a handful of lunatics with an academic degree." Olivernest smiled broadly. "You may also find it interesting that on Earth, there were carnivores among plants. Sundews, monkey cups, butterworts … to name just a few. They came in all shapes and sizes, but in fact they were marginal, just like the corals I mentioned before. Here, however, the opposite is true. All you can see"—he pointed at the green carpet, stretching to the horizon—"is the animals."

"In other words, something like land corals?"

"Not quite. But for simplicity's sake, we can assume so. Of course, being one of those lunatics I mentioned a moment ago, I spot significant differences between Earth's and Delta's fauna, you however, as a layman, can be easily fooled. Except that these organisms live on land, not in the sea."

"And what about plants?"

"In a short while, you'll see for yourself," Professor Fitz said with an enigmatic smile, making a minor course correction.

They started approaching a mountain range.

At its foot, Darski could see a gray mass spread over many miles.

"The Sea of Mists," Olivernest said, turning the autopilot off. "A really incredible place. Here lives the largest plant we've ever discovered in the whole Known Universe."

"This thing doesn't look like a plant to me," Henryan objected, with his nose against the porthole.

The head of the scientific department looked at him with amusement, of which Darski wasn't even aware because he concentrated all his attention on the suspended matter, rippling lazily and as if swallowing the emerald tops of creatures he could only call trees.

"Mists are clouds, only lying just above the ground."

"If I'm not mistaken, clouds are not plants," Henryan snapped.

"You're right, Captain," Professor Fitz replied. "We're looking at a regular atmospheric phenomenon, and the hunting ground of our beast."

He leaned over the console and pressed a button. All displays showed maps, divided into squares. For a moment, the virtual screens seemed lifeless. But then … Henryan saw a red dot in the top left corner, pulsing rhythmically as it moved toward the center.

"Here it is!" Professor Fitz stopped the graviplane six hundred feet above the gray swirl.

When Darski looked through the panoramic window, the mist—as thick as milk and completely opaque—seemed calm, wrinkling like water only here and there.

"Easy ..." Olivernest murmured. "Easy ... There!" he shouted so unexpectedly that his passenger jumped.

The mist bulged as if something large pressed at it from below. *Like a whale emerging from the deep sea,* Henryan thought. He was watching the gray mass which was rising higher and higher, but didn't give in—as though it weren't water vapor at all ...

A few seconds later Darski realized how very wrong he'd been until just now. It wasn't mist, but some creature living in it. Whatever it was, it started standing up, and that hump, that bulge, was its ... neck? Henryan could only guess that the giant was straightening its extremely long neck and expected to see something that would resemble a dinosaur's head.

He was in for a surprise, though. The thing emerging from the Sea of Mists turned out to be a sort of flexible pipeline with a blunt end.

"My baby ..." Olivernest touched the crystallite with his open palm. "I'll miss you."

Henryan muttered under his breath, then turned to his guide. "What exactly is this?"

"Let me introduce you to the most magnificent specimen of *Tripodus fitzii,* the queen of this planet's ecosystem."

"*Fitzii?*"

"The scientific community still follows the tradition of naming newly discovered species by the discoverer," Olivernest explained. "And this is my find, if I may say so. And my chance at immortality. Because it's the largest plant ever discovered in the Known Universe."

"It looks like a gigantic worm," Henryan remarked, still slightly dazed.

"You're looking at just one of its three limbs." Professor Fitz leaned back in his chair and switched the displays into another mode.

The "tentacle" swaying above the Sea of Mists was highlighted in red, and almost instantaneously two similar outlines appeared under the gray mass.

"How deep is it?" Henryan asked.

"The bottom of the basin is about twelve hundred feet below the surface of the mist," the head of the scientific department replied with a hint of admiration in his voice.

"This thing is nearly fifteen hundred feet tall?"

"The maximum branch span, measured this year, was one thousand, three hundred and forty-one feet. I wish I'd be still around when this beast reaches maturity."

"Are you kidding, Professor?" Darski laughed. "You're not old. And you'll easily live another hundred years, maybe more if you choose to hibernate."

"On this world, a hundred years is just the blink of an eye," Professor Fitz said, sighing loudly. "Deltiana was born before early man left his cave, and she'll still be around when we reach the Galaxy's edge."

"Deltiana?" Darski preferred not to discuss Humankind's further expansion into deep space.

"I call her that, in private ... Now look."

Henryan turned his head and saw movement in the air. Above the Sea of Mists, some dark shapes were gliding. They had to be enormous because they seemed big even from this distance. There were hundreds of them.

"What are they?"

"Spores," Professor Fitz said, and pointed at the "tree" tops.

Darski guessed that the spores were produced by these plan —animals. He still found the reverse natural order of things on Delta hard to believe, and was resigned to the fact that he might never understand how the heck plants here had taken over the role of carnivores …

While he was pondering this, the spores traveled a long distance. Carried by the wind, they floated high above the gray mist like bizarre balloons. They were nothing like Gurdian alag'terysms, however—there was no beauty in them, given to the products of civilization by thought, even if primitive, and presented the mere efficiency of Nature. Swollen, livid nodules enclosed by residual tissue from which they'd grown before they were dispersed by … Darski didn't know the name for the part of the Delta's "corals" that the spores grew on.

"Where did they come from?" he asked casually. "I mean, I haven't seen anything like it before."

"They develop in special loculi … body cavities … inside a … let's say, inside a trunk. When they are ripe, they emit gases, these fill the loculi and lift them high into the air where they float far and wide to colonize new areas."

Meantime, the spores hung over Deltiana, which somehow sensed their presence. A thick, pale tentacle stretched full length, its end bursting unexpectedly. For a moment, nothing happened, and then … Something black and shiny fired from the inside of the limb. It went straight for one of the gliding spores. The antenna, or rather a tendril covered in sticky slime, stuck to the balloon and pulled it down from the cloudless sky, giving way to the second, third, and subsequent whips lashing at the spore formation. Right before Darski's eyes, within seconds, a huge hole appeared in the sky.

"Deltiana has a hundred and twelve nematocysts," Professor Fitz explained when the loosely hanging tendrils began to hide again, with their prey of course. "My darling did not miss even once—not even once, I bet."

"What an incredible critter," Henryan said.

The head of the scientific department corrected him, "Plant."

"Okay, plant. So … it's tens of thousands years old, you say?"

"We think that the oldest specimen we've encountered is forty thousand years old."

"Are you telling me, Professor, that there are more of these … these … gundyguts here?"

"Here? No. That is … not in the Sea of Mists. But we've found as many as seven of them across the whole continent."

"Forty thousand years … Unbelievable."

"Why?" Olivernest shrugged. "The oldest tree on Earth was almost nine thousand years."

"Really?"

"You can look it up on Galactopedia."

"I'll take your word for it."

They watched Deltiana for a few more minutes, during which it made several failed attempts, then slowly dropped its nematocysts and vanished into the mist without churning it.

Professor Fitz first broke the silence. "Do you know what I thought when I came here and saw how Delta's ecosystem is different from Earth's, Captain?"

"I'm not even trying to guess."

"By studying Deltiana, I came to a shocking conclusion that this is the only correct evolutionary path. Not animals but plants are the crown of creation."

"Aren't you exaggerating a little?" Henryan laughed.

"Am I?" The head of the scientific department turned to him with a serious look on his face. "What would happen if I cut off your hands and feet?" he asked, but before Darski, somewhat taken aback, had a chance to answer, he added, "Or if I burned your body, except maybe your head? Or even better: if I poisoned and skinned you?"

"I would die, and so would you if I were to do any of these awful things to you," Darski said, not quite understanding what his guide was getting at.

"Exactly. But you can burn a plant, grub it up, cut a stump close to the ground, and you still won't kill it. It's enough that one tiny fragment remains in the soil and a year later, it will regrow in the same place. Let's not forget about the seeds; some are able to persist for hundreds or even thousands of years in the most unsuitable conditions. Dried, frozen, and then … boom!

There's a new life. We'll never match them in terms of vitality. They were the first to colonize Earth, which we've forgotten. Believe me, if God existed, he'd put on the top of the food chain not us, but plants, as it happened here."

"Maybe so," Darski admitted. "But there's a little problem. It's true that plants are incredibly resilient, however … they haven't developed any specialized organs and therefore will never acquire humanlike intelligence."

"I wouldn't be so sure. Deltiana"—he pointed at the mist with his hand—"may not yet think in an abstract way, but she certainly knows what she's doing. I wish you could see how carefully she chooses her hunting grounds. In a thousand of millennia, she might develop her own version of mind."

"And when that happens, she'll lose all the advantage of being a mindless plant," Henryan concluded. "She'll become as empathetic as we are."

This wasn't something Professor Fitz took into consideration, apparently, because he said, "In light of the current state of knowledge, plants can respond to many stimuli and feel fear, for example, but they don't have complex emotions. If they ever develop intelligence, it may be very different from ours."

Henryan shrugged.

"I'm afraid that biology isn't my cup of tea. I'm a soldier, I've been trained to kill."

Olivernest grimaced. "What did you mean yesterday when you said that the Aliens aren't trying to talk to us, they're just destroying everything they see or sense?"

"Well … They're treating us as vermin. At least, my boss says so."

"Aren't you curious why that is?"

"We all are, all the time," Darski replied. "However, no satisfactory conclusions have been reached so far."

Professor Fitz smiled triumphantly.

"And if they are sentient plants?" he asked rhetorically, giving Henryan food for thought. "Plants don't take pity. Some even kill their own offspring if a seed sprouts too close to them."

A very accurate remark, Darski thought. *Maybe the Admiralty unnecessarily tried to humanize the enemy ...?*

He was abruptly recalled from the contemplation of the Aliens' nature by the vibrating comlink.

"Sorry," he said to his guide. "I have to take this call. Hello? What is it?" he snarled when Toranosukenjiro's face appeared on the virtual display before him.

"The director of the mine insists on talking to you, Captain," said Hondo.

"Put him through."

"Yes sir."

The lieutenant disappeared, replaced first by the corporate logo and then almost immediately by a familiar view: the panoramic screens of the control room with Dupree standing in the foreground. Henryan sensed bad news as soon as he saw the expression on the man's face.

"What's going on?" he asked, forgoing the pleasantries.

"We have a situation, Captain," the director replied, undeterred. "The containers aren't airtight."

"So fix them," Darski suggested. He couldn't see what the problem was.

"It's not that simple." Dupree sighed. "These old junkers are full of hairline cracks. Fixing just one habitat's going to take a week."

"Dammit!" Henryan groaned. "Don't you have any new containers?"

"No," Dupree said. "Ore doesn't have to breathe, so the Board wouldn't dream of wasting funds ..."

A sense of unease seized Darski.

Things have been going so well, he thought. By now, at least three pseudohabitats should be ready for boarding. The transporters are on standby, they'll start to shuttle people any moment ...

"We're still looking for a solution, Captain. We could cut several containers into smaller fragments and weld them to the other habitats' sides. It seems to be the best idea, so far."

"Best how?"

"Fastest," the director of the mine said tersely. "It's highly unlikely that the cracks will appear in the same places, but even if they do, we can easily patch them up."

Henryan looked at Professor Fitz, who nodded.

Darski was hesitant, though, for they were pressed for time.

"How much longer is it going to take?" he asked.

"I'm not sure, but I think a couple of hours … for each habitat."

"Could you be more specific?"

"I'll get back to you," Dupree said and disconnected.

The Etoile Blanc Corporation logo appeared on the screen again.

"All good things come to an end," Darski declared. "Let's go back to the Tower."

Reaching for the controls, Professor Fitz said, "I'd like to show you one more thing, Captain."

"Sorry, but I have too much on my mind right now. Although I admit that this planet is fascinating."

"I'm not going to waste your precious time. I just want to suggest an alternative solution. In case your idea falls through."

Darski was intrigued.

"I'm all ears."

"Seventeen hundred miles northwest of here, we've discovered an enormous cave complex. It stretches over tens of square miles and goes as deep as fifteen thousand feet below sea level. It occurred to me that we could harbor a significant number of colonists there. Not for a very long time, mind, but they should be able to hang in there for a few weeks if we start moving equipment and food at once."

"Too risky," Henryan decided.

"In fact, less risky than you think," Professor Fitz said. "I've been considering it since yesterday; I've thought through all possible pros and cons, and you can believe me when I say that nobody knows Delta like I do. The only real problem is how to feed so many people, but if you have all the food left in the colony transported to these caves, we'll be able to wait the attack out, not leaving until you rescue us."

Darski narrowed his eyes. Last night at dinner, he'd said that the Aliens left the systems they purged almost instantly. The probes sent to Belt V found no trace of the enemy, even though they checked every monitoring station gone silent. True, they'd been programmed to return within a few minutes of the jump, but such short time allowed for data collection. Later in-depth situational analyses included the level of damage done.

"What I'm going to say next is classified, so maintain discretion please." Henryan looked Professor Fitz straight in the eye. "The Aliens destroy not only buildings and industrial installations, but also everything holding electronic devices, even the simplest ones. This widens the circle of targets, which include vehicles, satellites, and all things we would never think of. Like the bunkers on Gamma, which had been built shortly after the settlement of this planet. And they were hidden almost five hundred feet underground."

"Five hundred feet and fifteen thousand feet is not the same, Captain," Olivernest said flatly.

"Certainly," Darski agreed, "but we don't know how sensitive the alien sensors are, or how they work for that matter, so just to be on the safe side, I'd advise you against putting electronics in the caves."

"It complicates things a bit ..." The head of the scientific department stroked his chin. "But I think we can still do it."

Darski nodded, albeit uncertainly, which didn't escape Olivernest's attention. The captain was starting to like the idea; the big unknown, however, was how the Admiralty would react. Even he knew that the schedule was very tight. In Belts U and T, there were many smaller colonies needing to be evacuated soon. But if he laid his hands on an ark, or one of the bigger transporters, and made it shuttle back and forth, then ... Yes, it would be possible. Unfortunately, the logistics wasn't the only problem.

"Delta's going to be the first oxygen-rich planet the Aliens hit," he said. "It's hard to say what they will do. On Valis,

Valkyrie, and Vandal, they destroyed the infrastructure and waited for a few days to make sure no one survived. Delta's another matter. They might leave orbital weapon platforms behind, or even land on the surface. They also might turn Delta into their staging area."

"If the things don't work out the way you plan, everyone left behind will be a walking corpse," Professor Fitz spoke after giving the captain's words a moment's thought. "I want to give these people the ghost of a chance. If the Aliens find us, that's too bad, but if they don't, you'll come to our rescue. Besides, shifting the supplies to the caves isn't going to impede the main operation."

"That's where you're wrong. The evacuees need to be provided with food, and for two days at least. And we're talking about the same ration packs you plan to shift."

Professor Fitz shook his head.

"The colony's supply depots are filled to the brim with freeze-dried products. There's ten times more chow than we both of us are going to need. Don't forget that this populace was half a million strong."

"Are you sure these figures are right?"

"Yes. I asked Ninadine to check the stock levels this morning. You'll get her report when you see her. I suggest you start with depots three, five, and seven, in which supportive meals for mine workers are stored. In the meantime, I'll have my people clear the stuff from the shops."

"This would be looting," Darski said, appalled.

"The shop owners had left before you arrived, Captain." Professor Fitz shrugged. "So these are abandoned goods. Wouldn't it be a pity if they went to waste? Especially that they can save many human lives."

"Okay, let's say that I haven't heard anything."

"Heard about what?" The head of the scientific department grinned.

"Are these the only caves on Delta?" Henryan changed the subject.

"No, but they're the biggest."

"Good. If you want to salvage some equipment, put it in the other caves for now. As far from the place where you're going to hide as possible. If it gets destroyed, you'll know that the Aliens can detect all electronics, even underground. If not, you'll use it after they leave the system."

The display came back to life.

"Bulking out all the containers, we'll produce eight of them at the most. Seven, more like."

"Damn."

"Only they're going to be really big, for minimum twelve thousand people each." The director of the mine added with a half-hearted smile.

"Eighty-four thousand people …" Darski sank in his chair.

Dupree licked his lips nervously.

"Rutgernest, I mean one of my deputies, suggested that we could use our transporters," he said.

"The ones which used to take workers to the mine?"

"Yes."

"But how?" Professor Fitz wondered. "They're not equipped with extra-systemic drives."

"They can always be connected to the holds' air locks, just like the containers."

Henryan and Olivernest looked at each other knowingly. Both liked this idea.

"Brilliant," Darski exclaimed exultantly, but his expression turned serious almost instantly. The look on Dupree's face cooled his enthusiasm. "You seem worried …"

"This will require some significant alterations, for which we don't have time."

"How much time are we talking about?"

"Six to eight hours."

Great, just great! Henryan thought. *If the evacuation is to be successful, it must start in two hours, tops. Even if not all the containers will have gotten converted by that time.*

Professor Fitz raised his hand as if he was requesting permission to speak.

"Why don't you make these changes batchwise when the shuttles are unloaded on orbit? You'd have at least one hour to do the work."

Xavieric grimaced wryly, looked to the ceiling for inspiration as he often did, finally shook his head, although he didn't mean to disagree with Professor Fitz.

"It'll be difficult, but it's doable," he said with slight wariness in his voice.

"The trick to get things done is to do them in the right order. Besides, no one expects you to give the containers a paint job." Olivernest's last line cracked them all up.

The director of the mine ended the call, still shaking his head in disbelief.

When Toranosukenjiro reappeared, Darski asked him, "Is there anything else?"

"Yes, Captain. Dr. Pallance keeps calling. I've tried to brush him off, but he's very insistent."

"Whatever he wants, you can take care of it."

"I told him as much."

"And ...?"

"Privileged information, eyes-only, need-to-know and all that."

"Right ..." Henryan sighed heavily.

"He says it needs to be resolved before the hospital is evacuated."

Darski checked the time. Dr. Pallance was to report at the terminal in two and a half hours.

"If he calls again, put him through providing—"

"He's kept his comlink open," Toranosukenjiro cut in.

"Okay." Henryan, put under the gun, eventually gave in.

A few seconds later, he heard familiar wheezing. He'd deactivated holovision deliberately, not wanting the doctor to see where he was or who with.

"You've been trying to reach me," Henryan said impatiently.

"Ah, it's you, Captain." Dr. Pallance was visibly glad. "At last. As I mentioned yesterday, I'd like to bring your attention to —this is about one of our patients. Let me show you something."

"Is it really so important?" Darski asked. "My schedule is tight. Plus, Xavieric's just informed me that there are some serious problems with the containers."

Dr. Pallance seemed nervous. "Honestly, I don't know what to think, so I'd rather you had a look at this."

"Why are you so mysterious, Doc?" Henryan laughed.

"It'll take only fifteen minutes of your time. Seven minutes there, seven minutes back again, and if I won't convince you to stay longer within the remaining sixty seconds, we're going to forget the whole thing, all right? Now … When will you be ready to board the graviplane?"

"I'm away on a little trip, trying to find a place where those who stay behind could hide—"

"I see," Jerryan interrupted the captain, apparently afraid that he might end the call any moment. "Are you alone?"

"No. Professor Fitz is sitting next to me."

"Could you activate your personal force field?"

"Seriously?"

"Yes. What I'm going to show you is strictly confidential."

"Is this some kind of joke?"

"No, it's not," Dr. Pallance said with a deadpan face.

"Just a sec …" Forgoing the force field, Darski reached to his pocket for his personal headreader and turned it on.

One minute and fifteen seconds later, he ripped the device off his head. It was hard to gauge if he was irritated or interested, judging only by his facial expression. However, he opened his mouth almost instantly.

"How soon can we be back to the Tower?"

"In sixteen minutes if we fly over the bay."

"And to the military compound?"

"If I step on it, five minutes later."

"Will you spare me another half an hour, Professor?"

Olivernest noticed that Captain Darski was filled to the brim with nervous energy, now that the conversation was over, but he didn't ask what Dr. Pallance had shown him. Some secrets, especially military ones, are meant to stay secret.

"Certainly. The signal my people are waiting for can be sent from the air."

TWENTY-TWO

THE GRAVIPLANE FLEW JUST above the square roofs of mass-printed houses. Except for the prominent Tower and several high-rise buildings owned by the corporation, identical ground-story bungalows reigned everywhere else in the colony. Their orange, and sometimes pinkish structures in the shape of cubes stretched in every direction as far as the eye could see. The squat houses stood row upon row along identical streets, parallel to the maglev line. For a soldier, used to uniformization, this wasn't a particularly depressing sight—most military barracks looked just like that, though rarely were they as vast as this mining town. Could this landscape please the civilian eye? Darski wasn't sure, but apparently no one on Delta complained. Here, in the Inner Rim, people had other concerns.

The corporation provided its employees with basic amenities, but as for the rest, they had to fend for themselves. Their wages were good compared to other systems—too low, however, to even think of extensions. That's why the miners concentrated all their efforts on cultivating their backyard gardens because this gave them a healthier, more varied menu. And so, greenhouses, polytunnels, and ordinary beds stretched between the prefabricated fences, enabling the cultivation of the most popular of

Earth's fruits and vegetables, engineered of course to grow in extraterrestrial conditions. Delta was an agriculturalist's paradise; with axial tilt of forty-two degrees, summer never ended at this latitude, and with such rotational speed of the globe, a local year lasted twenty-three standard months, while a day was five hours, four minutes and fifteen seconds longer than Earth's.

The colony's outskirts were a less densely built-up area; the houses were larger, and while they still stood in walled gardens, the latter were of the traditional sort—made of stone. Even the streets seemed wider, probably thanks to the greenery-covered berms. At almost every crossroads there were entertainment and commercial pavilions. These were typical middle-class neighborhoods, populated by engineers, technicians, supervisors: the fourth- and fifth-level employees on the corporate ladder. Still insignificant, but more important than blue-collar workers. Some could even afford their own means of transport. Today, the sleek and shiny vehicles stood mostly in the parking lots near the maglev stations. They'd been abandoned just like most of the personal belongings because baggage allowance was set at the limit of a hundred and seventy pounds per person in case of arks and fifty-five in case of transporters. Anything over the limit had to fit in the evacuees' pockets.

Professor Fitz flew over the last buildings and passed the wall, at least forty feet high, beyond which Nature reigned supreme over Delta. Farther down, a fenced road led to a small military compound Olivernest had mentioned last night. At first, Henryan took his words for a slip of the tongue. He couldn't believe that High Command maintained a secret facility on a planet illegally leased to one of the largest corporations.

There's something very wrong here, Darski thought, staring at the distant truncated pyramid of a building standing in the middle of a vast complex, where he was about to land in less than sixty seconds. From what he knew, Dr. Pallance took care of civilian patients too. He was Etoile Blanc Corporation's medical consultant, spending several days a week on the other side of the wall, thanks to which he abecame a prominent member of the colony. This didn't really fit in with the captain's conception of the head of a top-secret government institution.

The graviplane descended slowly and touched one of the landing pads. The moment its retractable skids rested on the circular grille, the latter lowered into a spacious hangar. A few seconds later, Henryan came face to face with an obese man.

"Follow me," Dr. Pallance said without a proper greeting. "And you can wait here," he turned to Fitz, almost as an afterthought.

These two aren't the best of friends, that's for sure, Henryan thought.

Before he trotted after the doctor, he had to let the three paramedics escorting a stasis pod pass by, and only then could he head for the elevator, waiting to take him underground.

Level minus six, Darski thought. *Who builds underground hospital complexes in the boondocks, especially in time of peace?*

Dr. Pallance took the lead again. He limped slightly with his left leg, which Henryan hadn't noticed until now. He also sweated heavily, as if he wasn't used to such rush. The back of his head and his neck were covered in large, fat droplets.

What if this isn't just the sign of fatigue …?

After a short walk down the sterile corridor, they turned left and passed, one after another, two doors with an integrated genetic scanner. On reaching a small, cluttered office with a holodisplay instead of a window—which was nothing strange in underground complexes such as this—Dr. Pallance fell onto a swivel chair, showing his guest a seat on the other side of the desk.

"We can speak freely here. The esdees bailed out an hour ago, so no one will see or hear us, although the CCHV is still operational."

"Let's cut to the chase, then," Darski said, not quite believing the doctor's assurances.

He decided that he'd be careful about what he said and wouldn't even mention yesterday's meeting, just in case.

"Of course." Dr. Pallance activated the terminal and then moved the virtual display over the desk, enlarging it four times so that his guest could see every detail of the documents presented to him.

The drawings, austere and simple, weren't drawn by a child by any means. All showed a familiar, bulb-like, somewhat shapeless silhouette.

"Incredible," he murmured, flipping through the files. The sketches became more and more interesting. They depicted a hangar with a turret, to which many small vessels were moored, maps of circular corridors, and finally the figure of ... an angel. "Why didn't you show me these pictures before?"

"I'd completely forgotten about them," Jerryan said. "But yesterday, when we were discussing the evacuation plans, it dawned on me that the shapes from the bulletin ... I'd seen them somewhere. And I remembered everything. But I couldn't speak up ... Not with the others present ..." He paused significantly.

Right, us soldiers and them civilians, Darski thought, and laughed internally.

"Where did you get these drawings?"

"A patient of mine drew them," Pallance replied quickly.

"And you're absolutely sure he did it three months ago?"

"Yes. I had them archived. Look at the date the files were created."

Everything checked out; the drawings had been registered in early August, long before the first attack.

"But how is it possible?"

"I've no idea." Dr. Pallance shrugged. "That's why I turned to you."

"Who is this man?"

"His personal details were classified," Jerryan explained. "To us, he was Number Seventeen."

Reducing people to numbers, literally, had negative connotations for Darski. Suddenly, this room became even more ... ominous.

"Pardon my asking, but what exactly is this place?"

"It used to be called a black site, Captain ... For years, our locked ward was full of terrorists, subversives, and separatists. We were supposed to get intel from them. You wouldn't believe if I told you how many people are attracted to some criminal ideology or other."

"The detention of political prisoners just outside a colony with a population of nearly half a million wasn't such a good idea, I'd say."

"Would you? In my opinion it's a perfect place. Ulietta lies close to the edge of the Inner Rim. Flying out of here are only those who are privy ..." Dr. Pallance raised his hand to silence the captain who'd just opened his mouth. "Not to this project, but to the agreement between the Council and Etoile Blanc Corporation. All the rest work hard to support themselves and every day give thanks to gods and CEOs that their families, for the first time in their life, can see the sunrise, bathe in warm waters, and eat something better than protein mush. Besides, the hospital is a perfect cover. We treat the colonists, and they believe that we run a regular vet center."

The darkest place is under the candlestick, Henryan thought, but didn't pursue the matter. Time was getting on, and he had much more important things to do.

"As for the patient ... you wouldn't know why he was placed here, would you?"

"I'm afraid not. We usually receive detailed guidelines ... of course I don't mean us doctors, but the esdees ... There was only one recommendation in his case, however. Total seclusion."

"Didn't it make you wonder?"

"No. Sometimes, a month or even a week of seclusion is enough to soften up unrepentant hoodlums, but ..."

"Yes?"

"With him, it was different. And we've never received any new orders, so he's been sitting in the hole for almost ninety days now." Dr. Pallance shrugged.

"Can I talk to him?" Darski asked.

"I don't see why not. He's ready for the visitation."

"It might take longer than you think—"

Henryan knew that the military compound was being evacuated. A small hospital ship, sent by the Admiralty, had already reached Delta's orbit and the medical staff was now preparing a few hundred patients for boarding, mainly soldiers and sailors from open wards, who had been undergoing post-accident rehabilitation. Some of them had already been transported to the landing pad. In the meantime, the compound's support staff carried equipment and stasis pods with the sickest patients to the ambulances. The whole place bustled with activity.

"That's all right," Dr. Pallance said, waving his hand dismissively. "Number Seventeen is all yours from now on, Captain."

"I don't understand ... You can't just hand the man over to me. This is a secret prison, and he's been placed under your supervision."

"Maybe I can't, or shouldn't, but I have no choice. I'd be rid of him in about an hour if it weren't for these drawings."

"What are you talking about?"

"Within the next sixty minutes, the compound's evacuation is going to finish. When all the medical staff and patients are transported on board the hospital ship, we'll pack the prisoners in the 'coffins' and we'll leave the Ulietta system according to the schedule."

"I'm aware of that, Doc. I know what numbers you've been assigned."

"Look here ..."

Jerryan pulled up his inbox, selected one of the latest messages, and opened it. It was a short answer to his question regarding Number Seventeen's transfer:

Are you fucking kidding me, Pallance? We've sent you sixteen objects and you're going to fly out to Numenor with just as many. Over and out.

———

The interrogation room was cramped and claustrophobic; nothing like a hospital room. Gray polymer covered all the walls and the ceiling, there were no windows, or holographic displays, and the only sliding hexagonal hatch couldn't be opened from the inside. In the middle, on a fine grille, stood a wide table equipped with a simple console and a dual-screen holoprojector.

Henryan took a seat across from a slim young man with an oval face and fair hair cropped close to the scalp. His gaze was lazy, and his deep-set blue eyes were half-closed as if sleep was overwhelming him.

Dr. Pallance had mentioned that the guards would give sedatives to Number Seventeen; every prisoner leaving his cell was subject to such procedure. However, the drug should have worn off by now.

"I'm Captain Darski," Henryan said when the man looked his way with the eyelids up. "What's your name?"

"Number Seventeen," the prisoner croaked.

It was obvious he was having trouble speaking. Not necessarily because he'd been medicated.

"How about a real name? Don't you have one?"

"I do."

"Then tell me. Let's talk like one human to another."

Number Seventeen coughed loudly to clear his throat. "As if you didn't know ..." he mumbled, swallowing his own phlegm.

"I'm not an esdee,'" Darski said, doubtful that the prisoner would believe him. "I'm here because you might know something I'm very interested in."

"Who sent you here?"

"No one. It's just that ... I was in touch with Dr. Pallance, the head of this facility."

"Dr. Pallance?" The prisoner shook his head. "I don't know anyone by that name."

"Never mind," Darski put an end to the divagations. He was mildly annoyed, but he knew he couldn't show it. This was too important a matter to get fucked up. "Okay, let's do this again. I'm Captain Darski. What's your name?" he repeated and then added in a stage whisper, "I told you my name, now you tell me yours."

Number Seventeen stared intently at the officer's face. "To what do I owe this sudden interest? I told you what you wanted to know."

"I've no idea what you're talking about." Henryan gave up and decided to cut to the chase. "I don't know who you are, or why you ended up here, and, to be honest, I don't really care." Turning the holoprojector on, he pulled up the sketches. "Do you know what it is?"

"No," Number Seventeen replied.

Too quickly and too nervously, Henryan thought. Dr. Pallance was right: prolonged solitary confinement messed with people's heads so much that they didn't control their own reactions anymore. Even a blind man could see that the prisoner was lying.

"It's your drawings."

"So what?" The prisoner would have shrugged if the electro-magnetic constraints allowed for it. "I don't remember scribbling any such thing."

"I think you do," Darski said.

The second screen came to life, showing the confrontation between Khumalo and the liners. Not a sanitized holo, but a full recording, available only to High Command.

The prisoner's reaction didn't surprise Henryan; it was exactly what he expected. Number Seventeen turned pale, and pearly beads of sweat appeared on his forehead instantly. He gaped at the screen alive with apocalyptic scenes, as if he didn't believe his eyes. When Darski stopped the recording and the exploding ships froze above the table between them, the prisoner remained motionless.

"What was that?" he asked shakily after he came to his senses. "What did you just show me?"

"Something tells me you know more than you're letting on," Henryan snapped, pointing to the other display. He'd learned how to put pressure on people from his brother, and now he intended to use this knowledge. "But first things first. What's your name?"

The prisoner looked at him reproachfully.

"Stachursky. Nike Stachursky."

"Nike?" Darski was flabbergasted. "Are you from Earth?"

"No. That's a standard double-barrel, actually. Nik and Ike …"

Darski entered his first and last name and waited for what the Admiralty's database would spit out. Finally, on a small screen his interlocutor couldn't see, he noticed a flashing folder. The facial features matched, although the young man in the photograph weighed at least twenty pounds more and was smiling. Twenty-seven years old. The fourth best score of all the graduates, assignment to the Recycling Corps. *Since when does the Academy relegate top students to junk collection …?* Henryan found this thought disturbing, but he pushed it aside for the time being. Training on the FSS *Nomad*, the first mission in the New Rouen system. And that was it. If you don't count the last file, that is. Very brief, in fact consisting of only three letters.

"KIS." Killed in service.

The enclosed hyperlink, however, provided access to a report, in which a certain Captain Morrisey had described the accident scrupulously. Stachursky, Bourne, and two other cadets were practicing rescue capsule emergency launching. One of them entered a real startup sequence by mistake and launched their capsule straight into a wreckage cluster. The captain and two other crew members confirmed that the high-speed capsule had collided with the cluster multiple times, and most likely exploded. Stachursky was killed outright; Bourne, who'd ejected, was still in coma, in hospital on Kassel 6. On board collapsars, such accidents were not uncommon—especially among cadets whose IQ was rarely impressive.

When Henryan looked up at the prisoner, he was staring at the still cube with an alien liner flying from behind the sphere of plasma which a proud battleship had turned into seconds ago.

The captain understood that Stachursky'd been deleted from the Fleet's register as another victim of a long-forgotten war.

"Well, Nike ... Now tell me what you know about the ships that you've sketched so skillfully."

Stachursky gulped. There was fear in his eyes. "You won't believe me," he said after he'd gathered his thoughts.

"Wanna bet?"

"While recycling the wreckage in the vicinity of the fourth planet in the New Rouen system, I noticed another cluster in the Theta L-point. We flew to check it out—" He started to sweat profoundly. Those weren't happy memories. "We found a ship there. Damaged, drifting in the cloud of debris for about forty thousand years, as it turned out later ..."

Henryan first widened his eyes and then nodded, encouraging the prisoner to continue.

"We went on board, which was our captain's idea," Stachursky added hastily, "I was against this, but they outvo—"

"Come on, focus on what's really important," Darski said.

"Under one of these domes," Nike pointed to the bulges at the liner's bow, "there was a large recess which we called a hangar. I made some sketches of the mooring turret ..." He turned to the second screen, hesitated, and gestured at the right drawing. "We got into a complicated corridor system through one of the locks ..."

He traced the drawing with his finger and fell silent.

"And then?"

"We inspected everything. I guess I drew up a corridor plan too ... Eventually, we got to a sort of hibernation chamber, where we found a ma'lahn. Still alive."

"Still alive what?"

Nike pointed his chin at the figure of an angel.

"Him."

"Is this some kind of joke?"

"No." Nike looked down.

"Are you telling me that we've been attacked by angels?"

Instead of answering, Stachursky just nodded.

"See? You don't believe me. And I haven't come to the best part yet."

Henryan leaned back in his chair. After a promising start, they sank to new depths of absurdity. He was beginning to suspect that Nike was just plain crazy because of the trauma he'd suffered, and no longer able to tell the difference between fact and fantasy. However, he decided to listen to the rest of his story, for there was a grain of truth in it—the prisoner's drawings showed alien liners, there was no doubt about that. It was only necessary to skillfully manage this conversation, and then separate fact from fiction—or rather sick mind illusions.

"I'm sorry, you just took me by surprise. Go on. Do the best you can and I'll try not to interrupt you."

"What I'm going to tell you now, sir, is so incredible that you could easily think I'm nuts, but I am not.

"Scriptural angels look just like the being I've drawn not coincidentally, oh no. If you had a little better education, you'd be familiar with the name I gave you ..."

Darski ignored the waspish allusion.

"Many thousands of years ago," Stachursky continued, "we saw them regularly because they were our shepherds. Yes, the word 'shepherd' is the most appropriate here. Everything we've been taught about the origin of man is nonsense and lies, sir. Do you want to know the truth? It was the ma'lahn who brought our ancestors to Earth. The cradle of Humankind? Our roots go back to one of their farms where we were bred like cattle. Also for slaughter, of course."

The prisoner's mocking smile told Henryan that he wore an expression of disgust on his face.

"That's right. We were livestock to them, nothing more. And I'm not making it up. In the hold of the alien ship, we found tens of thousands of humanoid carcasses, frozen and cut up."

"That's what you figured based on some ancient scriptures and butchered bodies?" Henryan couldn't help himself.

"No. We didn't have to speculate. Murdermat told us everything."

"Who?"

"The ma'lahn whom we awoke."

"I see."

"Don't try to fool me. You don't get anything, and you didn't believe a word of what I just said, maybe except the first part. I'd known what this ship looked like even before I met you, hadn't I? We ... I'm talking about the *Nomad*'s crew ... could be sure that no one would believe us, so we didn't report the incident and kept all the details under wraps. It's all so fucked up that even I sometimes think 'Nike, the Theta adventure was just an extremely dumb dream.'"

Henryan nodded; at long last Stachursky said something that made sense. A second ago he wanted to turn the comlink off and leave.

An extremely dumb dream doesn't even begin to cover it, he thought. *The most moronic story anyone's ever told, more like. Nothing about it adds up.*

"Let's stay focused on the ship," Darski said, restraining his nerves. "What else can you tell me about it?"

Nike thought deeply.

"Your head's going to explode when you hear this," he said with a note of amusement in his voice, but became serious almost instantly. "In fact, it's not a ship at all. It's a living creature, surrounded by armor which—"

Darski winced. He should have laughed, there and then, but before he had a chance to lift the corners of his mouth, he remembered how the liners responded to the nuclear torpedoes.

If Nike isn't lying ...

"Just a sec. Are you saying that this ship has a will of its own?"

"Well, I wouldn't quite put it that way myself, but ... it sure can make autonomous decisions. It let us in."

"It let you in?"

"Yes. Its deflectors were still active, though barely functional. The ma'lahn use absorption fields," Stachursky added casually, as if it wasn't a very important piece of information.

"Anyway," he continued in the same breath, "we started bombarding the wreck with the L-point debris and suddenly, one of the domes opened letting us into the hangar. Then, while determining the layout of the interior, we noticed something strange. New layers didn't match the old ones. This could mean only one thing: the ship's structure was fluid. Moreover, at one point it became clear that some of the corridors were closing up on their own, as if the whole thing was made from some super-elastic material. We even had to burn through one such obstruction …"

Darski was seriously confused. Could the prisoner really have seen an alien liner up close? But how else would he know about the absorption fields, which were just a theory in the Admiralty's eyes. Did it mean that the rest of his story was also true? Henryan, who kept a cool head, found it difficult to believe that the Aliens looking just like biblical angels raised his ancestors for meat. Although … that would explain their current actions, wouldn't it? Since the livestock got out of hand, it was only natural that …

Come on, man, he thought. *This can't be true. Nike went through an ordeal which messed with his head so much that now he can't tell what's real and what's not.*

Henryan made some notes, however. Just in case.

"Okay," he said. "Without proof, no one's going to believe you, you realize that, don't you?"

"I guess …"

"So? Evidence?" the captain pressed on, but Stachursky only shook his head. Henryan leaned back in his chair. "Then we have a problem."

"You do," Nike jibed.

"Don't be so cheeky," Darski cut him short. "When I say we have a problem, I mean you and me."

"Oh? And why's that?"

"Let me put it this way … We are currently located in Belt U. On Ulietta, which will be attacked by the Aliens in about twenty hours. My problem is that I'm responsible for evacuation and can't see any way in which all the colonists might be saved. Your problem is that this compound is already empty. The staff and patients have been transferred on board the Admiralty's hospital ship. Only you weren't on the list of people eligible for transport."

Stachursky was still smirking, but visibly lost his confidence.

"Those who put me in here are capable of such cruelty," he admitted sadly.

"Who are you talking about?"

The prisoner sighed. Instead of giving an answer, he asked, "What exactly is my current status?"

"It's hard to say," Henryan said calmly. "If I write you off as insane, you'll be dead in twenty hours, still sitting in that chair …"

"Good to know."

"… but if you start talking sensibly and give me some information that'll help the Fleet, I'll get you out of here."

"And what next? The Admiralty will take care of me again. I'll be put in the hole, or better yet—I'll inadvertently fall out of an airlock, which I'll open with both my feet and hands tied up."

"You're talking as if everyone in the Admiralty hated your guts," Darski said.

"Don't they?"

"Let's take a step back. Now that the formalities are out of the way, tell me what you've been doing time for?"

"The *Nomad*'s crew not only cleared debris from orbits, but also made money on the side, looting all promising wreck," Stachursky said with some reluctance in his voice. "You may not know this, but … on New Rouen, there was a battle between the separatists' fleet and the Federation's striking force under the command of Admiral Taho—"

"History was one of my favorite subjects," Henryan interrupted him. "Get to the point."

"We got on board *Odin*, Tahomey's flagship. That clone-of-a-bitch Morrisey was obsessed by desire to possess memorabilia …"

"Get. To. The. Point!" Darski urged him.

"On one officer's dead body, I found a diary with a very interesting story from the times of the civil war ..." Nike hesitated. "It portrayed a certain war hero in a rather negative light. A still-living hero, I should add."

"The civil war ended more than a hundred years ago," Henryan said. "Those who took part in it are long since go—" Suddenly, he remembered that it wasn't right. There was one exception. "Are you talking about Admiral Dreade-Ravenore?"

"Yes," Stachursky confirmed.

"That must have been him who put you here ..."

"No. Upon returning from New Rouen, I wrote a report, and ignoring the chain of command, I sent it directly to Chancellor Modo and two other members of the Council. Three days later, I was arrested by esdees who then dragged it out of me, I mean the information where I kept Major Visolay's diary and all the backup copies. I'll add in passing that they didn't only use gentle interrogation techniques such as drug administration. Eventually, I was put into a stasis pod and ... woke up here. Then forgive me if I don't share your trust in our superiors."

"All right. You're forgiven," Darski said, still feeling that there was something off about Nike's story. Finally, he realized what it was. "This wasn't your first clash with Dredd," he stated rather than asked.

"How do you figure?"

Henryan ignored the incitement. "Why'd such a good student like yourself ended on board a collapsar?"

"I contributed to the wrong ... ahem ... body of knowledge," Nike responded enigmatically.

Darski was impressed. "Did you dig up dirt on Dredd?"

"No ... I fucked his youngest daughter."

"Whoo," Henryan groaned. "Sweet."

"It just kind of happened. I didn't exactly force myself upon her, you know."

"And by some wondrous twist of fate, you found documents that incriminate him during your first mission."

"Accidents happen, sometimes even happy accidents."

"So they do ..." Darski muttered in an absent tone, wondering how much of Stachursky's story he could include in his official report and not make a fool of himself in front of Rutta.

"What's gonna happen to me?"

Henryan jumped at the sudden question. He had no idea what to do with the prisoner. Smuggling him out of Ulietta could cause quite a stir if he'd really been exiled by someone from the Council, for it certainly wasn't a routine detention. The lack of documentation concerning his transfer was the proof of that. What could Darski do to help Nike? He was nobody next to the top brass. Besides, having gotten intobad books more than once, he walked on eggshells too. And Rutta would have a field day when he heard this absurd theory about angels and raising people for meat. Especially that there was no evidence to support it. However, if only Stachurskycut the bullshit, the colonel might be willing to offer him some sort of protection in return for the liner's technical specifications. The question was whether Nike would be able to restrain himself?

"I'll try to help you," Henryan said, drawling the words. "Now, listen to me very carefully ..."

TWENTY-THREE

FITZ SPRANG to his feet at the sight of Henryan leaving the elevator. Except for him and his graviplane, the hangar was empty, the lower deck drowning in garbage left by the hurriedly evacuated medics.

"What took you so long?" he asked and before Darski even replied, added: "Who's this?"

He pointed to a young man keeping his head on a swivel.

"He's coming with us," Henryan said without going into detail.

The head of the scientific department shrugged. "Okay."

However, the fact that Stachursky passed him in total silence piqued Olivernest's interest anew. He knew that Darski, initially opposed to Dr. Pallance's idea, had changed his mind upon watching some message. Could it be that this quiet young man was the key to the mystery?

They got on board and took off immediately after the hatch closed with a soft hiss. Fitz was a moderately gifted pilot, so at first, they were pushed into their seats when the graviplane was climbing, and then they felt the G-force accompanying rapid acceleration. Olivernest was firing on all cylinders.

"What's the rush?" Henryan asked when he sat straight and regained his breath.

"A lot happened while you were gone, Captain," Fitz said. "Your assistant kept calling me—"

"Why didn't he reach me directly?"

"There's no signal where you went. I know this because I tried to contact you a few times, to tell you that High Command were after you. I'd have joined you, but the likes of me can walk in the hangar at best."

Fitz clutched the control sticks tighter and with a tone of resentment in his voice, he added, "Even Jerryan, who was leaving the hospital, told me to go fly a kite."

"You said that a lot happened when I was gone. What else should I know about?"

"Dupree has finally realized that the increased mass of habitats means that ejectors will have to be recharged longer."

"How much longer?"

"Twenty to thirty seconds."

"Galacticunt!" Henryan cursed under his breath.

Half a minute, or even less, he thought. *So little, and yet it'll make a huge difference ... If the squadron doesn't manage to buy time and some empty habitats get launched, another five ore containers won't reach the orbit. The Admiralty won't condone this ...*

When he shared his thoughts with Fitz, the head of the scientific department considered their options.

"Captain?"

At first, Darski didn't register Nike's quiet voice. He turned his head only when the prisoner coughed significantly.

"Yes?"

"So ... this evacuation is for real ...?"

"Why would I lie to you?"

Stachursky was silent. He looked through the window at the sea of greenery below and the colony in the distance, where one of the transporters was climbing into the sky.

"Everyone else did," he said after a long while.

Henryan shook his head, indignant. "Everything I've told you is pure truth; I promise."

They were approaching the swath of water that separated them from the colony and the Tower. Fitz had already begun to slow down and started descending from cruise altitude to save them torments of heavy braking.

"The proof you asked me about …" Nike spoke suddenly.

Darski pricked up his ears.

"Go on."

"I might know how to find it."

"You just claimed it didn't exist."

"I thought it was them who sent you."

Olivernest cast a glance at the captain. He did it discreetly, not to arouse the passenger's suspicion. What he'd heard so far was enough for him to consider the young man insane.

"Let's see what you've got," Henryan said, ignoring Fitz's meaningful grimace. "When we land, I'm going to report to my superior, and I'd better have something to explain my long absence. Snap it up!"

"I think I know where you can find Major Visolay's diary … that is, one of its copies which Dredd didn't put his hands on. Maybe even along with some information relating to New Rouen. But first …" Stachursky paused to take a breath. "Your biggest problem is how to place a specific amount of helon ore into orbit, am I right?"

"Yes. But … what's it to you?"

"Nothing, in fact." Nike shrugged. "Except … It just so happens that I know where to find a few million metric tons of it. And I don't mean helon ore, but pure metal."

TWENTY-FOUR

THE ANZIO SYSTEM, ZEBRA SECTOR

10/24/2354

Rutta sat staring at the spot where Henryan Darski's slightly blurry hologram was just a moment ago. He still couldn't believe what he'd heard. It was so simple, yet so brilliant. But was it true?

He activated his comlink to call the command center.

"Colonel Rutta speaking," he said when the officer on duty answered. "Captain Seidici, I need the Recycling Corps' records ASAP. Specifically, everything that concerns the recovery measures after the civil war."

"What time span are we talking about, sir?"

"Last two years. No, wait, last twelve months should do."

Seidici typed something on his virtual keyboard, then looked up again. "There are no such files on our servers."

"That's okay, these operations were carried out in the external belts. You'll have to contact the Second Fleet's command."

"I see, sir. I'll submit an access-to-documents request straight away." Seidici was ready to end the call.

"Hold on, Captain. Before you do this, connect me with the DFS ... Department of Fleet Security. I'd like to speak to Lieutenant Gunternest Poetze. They can wake him up, if needed, or pull him off a gal. He's to report to me in fifteen minutes at the latest."

"Yes sir."

The glow of the screens shimmered and faded, but only for a moment. Rutta reached for his comlink again. This time, however, he activated an audio call, leaving the display blank.

"This is Farland." The grand admiral was flustered, judging by the tone of his voice.

Not surprising, the colonel thought. *CEOs' lobbying could get under everyone's skin, no matter how thick.*

"Theo, it's me," he said. "Could you pop in for a moment? We have to talk."

"Is something wrong?"

"Perhaps."

"Don't start, Franciscollin. I'm so wired that if I had my gun, I'd shoot the entire staff!"

"Darski tried it and look where that got him," Rutta joked to defuse the tension.

"Don't even mention the bastard's name in my presence!" Farland growled like a wounded animal.

"It's him we need to talk about. In private."

The grand admiral groaned. "What did he do this time? Is this why you couldn't track him down?"

"On the contrary, my friend. On the contrary … It may be that he's saved our butts. But to know what's what I'll need some time and someone with a higher level of security clearance."

Farland said something incomprehensible, directing his words to someone else. A second later, he turned to Rutta again. "I'll be right there. Let me just clean up this fucking mess I'm dealing with here …"

———

Thirty minutes later the Recycling Corps' records were displayed above the colonel's console. Rutta had been right: the Second Fleet command didn't have the slightest intention to share these documents with him. Had it not been for the grand admiral, the obstacle wouldn't have budged—and it was worth their while.

Darski's informant was right. The colonel could see it clear as day now. There were millions of metric tons of helon, pure as it gets, in the fields of long-forgotten battles for their taking.

The Recycling Corps' probes had cataloged a hundred and fourteen clusters of space scrap; eighty-four of them had already been reclaimed, and another sixteen had been zapped by collapsars in the direction of the central stars of the systems which people fought for more than a hundred years ago. They could still be recovered, just as the rest of the wreckage, waiting for its turn in L-points.

The colonel rubbed his hands together and looked triumphantly at Farland.

"See Eden 67?" he asked, opening one of the attachments. "The total mass of the cluster is estimated at seven point seventy-five million metric tons of scrap. As per spectrum analysis almost one million two hundred thousand metric tons of that is pure helon."

Farland nodded. "Clone-of-a-bitch," he muttered.

Rutta laughed cheerfully. "I told you! The guy's a hip shooter, but he has his head screwed on right."

The grand admiral, who didn't feel like praising Darski, decided to change the subject.

"Well ... what about the other thing?"

"Nothing so far, but that's understandable. You know how it is. Xiao needs a safety net; he won't make a single decision without hundreds of unnecessary consultations."

"Are you talking about sending a strike force to Ulietta? It's a different matter altogether. No, I meant our esdee friend and what he's supposed to do for us ..."

"Poetze's going to take care of things personally because

fortunately, the *Nomad* is in the docks of the Inner Rim's main base."

This didn't seem to put Farland at ease. "Let me know as soon as you hear from him."

Operations undertaken in another metasector, right under its Admiralty's nose, had always been risky. High-ranking officers hated it when someone was playing in their backyard. Especially if that meant making use of their subordinates.

"No worries," the colonel assured his friend. "Poetze is a pro."

TWENTY-FIVE

THE DULUTH SYSTEM, KILO SECTOR

10/24/2354

A cylindrical car went past successive technical bays, moving slowly inside one of the sixteen tracks running along an openwork mooring arm. The journey from the supersized toroid, housing the Second Fleet's central warehouse, to the last bay, Bay K38, and the *Nomad* waiting there, lasted almost fifteen minutes. During this period of time, the passengers wearing heavy space suits covered the distance of two miles—and it was one of the shortest arms of the Omega orbital station; the four- and five-mile-long quays were reserved for the largest warships.

Lieutenant Poetze and two noncoms who were accompanying him could see them in the distance; the cigars of majestic fourth-generation battleships and squabs of cruisers swarmed by the far-off arms. All those vessels underwent technical inspection, or took cargo on board before flying to the Outer Territories.

The sight of so many mighty ships was comforting. The lieutenant, just looking at them, was proud to be a soldier of the Fleet, a man traveling to distant stars, a cog in the invincible armada ... Until recently, that is. Now, he couldn't believe that such force had finally met its match: the enemy who was even stronger. The Aliens, whoever they were, had humiliated the Third Fleet, or rather one of its squadrons. But when they faced the Federation's Combined Fleets, they'd learn the hard way what it meant to raise people's hackles.

Gunternest laughed under his breath. He knew little about the war, which was taking place hundreds of light-years away. In order not to sow panic and fear in the unchallenged systems in other metasectors, the Admiralty had limited the flow of information to the necessary minimum—and they meant to keep it that way until the crisis was over. Quantum communications censorship had been implemented since the very first attack, and commercial traffic had been discontinued in the Inner Rim. Only those privy to the facts, the evacuees, and the Boards of the colonies accepting the resettled population knew about the ongoing war.

It was an understandable and even acceptable strategy, especially since a massive counteroffensive had been planned. Poetze unswervingly believed that it would change balance of power on the fringes of the Known Universe. A victorious climax of the heroic struggle would certainly uplift public opinion, whereas the attempts to describe the chaos of war, in which Humankind was the losing side, only made matters worse. The lieutenant regretted that he'd been let in on this secret so early. The crews of the ships he was looking at with such pride still lived in blissful ignorance. Their next mission's objective would be revealed to them upon reaching the Inner Rim systems.

As the car began to slow down, Poetze's gaze shifted away from the battleship, surrounded by hundreds of drones which were replacing its shield generators with newer, more efficient models, and he looked toward the angular collapsar. It was also a huge vessel, shorter and squatter, however, than the craft hanging nearby, which—Gunternest realized it only now—were half the size, but still several times more powerful than the first-generation warships used in the times of the civil war.

The car came to a halt at Bay K38. A moment later, the three men unplugged the tubes, connecting them to the vehicle oxygen tank, and left the passenger compartment. Stopping at the brightly illuminated hatch, Poetze moved closer to the control panel, waited until it came to life, and when a virtual keyboard appeared above the small pad, he quickly entered the password which contained sixteen alphanumeric characters.

The hatch remained locked. Hiding his surprise, Gunternest reset the control panel and keyed in the password again. The result, however, was exactly the same.

"Strange," he muttered, fastening a clip hook to one of the handles within his reach.

Being a traditionalist, he preferred mechanical locks to their modern, magnetic counterparts. The control panel failure forced him to let go of the handle and use both hands. He removed the cover, reset the device once again, waited a few seconds, then called the master's office, enabling the sound only.

"Senior Chief Petty Officer Taylorson Bagley speaking."

"Poetze from the security department," Gunternest skipped his military rank deliberately—mere reference to the SD should be enough to pummel the noncom into submission. "I'm right in front of Bay K38; I was going to make a routine check of the flight recorders, but there's a problem with the lock. The bypass code doesn't open the airlock."

"Are you sure you entered the password correctly—" The duty officer paused, realizing that he didn't know the rank of his interlocutor.

"Ask me one more stupid question, Bagley, and I'll invite you for a chat in our headquarters." Poetze didn't have to raise his voice, the very suggestion was more threatening than meaningless shouts.

Bagley was silent for a long moment. This and his panting testified to the fear that had overwhelmed him.

"It's not a system failure, sir," he finally said with palpable relief. "The *Nomad*'s been quarantined."

"What?" Poetze could hardly believe his ears. "On whose orders? And why hasn't the security department been informed?"

"Sir, all I know is that the quarantine was imposed by the Admiralty."

"When?"

"Eight hours ago."

"Thank you. Over and out." Gunternest disconnected the call.

A quarantine imposed on a vessel, which crew had disembarked a week before? By the Admiralty? Had he heard such thing under different circumstances, he'd have thought it was funny. "Svenrique," he said, turning to his men. "Check where the *Nomad*'s crew members are stationed now, will you."

"They were all detained and isolated," the answer came immediately.

Poetze grew anxious. This could mean only one thing …

"When did it happen?"

"About eight hours ago."

"Where are they now?"

"SD's headquarters. Level 8."

"Not the biohazard section?"

"No, sir. It says clearly here. Level 8," Corporal Thulin replied.

Poetze would have cursed if he hadn't cared so much about saving his face in front his men. The legendary Level 8 was the place where only extremely dangerous criminals were held. People didn't leave Level 8 just like that. Whoever wanted to silence the *Nomad*'s crew meant business—so any attempt to board the collapsar was bound to bring down on the lieutenant's head something much worse than his superiors' dissatisfaction.

"What about their private quarters?" he asked with apparent indifference.

"Quarantine, quarantine …" Svenrique muttered. "All are subject to quarantine."

This isn't going anywhere, Poetze thought, and began frantically considering his options. He didn't want to disappoint Colonel Rutta, not after what the man had done for him, but he didn't want to get the ax—or should he say, laser—either. And this was how any attempt to interfere would end.

He'd made it so that the *Nomad* was selected for a routine check by the security department system. As such checks were carried out on a regular basis, it could be thought mere coincidence, especially since this particular collapsar had last been given a thorough check a really long time ago. Moreover, he was appointed as an inspector and could be sure that no proof of tampering with the random generator would ever be found. So Gunternest was safe, and he didn't have any reasons to worry— that is, until he drew attention to himself by trying to open the lock again. Unless …

"Judavid," he said to the other noncom. "Call the medical section and ask them if they know about the quarantine imposed on the *Nomad* and its crew."

Wurstbeutel was on standby, so he made the call instantly. Just as Poetze thought, the officer on duty didn't know anything, but cross-referred to some records, he paled and started issuing orders with the speed of a blaster. That was exactly what the lieutenant wanted. Now, he just had to file a report, and no one would suspect him that he went rogue. On the contrary: while performing his duties, a law-abiding esdee noticed a breach of procedures and reacted in accordance with regulations.

All he had to do now was wait. Soon, Bay K38 would swarm with medical personnel. Poetze could only hope that they'd come before the people sent by those who were the reason for all the fuss.

———

Twenty-six minutes. The medical section needed as much time to assemble a team and send them on their way. Finally, a car with four people inside stopped at Bay K38. All the medics wore yellow space suits, so that they could be distinguished from other emergency services, which were sure to appear soon.

However, the gendarmes headed to Bay K38 were in for a

surprise. Judavid helped the medics to carry their equipment first, and then programmed the car to stop at all the airlocks on its way back. So, its return journey was going to take longer than normally. Just a few minutes longer—the difference unnoticeable in case of the gendarmes, but gigantic in terms of Poetze's plan.

Less than sixty seconds after the car's departure, the medics opened the airlock leading on board the *Nomad*. There was one tiny drawback to the password disabling the access to the collapsar: it could be easily canceled by emergency services. The lieutenant was counting on just that. That's why, pretending to be a worried esdee, he breathed down the chief medic's neck.

However, when the airlock lights glowed, the seven-foot-tall chief medic turned to Poetze, stopping him with his large hand.

"It's a quarantine zone," he said in a menacing tone. "We have to identify the source of contamination before anyone else can board the *Nomad*."

"Of course." Poetze took a step back as if he suddenly got scared. "Let me secure the airlock at least, so that there's no accidental breach of the cordon."

The chief medic gestured at one of his companions. "There's no need, Lieutenant. My analyst will stay outside."

"If so …" Poetze turned to his subordinates. "Svenrique, call the car."

"Yes sir!"

Gunternest addressed the chief medic again, "We'll keep your man company until the car returns. It must be picking up gendarmes as we speak," he added, dropping his voice to a confidential whisper.

"Do what you want, just don't get in our way. Under no circumstances can you board this collapsar."

"Come on, Doc!" Poetze stretched out both his hands in front of him. "We don't wanna catch anything …"

The chief medic ignored him completely. Nodding his head at his companions, who were only slightly shorter than him, he turned on the mobile analyzer by means of a remote and followed it toward the inner hatch. Poetze obediently withdrew from the airlock, so that the *Nomad* could be locked again. After the three medics boarded the collapsar, the analyst released the "contaminated" air into the void and opening the airlock once again, he set about to installing his equipment.

The nearest computer terminal on board the *Nomad* was located at the control panel of the inner hatch; the analyst was going to link it with his instruments, meters, and recorders.

"Judavid, move it, Doc needs your help!" Poetze yelled when the man in a yellow space suit reached for the wires. "Svenrique, don't just stand there!"

"I'm fine," the analyst grunted, as Wurstbeutel yanked the plug out of his hand.

"No problem, Doc," the lieutenant said. "My people are here to serve and protect!"

The analyst glanced over his shoulder and sent the esdee a contemptuous look. Poetze could only spread his hands as if saying: "Well, we're trying to be helpful for once." People associated the security department with many things, but certainly not with help. That's why the analyst, even though he preferred the esdees to leave him alone, refrained from kicking them out. He never knew what they would write in their reports later, and getting on the SD's blacklist was like playing Russian roulette with a blaster.

The esdees' carrying-on served its purpose. They distracted the analyst long enough to plug in their own holopad and upload the virus, before eventually they linked his equipment to the terminal. They'd been trained to do such things, so it took them only a moment of time when the analyst stared at their superior.

"Beat it!" Poetze yelled at them. "You'll keep watch on this side of the hatch until the gendarmes appear!"

He knew that the analyst would lock the outer hatch the moment they went out anyway. And indeed, it closed properly with a soft hiss right behind their backs.

Poetze told his men to stand on both sides of the locked hatch, and looked along the K-arm as if straining his eyes to see the arriving car. All of this, however, was just a smoke screen.

The lieutenant created a virus, or rather a tracker, to scan the *Nomad*'s database and select the files originated during the period Rutta had in mind. The malware was also supposed to find everything that had been hidden from view, sent, or encrypted by the crew members, the captain in particular. Then, the data obtained in this way would be sent to one of the vessels in the nearby anchorage by the means of directional compressed transmission. From there, via the communications center, the message would reach the mess terminal, and then would be automatically circulated in the system, infecting hundreds of other computers. Just like spam.

Gunternest didn't have to anonymize himself so much because his self-deleting software wouldn't have been detected even if someone had inspected all the *Nomad*'s databases. He preferred to protect himself on all fronts, though, because this time the game was played with someone at the very top.

Even his subordinates had no idea what they'd really helped him with. If anyone asked—and that was less than likely, in the lieutenant's opinion—they'd say that they'd simply done what was expected of them, namely, carried out the scan of all the memory blocks in search for malign and subversive information. Why secretly? The medics didn't let them on board the *Nomad*, even though an order is more important than some idiotic quarantine.

The funny thing was that any random check would support their version of events. For the malware had been tagged to a standard esdee's tracker, and a report informing of the inspection results would be sent directly to the security department headquarters.

TWENTY-SIX

THE ULIETTA SYSTEM, ZEBRA SECTOR

10/24/2354

It was still sixteen standard hours to the estimated time of the Aliens' arrival—ETAA.

Finally, Darski found a moment to catch his breath. Fifteen minutes to take a shower, and fifteen minutes to eat something. That was the plan, but nothing would come of it, Henryan could feel it in his bones. Whenever he wanted to rest, something went wrong. But a biological organism isn't a machine; it can't constantly be in overdrive and not feel fatigue. And a time like this, dopiness and lack of focus could result in even greater losses than going under the radar for half an hour. This was what Henryan told himself when he gave orders to his assistant. He kept repeating it like mantra, while walking briskly to his apartment.

Unfortunately, his instincts had been correct. No sooner had he adjusted water temperature than his comlink rang out. The corporation equipped its employees with the best equipment, so he could answer the call anywhere, the lavatory including— where by the way someone put a holograph wallpaper showing the office part of the apartment, which prevented callers from knowing that the person they were talking to was presently answering the call of nature.

It was beyond Darski how anyone could have a conversation in such awkward circumstances, but apparently different rules applied in the business world than in the Fleet. Luckily for him, the display could be activated in the shower too, so he did just that to see who bothered him this time. Looking at his assistant's face, Henryan grimaced at the thought that he'd have to shut off the hot water and get dressed in a hurry. He made up his mind on the spot. Fuck it all, Toranosukenjiro was one of the boys, and besides, he knew why the captain had returned to his apartment.

"What's going on?" Darski asked, enabling the sound only.

"Delivery from on high," Hondo said and squinted his eyes. Undoubtedly, he heard water. This Foley effect simply couldn't be excised from the transmission. "An encrypted message. For your eyes only. From Colonel Rutta."

Could it be that Bruttal laid his hands on what I'd asked for …? Suddenly, Darski felt a warm burning feeling in his chest. It certainly wasn't the effect of a hot shower.

"Forward it straight to my personal terminal in this apart-ment," he ordered, turning off the water hurriedly. "And send Stachursky to me."

"Yes …"

Henryan hung up on his assistant in an unceremonious manner. He was bursting with curiosity. In his last conversation with the colonel, he quoted Stachursky's words about millions of metric tons of helon, which the Federation could still regain from the numerous battlefields of the civil war. Healso asked Rutta to rustle up the data from the *Nomad*'s onboard computers—as discreetly as possible. This was how he intended to repay his informer, provided the information would prove true and valu-able enough. Nike, as it turned out, had not lied. His suggestion was so interesting that Rutta cut a deal and procured Morrisey's backup files. As long as the message contained the copies of the files obtained from the collapsar, and not just another reprimand.

Henryan activated the blower to dry himself off in a stream

of warm air, in the meantime deciding that it had to be the files after all. He didn't expect any orders, and even if High Command had issued them, they wouldn't have been sent as an encrypted message.

Hondo brought Nike before he finished buttoning up his freshly printed uniform, so both of them had to wait at the door for a few seconds.

"Toranosukenjiro, hold all my calls. I'm not available to anyone, even Ninadine. If something comes up, take care of it. You can send me reports, but only the most important ones, do you understand? Otherwise, you're on your own."

"Yes sir!" The door slammed shut in Hondo's face.

Nike, who until now had been sitting in his quarters, staring at the panoramic window, seemed bewildered by this sudden change of scenery. He followed Henryan obediently and let himself be seated at the computer terminal.

Darski downloaded a ton of messages, searched for the one Hondo had mentioned, and opened it without hesitation. There, waiting for him, were two encrypted files—one several terabytes and the other much, much smaller. He started with the latter. Decrypting it took no time because Rutta used the same code as on Xan 4.

Soon, Henryan was watching a short video message from the colonel.

"I've no idea who your guy is, but tell him that there are other people who desperately want this data. Eleven hours ago, the *Nomad* was quarantined at the behest of someone from the Admiralty and its crew were taken in and locked up in the most secure part of the SD headquarters' prison. Equally well, they may be already dead. My men risked a lot to get these files, so be careful with them; they can't see the light of day. I won't stick my neck out, especially for some corporate asshole. I agreed to this only because his suggestion could solve all our problems."

Rutta was usually closemouthed, but whenever he spoke, he managed to convey both the important information and his opinion on the matter. Henryan valued this trait above all else in his superior. Unswerving professionalism.

Nike followed every move of Darski's fingers when he proceeded to decrypt the second file. But then another problem showed up. The password-protected file contained hundreds of subfiles—two thousand three hundred and seventy-six, to be exact. Some of them were multilevel directories. *Nothing strange about that,* Henryan thought. *I'm looking at all the records added to the Nomad's database after the cluster had been found in the Theta L-point.*

He moved over, making room for Stachursky.

"A little job for you," he said.

Nike positioned himself centrally in front of the terminal, not even looking at the captain. He immediately started to sort the files according to the criteria known only to himself, instead of browsing through them in the given sequence. It was clear that he knew what he was doing. When he finished, the data was divided into three separate sets. Now he just had to further examine each of them.

Darski watched him for a few minutes, but he quickly got tired of staring at the codes, flowing downward on the screens. He decided that a glass of Valisian rum wouldn't hurt. Especially since Hondo had already sent three messages.

The first one concerned Ejector Four, which was starting to malfunction even though the load had been reduced. The chief engineer said that within next four or five hours it would have to be shut down, in order to avoid a disaster. In the second message Fitz reported that the recruitment among the last few dozen thousands potential evacuees had already begun. It didn't go as smoothly as he hoped, however. The colonists, still unaware of the extent of the threat they faced, preferred to wait in the hopes that a transporter would arrive at the very last moment by some miraculous twist of fate and take them on board, rather than risk being irradiated. And High Command would never reveal the truth about the Aliens before the attack.

So they would have to resort to wheedling. And Darski

intended to help the head of the scientific department, making congruous announcements as soon as his session with the Admiralty's ex-prisoner ended.

As to the third message, it was good. Having sent another thousand volunteers to the moon, they accelerated the working pace and finally began to catch up with the original schedule. Three pseudohabitats were ready for launch, another two would be in the next couple of hours. Yet another three were being built in space, but all required a great deal of work on their caulking. Within the next sixteen hours, two of those would be completed, and the last one would be fit for transporting the volunteers currently working on the moon. These people were ready to risk their lives as long as the Fleet guaranteed their loved ones places in the proper habitats. That was doable, although Darski decided to leave the logistics to the corporation.

"Gotcha!" Nike announced as the captain was sending his last reply. "Just like I said. That clone-of-a-bitch Morrisey copied the contents of Major Visolay's diary without my knowledge."

"I'd rather see the proof of your meeting with the Aliens ..." Darski didn't hide his disappointment when he understood the reasons behind Stachursky's exuberance.

The evidence of the old admiral's criminal activity over a hundred years ago had no meaning to him.

"Easy, Captain." Stachursky looked at him for the first time. "If Morrisey had copied the diary, he'd also have kept all the rest of recordings from that period. In case he could make money on them."

"Keep digging in that shit until you dig something up," Henryan ordered before returning to his mail.

"Captain, why don't you download this file to your holopad," Nike offered. "Finding proof gonna take time. I'm sure the clone-of-a-bitch chopped every record up in such a way that it's not possible to merge fragments into one whole document. Not without a passkey, anyway."

"But you found the diary, right?" Henryan reminded him.

"Only because Morrisey kept it intact. He wasn't gonna hide it from the world, like copies of the deleted records."

"Stop talking and get down to work, will you?" Darski admonished the ex-prisoner.

A moment later, he opened Major Visolay's diary with the intention of reading a paragraph or two while waiting for the search results …

THE FORGE

"Name." A bald sergeant who sat at the door didn't even look up when I approached.

"Johanatol Doni."

"You go in, there's a wall-mounted screen on your right, you undress, and await further instructions."

"But ..."

"You go in," the baldy repeated impatiently. A violent wave of his left hand accompanied his words. "Now!"

I went in. I remembered this room. I'd spent a lot of time here, years ago. It used to be my classroom. But now, stripped of its visiomats and desktops, and with propaganda posters hanging on the walls, it looked strange. It even smelled different. Intimidating and odd.

"Move it!" ordered one of the uniformed men sitting at a long table, with a holoboard in the background.

I undressed behind the screen, then following the displayed instructions, I got inside an auto-med unit. It did a quick, but full scan—a rarity today. But the army spared no expense. When I put my clothes back on, another sergeant—this one thin as a rail, for a change—brought me before the military medical board. With these gentlemen's stars, proudly gleaming from their shoulder straps, you could create a map of any sector. And with their medal ribbons—a line connecting New Brisbane with its nearest moon. Generals. Veterans. Although I could have passed the youngest one of them in the school corridors, and the eldest certainly didn't reach my father's age yet. The wheels of war had been grinding all. Well, wasn't that the reason why I was standing in front of the seven specimens of top brass now, buttoning up my shirt?

"Class Alpha," pronounced a four-star fatso sitting close to the window. It was him who got my medical test results. "Congratulations on your great physical shape."

"Thank you," I said hesitantly. I had a feeling that his words didn't bode well for my future.

"And I congratulate you on your assignment," added a six-star muscleman, who sat at the opposite end of the table, right next to three nearly identical looking blonds.

"Draftee Doni," he continued, "you've been assigned to serve in an elite group of spaceborne troops. You'll find yourself among the best of the best. Tomorrow at sixteen hundred hours standard time, you'll report for duty at Spaceport Terminal 1, check-in counters from 606 to 692. Dismissed."

He closed my personal file and moved on to the next one.

"Hold on a second," I said.

They froze. All of them. Including a puny sergeant, who was already heading toward the screen. There was obvious consternation in their faces.

"You have something to say?" asked the one with six stars, his tone full of incredulity.

"Yeah ..."

One of the five-star triplets, visibly irate, intervened, "This is violation of the regulations ..."

"I don't give a shit about your regulations!" I said firmly. "The Federation Constitution is more important than anything you might put in it."

The members of the medical board exchanged significant

glances. They already knew what I was aiming for. I wasn't the first one.

"You think you can lecture us on civil rights, son?" huffed the youngest of the officers. His voice cracked slightly on the last word.

"Yes."

Taking advantage of the fact that they still hadn't regained their composure, I continued, "I've got the impression that you relish your little war so much that you ignore the law recognized by civilized world. I can refuse to be conscripted; this is my constitutional right!"

I took an appeal letter out of my pocket, its text scrupulously composed during evening meetings in the dorm. It landed on top of a closed personal file with my name. The six-star general's face reddened, when he read the first sentence.

"This is treason!" he hissed.

"No. This is a legal opinion, based on statutes of a higher level, enacted by the Senate of the Federation."

The six-star general turned purple and began to rise from his chair, taking on a menacing look. While this beefcake of a man, in his shiny uniform bursting with muscles, rose taller and taller, I shrank away with every passing moment as if by magic.

"You lousy bastard ..." The torrent of abuse, which had started quite gently, stopped all of a sudden when the eldest general's hand rested on the giant's forearm.

"Gentlemen, I'm afraid that Draftee Doni's case requires slightly different approach," said the four-star vet, glancing at his watch. "May I ...?"

They nodded reluctantly. First the triplets in unison, the rest a moment later.

"Watch the door, Sergeant!" ordered the four-star fatso from under the window, who'd classified me as Alpha and just came to my rescue.

The scrag clicked his heels, galloped to the entrance, and took post behind the screen for good measure.

"Draftee Doni ..." The vet read the letter quickly, and then turned to me, speaking in a softer, much more polite tone. "I can see you prepared yourself for this meeting well. What's more, the provisions you refer to can indeed be a significant obstacle to your military service. However ..."

He paused and cleared his throat.

"I will not mince words," he said. "We're at war, son. Your friends are already fighting and dying. In a good cause, no less. For Earth, for the safety of us all. For your family to ..." The sly dog paused again to run his eyes over my dossier.

There'd been a lot of casualties in this war; nearly everybody had lost a loved one. I decided to take advantage of this moment of hesitation.

"You're right, sir. There is a war. Your war, not mine. Nobody's attacked the Federation. Several outer belts wanted to make their independence official. To confirm the status quo. The Senate controlled less than a half of the territories acquired by the colonialists in the last four decades. In fact, the Senate didn't give a shit about them so much that it bypassed most colonies when allocating the budget. At the same time, it milked them all it wanted and when they started to rise up, then—" I took a deep breath. "Then, instead of letting go, it sent you, spluttering hatred machos, to restore order which you won't be able to keep in the long run!"

"It's ... It's ..." The six-star muscleman became blue in the face.

The fat vet silenced him again. "This is your version, Draftee Doni. Do you want to hear mine?"

"No, I don't. Something tells me that it wouldn't be much different from the propaganda pap that oozes from every comlink twenty-four seven."

"Why don't you listen to what I have to say, anyway?"

"Okay," I gave up. I didn't want to overstep my bounds. Although law forbade the members of the medical board to carry firearms, the muscleman would easily break me in half and tie me up into knots—not only figuratively, but literally too. And he probably wouldn't even break into sweat in doing so.

"Thank you." The vet put my letter down. "I was on Scotia when the separatists declared independence of the outer belts. I won't go into the story behind that act; you drew your own conclusions, I drew mine, relying on my service experience in those systems, and you can believe me when I say that I spent a really long time and met many wonderful people there. Give me a moment, will you …?"

I also noticed that on hearing this, the six-star mutant's eyes nearly popped out of his head, not to mention that the rest of generals seemed desolate. However, the one look the vet sent them was enough to silence any murmurs.

"Yes, there too live wonderful people. You know it and I know it. I think my colleagues would allow themselves to admit that if only the circumstances were a little different." He cut off the voices of protest with one sharp gesture. "But that's not the point. It wasn't our good friends who decided to secede from the Federation, taking control over almost one-third of all the colonized planets. Do you agree?"

As he addressed me directly, I nodded automatically even though I didn't really understand what he was getting at. I'd have said something, but he didn't let me get a word in edgeways.

"Well, I daresay nobody listens to our friends. The worst elements came to the fore … You said the Senate didn't give a shit about the distant provinces and you're right. For years, we were trying to develop the security apparatus in those systems, but—" He raised his hand to indicate that I couldn't speak, not yet anyway. "You must know, young man, that practically half the outer belts had been outside our jurisdiction before this war started. And this gave way to gray economy and crime spike."

"You don't mean to say that the secession and the war came about because of common criminals?" I managed to interject when he paused for a moment to gather his thoughts.

"This is exactly what I'm saying," the vet replied. "Both sides in this conflict have played dirty, us included, but we"—he gestured at himself and the six men sitting at the table—"we are the good guys, take my word for it."

"Right …"

"Right. If you went for the entry physical in one of the outer belts, you wouldn't have this conversation. There, refusing induction equals a shot to the head. In the front yard, with as many witnesses as possible."

"Agitprop."

"You think so?" The deadly tone in his voice gave me chills.

Even though, I wasn't one to give up easily. "I think so."

"But you're not sure?"

"I don't have to be sure. I'm not getting married. Besides, there's something like 'benefit of the doubt' …"

He looked at me with his piercing blue eyes and smiled.

"I'm not able to tell you about everything I saw in nineteen and twenty, but I can tell you this: Idealists like yourself see the world only in two colors. And truth is, there are billions of shades of gray between what's black and what's white. When people like you face the reality, tragedy ensues—"

"I'm not afraid to confront reality."

"But you should be, son. You should be."

"I'm sorry, but I think we drifted too far from the topic," I said quickly. "You're looking at a letter which clearly demonstrates that you can't induct me without breaking at least four articles of the New Brisbane constitution. And that's the only fact we should be talking about. Our feelings and impressions aside. This isn't my war, and I want no part of it."

"Well …" Glancing at his watch again, the vet reached for my letter. "What's going on up there"—he pointed his head toward the ceiling—"is so horrible that sometimes, even I can't believe it. And I've seen much of this … agitprop, as you put it … with my own eyes and actively participated in some of it too. That's why I know that we need to win this war, bring peace to the whole Known Universe, and then change our policy toward the outer belts. And we will. Whereas you, son, will take part in this giant operation of the Federation, just as millions of your friends," he concluded and tore my letter in half.

I was expecting this, so all I had to do was put my hand into my pocket again and take out another copy and waved it in his face. The vet gave me a pitying look.

"It's sixteen oh one standard time. A minute ago, the Senate discontinued proceedings and ceded power to the Military Council of Federal Salvation. The provisions of the constitution no longer apply, I'm afraid."

"Pardon?" I was dumbstruck.

"Had you slammed the door," the vet gestured at the exit from the room, "instead of getting into discussion with me, you'd have gotten a two-week deferment. At least, given the number of appeals we now have to consider. If you were really smart, you might weasel out altogether. But you decided to present your arguments ... just to impress your buddies, I guess."

The muscleman guffawed.

"I didn't know that—"

"You don't know many things, Private Doni," the six-star general said with satisfaction in his voice. "But we're going to take care of your education from now on. You'll finally see through your so-called friends ... that is, if you get it through your thick skull before the first bullet shot by them blows your brains out. Congratulations, you've just joined the 6th Space-borne Division, crème de la crème of the Federation Army. You'll have the honor of serving on the frontline. Dismissed!"

I guess I went pale. Anyway, the five-star generals evidently cheered up, and the stick of a sergeant came over to show me out. When I looked at the vet, I didn't see glee in his eyes. He extended his hand with a ticket in it.

"I'm not some dim-witted clone-of-a-bitch," he said, ignoring the triplets' reaction. "Besides, you were here before four o'clock. You're to report for duty in two weeks' time, son. Use that time for getting your affairs in order. No need to thank me."

———

Thanks to him, I had two extra weeks of life. Fourteen days. On the one hand, not that much; on the other—all of eternity. I used this time well, although my liver, and several other organs, might disagree. I said goodbye to half the guys on my block, and quite a few girls. Including those that were staying home. Somehow, in the welter of events, things turned out this way. I was the last one with a deferral, after all; practically a hero. But my fame faded with every passing day. There was too much happening. Too many good people departed, also in a very literal sense. By the time I packed my duffel, we had a visit from some sad ladies in black pantsuits. They showed up within a week after the first transporter full of draftees took off. Manfredward Gemme, a chubby nerd, a year younger than me … I think. I'd been in the mining school for almost twelve months when he rolled up, that's for sure. Anyway, he volunteered for the army at the very beginning of the mobilization and was killed during the first FTX at the transit station. Although "killed" wasn't the word most people would use in this situation. Manfredward had a heart attack when he heard the sirens. In the resulting confusion, it took an hour for somebody to realize that the fatso, curled up behind a stack of plasma ammo cartridges, was no longer a candidate for a Federation hero.

Nobody liked Manfredward on our block, but his death came as a shock to many of us. Even I hurt when I realized how blind fate could be. The fatso was the first victim of this war personally known to us. The first, but not the last. By the day I left, the black graviplane had come to our colony six more times. Two days after Gemme, we paid our last respects to Montyberian, Tadam, and Mabelise. Their transporter crashed on the surface of a planet, which name I couldn't even pronounce properly. No sooner had we sobered up after the funeral party than the harpies in black brought news again, this time about Joandrea's sister. Her mother wouldn't say anything, and we didn't ask. But we drank. To her and to the others.

The day before my departure, the information that Abra-madeus Foss died a heroic death reached us. That guy had always been crazy, so nobody was surprised that his fighter crashed into a cruiser. We could only hope it was an enemy vessel. Damn it, I didn't even know who the seventh victim was. The black graviplane passed us on our way to the spaceport. When the massive body of the vehicle flashed in my parents' zipper's window, Mom started crying and didn't calm down even after I swiped through security and was gone. I still could see her standing snuggled into Dad's shoulder, with a tissue pressed against her nose. She was the only one who wasn't waving goodbye as we went out, onto the warm tarmac of the spaceport.

———

If you think that the army is organized better than any given nonmilitary group, you couldn't be more wrong. I understood this even before I got on board a shuttle.

I hardly knew anybody in my squad—the faces of five or six guys looked familiar, but specific names and biographies I asso-ciated only with Levaristo Shorza and Marianton Kozak. Both had wriggled out of the draft a few days before me. Both had helped me to wriggle out. The vet knew what he was talking about; the Admiralty needed less than two weeks to "consider" most of the appeals.

We said hello with a look of a condemned man on our faces ... because this was exactly who we were: the condemned. If seven persons from one colony moved to the alley of honor in just two weeks, what was going on up there must have been a real bloodbath. Anyway, the three of us hang back, distancing ourselves from the murmuring crowd of eighty men and women, give or take. Almost everybody was my age; no young 'uns in their late teens. Levaristo noticed this too.

"Reclaimed cannon fodder?" he asked so loudly that people standing in other groups could easily hear him. Some just smiled crookedly, others nodded their heads. "A fine crowd," he proclaimed with a big smile on his face.

"What's so funny?" Kozak pouted.

In comparison, he suffered the most when he was drafted into the army. For one thing, he didn't give a shit about the Federation, and, for another, he'd just gotten his girlfriend pregnant. Some said, spitefully, that it was deliberate, to wriggle out of the draft, but even if that were the case, the army turned out to be insensitive to the girl's charms. Marianton wasn't deferred even for one day, he was only granted paternity benefits, including a small sum of money that would be wired to him along with his soldier's pay. But only after the baby was born— and that meant almost nine months in the battlefield before he could see the extra penny. Well, unless it was all about the family. Death gratuity was higher in case of servicepeople with kids. Rumor had it that Manfredward's old man bought a new zipper with the Admiralty monies; and for such a softie, who'd died before putting on a uniform, they couldn't pay as much as for a hero killed in action—

Suddenly, I realized that even though I was a full-on pacifist and one of the doves opposing this war since its first day, I stood in a crowd of like-minded people, humbly awaiting what the future had in store for me. Was it possible that two weeks of soaking had laid waste to my brains? No, not really, especially since I could still think ... What's gonna happen to me? In a month, or two? If I don't die straight away, that is. When they send me to the frontline, I'll have to shoot at people who rightfully want to free themselves from the rule of the biggest fuckers in the Known Universe. Yes, for the first few days, I and my buddies, we'd been making far-reaching plans. That we would dismantle the army from the inside, open people's eyes ... but our eagerness quickly drowned in the sea of booze and fun. We focused on taking advantage of the last days of freedom. Now I knew that I wouldn't achieve much. And not only because I couldn't be bothered.

Yesterday, my old man—always watchful—brought me some

news about recent changes in the law. It would cost me twenty years of hard labor in orbital shipyards if I expressed my support for the unionists, even as vaguely as in front of the medical board—provided I spoke as a civilian; if I did it in the trenches, I'd be sentenced to death. That's why, seeing Mom's scared face, I decided not to push it. They wanted me to be a cog in the war machine, okay, I would be one. But the smallest and the least necessary. I'd remain a passive observer for the most part and would kill anybody only in self-defense.

Perhaps it wasn't the smartest decision, but Levaristo and Marianton agreed with me when they gained a better understanding of the situation. We would challenge the decaying Federation and its fucking army.

"The 6th Spaceborne Division! In close order, form two ranks!" All conversations were cut short by a loud command.

We turned our heads to see a tall, well-built sergeant who just emerged from a hatch of the shuttle. Reaching for our duffels, we obediently walked to the side of the vessel that was supposed to carry us into orbit, and maybe even further. There, the stuttering sarge read the roll call, getting half of our names wrong. With every mistake, he stuttered more, but it was all right by us. We got a few extra minutes of freedom. But all good things come to an end. Sarge also reached the last name in the list, which clearly pleased him. He was back on solid ground.

"Before you board, you'll receive your uniforms from the quartermaster on duty. They'll be here in a moment. For the time being, nobody falls out and nobody smokes." He pointed at the signs adorning the hull of the shuttle.

"What about talking?" Shorza asked with a perceptible irony in his voice, most likely lost on Captain Obvious.

Sarge glanced around to fish him out of the crowd, then looked at him menacingly, and finally nodded, as if after a long deliberation.

"You can talk. But no screaming or laughing! The 6th Spaceborne Division is not a nursery for retarded brats!"

"So how come you ended up here?" muttered a guy standing

next to me. Just a few words, and I already liked him. What a quipster.

The rest of us sniggered softly. Sarge heard it all right, but decided to pretend that it was a nervous laugh on our part, for fear of him. Anyway, he puffed up with pride and held his head up high.

The delay of the quartermaster put us in a blissful mood. Freedom tasted sweet, especially now, and we could only regret that we weren't allowed to celebrate it with a smoke. However, thirty minutes on the hot tarmac were gone in the blink of an eye. Eventually, a short convoy of gray vehicles emerged from behind the nearest hangar. They stopped in front of "our" Sarge and within minutes, we witnessed a brusque conversation between him and two privates from the quartermaster's office. We couldn't hear a word of what they were saying, but my neighbor—the same guy who made fun of Sarge a moment before—acted out their dialogue.

He started off with the first private, "Did you order eighty unicorns, sir?"

"I ordered eighty uniforms, galacticunt!" he replied in lieu of Sarge.

"But the order says 'unicorns.' White with pink manes."

"You can shove one up your ass, you stinker! Horn forward!"

"I might as well, but you have to pay for it beforehand."

"It was an express delivery," piped in the other private. "A tip would be nice!"

Sarge did an about-face and headed toward us, steaming. His square jaw was measuredly moving from left to right and back again. If he'd been a ruminant, he'd have ground his teeth to the gums during this short walk.

"Ten-hut!" he bellowed, and clicked his heels as if the order applied to him too. "There's an issue with your uniforms, but we'll deal with it after we get you to the barracks on Delta in the Triton system. You'll just have to make do with secondhand uniforms for now. Some retard from the quartermaster's office"—he uttered the last words with obvious hatred—"has jumbled the packing lists up again. Your brand-new uniforms have been sent to the base, and we got replacements. You have thirty minutes to find the right size. Leave your own under-wear on. If it's not a good fit, don't complain! Unless the cover-alls are too small for you, which I find doubtful, just looking at you—"

"We'll definitely need pants with a saggy crotch, so that there's room for our family jewels," the quipster whispered.

"Who said that?!" Sarge roared.

The quipster took a step forward.

"Do you think it's funny?!" Sarge yelled.

"Yes sir!" I cried out as loud as I could.

Marianton and Levaristo followed suit, and the rest joined them within moments.

Sarge froze. He glowered at us, bit his lip, then straightened up and said contemptuously, "So you think you've got balls? Good, I'll have something to kick during the training!"

There now, the sod that seemed to be the least bright alum of a postgraduate course of syncing a blade foresight with a peep rearsight was radiant with wit all of a sudden. Or half-wit, as was to be expected from such an old army mule.

In any case, we got away with this. We lined up for measure-ment, and as the quartermaster was handing the uniforms out to us, we were moving to the side one by one, disappearing in the shadows under the shuttle's wing. We could change there in peace—that is, not counting Sarge who was still hooting at us on and off.

Before time was up, we stood in close order again. Two rows of khaki coveralls with all the trimmings: badges, medal ribbons, even name tags—with strange sounding names on them. And the ranks! We even got a few NCOs. I was just a sergeant, called Lamonte, but the quipster was made a full lieutenant.

Luckily for us, there were more uniforms than we needed, so nobody had to wear too tight pants. Nobody looked like a three-time loser either, though a skillful tailor like my old man would have known that the clothes we were wearing weren't our own at first glance. Except that in the war nobody asked tailors for their opinion. And that was a shame.

We got on board the space shuttle after a short briefing and another headcount. This time, Sarge couldn't be bothered to read our names. The flight didn't take long, even though for many of us it was the first time we'd left the New Brisbane's atmosphere. Unfortunately, the army rattletraps didn't have a single window to look through and admire the beauty of our small planet. I had no idea what plasteel properties are at that time …

A few hours later, we could leave the cargo hold, smelling of grease and puke, and move to a bright airlock of a troop carrier. From there, the crew members led us straight to cryogenic chambers. They told us to strip down to our underwear, which meant that the flight wouldn't take more than two, three days.

I settled down in soft foam, waited until all the electrodes were in place, and closed my eyes. My last thought was, "When I open them again, I will be a soldier."

———

You come out of hibernation gradually. Don't believe the stories about seasoned veterans who make hyperspace jumps and are able to fight fifteen minutes after leaving their cryogenic chamber. That's bullshit. Knowing that even before the draft, I calmly submitted to the post-hibernation procedures, sure that I'd come round eventually.

I didn't remember the moment we were led out of the troop carrier; I had no idea how I found my place in the four-sided formation. The moment I first became fully aware of my surroundings, I cursed whoever made us stand in this heat in full uniform. I patted down my pockets, but didn't find my glasses. Strange … My eyes stung like hell, but there was little I could do about it—at least not until the quartermaster gave me my duffel back.

"Attentiooon!" somebody bellowed. Judging by their nasal voice, it wasn't our Sarge.

We clicked our heels obediently. I heard a loud whistle on the right, then some creaking and finally somebody's heavy footsteps. Very close, just over my head. Annoyingly enough, I couldn't wipe my eyes. I didn't want to get into bad books before I even started my army career. They said "attention," you held yourself straight as a ramrod and didn't even blink. Besides, I could see a bit. The outlines of a tribune and some blurry silhouettes of people, standing on it.

"At ease!" somebody's deep bass voice rumbled through the formation. "Hello, GIs …"

"Hello, sir!" I shouted raspily, along with well over a hundred others.

The formation was much bigger than when we left New Brisbane. Why was I even surprised? Hyperspace travel wasn't cheap, and the replenishments couldn't have come only from our shabby planet.

The burning in my eyes was slowly subsiding; now the biggest problem was the sunshine hitting my face. And the tears, which were still flowing down my cheeks.

"My name is Colonel Greenlee," said the man standing on the tribune. As I leaned slightly to the left, the solar disc hid behind his sizeable figure and I could look around. "In the name of the Federation, I'll guide you to victory!"

"To viiictooory!" we roared automatically. All we wanted at that moment was to escape the heat.

"Long live the Federation! Long live the 6th Spaceborne Division, the queen of the whole army and slayer of the separatists!"

"Long live—!"

"Death to the traitors!"

"Death …!" I noticed that this battle cry didn't draw a very strong response. And not surprisingly; most of us despised the Federation much more than the rebellious colonists.

"… until there's no trace left!" Colonel Greenlee continued, undismayed.

I didn't know how to respond to this, and neither did many

of my companions, so it came out all wrong. A bunch of people just blatted simultaneously.

Apparently, the colonel didn't like it very much. He fell silent and as is the custom of every officer, he started looking down on us. I squeezed my eyes shut to get rid of the tears, then lifted my eyelids and …

"Fu—" The words died in my throat.

Thirty feet away from me, on an openwork platform, stood a slant-eyed man in a khaki uniform who most certainly wasn't a part of the spaceborne forces of the Federation. Moreover, he was accompanied by a line of soldiers carrying guns aimed at us. My companions began to get their bearings too. There were shouts and screams, growing louder with every second. It took not one, but three pulsator shots to restore order in our ranks.

"Welcome to the Forge!" the colonel said emphatically. "For you the war is over, I'm afraid. The valiant troops of the Rim Union—"

I'd never heard this name before, but I was not surprised; the government propaganda had been concealing the truth for a long time. After all, labels such as "rebels" or "traitors" sounded much better to the authorities' ears than proper—and proud—names like Rim Union.

"—have managed to track and seize the troop carrier, on board which you were sent back to the barracks after your vacation leave. One hundred and sixty-five representatives of the Federation's most elite division captured at one go …" The colonel paused and took a deep breath before he continued, "Our Higher Command decided that we couldn't afford to miss this opportunity to retaliate against the Federation, and especially its most elite division. The massacres you committed—"

"What's he on about now?" Shorza asked me in a whisper.

"I've no idea," I whispered back, almost without moving my lips. "He might be taking us for the Sixth's soldiers—" Suddenly, it dawned on me. "Fuck, it's the uniforms!"

"—Gideon Gamma, Alpha Tanganyika …" Colonel Greenlee continued. I'd lost the thread because of my brief exchange with

Levaristo, but apparently the colonel was alluding to the war crimes committed by the Sixth. "... Romulus Gamma—"

"It's a lie! We've never been to Romulus!" shouted one of the guys on the far left.

Greenlee clenched his teeth and tightened his jaw and facial muscles. Then slowly, very slowly he turned toward the soldier who had interrupted him.

"Are you saying, you federastic piece of shit, that I'm a liar?" he asked with venom in his voice.

"I'm saying that the Sixth's never operated on Romulus," the same guy said impudently. "And I should know. I've been with the Sixth since sixteenth."

The Union's officer didn't speak, he just waved his right hand. A soft cough somewhere in the air coincided with a thud coming more or less from the place where the fervent words sounded seconds ago. Momentarily, there were screams. I fought the fear and looked in that direction. The guycollapsed where he stood. I only saw the soles of his boots and the rumpled fabric of his suit. And blood. It was everywhere. On the faces of the soldiers who'd stood behind the shot man, on the sand around them. He must have been hit by a concentrated charge. At the sound of another volley, I fell to the ground. This time it was longer and louder, and came from more than just one pulsator.

"Whoever leaves his place in the ranks will be shot on the spot!" Greenlee said. "Whoever calls me a liar will follow in the footsteps of this piece of trash. Got it?!"

"Yes sir!" I shouted along with the others, getting up from the ground gingerly.

"Romulus Gamma, eight days ago," the unionist picked up where he left off.

"At precisely noon standard time, a squadron of capsulers with the telltale burning 6 on their bows appeared over the four largest cities of the colony. The landing troops reached the surface of the planet thirty-six seconds after the kinetic bombardment, which lay waste to all the agglomerations. Once again, the Federation triumphed over innocent people, women, and children. Seven hundred and thirty-seven thousand were killed. Almost six times as many injured.

"There were no military objectives on Gamma. The Romulus System joined the Rim Union only a week before, by virtue of the Unification Treaty. They didn't even have time to announce mobilization.

"You might not have known about this since you enjoyed your well-deserved rest after you'd suppressed riots on Tanganyika moons. Besides, I'm pretty sure that the Federation's authorities don't spread such kind of information."

These words created a stir in our ranks. Even I heard that we'd … ugh … that the Federation had won back a couple of systems recently. Greenlee was right: agitprop didn't include this sort of information. When the unionist fell silent, we began to whisper nervously among ourselves.

"Does anyone want to say something?" The colonel thundered from the tribune.

Nobody spoke. I thought I'd try to explain the situation, but then I remembered a soft cough from just a moment ago, and saw Mom in my mind's eye. You're a cog, tiny and nonsignificant cog, I told myself. Let somebody else stick their neck out—

"Yes!"

I looked in the direction the voice came from and saw that the guy definitely wasn't from New Brisbane.

"Go ahead."

"I'm afraid there's been a misunderstanding … sir!"

"Misunderstanding, you say?" Greenlee was sincerely amazed. "What kind of misunderstanding?"

"We're mainly conscripts, and have never seen combat," elaborated the guy standing in the second row, four places from me. "We were drafted into the army as a consequence of the recent decree of the Military Council of Federal Salvation. We've been against this war since the beginning—"

The colonel raised his hand again. There was silence, and the overeager guy covered his face with his hand as if this could block a charge of energy capable of burning a fist-sized hole in a two-inch-thick plasteel armor. But the shot wasn't fired. Instead, a file was handed over to Greenlee.

"Staff Sergeant Rosso, if I'm not mistaken ..." On hearing this name, the smart-mouth shook his head nervously, but Greenlee ignored it and with his nose in the file, continued, "Jamesteban Rosso. We have all your files, son. Despite the foul efforts of the captain of the troop carrier that carried you, we recovered a lot of data from the craft's computers, including these concerning the Sixth's list of staff. Maybe a little incomplete, but still. Let's see what we've got ... Rosso. In service since sixteenth. Distinguished himself in the campaign of Karnak. Served on Gideon, without meritorious conduct, and finally on Tanganyika. Recommended for promotion. It also says here: 'An excellent, disciplined soldier; never once failed to obey an order during the pacification of mining settlements.' I think I know why you came up with your little story, son. The pacification of Umbutu's mining settlements ... One of the darkest pages of this war."

"Sir, whatever happened there, it wasn't me. This is not my uniform! My name is Tristich, I'm from—"

"Shut up, you cowardly bastard!" Colonel Greenlee bellowed, giving the file back to his assistant. "Do you really think I'll believe your far-fetched story? You deserve to die a thousand deaths for what you did on Tanganyika's moons. And you will, I can guarantee you that you will."

"But I—"

"Another word, and I'll make sure you repay your debt to the Rim Union at once!"

Tristich looked at us pleadingly, but even though we all were in the same boat, nobody came to his aid. The stench of death was too much for us; nobody wanted to stand in the line of fire. I didn't know what excuse the other guys had, but I deeply believed that we would explain the whole situation, only not then and not there. Not under such circumstances. After all, it was a mistake. None of us—

"Now that we've cleared it up," the colonel said, "we can move on to the next item on the agenda. As the most hated enemy of the Rim Union, you fell into my hands. Here, at the Forge, the fate of this war is being decided. Take a look around," he ordered, and paused, encouraging us to glance about with a gesture of his arms.

We were on a vast plain; behind us, on the landing ground's tarmac, less than three hundred feet away, stood a charred planetary transporter, carrying the markings of the separatists. To the left of it, I saw a dozen simple, single-story barracks built of poro-concrete. Behind them, there was a dome of a huge bunker, and a slender tower with something resembling a hat on top— one of four similar structures placed in every corner of the compound. No fences, no coils of barbed wire, nothing at all that would separate us from the endless plain.

"You must be wondering why the camp, where you're going to spend the rest of your lives, isn't encircled by anything that would resemble a fence," Greenlee said the second I asked myself this very question.

Judging by the looks on the other guys' faces, many of them were mulling it over too.

"How about a little presentation? Mr. Rosso!"

The draftee called Rosso didn't respond and I couldn't blame him. I'd already forgotten the name of the soldier whose uniform I was wearing.

"Sergeant Rosso, I'm talking to you," the colonel said louder, pointing his finger at Tristich.

"But I'm not—"

"Shut up! You've been warned: If you make that excuse again, you'll repay your debts here and now! You shouldn't have ordered your people to shoot when the civilians wanted to surrender, knowing that they stood no chance against the armed and armored ruthless enemy."

Tristich was devastated. He searched for help, but didn't find any for everybody was staring at the ground, so as not to become the sadistic unionist's next target.

"Ha," Greenlee snorted. "The Federation's elite division … Crème de la crème … Heroes …" he taunted us.

When the colonel raised his hand once again, I was confident I'd hear a pulsator cough. But nothing happened. In the silence that fell over the square, I only heard my heart beating in my ears. "Sergeant Rosso, right turn and double time, march!"

Anxiously, Tristich looked back, then glanced at the tribune. The colonel waved his hand and one of the soldiers put the pulsator to his shoulder. That was all the frightened conscript needed to hoof it; within moments he was pushing his way through the ranks. When he finally was in the open, he quickened his pace and began dodging. He was slim and fit. Shooting him might have been difficult even for an experienced shooter. Especially since the distance grew with his every step.

I stared after running Tristich for a moment longer, then shifted my gaze to the tribune. The soldiers surrounding the colonel lowered their weapons. They stood still, no tension on their faces. I glanced at the towers. Did they have robotized firing posts on them? This would explain the unionists' calm.

Meanwhile, Tristich had already covered quite a distance. He went past a yellow flag, one of a few that I noticed just now. They were very small and close to the ground; if not for the fact that the escapee had been pushing straight onto one of them, I'd have missed it. Tristich took two further steps, and fell. We thought he'd tripped over something, but a second later we heard his whine. He squirmed on the ground, tried to get up, finally sat down heavily and, bent like a rag doll, stayed in this position.

The colonel nodded at two soldiers who immediately left the platform and climbed into the graviplane.

Greenlee addressed us from above. "Wouldlike to know what killed Sergeant Rosso, a man who unhesitatingly shot an old woman in the back of her head, or threw a grenade into a classroom full of children?

"I'll tell you. Since each of you may suffer the same fate, you should know. There is no escape from this camp. We don't need fences or guards to keep you on premises. Before we initiated the reviving procedure, we engrafted a few tiny implants in your body. Just one step beyond the flag-marked boundaries of the camp and four micro-explosive devices will turn your arteries into an unrepairable sieve. In other words, you'll bleed to death within seconds."

The graviplane flew back to the tribune, Tristich's body hanging off its side. Before the soldiers lowered the corpse to the sand, we could see big stains of blood adorning the shoulders and thighs of our companion's coveralls.

"You have no rights from now on," Greenlee continued in a voice devoid of any emotion. "The Rim Union has found you guilty of committing war crimes and has sentenced you to death. The execution was carried out immediately and publicized in all major news reports."

He paused and looked down on us, smiling to himself. "That's the honest truth. No one's going to look for you, whatever you might think or hope. You're as dead to the whole world as these two federal buggers."

"What are you going to do with us?" asked somebody from the back rows.

"You will find out in due time."

To my amazement, Colonel Greenlee didn't order the daredevil to be silenced.

———

A few minutes later, the troop carrier flew away. The colonel and his people watched as it vanished into dense clouds, and then they climbed into their graviplanes and headed for the bunker's dome. Nobody said another word; nobody told us what to do.

"We're fucked," Shorza whispered. He couldn't take his eyes off of the bodies lying in the dust.

Kozak, green in the face, crouched next to us. He didn't speak, only stared glassily at the horizon. I sat beside him on the bare ground. I wanted to say something comforting, but I couldn't think of anything. No matter how hard I tried, I wasn't able to come up with a single sensible sentence.

"Listen up!" a voice sounded on the other side of the formation. "If we stick together, they won't break us easily!"

"Speak for yourself," somebody else said.

"Those clones-of-bitches didn't tell us the whole truth," argued the first speaker. "We're alive and kicking, so they must have some plans for us."

A few people backed him up, there were murmurs of approval coming from all sides.

"Soldier boys ..." muttered the quipster in the uniform of a lieutenant.

"What did you just say?" asked the first speaker.

I looked at him when he stepped forward from behind others, most of whom were strangers to me. He certainly wasn't a member of the New Brisbane group.

"You heard me," the mock lieutenant replied.

"Who do you call 'soldier boys'?" The guy was tall, well-built, and had fire in his eyes when he came face to face with our homey. They were glaring each other down from a two-inch distance. If one of them had a bit more prominent nose ...

"People who—what was it?—throw grenades into classrooms full of children," the mock lieutenant said in an icy voice.

"The Sixth don't murder civilians," his opponent hissed, all red in the face.

"You didn't pacify the Tanganyika moons?"

"Not the way you think."

By now, most of the guys had gathered around them. I got up and pushed my way to the front row. Those whom I knew stood behind the "lieutenant"; the rest—the Sixth's real veterans—clung to the back of their comrade. There were eighty of us, and only twenty of them, but if it came to the crunch, I wouldn't wager a penny on the New Brisbane team. And the fight seemed imminent.

"We have to bury the dead," I said.

They both looked at me, as did the rest, but pulled away from each other as I went past them, walking toward Tristich's body.

My badly grazed hands hurt like hell when we headed for the barracks in a disorderly bunch. Burying a man in a dry, hard soil, especially with no tools available, is not an easy task. Admittedly, we had a few small stones to dig with, but still. After an hour of such teamwork, during which we constantly changed, we managed to make a shallow pit. It was not more than twelve inches deep, but it had to do. We lowered our friend's pale, horribly stinking body to the hole in the ground and covered it carefully with all the stones we could find within a dozen-yard radius. Levaristo made an awry tiny cross from the stalks of withered plants. When we finished, some of us fell to the ground, heaving a sigh of relief, and the others went to help the soldiers. They were far less numerous, and their task was even more difficult than ours, for their comrade's body was practically torn apart.

When both men rested in peace, we paid our last respects, falling silent for a minute, and then headed for the barracks.

They were a mile away. Under normal circumstances, it would take no more than a couple of minutes to reach them on foot. But we needed almost half an hour to get to the nearest building. We hadn't recovered from the hibernation yet and were exhausted by hard work in the hellish heat. The sun, which was tinted strange blue and at its zenith, had taken a toll on everybody. We were having trouble lifting our feet. Every now and then, one of us sat on the ground, or even fell flat on their face. We didn't leave our companions behind; we waited until they got up or helped them up when they seemed incapable of coping on their own.

About twenty minutes into the march, somebody shouted at the rear. All eyes turned in that direction. A chubby guy pointed his finger at the cloud of dust behind a vehicle that was heading toward the tribune, much less imposing from this distance. We stopped and watched as several unionists jumped to the ground and expertly dug up the graves. A few minutes later the two bodies were in black bags and found their way onto the back of the vehicle.

"Clones-of-bitches …" a sergeant muttered under his breath. It was the same guy who bristled at the "soldier boys" comment. "As I said, they are playing with us."

With these words, he turned around and walked on toward the barracks of the camp.

———

We weren't expecting a reception. Not such, at least.

By the time we went past the first barrack, its door had opened, and we saw several men in dingy Federation coveralls. Judging by the patches, they were all pilots. I was too tired to pay attention to details, but something struck me about their appearance. Only later, in the evening, I realized that they looked too clean and too healthy for incumbent prisoners of an extermination camp.

Soon, others started pouring out from the rest of the buildings. There were not many of them, not even twenty. They stood in the distance, silent and emaciated. They watched us attentively, but they didn't come any closer.

The oldest of the pilots, a thin man with the rank of captain and grizzled hair, surveyed our group with a searching gaze. We stared at him, wondering who or what he was looking for. The mystery was explained when the officer stood in front of Thomashley Doherty, our "lieutenant," and asked, "Are you in charge here?"

"I think you must be mistaking me for Colonel Greenlee."

The captain gave him a strange look.

"I mean—"

"I know what you mean," Doherty interrupted him. "My answer is: No, I'm not in command of these people, I'm not a lieutenant, it isn't my uniform, and I don't feel like explaining any of it right now."

That left the captain dumbstruck.

"Okay, I see, sure." He turned to his comrades. "What are you waiting for? Show them to their lodgings. NCOs in Block 6, the rest in Blocks 1, 2, 4, 7 and 11."

———

Having noticed that the prisoners form a tight-knit community, I decided it was the best way to survive in this place, and so I found myself in Block 2 along with a bunch of other guys from New Brisbane.

Our barrack had three parts. You walked into a bedroom with thirty-three bunk beds, a dining room—with two long tables and a simple food dispenser—was located behind a thin partition, and at the very end of the building there was a bath-room containing toilets and showers. We couldn't be more happy to see the latter, but soon came the realization: they were just for show. We were told that water flowed from the taps only twice a day, for a total of ten minutes each time, which with eight cubicles wasn't very promising. It was the same story as with food. The dispenser offered three modest, synthetic meals during the whole day—and that lasted nearly thirty standard hours. For those of us who came from New Brisbane, it wasn't a problem because a local day was only one hour longer than on our home planet, but some of the Sixth's soldiers could find it bothersome.

We got settled in a flash, took a very quick shower, then ate some brown, smelly slops. Thirty minutes later, following the instructions given by one of the prisoners, we marched out to the roll call yard.

The captain and his two assistants were waiting for us in the middle of the yard. The rest of the prisoners kept back in the shadows of the barracks. When we stopped and looked at the captain expectantly, he greeted us, "Hello, my friends! I can only imagine that you have hundreds of questions about this camp and the situation you've found yourselves in."

He held up his hand to silence the growing buzz. "All in good time, all in good time. First let me, as the senior officer in this camp, fill you in ..." He paused, waiting for us to calm down. "My name is Captain Rustymon Bidley and I was shot down by the unionists during the Battle of Beta on Narvik on January 16, two thousand, two hundred and thirty-five."

He had to pause again. "A month later," he continued when the murmur died down, "after a show trial where I was sentenced to death, I found myself in this camp. For nine months, that is since we lost Colonel Keptler, I'm the senior officer here. One might say, I'm in command of all the Forge's prisoners." He pointed at his companions. "I'm going to expect compliance and discipline of you too. You may have been captured, but you're still soldiers and as such you can't lose heart."

For a moment, he looked as if he wanted to add something, but eventually he just shook his head.

"I'm not the best speaker in the world, so that would be it on my part. If anyone has a question, please raise your hand."

We all raised our hands like hyperactive kids in the first grade.

Bidley pointed a finger at one of the Sixth's veterans.

"What is this place, sir?" asked a corporal who I laid my eyes on for the first time this very moment.

"If you mean this planet, I don't have any concrete information for you. There are no astronavigators among us, and we weren't able to determine the sector of space we're in on our own—"

The corporal interrupted him, "I meant the camp."

"The Forge isn't your typical POW camp," Bidley said carefully. "I guess Commandant Greenlee has already told you that all of you were sentenced to death and the executions were carried out a long time ago. That clone-of-a-bitch loves to shock new arrivals.

"Unfortunately, in this case it's true. They faked your death. I'm not kidding ... Okay, no more beating about the bush. The unionists didn't gather you here to give you a second chance.

What's in store for you is … First harsh training, and then—then they'll start hunting. For you."

The two assistants had to cut the racket before the next question could be asked. This time it was Doherty who spoke. As the "most senior" in our group, he was given the floor first.

"What do you mean, hunting?"

"Maybe my wording is a little unfortunate, but it reflects your situation best. It's always the same. At roll call in the morning, some names are read out, usually four to six. Then, the selected prisoners are transported to the bunker, where Colonel Greenlee gives them detailed instructions regarding their mission. It can be something complicated, but for starters, unionists tell you, for instance, to get from point A to point B. Finally, you're taken to some distant place on this planet, and the hunt begins. You'll find yourselves on foreign territory, without weapons or food, equipped only with a map. Enemy soldiers will stalk you. If you complete the mission and survive, you'll be taken back to the camp. For the next thirty days, you'll be enjoying immunity. But if you get caught …" He paused meaningfully.

An uproar swept through the ranks. Especially on our side. As conscripts, we knew practically nothing about advanced combat techniques, or camouflage and concealment techniques for that matter. Because the theoretical training during hibernation on board the troop carrier didn't count. I glanced at the vets, standing in the shadows. There were seventeen of them, not many, given the capacity of this camp. Things like that made you think.

"Did anybody manage to survive such 'hunting'?" asked another soldier pointed by the captain.

"Yes," Bidley nodded. "Losses are usually around seventy percent. Three out of ten people get back to the camp. Sometimes even more. We're doing everything we can to train you. So that you're better than this unionist scum …" He spat at his feet contemptuously.

"What's the point of such training if we are to die anyway?"

said a short brunet standing in the first row of our group. I've seen him before. Probably in the school corridors. "Isn't it better to sit on our asses and let the unionists kill us right away rather than provide them with free entertainment?"

"No, son. You're wrong." The captain scowled at us. "It's not about providing them with free entertainment. This war will end, sooner or later. And I'm sure we will win it. That's why I'm so determined not to let all of you die. Thanks to your testimonies, people will learn the truth about the Rim Union criminal regime. Perhaps with this sacrifice, at least one of you will witness Colonel Greenlee's execution."

The prisoners standing in the shadows brightened. They hoped so too.

"Sir, you keep saying: 'you' ..." I blurted out before the captain could point to the next person. "Does this mean that these rules don't apply to yourself and your people?"

Bidley smiled.

"If someone survives ten missions, they become training staff for the next twelve months." He pointed to the blue band on his right sleeve. "Those poor clones-of-bitches didn't stand a chance against me," he added with unfeigned pride.

I wasn't amused. All the vets had blue bands on their sleeves.

———

The meeting drew on and on, but we learned little more. Life in the camp was mainly about sleeping, eating and strenuous exercise. The missions, or "hunts," had no common denominator. All were different, or so the survivors said. The captain also told us that "new arrivals" usually had the first week off, but as transports of fresh cannon fodder had started coming in less regularly now, and the Sixth was the grit on the lens of many unionists, we couldn't really hope for much slack. When yet another guy spilled the beans about us being practically civilians, Bidley nearly freaked out. He wrapped up the meeting in the roll call yard, telling us to get some rest and choose two liaisons with the informal Camp Command. Preferably somebody of the highest rank, or at least most respected by the rest of us. We had time until 25:00. The captain scheduled a briefing at this hour in his barrack.

And so we had a problem. Us, not the old sweats from the Sixth.

We really didn't know how to go about the elections. Finally, we gathered in one barrack and began to deliberate. An hour passed, two hours, then we took a short break to have dinner, and the whole thing started all over again. We were as disorganized as they come. Each group of friends suggested their own representative because the function of a liaison seemed a pretty good setup. "Seemed" was a key word here, for we could only hope that it guaranteed exclusion from the "hunt" lottery. At least in the first phase of training. Bidley suggested something like that between the lines, or somebody had gotten it into their head.

Just before 24:00, when yet another candidate fell through, the guy who'd been rejected moments ago stood up, looked at us and said, "Listen up! There's someone who has balls among us. Not only that, but he can think too. Even under tremendous stress."

Suddenly, it was so quiet in the barrack that you could hear a pin drop.

"Who do you have in mind?" Doherty asked hopefully.

"Him!" the guy pointed in my direction. "When you were at each other's throats with that sergeant, he reacted astutely and defused the situation—"

This was the moment when I realized that my hopes of remaining a tiny, nonsignificant cog in the war machine were crumbling to dust.

With each murmur of approval, I felt a growing chill on my back, even though it was incredibly hot and stuffy in the barrack.

"What's your name, buddy?" Doherty asked.

"I'm not cut out for it," I snapped, but what are friends for.

"Doni! His name's Johanatol Doni!" Levaristo cried out.

"He's right for this job, I'm telling you ..." Then, seeing my face, he added in a much softer voice, "What?"

"You see?" My promoter spread his arms wide. "He's the first one who's not gagging for the job."

"Then why cause him grief," said somebody from the back row, but was silenced by a chorus of voices.

"Shut up!"

"Let's cut the crap," Doherty said. "In my opinion, Doni is perfect for this job. Who agrees with me?"

A show of hands—so bang goes my anonymity. Involuntarily, I walked into the spotlight, which meant that I was exposed now.

Even Kozak seemed to liven when I rose from my bunk, although until just now, he'd been apathetic and silent.

"And the second liaison?" he asked, shouting over the growing frenzy.

Everybody went quiet. They realized they were only halfway home.

"How about ... I choose a partner myself?" I hoped my insolence would dampen their enthusiasm. Unfortunately, my hopes proved ill-founded.

"See? Didn't I tell you that he's perfect for this job?" Then my promoter added, "Sure, bro! Go ahead ..."

———

Thirty minutes later I was walking across the roll call yard with Doherty, who seemed to me the most reasonable guy in our group. I didn't know anybody else, apart from Levaristo and Marianton, of course, but they weren't fit for this kind of job. So, I decided that Thomashley would be my right-hand man. I hoped that at least one of us had the guts to stand up to Bidley, if need be.

We had fifteen minutes to get to know each other a bit better. I told him about myself, he said a few things about his own past. Thomashley was a year older than me and lived in a nearby settlement, we went to the same school, but on different shifts. We had quite a few mutual friends, which wasn't anything extraordinary in tight, small communities such as New Brisbane. I ferreted out two clauses relevant to our appeal, and so did he. That's where we stopped.

The door leading to Bidley's barrack was guarded by one of his assistants, a black giant with gray hair called Navin. Theodoreed Navin. Without unnecessary fuss, the lieutenant took us to the dining room, where the real Sixth liaisons were already waiting; the mouthy troglodyte, with whom Doherty had clashed at the tribune, and another sergeant.

We nodded at them casually, and the captain invited us to take chairs before he said, "Since I know everyone here, I'll make the introductions."

A moment later we knew who was who. The troglodyte was called Ianthony Skalski, and his equally moronic-looking companion—Clayrton Barron.

"Can you tell me, lieut—" Bidley paused and quickly corrected himself. "Private Doherty, why don't you explain what's with this dress-up?"

Thomashley described the events on New Brisbane briefly, skipping altogether the part about our objection to compulsory military service. And rightly so, if you ask me. After several years in this place, none of the soldiers would have understood if we'd told them that we support their captors.

The captain stared at Doherty in disbelief, then shook his head resignedly. "I had no idea that such a fuck up is even possible," he finally said.

"That's nothing," Barron cut in. "Once, we got three hundred tons of kinetic ammunition."

His tone suggested it was a good joke. We didn't get it for obvious reasons, but Captain Bidley and his people seemed equally confused. When Barron noticed this, he cared to elaborate, "We don't have heavy weapons. We're launched in G-pods straight into the battlefield, and there we fight mainly with

DEWS, directed-energy weapons. You can't fire a multi-ton missile from something like this."

The captain rubbed his face, although he didn't seem tired.

"Such stories make me doubt if anyone ever comes to our rescue," he said.

"It's not the most pressing issue at the moment," Doherty remarked. "You have eighty civilians in the camp, and the unionists are going to put the screws on us any day now."

"I know." Bidley nodded and bit his lip nervously. "However, if Greenlee finds out who he's dealing with—"

Doherty didn't let him finish. "Colonel Greenlee doesn't care about the truth. He didn't believe us when we tried to explain the misunderstanding."

"He claimed he'd recovered some data from the troop carrier's computers," I said, and pointing at the name tag with "Lamonte" on it, added hastily, "Including 'our' personal files."

"Colonel Greenlee lied." Bidley waved his hand dismissively.

"I don't think so." Doherty backed me up before any of the sergeants could speak. "He read some unglamorous facts from … our former colleague's assumed CV. He gave the impression of someone well-informed."

The captain looked at us more closely.

"How well?"

"Well enough."

Bidley let out a loud breath. "The good thing is you won't sing during interrogations."

"What interrogations?" I crowed.

"Son, did you really think that Greenlee would leave you alone? The aces of the most elite division in the whole Federation? Capturing almost a hundred of such soldiers gives him an incredible opportunity to winkle out many secrets of our army."

Doherty went pale. He'd gotten an NCO's uniform, as the only one in our group. Even among the twenty soldiers of the Sixth, the highest-ranking NCOs were only sergeants.

"Galacticunt …" Skalski muttered. He just realized it wasn't the hunts that were the greatest threat here. "Sir, why didn't you say anything earlier?"

"I'm telling you now. Decide for yourselves if you want to pass this information on. Personally, I'd advise against it."

"Why?" we asked in unison.

"How do you feel knowing about interrogations?" Bidley asked.

We didn't have to reply, and not only because it was a rhetorical question on his part; he could see the answer in our faces. How right he was! Prior knowledge that the unionists were going to put the screws on us would certainly lie heavy on many of the conscripts. They wouldn't have gotten a wink of sleep. That's why Thomashley and I unanimously decided not to tell them anything.

"Isn't there some way around it?" My companion seemed brokenhearted.

Bidley closed his eyes. "I think that eventually, they'll realize you're just conscripts," he said. "But it'll take several attempts, maybe more ... If not for the personal files Doni mentioned, I might be able to convince them that they'd captured replenishments. But since Greenlee has everything in black and white, he'll press you real hard for intel. I know the bastard long enough."

"So, we're fucked," Doherty summed up.

"You've no idea, son."

———

Thomashley was right. He was also the first to go. The very next day. We all got up at eight, long before sunrise. Thirty minutes later the roll call began. All that military crap. The headcount, the report, task assignment. I gathered that something was wrong from the fact that Bidley never directed his gaze toward us. Not once.

He read the list of daily orders, and then—as if in

afterthought—added, "Lieutenant Manfredward Dunst will report at the East Passage at 07:00 hours."

We remained indifferent, but within seconds I realized that none of the vets was called Dunst. Thomashley on the other hand wore a tag with this surname on his chest. The captain's behavior only confirmed my suspicions. He turned on his heel and saying nothing else, went back to his block.

Doherty didn't move from his spot when the roll call ended, and everybody went about their business. I stayed with him. That was the least I could do. I didn't want him to be alone now.

It was already ten to seven, so we had just enough time to get to the East Passage.

"We should be going," I said, placing my hand on his shoulder.

Thomashley was shivering all over. He might not have been so scared if he hadn't known what to expect.

"No," he said, shaking off my hand.

"Are you crazy?" I hissed into his ear. "If you're not there in ten minutes, they'll blast off the micro-explosive devices planted in your body."

He looked at me, his mouth trembling, his eyes moist, sweat beading on his forehead.

"At least it won't hurt as much," he pronounced.

Too right, I thought. I wanted to say something, but one of Bidley's assistants waved his hand at us.

"Hey, you!"

I grabbed Doherty's arm and yanked him toward the captain's block which was in the opposite direction from the East Passage.

Bidley was waiting for us by the door. "Private Doherty," he said firmly, "you just don't get it, do you? The rules here are clear—"

"I'd rather die within seconds than after hours of agony."

"Yeah? Even if that means that three of your friends die too?"

Thomashley looked up at the captain.

"I don't have any friends here," he said in a flat, dispassionate voice of a man reconciled to his fate. Then, suddenly, he awoke from his stupor. "What are you talking about, sir?"

Bidley extended his hand with a piece of paper. "Read this order." Doherty didn't move. Not to make things worse, I took the order from Bidley's hand and read it. There were three other names apart from the unlucky lieutenant's. The following people would die if Thomashley didn't report as told: Squall, Baldini, Cronauer. Those names meant nothing to me, although the last one rang a bell. Cronauer, Cronauer ...

Galacticunt! Marianton wore it on his chest!

"You've only got seven minutes left," the captain said.

"I don't give a shit," Thomashley grumbled.

I felt for him, I really did. But he was a stranger to me while Kozak was one of my best friends.

"Sorry," I whispered, taking a step back, and punched him in the temple.

He'd been so numb that he didn't even duck, although he must have known what I was going to do. He staggered, but kept his footing. *I'm a poor excuse for a fighter*, I thought, supporting Doherty just in case. One of the assistants grabbed Doherty's other arm.

We headed for the camp boundary, dragging him between us. At first, Thomashley tried to pull away, but eventually, he stopped kicking.

"What's wrong with him?" asked Lieutenant Lisky, breathless.

To answer him, I had to stop for a moment.

"You, of course, would go to the interrogation of your own free will ..."

In the meantime, a graviplane took off from the bunker's dome, heading straight for the eastern boundary of the camp. We still had three hundred feet to go.

"You two are quartered in the same block?" Bidley's assistant asked me.

"Yes," I replied, surprised by his question.

"Did you see him at breakfast?" Lieutenant Lisky pressed on

"Yes."

"Did he eat?"

"Not much."

"Clone-of-a ..."

We were already approaching the yellow line, beyond which there were two unionists standing next to their graviplane.

"Is this Lieutenant Dunst?" one of them asked, aiming his gun at us.

"Yes," I said.

The unionist looked at Thomashley curiously, then shifted his gaze to Lisky.

"He had little for breakfast." Bidley's assistant shrugged his shoulders as if these five words explained everything.

To my astonishment, the unionists took them at face value. Then they grabbed Doherty, still unsteady on his feet, put him on board the graviplane, and left for the bunker without another word.

For a long moment, we just stood there in a cloud of dust, catching our breath, and when the air cleared enough for us to see the camp's buildings, we headed back.

"What's with this breakfast thing?" I asked, midway.

"Food dispensers add sedatives to the meals of those prisoners who are to be hunted or interrogated on a given day," Lisky explained after a moment's hesitation. "So, they are usually meek as lambs and follow orders."

———

Thomashley returned right after dinner. I realized that something was wrong when the block suddenly became silent. I sat bolt upright and glanced toward the door. Everybody else was already looking that way.

"Someone get a first aid kit!" Lieutenant Navin ordered before crossing the threshold.

"Which is his bed?" Lieutenant Lisky asked at the same time.

Shown one of the top bunks, Navin and Lisky winced.

"Bring him over here," I suggested, jumping to my feet and spreading out the blanket.

Before they put Doherty in a comfortable position, somebody brought the first aid kit. Navin took it from the red-haired guy's shaking hands and pushed the Good Samaritan back into the crowd as if he were dealing with a mannequin. Now, everybody was gathered around my bunk, motionless, silent, wide-eyed.

I didn't see Thomashley's whole body, but the sight of his hands and face was enough to make me sick. The clones-of-bitches ripped off all his fingernails and broke at least two of his fingers. You could see it with the naked eye.

Doherty's face looked even worse. A swollen jaw, bruised mouth with toothless gums, puffy eyes, hardly visible because of the purplish swelling which spilled out to the cheeks and neck. One ear dangled out at an unnatural angle. The pug nose disappeared completely under a swelling, dark blood still oozing from one of the nostrils.

"Water! We need some water!" Lisky said.

"But how ...?" I asked, snapping out of my trance. "It's after dinner, and the showers—"

"From the toilet, man!" The lieutenant impatiently waved an empty canteen.

I handed it over to Marianton, along with my towel.

"Shake a leg!" I pushed him toward the bathroom. "Just remember, the toilet needs scrubbing first!"

He nodded and disappeared behind the partition. Meanwhile, Lisky carefully examined our friend's injuries. It was clear he didn't give Doherty much of a chance. As he pressed Thomashley's chest lightly, he started writhing in pain and coughing spasmodically. Bloody bubbles appeared on his lips.

"Galacticunt!" The lieutenant withdrew his hands abruptly.

Doherty was gagging. He moved his lips silently, struggled to get up, but each movement only intensified the pain. With yet another violent spasm, a stream of dark, almost black blood trickled down from the corner of his mouth. A second later, he fell back on the pillow heavily. He didn't breathe at that point.

"Here you go!" Kozak screamed in my ear, beaming. "The water you've asked for ..."

The canteen hung in the air. Nobody reached for it.

———

The next day at roll call, we stood in complete silence. Our friend's body was lying alongside the formation, tightly wrapped in a blanket. Lieutenant Lisky had told us to carry it to one of the passages after we were dismissed. A walk to the camp boundary at night might have been misinterpreted by the guards.

Again, we went through a routine headcount, reports, and daily orders. By the time Bidley finished, I'd been sweating all over.

I understood my hunch was right, when Bidley read three new names, "Sergeant Troy, Corporal Sauncey, and Private Honzo will report at the West Passage at 07:00 hours."

One vet and two guys from our group of eighty ... seventy-nine, that is. Sauncey, I knew him by sight, he lived next door and could play ball well. He even was on the school team. Honzo, I didn't recognize his face.

I hadn't noticed until now that the captain didn't put the order away. When he swallowed nervously, I knew it was a bad sign.

"Senior Sergeant MacMarsky will report to the East Passage at 07:00 hours." Bidley pocketed the document.

The guy standing next to Shorza looked around with unseeing eyes. I'd told the orderlies from the other blocks to make sure that everybody ate their serving at breakfast. They hadn't asked me any questions. All of us were still shell-shocked after what the unionists did to Doherty.

When the prisoners went about their business, only seven people stayed in the roll call yard. Me, Skalski, Bidley, and the four guys whose names had been just read out.

"You were damn right, sir," Ianthony said as we approached the captain. "They didn't cut us any slack."

In the meantime, Lieutenant Lisky corralled the three prisoners who were supposed to report at the West Passage. They followed him now meek as lambs, carrying Thomashley's stiff body on their shoulders. Navin put his arm around MacMarsky's neck and led him in the opposite direction. Bidley looked after them for a moment, then turned to us.

"I know what they did to Doherty," he said slowly. "Greenlee went all the way this time. For months, there have been no fatalities resulting from interrogations. Several soldiers were crippled, but never something like that …" He shook his head in disbelief.

"Sir, perhaps you'll be willing to put in a good word for the boots now," Skalski suggested.

"How do I do that?"

"They've taken another one today," the sergeant continued. "And he won't tell them anything either, whatever they do to him—"

I cut him off. "A man in pain will confess to anything."

Skalski looked at me with disgust. There was no place for fear or treason in his heroic mind. I wondered if he would change his mind if somebody pulled out all his teeth and ripped off all his nails without anesthesia.

"Doni is right,," the captain took my side. "They're civilians. They can't even answer a question about their service number."

He had a point. I didn't remember my service number. After the awakening, our dog tags weren't returned to us …

"True," Skalski agreed at once. "But sir … maybe you could —It's a good time to ram home the fact that Greenlee won't beat anything out of them."

He got me wondering. Why would this troglodyte care for us so much? After all, he called us "boots" which meant that he despised all conscripts.

"I'll see what I can do," the captain promised before saluting and walking away.

"Thanks," I said when the two of us were alone.

"What for?"

"For sticking up for us."

Skalski came up to me, and stopped, although not as close as with Doherty the other day. He looked me straight in the eye and said, "Private Doni, you may not have noticed yet, but these clones-of-bitches are picking us up by ranks, starting from the top. If they really have these personal files, Sergeant Tyrrus will be next … pardon me, but I don't know the name of the boot who wears his uniform now. Then it'll be my turn."

Well, I could have guessed that he was just protecting his ass.

"I'm in the top ten too," I muttered.

"You don't get it, boot." Skalski moved even closer. "As long as they take you, the situation is under control. You may confess to fucking your own mothers, but any good investigator, and they certainly have such ones here, will immediately know what's true and what's not. But when I go to the interrogation, I'll be in for a wild ride. I saw what they did to Doherty, so I know they'll drag what they want out of me. And if that happens, they'll realize that not everyone is a boot here. They won't stop torturing us until they know everything. We have to convince them that we're all civilians, otherwise many of us will be skinned alive. That's why I'm pushing the captain hard. If he talks with them about it today, they should let us be."

———

It played out differently. It always does. Especially if something is so important. At about six in the afternoon, when we were just finishing our training session, a sound alert called us back to the barracks. The announcement was short: Anyone who remained in the open after the sirens went silent would be killed.

I'd herded the guys to our barrack and closed the door behind them long before the camp was enveloped in silence. We sat on our bunks, staring at each other in horror. We didn't understand what was going on, but we had a hunch that it couldn't be anything good.

Five minutes later Kozak raised his hand and asked, "Can you hear it?"

I didn't hear anything, and neither did most of the guys, but Marianton was rolling his eyes and waving his finger as if picking up some distant sounds.

"What are you—" I began, but he put a finger to his lips, silencing me.

And then I heard it, or rather I felt it. Light, familiar vibration, immediately followed by rumbling noise. Nobody could miss that.

"A transporter!" Levaristo cried out.

Marianton nodded, grinning from ear to ear. His hearing was pretty good, I had to admit.

"Our troops?" somebody asked hopefully.

"Ours," Shorza confirmed, and when the cheers faded at last, he added, "You'll see them at roll call tonight." He was right. An hour later, the alert was over with a loud clang announcing to all that the barrack door was unlocked again. The guys stayed put, though. Someone had to set an example. I even knew who …

I opened the door and looked outside warily. I saw a cloud of dust near the bunker. It was settling very slowly. To see the landing pad, I had to walk to Block 7. A few soldiers watched me through a crack in the door. I nodded at them, saying that it was safe, and went round the corner.

A troop carrier stood on the landing pad. Its hatch was open, a wide gangplank was resting on the ground. By the tribune, on which Greenlee was standing again, I saw a cluster of miniature silhouettes.

"A new delivery."

I started. I hadn't noticed Skalski creep behind my back. Focused on the horizon, I missed the moment when a large group of soldiers from Blocks 3 and 7 surrounded me.

"Not very impressive," somebody else said.

There were far fewer of them than us. Between the conscripts and the soldiers, not even half of the barracks were occupied. Had they brought in two hundred newbies—and to think that

I'd been here for just three days, and I already felt myself to be a vet!—it still wouldn't be too crowded in the camp.

"They're coming!" yelled one of the conscripts, judging by his voice.

Clouds of dust behind the graviplanes clearly showed that the welcome meeting was over.

"That was fast," Skalski remarked.

"He didn't dillydally with us either." I shrugged my shoulders before I started walking toward the front row of the barracks. There, I sat on the bare ground to wait for the newbies. "Nobody shot at them," the sergeant said.

"They must have been more civil ..." I muttered, and laughed under my breath. The pun wasn't intended.

They walked faster than us. And different somehow. In a column ... After they'd covered two-thirds of the way, I could judge their numbers more accurately. Thirty soldiers. For they were seasoned soldiers, I had no doubt about that.

Bidley stepped out of his den when the head of the modest column halted in front of his barrack.

———

We met an hour later at Bidley's, as usual. I, Deymoon—my recent promoter, whom I chose to replace Doherty—Skalski, Barron, and one newbie. A young guy with the rank of second lieutenant. His name was Estebandreas DeVerro.

The captain introduced us, then gave the floor to the newbie.

"It was our first mission right out of Academy," DeVerro began hesitantly.

"Our platoon was part of the 3rd Engineering Brigade. We were to land in Kovo, the second largest city on Delta in the Triton system. According to the intel, the 17th Spaceborne Division captured it the day before and drove the unionists to the nearby mines. We had to secure the area and set up a transport base for heavy equipment.

"So, we left the orbit. A total of six Hectors. We were flying the first one. The moment we touched down, all hell broke loose. In three seconds, the shields were gone, the main rotors blown up. Hectors 2 and 3 also got hit pretty bad, but they were still in the air. They managed to retreat under cover of friendly fire."

Skalski and Barron shook their heads unanimously.

"We fought back from inside the wreck for a while," the newbie continued, "but we didn't stand a chance against the active armors of the Rim Guard with just needle ammunition. They popped us out of the hold like peas of the pod." The idiom he used suggested that he came from an agrarian planet.

"And that would be it …" Bidley said, also shaking his head. "What about the pilot?"

"He was wounded. The unionists killed him on the spot. And my six men too."

"Lucky dogs," Skalski murmured.

"Sorry?"

"Nothing." The sergeant shrugged. "Welcome to the Forge."

———

In the evening, when I was getting ready for bed, somebody tapped me on the shoulder.

"It's just us," Levaristo whispered, perching at the foot of my bunk. In the dim glow cast by the lights, I could barely see the outline of his silhouette. A few seconds later, Marianton joined him.

"What do you want?" I growled, angry that they disturb my sleep.

"We have to talk."

I lifted my head and leaned on my elbows. "What about?"

"About all this …" Levaristo's shadow stirred a little.

"We've been talking to the guys," Marianton added quickly. "If we don't figure it out, something bad will happen."

"Bad things are happening already," I said.

"I mean something much more serious." Shorza lowered his voice even more and leaned toward me. "Many guys are at the end of their rope. We have to act, otherwise they will fall apart any moment now. I know of at least three guys who are thinking of crossing the yellow line ..."

Suicide?! But—My surprise wore off quickly. Doherty had a point. It was better to die quickly than to suffer for hours. Faced with such a choice, I'd probably go for an easy death.

"That's nothing." Kozak raised the stakes. "Kamal and four friends of his came up with another idea."

"They refuse to eat breakfast because they want to be in fine fettle when their names are read out. What they're going to do is to take control of the graviplane and crash it with the unionists and themselves on board."

"Morons!" I hissed. "Captain Bidley said clearly: if any of the guards gets hurt, Greenlee will have the micro-explosive devices activated in the bodies of each guy from the block of the perpetrator."

"I tried to reason with them, but they just gave me a strange look and—"

"And what?" I asked.

"And said that both you and we are the unionists' minions."

That left me pretty much speechless. Kamal was one of the major instigators of the whole appeal thing. It was mainly thanks to him that we got our act together and created the template of an appeal letter. On the other hand, he was a real hothead. Never went with the flow. He must have hurt like hell when he saw what this war was really like.

"Go to sleep," I said to them. "I'm going to sort it out tomorrow. One way or another."

———

The new arrivals saved our asses. At least for the time being. Admittedly, Greenlee brought "Sergeant Tyrrus" in for questioning, but the interrogation took only a couple of hours and led to minor injuries. Three nails, five teeth and some bruises. A piece of cake, when compared with what happened to

Doherty and MacMarsky. By the way, the latter still hadn't come to …

On the fourth day, nobody's name was read out at roll call. No interrogation, no hunt either. Our friends' performance in the field must have been really poor. Not surprisingly, since most of us had never left the colony. New Brisbane wasn't a friendly place. Its atmosphere was too thin, the temperatures too low. All lives revolved around the mines.

When the roll call ended, and the captain saluted and headed for his block, Skalski looked at me triumphantly. Lucky dog. He weaseled out at the last minute.

I went to the training ground, following in the wake of the team I'd been assigned to. Lieutenant Navin was waiting for us at the command post, where the obstacle course began. I told the guys to fall in, did the headcount and approached the lieutenant to make a report. For the first time since I'd found myself in this place, I felt good. The tension in my neck was gone, my mood improved. I even allowed myself a hint of a smile and a certain nonchalance when I saluted.

"Private Doni begs to report Team 2 ready for practice! All present and accounted for!" I recited the formula I'd learned by heart and stood beside Navin.

"At ease."

The lieutenant sat down on a table with six helmets, a few sets of dip harnesses and some dummy weapons. "Deymoon, Payt, and Kosma. Once you've warmed up, you'll do a timed run to the bunker and back." He pointed to the largest pile of sacks at the end of the yard.

The distance was almost a thousand feet, with at least a dozen obstacles of various sizes along the way.

"Kamal, Shorza, Doni," the lieutenant read out our names. "You'll be next."

Levaristo winced; he hadn't been into running, even though he could be very good at it. Slim, broad-shouldered, long-legged. A natural-born long-distance runner, or maybe a sprinter. But he preferred holo games to physical activity. Nobody in our colony was better at fragging than Shorza.

Kamal was the total opposite. Two heads shorter than Levaristo, potbellied, and slightly stooped. Only a madman could see an athlete in him. And yet, I didn't know a better wrestler. Stubborn as a mule, covered in sweat, he slithered like a snake and always found a way to defeat his opponent. It must have been the reason why he thought he would be able to disarm the guards and take control over the graviplane.

I looked at him. He moved his jaw rhythmically, chewing on a breakfast griddle cake. Levaristo had it right; the guy was getting ready for action. He'd made something resembling a case from foil, and that was where he hid the grub. Then, he nibbled on it on the way to the training ground.

I knew it would be very difficult, maybe even impossible, to persuade him not to attack the guards, but I had to give it a try anyway. Bidley didn't lie; any move against the unionists was going to end with a massacre.

"Ready … set … go!" Navin waved his hand in which he held a stopwatch, and the first trio started running.

When they cover a hundred feet of flat terrain, they'll reach a low wall, then there'll be a rope, a balance beam, and a dozen other, equally idiotic obstacles resembling the jungle gyms of our childhood.

"Hi, Miken." I walked over to Kamal, who was watching the runners while cleaning his teeth with his tongue.

"Hi," he said succinctly and aggressively.

"You know that—"

"I do!" He interrupted me without taking his eyes off the track.

"You didn't even let me finish the sentence, so—"

"I know what you're going to ask me, Doni," he cut me off again. "And my answer is no!"

"If anybody dies, it's on your head."

"No," he replied. "Nothing's on my head. I'll just save them a lot of suffering, in the bunker or in the field."

"We're talking thirty guys here. Our friends."

Finally, Kamal looked at me.

"Do you really believe that we'll get out of here?"

I nodded, slightly and without conviction. He just sneered in reply. He didn't have to say anything.

I looked over to the obstacle course; Deymoon was already running back, Payt and Kosma were pumping their legs and arms, emerging from around the bunker. In two, three minutes it'll be our turn.

We approached the starting line, adjusting the harnesses and helmet straps. Everything had to be just so; there was no room for imperfection. Deymoon ran past us, breathing heavily. The other two guys still had four obstacles to best.

Thirty seconds. I took a few deep breaths, relaxed my neck and shoulder muscles. Ten seconds. I looked left to Kamal.

"Think it over," I said.

"Fuck you," he spat, and broke into a run as Kosma slumped to the ground right behind the finish line.

He ran half bent, with a pulsator dummy in both hands, dodging and ducking along the way. He outran me in a heartbeat. Levaristo stayed behind. Withadditional ninety pounds on him, he was already starting to poop out. Here, it was about the whole body, not just deft fingers.

The first obstacle. A wall. Kamal slips on the first attempt. He's too short to reach the top of the wall with his foot. I go past him. A perfect jump and I'm already on the other side. Although I lose my balance landing on the uneven ground, I don't lose the advantage I've gained over Kamal. He has to step back to best this obstacle.

Okay, now the rope. Eighteen feet to climb. He's gonna get me now. That wiry clone-of-a-bitch is as strong as a robot. I bounce, grab the rope over the knot, and hang on to it with a moan. The harness seems to weigh a ton. Feet, I tell myself, you have to use your feet. So, I grope for the first knot with my toes; good, it works. I'm halfway through when Kamal swooshes past me. He doesn't care about his feet, he just plows the air as if it were water, and he a swimmer. Horizontal, vertical; it makes no difference to him. A swing, a hoist, another swing, and another hoist, and he's already three feet up the rope. I swear under my breath. This time, he's gonna beat me to it.

Before I run onto the balance beam, he starts to climb the net, two obstacles ahead. I turn over my shoulder and see that Levaristo is almost at the top of the rope. I have to hurry ...

I reach the bunker wall a dozen paces behind Miken. His potbelly caused him a bit of trouble crawling under the low barbed wire, so I almost caught up with him there. On the way back, we beeline for the finish line. One-thousand-foot track and no obstacles. There is a good chance that I'll get the clone-of-a-bitch.

I brace myself to give it my best, though my heart is already beating like a drum and my breath gets shorter every second. Halfway, I'm five, maybe six paces closer to Kamal, but he doesn't slow down ...

They took him out when he was passing the rope. Slightly leaned forward, with his weapon in both hands. He was right in front of me. Three, maybe four paces ahead. And then, all of a sudden, he wasn't there anymore. At first, I thought that he'd stumbled and fallen to the ground, but a moment later, through the pounding in my ears, I heard a loud shot. I didn't lose momentum until I ran a few more paces. Finally, I stopped dead in my tracks, turned around, and looked at the twisted, motionless body. Blood trickled from under the helmet. The soil, as dry as a bone, didn't want to drink it, so the maroon puddle grew bigger at an alarming rate.

Before I could gather my thoughts, I saw Levaristo's terrified face. He dropped his weapon and ran straight at me, shouting something I couldn't hear. I stood there, completely stunned, barely breathing, and thinking ... thinking that if I didn't move, Kamal's blood would reach my boots—

A strong jerk brought me back to reality. Shorza's reflexes were impressive ... Just seconds ago, he was behind us both, so he could see what had happened better than I. He instantly realized that we'd been shot at from the bunker. That's why he lunged at me, grabbed my arm, and pulled me behind the wooden wall. Little protection, but better than none. We were lying there, panting and groaning, just three steps away from our friend, bleeding to death.

———

There was no way around it. We had to continue with the training. Lieutenant Navin had been informed that the unionists would eliminate the entire group if anyone refused to participate in the next race. Three others died in the jungle gym that day. Pointlessly, without the key as to why them ... Almost like somebody wanted to play God. The bunker sniper was silent for four hours, then shot two guys in one race and another one just before we returned to our block when we fell in to do the headcount.

We ran in fear of our lives, looking over our shoulders toward the barely visible dome. At noon, it was so hot that the juddering air made it impossible for us to see any details of this structure. Maybe that was the reason why the sniper had given up temporarily. Maybe that was the reason why he caught up on shooting later, when the temperature got bearable again.

I couldn't be sure, and I didn't want to be. This monster's motives were beyond me. Brutal interrogations were one thing, although they also belonged to the category of inhuman behavior, but killing defenseless people was something altogether different.

However, what else could we expect from men who enjoyed hunting for prisoners?

The camp was reeling. After we'd come back, carrying four bodies, and gathered in the roll call yard, we were joined by the vets. It must have been something new for them.

Skalski pushed his way through the crowd and walked over to me.

"Is this true that they shot at you when you were training?" he asked as if he couldn't see the fatalities.

I nodded and went past him indifferently. I'd had enough; if only I could kill a unionist, I'd do it with my bare hands, right then and there, regardless of the consequences.

Miken was right. Nobody would ever get out of here. If not them, it would be our own fear that did us in. Soon, half the guys would cross the yellow line. It was better than hours spent in the open with the knowledge that at any moment, someone aiming at your head would pull the trigger—just like that, on a whim.

When I walked toward our block, I heard loud voices. Skalski was shouting himself hoarse. He swore, cursed, infected others with his rage. Not very reasonable, if you asked me. Before I closed the door behind me, I heard somebody's whine, then somebody else's. I stopped, but didn't turn back. A few seconds later, wailing sirens drowned the screams of agony. The door slammed open, and a crowd of terror-stricken guys burst into the barrack. They bumped into me, hurrying inside, so I sat down on the first free bunk. Right next to Marianton's. He was panting heavily, his eyes as big as two saucers.

"They activated the micro-explosive devices," he gasped before catching his breath. "At random. It was a massacre!"

———

When I got up the next morning and left the barrack, I noticed some maroon stains in the sand. This soil didn't drink human blood easily. The traces of death remained visible for a long time …

I looked toward Bidley's barrack. The captain was already on his way. He held a crumpled piece of paper in his right hand. Never had I seen him like this, maltreating the orders. *Aha*, I thought. *We are to see a little revolution today …*

The roll call yard slowly filled up with us the prisoners. The bodies of the victims of the previous day were lying alongside the formation. I counted nine of them. Five from our group of conscripts. Two from the 3rd Engineering Brigade and two from the 6th Spaceborne Division. Skalski survived. He stood next to our formation with his eyes fixed on the ground and his jaw moving steadily. Either he chewed on what was left from breakfast in his mouth or talked to his deputy under his breath. It was hard to tell from a distance.

"Fellow soldiers, attention!" The roll call began with Lieutenant Lisky's command.

I tuned out, my thoughts drifting as the captain was assigning the tasks. I realized something was wrong only when I felt Levaristo's hand on my shoulder.

"Buddy ... I just don't ..." he stammered, standing in front of me with his eyes full of tears.

"What is it?" Snapping out of my reverie, I looked around myself and saw some more frightened faces.

"You're going to the bunker," Marianton said.

I'm going to the bunker. Of course. The East Passage. I waited until Lieutenant Lisky approached me, and I let him lead me toward the yellow line. The flags fluttered in the wind so gracefully. They were so vibrant with color.

The lieutenant patted my shoulder; he was such a good man. So caring. He'd surely wait with me until the unionists arrived. It looked like a beautiful day. I put my face up to the blue sun.

"Sergeant Lamonte?" someone barked out a question.

"No, Private Doni," I answered truthfully, and turned to the two guards who gave me a strange look, then stared questioningly at the lieutenant.

"The colonel knows," Lisky said, and that did the trick.

I felt a slight push in my back and before I knew it, I was sitting in a hot graviplane, smelling of oil. The pilot increased the magnets' power and the vehicle pulled away from the ground. Man, did I love such flights! I'd rarely had the chance to fly on New Brisbane, but each time it was an amazing experience.

The graviplane swayed violently, once and then again. The guards started screaming toward the cockpit. One of them lowered his weapon and repeatedly hit the transparent plasteel with his open palm. The pilot just shrugged and landed right away. Pretty hard, if you asked me. Even I'd have done it more gracefully.

"Saucer 4 to Forge, I have a power failure, unless it's the coils —" I heard in my earpiece.

What a pity, I thought. *Flying was so cool ...*

Flying to the bunker?! I looked toward the majestic dome. It was maybe a mile away. A fifteen-minute walk. I tried to stand up, but one of the guards grabbed my arm.

"Where are you off to, pookie?" he asked.

"To the bunker," I said, trying to stand up again.

"Sit your fucking ass back down, now!" he growled, so I did as told.

It took a while. I didn't know how long exactly, but definitely long enough for me to start losing my serenity in the scorching heat, even though I reclined the seat into a lie-flat position. The day didn't seem so beautiful anymore, the colors also began to fade. Something cut into my backside, and the handcuffs chafed my skin. The sweat did its part, every scrape burned like hell.

And then a swoosh. And a bang, as if something exploded. The guards started to scream. The pilot crawled out from under the graviplane and reached for the radio.

"Saucer 4 to Forge, UFO 4 to Forge, why aren't you waiting for us, over?"

"You know Ravenore ..."

"Wish he—" The pilot didn't finish. "Tower 3 is down, the locking system's gonna crash with the next raid. Get us out of here!"

"I'm sending Saucer 3. It'll reach you in two minutes."

"Hurry up, Forge. I can see the fighters are already coming back!"

The pilot waved his hands at the guards.

"Move it!" he told them, glancing toward the barracks fearfully. There was a sudden commotion there. "Let's bail out of here while we still can."

"And what about him?" the guard who'd contained me asked.

"That's your problem, not mine!" The pilot turned on his heel and headed for the dome, from which another graviplane was just taking off.

The old guard reloaded his weapon.

"Leave the punk be," said his younger counterpart, jumping to the ground. "He can improve the statistics, at least in the commander's eyes."

I still had a barrel in my face. I closed my eyes and heard a quiet, "Bang, bang!" …

When I lifted my eyelids, I was alone. The hoaxer followed in the footsteps of his younger friend. I still didn't understand what was going on around me, but I was slowly beginning to realize where I was. And what they did to me.

I hadn't felt too well that morning. I'd eaten less than half of the stinking slops for breakfast, so the sedative hadn't done its job properly. If it hadn't been for the graviplane failure, they'd have delivered me to the bunker while I was high. Instead, that piece of scrap they called a graviplane went tits up and … Well, what?

I got up and at the same time two blurry shapes flashed over my head at high speed. A second later, the tower on the other side of the camp turned into a ball of blinding fire.

"Galacti—"

Fucking drugs! What do they add to these slops they're trying to feed us?

I rubbed my face with both hands, but the vision didn't disappear. Two towers lay in ruins, the commotion in the camp was in full swing, the pilot and the guards were rushing toward the approaching graviplane.

Could it be that …?

No, impossible, I answered myself, looking after the two tiny spots. They turned back again, drew a half circle in the sky and … The radio in the cockpit next to me crackled.

"—moved all the locks?" someone asked.

"Yes. You can land." I knew that voice. It was Colonel Greenlee who was speaking. "We've forged great heroes for you!"

"You're getting better and better at this job, Captain."

"Colonel," Greenlee corrected him.

"Oh, you and your ideas … We used to need a month—"

"Those punks? I had an easy ride with them." There was a tone of contempt in the colonel's voice.

"The next batch will be a tougher nut to crack, believe me."

"I'm looking forward to it." Laughter traveled through the ether.

The conversation stopped at this point.

I straightened up and looked at the two massive transporters, with the Federation's markings on their sides, which were just sinking slowly onto the landing pad next to the tribune. A crowd of people rushed toward them from the camp. A few guys ran in my direction as well. I jumped to the ground awkwardly. I was still dizzy; nothing was quite clear yet.

Levaristo and Marianton cornered me far beyond the yellow line. Before I knew it, they dragged me toward the landing pad. We reached the gangplank as last ones. The other transporter was already getting into the air when we—gasping and sweating —entered the dark maw of the hatch.

"Where have you been?" A giant wearing a uniform of a commander of the Fleet bellowed at us. Well-built and with grayish cropped hair, he looked like a recruiting poster. I knew I'd heard his voice somewhere before.

"We pulled our friend out … Out of the graviplane …" Marianton said, dropping onto the grating.

"Out of the graviplane?"

"They took him to the bunker for questioning, but the graviplane broke down on the way there," Levaristo explained. He'd already come round after a long sprint.

"Lucky you." The officer patted my shoulder. "A few seconds more and you'd stay here forever."

"Commander Ravenore!" The pilot's head appeared in the

hatch leading to the cockpit. "We have six objects at four o'clock. They'll be here in three minutes."

Ravenore ... Ravenore ... Where did I hear this name?

"Let's move it!" The officer nodded at the hatch operator. "We didn't set you free to let them shoot you down!"

Somebody sat me in a G-chair next to Levaristo, buckled me up, and disappeared down the fuselage. I turned my head. A row of vacant seats stretched all the way to the ramp.

"Did you hear the news?" Shorza asked me.

"No."

"The commander says we're not going back to the 6th. We'll get a month off, and then they'll assign us to other units."

"How did they find us?"

"Skalski heard one of the pilots say that they'd tracked down the transport carrier with these guys from the engineering brigade in Kovo. Before the unionists got the hell out of there, they managed to plant a few spy drones and took it from there ..."

I didn't listen to his chattering. The drug had stopped working and suddenly, as if by magic, all became clear. There were no spy drones, nobody followed anybody. Finally, I knew where I heard that voice.

I looked around at the beaming faces of the guys from the 3rd Engineering Brigade, the 6th, and New Brisbane. Give them weapons and—

The clones-of-bitches forged fucking heroes out of us!

TWENTY-SEVEN

IN A STATE OF STUNNED BEWILDERMENT, Darski put the reader down and reached for the bottle to pour himself some more rum. The decanter, however, seemed flabbergastingly light in his hand. Of course it did—the crystallite vessel was empty. Absorbed in reading, Henryan didn't even notice that he'd finished off the liquor.

He checked what time it was and swore under his breath. He'd spaced out for over an hour. One glance at the display calmed him down a bit, though. Hondo hadn't been in touch, which meant that he was coping fine.

Attaboy, Henryan thought, and immediately remembered the other young man.

Glanced over his shoulder, he saw that Nike sat at the console with his hands clasped over his stomach as if he was resting after a lavish meal. He looked pleased.

"How was the read?" he asked Darski.

The captain shook his head in disbelief. He had no idea what to say, so this gesture was his only comment.

"Why aren't you browsing the files?" When he spoke, his voice was a little hoarse.

"I'm done," Stachursky explained, straightening in his chair.

"Did you find it?"

"Yes."

Henryan leaped out of his chair, then walked over to the wall-mounted shelving unit to get pills neutralizing the excess of alcohol buzzing in his veins, washed two of them down with a sip of water and froze for a moment, closing his eyes. The drug was powerful, it usually worked within minutes.

"Why didn't you tell me?"

"I wanted you to read it all. Now you know why the clones-of-bitches wished to get rid of me."

"This story is about events from a hundred years back," Darski said, taking a free seat in front of the console. "Few people care about it today."

"Really?" Nike put on a big, exaggerated grin. "I think that many of the Federation's founding fathers were involved in such crimes. Maybe it won't hurt the Council, especially in the face of the invasion, but some heads should roll anyway. The legend of the squeaky-clean quality of the government will die. Wouldn't it be something?"

"Politicians are like plants," Henryan muttered, surprising Nike with this comparison. "I've been talking to the head of the local scientific department recently," he explained. "In his opinion, plants are a hundred times more resilient than even the best-adapted animals. You can burn them down, cut them down, but if time allows, they always grow back. And some are really long-lived. Did you know that the oldest tree on Earth was nearly ten thousand years old?"

Nike's eyes widened.

"I've never really thought about it before, but if you say so …"

Darski didn't listen to him. He was thinking about the beings, in which the Aliens were traveling. Did they belong to the category of fauna or flora of the Universe? When theytalked for the first time in the hospital, Stachursky said that the liner's entire interior—apart from some of the rooms and corridors which seemed to be structural—was filled with bizarre, pasty, self-sealing mass. And in that case …

"Let's see what you've got," Henryan said when the buzz in his head slowly started to subside.

Nike opened a window containing several folders.

"Everything is right here," he announced triumphantly.

TWENTY-EIGHT
THE ANZIO SYSTEM, ZEBRA SECTOR

10/24/2354

Rutta was dumbfounded. He sat in front of the screen with his mouth half-open, watching yet another holo sent by Darski. He didn't believe his own eyes.

This particular holo showed the camera footage recorded by one of the *Nomad*'s crew members while on board the alien liner. Ineptly compressed, it was a little blurry and disrupted, also too dark for the colonel's liking, but with a measure of goodwill, he could see an empty room with a cylinder hanging under the ceiling. One of the men within the camera range, dressed in a full spacesuit, was checking the scanner's readings. A moment later, he pointed at the cylinder with his head. Another man approached it warily and tapped its shiny surface with the tip of his phaser. Nothing happened, so he put his weapon away and tried to rock the cylinder with both hands. All he managed to do, however, was to lower it a couple of inches when he hung on to it with all his strength. Eventually, he let go of it and the cylinder returned to its original position.

"Antigrav, stone me ... " the man gasped, kneeling down to look at the cylinder's bottom part.

Yet another man, with a sensor in his hand, walked around the mysterious object.

"It seems to be perfectly smooth," he reported. "No cracks, grooves, or temperature differences."

"Tough. We're gonna pry it open anyway," decided the one who'd been kneeling seconds ago.

A woman's voice came in, "We'll have cut through the bulkhead in a few seconds. Here we go. The visuals of—" Her voice was suddenly drowned by static. The glowing growths flickered, their light intensifying. The guy who seemed to be the boss jumped away from the cylinder; the rest raised their weapons.

The cylinder was changing its color; the upper part darkened very quickly, and the surface began to ripple.

Rutta heard only scraps of words spoken by the woman. Suddenly, the cylinder began to bulge as if something pushed against it from the inside. The shell tore open under the pressure of almost human, six-fingered hands. Someone fired, a gush of energy enveloped the cylinder, charring it and burning a hole in one of the cylinders standing behind.

"Lost your fucking minds?!" lashed out the boss.

Meanwhile, entire forearms appeared in the rent. They were horribly thin, considering their length. Gray skin, clearly visible gnarls of muscles. The creature seized the edges of the opening, and began to pull itself up.

First, Rutta saw the Alien's head. Long, thick, metallic protrusions fell over the thin shoulders like hair. Seemingly, the creature's face resembled that of a human. The eyes, nose and mouth were where in the right places, but everything was totally … ALIEN.

The eyes, which lacked irises, were all black, the nose was underdeveloped and without any nares, the wide lips reached the golden protrusions on both sides. The colonel, however, focused his attention on the organ, located in the middle of a high forehead, which looked like tightly closed lips or eyelids.

The creature glanced around the room, then moved its mouth soundlessly, and finally, waved its hand as though driving the intruders away. But the men just stood there as if hypnotized and stared at an almost ten-foot-tall figure in a loose-fitting, gray as its skin, robe.

Finally, one of the astronauts took a step forward and raised his hand in the universal greeting. The being looked at him, tilting its head. A moment later, two curved shapes emerged from behind its back. Furled wings! When they spread out, the colonel could see some complex patterns on a downy, snow-white background.

"It's an angel," whispered someone in the recording.

"Angel ..." Rutta echoed.

A sort of smile widened the Alien's lips. The being unfolded its arms and suddenly—

Rutta watched this moment again, in slow motion. The wings shot up, and the mouth opened wide to a scream, showing hundreds of sharp fangs. The holoprojector automatically turned down the volume, saving the colonel a lot of pain inflicted by the shriek or, rather, howl. Meanwhile on the screen, the crystallite visors of the men's helmets cracked one by one; people swayed under the power of this sound, dropped like logs.

The Alien jumped down onto the floor, leaned over, and seized the nearest astronaut by the arm. Then it cleared his helmet visor of the crystallite shards and lifted him to its face. They touched foreheads and remained so, motionless for a few seconds. Eventually, the creature moved toward the door, flinging away the man standing there. The camera caught its face and the fleshy lips on its forehead, now agape.

Rutta leaned back in his chair heavily. Even though it was the tenth time he watched this recording, he still couldn't believe he was looking at the events which had taken place a few months ago. Equally well, these could be some scenes from an adventure holo. For his peace of mind, he ordered the system to compare selected shots, but even the computer found nothing. That meant the recording wasn't a fake. Besides, Darski had no reason to lie. His report contained a great deal of substantiating details, including the explanation of what he had been looking for in the *Nomad*'s archives in the first place.

Major Visolay's diary was also in the possession of the colonel, but for now, Rutta had read only its summary. The rest had to wait. There was nothing more important than the alien thing now.

"Theo …" He almost choked when he saw the grand admiral's face on his screen. "You need to see something."

TWENTY-NINE

EARTH, ALPHA SECTOR

10/24/2354

"We are talking with you, not about you, only because you have been with us from the start and have served our cause multiple times." Chancellor Modo's distinctive voice carried a lot more than just anger.

Damiandreas Dreade-Ravenore bowed his head. He had to clench his teeth not to explode. For decades, he had been the one to lash out at others, so the situation in which he had to patiently take this ass-chewing was beginning to overwhelm him. He couldn't and wouldn't listen to any more impertinence. On the other hand, he wasn't an idiot and he understood perfectly well why he was being pilloried by the Council.

"Don't stand there like a pillar of salt, whatever that was!" Juliusain Kaup, the Federation's secretary of defense, spat out. "What do you have to say in your defense?"

Dredd glowered at him.

I'm so paying you back for this, you rotter, he thought.

"I just did what was necessary," he hissed through the clenched teeth.

"Really?" Kaup didn't let him off the hook.

In the dim overhead light, the secretary's elongated face

seemed demonic. The shadows cast by the deep furrows on his cheeks, aquiline nose, and eyes so deeply set that they were barely visible, could unnerve anyone, but not Dredd: the Orbital Academy's rector and a repeatedly decorated war hero from the times long before all the members of the Council were born.

"Really!" This time, Dredd didn't hold back his anger. "If the information about Ulietta's evacuation had reached me with proper notice, I wouldn't have had to look for interim solutions."

"Interim?" snorted Giancarlouis Benadetto, the treasurer. "Ill-considered, more like."

"I wonder what you would have come up with if you'd been in my place," Dredd blurted out without thinking.

"My friend ... First of all, I would have never found myself in such a tight spot," said Gerdanielle's bulldog. He was called that, of course, behind his back, because of his roly-poly stature, three chins, and a bloated ebony face with a flat nose disappearing between the two sacks of his cheeks. He was visibly amused.

Modo raised her hand, cutting off yet another retort of Dredd's.

"This shouting match will get us nowhere," she boomed. "Let me remind you that we have gathered here to cut our losses, not to shout over who is at fault, because there is only one person responsible for this fucking mess, and this is you, Damiandreas."

"All of—" Dredd began, but he fell silent the moment Modo smashed her fist down on the ancient table that separated them.

"No. This time, it is you who is to be blamed," she continued, raising her voice even more. "I thought you were our equal, but it turns out you are just another fool. A piece of trash who places his perverse satisfaction above the concern for the government's authority."

"But I ..."

"Do not interrupt me!" The shout echoed in the dome-covered chamber. "You cut me off again, and we are done here."

Dredd bowed his head so that he could further grit his teeth in helpless anger unabatedly.

"That is better," Modo said in a calmer tone. "Three months ago, we let you act on your own and go off the book because you promised us you would make our problem go away and no scandal would break. You should have done away with this Stachursky guy after he had said everything he knew in the interrogation. You should have," she repeated, "but you did not. For you hoped—since he no longer existed to the world—that you would continue to abuse him. Do not deny it, we all know your motives very well. We have seen the Area 511 footage."

At that, Dredd raised his head suddenly; that was news to him.

"Yes," Chancellor Modo snorted. "This is our prison, and we have full control over it. Nothing goes on there without our knowledge, even if someone turns off the recorders."

Dredd couldn't take it anymore. "Were you spying on me?!"

"No. No one cared about your personal vendetta until you put the Admiralty and the Council in a bad light." Seeing disbelief in his eyes, Modo added, "The prison surveillance system has several independent levels. The top one, available only to the Council, cannot be deactivated, but only a chosen few know that."

Dredd bowed his head. Once again, he was given to understand that he wasn't counted among the members of the inner circle.

"This dickweed raped my youngest daughter," he muttered.

Benadetto cackled.

Ignoring her colleague's reaction, Chancellor Modo said impassively, "We found out about your conversation with Stachursky today, when we received a full report from the security department. But let us give it a rest, shall we? I mentioned this only because I did not want you to dig yourself into a hole any further."

Dredd got the hint and nodding slowly, finally looked her in the eye.

"Excellent. Let us get down to business then." She glanced at the screens in front of her. "You disgraced the Admiralty with your incompetence. The whole staff of the Second Metasector know that you have been trying to get rid of the *Nomad*'s crew. Quarantine, really?" she sniggered. "Where did you get such a dumb idea from?"

"Nowhere," Dredd growled back. "Yesterday, I got a tip from my friends that someone offered high-ranking officers some relics of the civil war. Among other stuff, there was a diary discrediting one of the most prominent people in the Federation. I easily guessed that person's identity. It was equally easy to determine who the seller was. So, I had Morrisey and the rest of the crew arrested in order to block the transaction. Things got complicated when an hour later I was informed about the evacuation of our center on Delta in the Ulietta system. I had to act quickly and decisively. Quarantine was the only way to cut everyone off from this vessel's computers."

"Seriously?" Kaup mocked him.

"Seriously," Dredd snapped. "I didn't have time for machinations like—" He bit his tongue to keep a bad situation from getting worse.

"By all means, say what you wanted to say," Benadetto urged him with a smile on his face.

Dredd held his peace, staring at the floor. "Give me twenty-four hours, and I'll fix it," he said finally, breaking the silence.

"No," Modo said.

"No?" He looked at her, bemused.

"There is nothing to fix," she added, leaning toward him. "Things went too far."

"I still can get rid of Stachursky and possible witnesses!"

"Can you? Are you saying that you will do away with half the staff of the Second Fleet and the entire staff of the Third Fleet, including Grand Admiral Farland? You will deplete our resources when we are at war, just to save your own ass?"

Dredd was beside himself with astonishment. "What are you talking about?" he asked.

"She's talking about that shit show of your doing," Kaup said acrimoniously.

Modo glared at him, so he fell silent, but straightened up and smiled to show his superiority.

Turning to Dredd, the chancellor said, "You might not know it yet, but Major So-and-So's diary saw the light of day a few hours ago. Both in the Inner and Outer Rim."

Dreade-Ravenore turned pale.

"That's not possible," he muttered. "The crew didn't know about Morrisey's backup, and he was so sure of himself that he hadn't taken any precautions against the risk of mishap. The top esdee investigators from the Second Metasector's staff vouched for it. After the access to the ship had been blocked, only the epidemiologists could go on board the *Nomad*."

"Are you sure?" Benadetto smirked.

"I'm positive," Dredd replied. "The esdees who made a stink stayed outside until the gendarmes arrived."

"Are you trying to tell me that all of this is Sergeant Poetze's fault …?" She glanced at the screen to get the esdee's name right.

"If he hadn't performed a random inspection on that day—" he began, but Modo didn't let him finish.

"Enough!" she screamed, and everyone cowered down inside themselves. Then, leaning back in her chair, she said more calmly, "You really are as stupid as they come. A self-centered narcissist who will never admit he has made a mistake and would sooner debase everyone than apologize. That is what your subordinates think about you, by the way, if you want to know."

Dredd ate dirt, or so it seemed. In fact, deep down, he'd already started planning how to get revenge on the chancellor and her minions. *A time will come when these scumbags will pay for everything …*

"Okay, let's get this over and done with," Benadetto said, taking advantage of the moment of silence. "We have a few more things to talk about."

"That's right," Kaup backed him up hastily.

Modo lifted her head; she wasn't looking at Dredd anymore,

even though he was the Orbital Academy's rector and the greatest war hero of the Federation.

"You only have one way out of this. You must resign from office and give up all your titles."

When she saw that Dreade-Ravenore turned blue and took a deep breath as if he was about to scream in their faces, she warned him, "Do not even bother trying! Out of consideration for your contribution, we will let you take a backseat, but remember, there will be no acts of grace or quiet comebacks in a few months. Forget your vendetta too. From this moment, Stachursky enjoys immunity, as if he were a member of the Council. Am I making myself clear?"

He didn't answer, he was just staring at her in utter amazement.

"The stakes are too high, Damiandreas. Do you understand?" she added. "We cannot let you screw it up for us."

"What stakes?" he asked, stuporous.

"There are many things you don't know, my friend," Kaup said in all seriousness.

"And you'll never find out," Benadetto piped in with unfeigned satisfaction.

"Don't even think you can sideline me on this," Dredd began, scowling at them all. "I know about you enough—"

Modo leaned forward in his direction.

"One more word, and you will say goodbye not only to the Academy, but to your whole family."

"You won't dare touch my children," he gasped, his eyes bulging as if due to apoplexy.

"Not us," Kaup assured him. "Our people, though, will make sure they'll die the most painful and cruel death. They and their loved ones," he stipulated. "We'll make it look like the separatists' attack. But first, we'll reveal your role in the Forge project. So that the public has no trouble believing the sincerity of the people's wrath."

"And you'll learn about everything from the holo, waiting on death row," Benadetto cheered him up.

"You have five seconds." Modo joined her hands as if in prayer.

Dredd tried to stop the thoughts from swirling in his mind. He knew that these people didn't make empty promises. A few years back, they'd prepared a similar fate for the family of one of the most famous patricians, who fatally desired to sit in the chancellor's office without running for election. Gerdanielle owed her present position to him. And to be more specific, to the poison that he'd administered.

"Okay," he said resignedly. "I'll leave, but—"

"No buts. If you do not play any games, we will do our best to keep the number of leaks about the Forge to a minimum. One stupid move, one stupid word on your part, the lightest shadow of suspicion that falls upon you, and there will be no one left in the entire Galaxy to carry your genes. Get it into your head, Damiandreas, because I am really going to give such an order."

In the semidarkness, a row of large displays appeared around them, on which Dredd could see all his daughters, his only son, even the descendants of his first wife. There were several dozen holograms, each depicting people in various situations: sleeping, working, eating … Only the clock visible in the top left corner of every screen showed the same time. All his relatives were watched by nanodrones. Modo and her sidekicks were prepared for this conversation well. Eventually, Damiandreas realized that he stood no chance against them. The result of this engagement had been predetermined.

"Why are you taking this scum's side?" he asked when he heard the door behind him swing open with a loud bang. "How did he force you?"

"We can't be forced to do anything," Kaup laughed.

Benadetto accompanied him.

"One day, you will understand," Gerdanielle said enigmatically, silencing her companions with a raised hand.

THIRTY

10/24/2354

Nike stood motionless in front of a window in his savior's apartment. His feet wide apart, his hands clasped behind his back, he stared straight ahead like the captain of a ship sailing right into the storm. Although nothing in his demeanor suggested he was anxious, he shook like a leaf deep inside.

Darski's stratagem had every chance of success, but the question remained: Would the people remorselessly eliminating their opponents want to talk to the "late" cadet? Would they take his side against a man who was so close to the Federation's authorities?

Stachursky very much doubted it, but waited for the answer from Earth patiently, as did the captain and all the officers from the distant metasector's staff, who were actors in this show. It was a simple bluff. Either the Council would accept the terms of the ultimatum, or Nike would die by his own hand without prior sharing anything he knew about the Aliens with anyone. The threat sounded serious, for at this point—with the *Nomad*'s crew eliminated—Nike Stachursky was the only living witness of what had happened in the New Rouen system. Chancellor Modo and her henchmen knew that in case of his demise, they'd be left empty-handed, since the mysterious agent, commissioned to retrieve the data from the collapsar's onboard computer, assured his principals that all the files were gone.

Shame it was just a ruse …

The metasector's staff, after all, were in possession of some substantial intel and it didn't really matter that only a very select handful of people were privy to it. In this situation, it was Nike, and only Nike, who would lose everything if the deal fell through. The Council would still receive the information which Nike was supposedly to take with him to the grave. And as for Nike himself … Well, Cadet Stachursky would disappear again, this time forever, but of course since he'd long been declared dead, no one in the entire Galaxy would shed any tears. Even his parents in the Outer Rim. They'd already gotten a box with his things, a touching letter from the Admiralty, and maybe some consolation compensation.

Nike chuckled under his breath. His parents were probably the only ones who would miss him. For Monicatherine, he'd been no more than just a sex toy, like other cadets before him and after him … In retrospect, he began to regret that he'd allowed himself to be seduced like some pimply teenager, even though he'd been aware of the risks involved. At the time, however, he'd been laboring under the delusion that he was unique, better than his predecessors, and that he would stay in the saddle—that was how she'd referred to their relationship. Okay, it was a wild ride, but he cut it. He and Monicatherine had been together until the end of the last semester, and then … Then he'd paid a high price for his infatuation. Exiled first to the *Nomad*, and then to this place, wherever this place was; to a "paradise lost" which charm remained mystery to him—

He started when the sliding door hissed behind him, but didn't look over his shoulder for fear of who he'd see. If the esdees came for him, this beautiful view would be the last nice thing before he got sucked out of an airlock on low orbit. If it was the captain—

"Cadet Stachursky?" someone said in a nasal voice.

Nike turned around slowly, feeling that his muscles were acting up something fierce. He was terrified. But he had to look the truth in the face ... To his great relief, it was familiar: freckled, with a wreath of copper hair.

"Yes?"

"Follow me," Hondo said, stopping at the threshold.

"Where to?" That was all Nike could say.

Darski's assistant didn't reply. He spun on his heel and a second later, was gone. Stachursky swallowed and, still weak in the knees, headed for the door.

"Move it!" an impatient shout echoed around the walls of the corridor.

Nike was so perturbed that he didn't know if those words were addressed to him, or to the esdees outside. The distance between him and the exit seemed to increase rather than decrease with each step.

"What is it?" Hondo appeared at the door again. "Do you want to piss them off even more? I said, move it."

Nike quickened his pace against his will. He walked out of the apartment, turned toward the elevators, and fell into step with the lieutenant who didn't take his eyes off his holopad.

"Where are we go—?" he asked, but before he finished, Hondo's response came in a grunt.

"And what am I, a visitor center?"

Then the captain's assistant started talking to someone on the comlink.

It looked like he was calling a shuttle; not a civilian one, but one of those belonging to the military. Nike realized that his bleak vision of an airlock opening to the void would come true after all ...

They took the elevator to go down a few stories, then walked along a circular passageway with no windows until they reached a large room filled with broadcasting equipment. Hondo pointed at a chair on the platform, and when Nike sat down, someone activated the force field separating his seat from the rest of the room. Suddenly, the cadet found himself in a golden iridescent cocoon. Before he could panic, a hologram of a woman with a long, emaciated face appeared in front of him. He didn't recognize her—it must have been the nerves—but when she spoke, everything became clear.

"Do you know, son, how much we pay for every second of this transmission?"

He nodded, unable to utter a single word.

Modo looked at him more closely. She noticed a collar around his neck and a detonator in his hand.

"Very well," she continued. "Do not make me wait next time because it will cost you dearly."

He nodded again, which seemed to irritate her; anyway, she got straight to the point. "We have considered your proposal …"

She paused for a moment. At least, Nike hoped that she had, for blood was pounding in his ears so loud that he might have missed the second sentence. He was lucky, though; Chancellor Modo only moved her lips as if to speak. The effects of poisoning hadn't subsided completely yet, and one of them was dry mouth. She had difficulty detaching her tongue from her palate.

"In light of the documents we had been presented with, we had no choice," she said, in a tone of indifference. "In today's meeting, the Council asked Rector Dreade-Ravenore to immediately resign from his post. He also voluntarily renounced all the honors and titles received after hibernation, and assured us that his personal vendetta was over. We the Council guarantee you that you will never hear of Ravenore again unless you want to. The Third Metasector's staff has already received the documents revoking your death certificate. The official story is as follows: one of the rescue capsules miraculously got through the wreckage zone and landed on Delta, where after a few months of forced hibernation you were picked up by the crew of another ship which appeared in the New Rouen system and accidentally intercepted an alarm signal. As compensation, you will receive a certain amount of money, and you will be awarded a medal. The Admiralty will advance you to the rank of second lieutenant."

"Thank you …" Nike croaked through the lump in his throat.

"In return, we expect," she continued, not letting him cut in, "that you will hand over all the information about the Aliens and that you will stop further dissemination of the diary defaming the Federation."

She paused, eying him menacingly. "If anyone ever finds out the truth about the Forge, our agreement will be canceled with immediate effect, and on your own head be it. Understood?"

"Yes," he mumbled.

"What?"

"Yes ma'am," he repeated.

She huffed and disappeared a second before the force field was deactivated.

Nike remained in his seat, stunned, until Hondo shook him vigorously.

"Move it, man. The shuttle is waiting."

"Where are we going?" Stachursky looked around at the communications center as if he had just woken up.

"To the *Cervantes*."

"What about Captain Darski?"

"He'll join us later. As soon as he's dealt with all stuff on the moon."

THIRTY-ONE

THE PASSENGER COMPARTMENT of a space shuttle could accommodate thirty-two people, but this time there were twice as many in there. Nike crouched in the corner behind the last row of seats, keeping his distance from a group of frightened women and children. Hondo had told him that Captain Darski intended to send as many people as possible on board the *Cervantes*, so it was no wonder that numerous small vessels circulated between the surface of the planet and the cruiser in orbit incessantly. Stachurskyhitched one of the last rides, for even such a big warship couldn't accommodate more than fifteen hundred extra passengers.

For the first couple of minutes, the shuttle flew smoothly as if pulled on a string, but then it began to vibrate a little, and finally it bucked several times. The passengers, clinging to the ropes stretched between the rows of seats, screamed each time the deck slipped away from under their feet and backsides. Nike knew that these weren't the signs of an impending disaster. While still at the Academy, he'd experienced much worse turbulence whenever he headed for Earth. So now, he just counted down the passing seconds, certain that everything would be back to normal when the shuttle left the atmosphere.

He was right; the maneuvering thrusters fell silent, gravity decreased, and it got noticeably colder. Nike closed his eyes. He wondered how much he should tell the Fleet's representatives. Definitely not everything. Since his first conversation with Captain Darski, it had been clear to him that no one in the meta-sector's staff would believe his whole story. Even Stachursky was having a hard time believing it, and he'd seen the ma'lahn with his own eyes.

He cringed at this memory, but involuntarily looked back to the moments which still stood out in his mind …

THIRTY-TWO

THE NEW ROUEN SYSTEM, VICTOR SECTOR

06/27/2354

"—Since I'm going to die today and heaven apparently can wait, it's time to keep my promise to Damiandreas, Mr. Daughterfucker."

Before the still smoking barrel of the phaser rose high enough, Annataly stepped between Morrisey and the man he was aiming at.

"Put it down, you fool," she said through clenched teeth.

"Or what?" Morrisey snapped back.

"Or this!" She shoved her gun in his face, smashing the already cracked visor.

"Better watch your step, bitch!" he hissed, enraged by this unexpected attack, but she didn't back off.

"I'm going to count to three," she told him icily. "One …"

"Listen up!" Iarrey yelled, but they ignored him.

"Get that thing out of my face, bitch."

"Two …"

The first officer didn't give up. "Shut up, and listen!" he repeated.

They didn't lower their weapons, but at least both fell silent.

Iarrey, who'd already taken off his helmet, pointed down the corridor.

"Listen ..." he said once again.

Standing in the dim light of phosphorescent growths, they strained their ears. At first, they couldn't hear anything but silence, yet then Annataly started. Barely audible grumble carried in the distance. Nike reached for his holopad, entered a few commands, and activated the nearest probes' audio sensors.

"—yooomaaansss—" The equipment picked up, processed, and played the electronically enhanced sound.

"Yoomans?" Morrisey muttered, slowly moving away from Annataly.

"Hooomaaansss—" They heard another whisper.

"Humans," Nike guessed.

At the third try, the whisper came in louder and clearer. "Hoomans ..."

Everyone, except Stachursky, aimed their weapons at the black throat of the corridor.

"You mentioned that you'd found a hold full of humanoids," Morrisey said, trying to penetrate the darkness with his eyes. "Is it one of them?"

Annataly gave him a contemptuous look.

"That would be a first," she announced in a loud voice.

"Someone killed and gutted forty thousand years ago walks and talks, speaking comlang, no less!"

"Shut up, all of you!" Iarrey said, glancing over his shoulder to Stachursky's holopad.

"—tsss ... aaaawwwwk ... hoomans—"

"Does someone want to talk to us?" Morrisey walked past Annataly and looked at the display too.

The probes couldn't locate the source of these sounds. They seemed to come from all directions at once, as if the corridor walls were swarming with loudspeakers.

"Sure looks like it," Iarrey answered the captain, then put his hands to his mouth and shouted, "Come closer, and we'll talk!"

"Is that the winged clone-of-a-bitch?" Morrisey flipped off the safety catch of his phaser.

The first officer didn't lose his composure. "Who else?"

For a moment, there was perfect silence, and then they heard a soft whisper again.

"Ohhh … aaansss …"

"What now?" Morrisey nudged Nike. "Can't you calibrate this shit?"

Before the cadet had a chance to respond, the device came to life again.

"Nooo gah—aaans."

"No guns, my foot." The captain stepped forward, sweeping the darkness with the barrel of his weapon. The rest of the crew huddled behind his back.

"I-I-I … h-help …" Each word was spoken more clearly, as if the angel was learning comlang fast.

Annataly turned abruptly and in one fell swoop, she grabbed the phaser, simultaneously pulling it down and twisting around its axis.

Morrisey groaned. He had to loosen his grip so she wouldn't break the fingers in his good hand. "What are you doing?" he hissed.

"I'm saving your life, you limp-dick!" she barked back angrily.

"Yeah, right."

"This creature can't kill us more effectively than our collapsar," Iarrey said.

"Tell this to Bourne," the captain scoffed, still massaging his hand.

"I will. As soon as he comes round." The first officer cut this conversation short, and focused his attention on the holopad again.

He hung his phaser on his shoulder, safety on. Davidoff-Rozerer put her gun in the holster.

"We're unarmed!" Iarrey yelled. "You can come out now!"

This time, there was no answer for a long while; the

holopad's loudspeaker was silent too. However, a flashing red dot appeared on the display. Something was approaching them, slowly, cautiously—

"Dooon'ttt ... sh-sh ... shooottt ..." they heard. "I-I-I ... waaant ... help ..."

"We're not going to shoot you, I promise!" Iarrey shouted.

Morrisey swore under his breath, but that was it; disarmed, he was helpless.

Suddenly, one of the growths about a hundred, a hundred and twenty feet along the corridor flickered; its steady glow flooded the walls in seconds. The darkness receded, and finally they were able to pick up a familiar shape in the distance. The Alien, wearing the same loose-fitting robe as before, stopped maybe fifty feet away from them—with its arms spread open and the wings protruding from behind its shoulders.

"I-I-I heeelp youuu ..." the Alien said in a distinctive voice, making the holopad unnecessary.

"What with?" Morrisey snapped.

"A word to the wise: Shut up, Henrichard!" Annataly chewedthe captain's ass out.

"I-I-I heelp youu coome baack." The Alien stretched out his vowels, but besides that, his way of speaking was easy to understand now.

"How come you know comlang?" Nike asked even before Iarrey opened his mouth.

"I-I-I absoorbed it," the angel replied, pointing its bony finger at Bourne lying against the wall.

So this is what the bizarre organ on its forehead is for, Nike realized.

"What have you done to him?" Iarrey glanced at the unconscious lieutenant.

"Absorbed," the Alien repeated.

"Is he going to be okay?" the first officer pressed on.

"Explaain."

"Will he regain consciousness? Will he be like us again?"

"I don't know," the angel said in its slow, mechanical voice devoid of emotion.

"You don't know? How's that?" Morrisey blurted out.

"It was the first time I've absorbed a hooman," the angel said and took a few steps forward.

It stopped again right under the connector between two corridor sections, no more than thirty feet from Stachursky. They could see it better now. He towered above them, almost twice as tall as petite Annataly.

"Explain: absorbed," Nike asked.

When the angel fell silent, they assumed it was looking for words to describe a process natural to him. Finally, they got the answer, "I probed the mind. To leaarn aboout you."

"Okay, enough of idle talk." Henrichard pushed between Iarrey and the navigator. "The collapsar's already powering up. How would you like to help us? Speak up!"

No one silenced him this time. The fascination with this amazing creature had to give way to the prose of life. There wasn't much time left, and they still had millions of questions.

"I'll give you a dhri'll," the Alien said.

"What?"

The Alien touched the corridor wall and its surface bulged slightly, forming an oval plane, which purpose became clear to them a moment later when they saw a picture. It wasn't a holo, just a 3-D image of one of the small vessels moored to the turret in the hangar.

"A dhri'll. Two hoomans can fly."

While they were watching, the small vessel took off and flitted through the space toward a tiny dot which grew bigger and bigger until it took the shape of the *Nomad*.

"And how is that supposed to help us?" Iarrey asked.

The angel didn't answer. The plan it had in mind was revealed by the animation. The vessel approached one of the *Nomad*'s emergency airlocks, moored to it, exserting a strange "collar," and then the camera moved inside. The people who traveled on board the small vessel cut out a circular opening in the three-foot-thick plasteel.

Simple and effective, although not very practical, Stachursky thought.

"Let me make a tiny correction," he said to the Alien, looming in the semidarkness. "We don't need to cut anything. All we need is access to the lock."

"Explain."

"Next to the emergency airlock, there's a mechanism allowing the hatch to be opened from outside. If we dock in such a way that we have access to it, we'll board the *Nomad* without cutting anythi—"

"We don't have the time to mess around," Morrisey interjected impatiently. "Let's go!"

"Henrichard's right," Iarrey said. "The more time we spend talking, the less time we'll have on board the *Nomad* to do what we must do."

"I agree," Annataly muttered.

"Me too." Nike preferred not to step out of line.

"That settles it. Let's go." Morrisey looked at the angel. "Don't just stand there, lead the way to that clunker boat of yours."

"First the deal," the Alien said, turning the device off. The wall became smooth again.

"What deal?"

"I help you, you help me."

"What do you want in return for this little ship?" Henrichard moved even closer toward the angel.

"Energy," came back the reply.

"Would you like to hook up to our reactor?"

"Not radiation. Energy restoration."

"How?"

"The star. Take my t'iru to the star."

Morrisey seemed exasperated. "What is t'iru?" he asked.

The Alien moved both his hands in a wide arc upward forward and then downward.

Iarrey nodded to himself, a cunning smile crossing his face.

"It wants us to pull this wreck closer to the star so it can charge the batteries or whatever they use."

"Yes," the angel said.

"How do we do it?" The captain looked at the first officer, but he just shook his head. Turning back to the Alien, Morrisey added mockingly, "Do you have a thousand miles of rope so we can tow you? The kind which doesn't get annihilated by the thrust of an ion drive?"

"Deal or no fly."

"Annataly, would you be so kind as to explain to Mr. Angel, or Mrs. Angel, that we still have a few aces up our sleeves and we allow no one to call the shots ..." Henrichard smiled crookedly, pointing at the phaser they'd taken from him a few minutes before.

The navigator shook her head.

"Be serious for once, old goat. It knows it's going to die without our help, we know we're going to die without its help. This is called a stalemate. And you're threatening our Alien with death? Even when it's about to get crushed along with this ship within half an hour? Don't be ridiculous ... Better find a way how to meet Mr. Angel's demand."

"I just might know what we should do," Nike said without thinking.

THIRTY-THREE

AFTER A SHORT BUT FIERCE DISCUSSION, they split up into two teams. Morrisey, Stachursky, and still unconscious Bourne stayed in the mooring turret as a guarantee while Annataly and Iarrey, taking all their weapons, set off in pursuit of the *Nomad*. They didn't have to worry about mastering the controls of an alien vessel. The angel told them that he'd redirected the required amount of t'iru energy to the st'uru—whatever the st'uru was—so everything would happen automatically, including the docking. All they had to do was to board the ship, deactivate the collapsar, and set the *Nomad*'s course to the Theta cluster.

As soon as the dhri'll took off, the Alien led the men to the lowest level of the turret and opened an airlock of a large, bizarre-looking vessel which purpose still was a mystery to them. In its upper, semisphericalpart, there was a circular room, most likely a control room. The Alien sat down in one of the six shapeless chairs arranged concentrically around a corrugated, fairly thick pillar occupying the very center of the hall. Morrisey and Nike climbed into the uncomfortable seats opposite Mr. Angel, as they called him now. They left Bourne lying beside them, to be able to keep an eye on him too.

When the Alien touched the pillar, it warped with lightning speed just like the corridor wall before, forming a streamlined console and a screen hanging right above it. In front of the seats occupied by the men, the folds were also replaced by flat, only slightly curved surfaces, on which a second later, both the captain and the cadet could see the cockpit of the dhri'll and the two people sitting in it. This time, however, it wasn't an animation.

When everything was ready, the Alien said, "You can speak."

"What about?" Henrichard seemed confused.

"To them."

Without waiting for further words of encouragement, Nike leaned closer to the screen in front of him and asked, "Annataly, how do you copy?"

"Loud and clear," she replied.

He also heard her as if she was sitting in a chair next to him.

"Any problems?" the captain inquired as soon as he regained his composure.

"Yes," the first officer said. "It's a little dull around here, and this flight will take a while."

"You can speak," the Alien repeated.

Henrichard scowled at it.

"A glitch, my friend?" he snapped. "Have you redirected a bit too much of energy and all?"

Now that hegot his confidence back and was almost certain they'd make it, Morrisey perked up. That was one of the reasons why everyone had insisted that he should stay on board the wreck. It was the only place where he didn't have access to any weapons.

"No."

"Then why are you repeating yourself?"

"You can speak to me," the angel elaborated, stone-faced.

Nike smiled inwardly. In the next fifteen minutes this creature would answer many of their questions. Important questions. Very important …

Before the captain had a chance to make another rude remark, he hit the ground running, "Does God exist?"

"I can't answer a question such posed," the Alien replied, raining on Stachursky's parade. "I know of at least forty civilizations meeting human criteria for divi ..."

"Wait a second," Morrisey interrupted it. "Let's start with something simpler and more useful. Tell me what your name is, provided you use names or nicknames in your choirs and roosts."

"Muurdermat."

"Murder, for short ... Lovely!" sniggered the captain.

He was furious. At this point, he wanted only one thing: to tear Father Pedroberto apart with his bare hands and then strangle Stachursky, seated two chairs over to his right, so that in the end he could take care of this ten-foot-tall, winged clone-of-a-bitch. However, since all of this was a pipe dream at best, he let off steam verbally.

"Ma'lahn don't use abbreviations, human," the Alien said, unfazed.

"That's what your race is called? Ma'lahn?" Nike craved for knowledge that this comer from distant stars must have had.

"Race meaning: humans?"

Murdermat spoke comlang correctly, but still had trouble expressing some of his thoughts.

"Yes."

"Then I'm ma'lahn."

"Cool." Morrisey took over. "Your home planet, is it far?"

"Far."

"Can you be more specific?"

"You don't have a name for the place I come from."

Quite right. Humankind hadn't named any of the stars in the center of the Galaxy or in its other arms yet. Some may have been assigned catalog numbers, but Bourne certainly didn't know these.

"Your—" Annataly had to search her memory for the right word. "Your t'iru ... It's not just a spaceship, is it?"

"T'iru is a symbiote. A living machine."

"A cyborg?" Nike prompted. "A cybernetic organism," he elaborated when Murdermat didn't reply immediately.

"No. It's more complicated. Life in the machine."

They had to content themselves with such a vague definition, for the different levels of human and ma'lahn civilizations' advancement made proper communication impossible.

"Down there, in the hold," Davidoff-Rozerer spoke again, "we found thousands of dead and disemboweled humanoids."

"That's what we do," Murdermat admitted less mechanically, as if Annataly struck a chord in him.

"We?" Nike didn't miss the opportunity to pursue the topic.

"We, ma'lahn."

"Wait, wait … Are you trying to tell us that you fly all over the Galaxy with gutted cavemen?" Morrisey couldn't help himself.

"We don't just fly with them," Murdermat said, and fell silent for a few minutes. "How should I p-p-put it?" he stammered, although he'd already been able to pronounce even the most difficult words with surprising ease. "We b-b-breed them, slaughter, and sell their meat."

There was dead silence. This creature, even though it came from a far more advanced civilization, turned out to be some kind of an ancient butcher. And to cap it off, his "stockers" were early men.

"Those corpses … they were our … our ancestors," Annataly said finally, words catching in her throat.

"I know." Murdermat confused them even more.

"Why don't you tell us what else you know about it?" Morrisey asked, easing up on him for once.

"We search for suitable, inseminated, oxygen-rich planets, then we put gl'wero colonies there … gl'wero are the beings you found in my t'iru … and we breed them like you bred cows in not-so-distant past."

Iarrey couldn't believe his ears. Also, he was the first one to shake himself out of the stupor they all had fallen into. "Do you mean to say that we're distant descendants of galactic slaughter cattle?"

"Yes. Thanks to analyses carried out by t'iru, I know that your DNA contains the signature marks encoded by us."

The captain jumped off his seat. "What exactly are you saying?"

"Gl'wero, which you seem to descend from, were created by us."

"Wait ..." Even though he looked equally agitated, Nike remained seated. "On how many planets did you breed these gl —gl'something?"

He wanted to dispel doubts about the origins of frozen bodies, or carcasses, as they should be called.

"On six planets altogether, but on only one in this arm of the Galaxy."

They winced as if they'd been hit over the head with a brick. As this piece of information raised hundreds of questions in them, they began to outshout each other.

"Shut the fuck up!" Morrisey cried raucously, lifting his arm as though he was about to hit someone to emphasize his words. Instead, he pointed his metal index finger at Murdermat. "Go ahead and tell us everything you know about it. Or there won't be any deal!"

Seeing that both the navigator and the first officer backed up the captain, Nike decided to do the same.

"I will tell you," Murdermat said after an even longer moment of silence, showing no emotion whatsoever again. "We created the first gl'wero by combining the DNA of the three most popular breeds of cattle known to us." When he saw their reaction, he immediately added, "I'm using simplified terminology to make myself understood."

"Okay," Morrisey said. "Go on."

"The results surpassed all our expectations. Over one hundred and eighty thousand years, by the hooman convention of measuring the time, we sold gl'wero to dozens of races. Then we repeatedly refined the combination of genes, striving for even higher quality meat. Unfortunately, this led to an ethnic—ethical conflict. We were faulted for creating Generation 311 of our product, which had crossed the fine line between a beast and a sentient being."

"And rightly so, as you can see," Iarrey murmured.

"Not necessarily. Back then it was just an unsubstantiated theory. Anyway ..." He paused for a moment, searching for the most appropriate term. "The Ssessmo Swarm made us stop further improving of our product's DNA. But we believed in the rightness of our actions and didn't give up.

"The demand for the Generation 312 was so great that my sench'ten began to specialize in setting up illegal farms, or mills as you tend to put it, in the most remote parts of the Galaxy. I was assigned to tend to the herd in this arm. Before my t'iru was attacked, I'd been in charge of breeding gl'wero and responsible for regular delivering the obtained meat to clients.

"I can't say what's been going on in the last forty-seven thousand years, although I have some suspicions."

"A lot has been going on, as you can see." Morrisey recovered his good mood and returned to his seat. "That swarm of yours was right."

"I don't subscribe to your point of view, hooman. I noticed changes in your genetic code, changes overwritten by someone else, who—intentionally or not—accelerated mutations which helped develop sentience."

"When did you manage to do this research?" Annataly asked.

"T'kharo of my t'iru ... the nanoscanners of my ship ... took your tissue samples after I'd been awakened."

Iarrey and Morrisey both held their breath for a moment, realizing that there could be billions of nanoobjects and/or nanocreatures around them.

"What do you mean: overwritten?" Nike, as usual, was interested in facts.

"Someone altered the DNA patterns we'd created. I think they were seirafu. Anyway, it was them who attacked me in this system. Having gotten rid of me, they took control over the herd and conducted further experiments to prove that the allegations against us were true."

"Our scientists have a slightly different opinion on this," Morrisey jibed.

"By the way," said Annataly, her tone suggesting that she wanted to catch Murdermat in a lie. "When did you establish this particular farm?"

"Four and a half million hooman years ago."

Whenever they thought they'd already heard the most incredible thing and the Alien couldn't say anything more surprising, he uttered words showing them that a true surprise was yet to come.

"If so, you had all the time in the Universe to notice that the hominids in your herd began to use tools. Isn't it a trait that distinguishes sentient beings from animals?"

"Many animals, even on Earth, use primitive tools," Murdermat said. "Have you not ingested the meat of species whose intelligence exceeded multiple times that of gl'wero?"

"Absolutely not!"

"What about octopuses, dolphins, monkeys?" Mr. Angel started naming them.

Nike had to admit that this creature's ability to probe minds was amazing. Murdermat's fleeting contact with Bourne was enough for him to absorb all the knowledge that man possessed. Now, he was talking to them as if he'd spent all his life among people.

"If your farm was located on Earth, why were you attacked here, a few hundred light-years away from it?" Stachursky asked suddenly, breaking the long silence.

"I was trading here. I delivered the obtained meat to the intermediaries, and they passed it on to different sench'tens. We did it to cover our tracks and avoid bringing our enemies to the herds. The location of this particular farm was classified millions of years ago. Only the ma'lahn who'd been told to tend to it knew about it. One hundred seventy-two thousand years ago, I was entrusted with this task. When I was eliminated, seirafu must have taken over. Unsupervised, they were free to manipulate your ancestors' DNA all they wanted."

"One hundred and seventy-two thousand years ago?!" Morrisey ran out of patience. "How long do you guys live?"

"Until we die."

Yet another answer—seemingly simple, but explaining nothing.

"Are you saying that you're immortal?"

"I am mortal. I can be killed."

"But if nothing bad happens to you, you can live forever?" Morrisey pressed on.

"There are no such cases recorded by our history."

"But is it possible? Theoretically speaking?"

"Lack of data prevents me from answering this question."

"Tell me then how long the eldest ma'lahn lived?"

"Dyaheve, the patriarch of our sench'ten, is … I mean was … one million, two hundred and sixteen thousand, three hundred and fifty-seven years old when my t'iru was damaged by seirafu, and I was forced to go to z'en. I don't know if he's still alive."

"Who are seirafu?" Nike asked.

"They're ma'lahn like me, only different."

As this was a really shitty explanation, Nike decided to pursue the subject. "Could you be more specific?"

"Rivals—" Murdermat began, but this time he didn't. "It's time," he said, pointing at the screen.

THIRTY-FOUR

APPROACHING the side of the wrecker, the dhri'll came to a halt. Annataly and Iarrey straightened in their seats. They waited. Suddenly, the wall of the alien vessel furled, just as the membrane door on board the t'iru.

Annataly was the person for the job because from their group of five only she still had an intact helmet. When Iarrey handed her one of the almost depleted phasers, she switched it to full blast. Father Pedroberto had certainly been notified of their presence, and even though the wrecker had no external weaponry, he might have prepared an unpleasant surprise for them just outside the airlock or in one of the corridors. Morrisey and his crew could only hope that the remaining cadets would be too scared to help the rebellious multilicensed priest. Hope, however, as the proverb goes, is the mother of fools. That's why the navigator, who considered herself a very intelligent person, had developed three alternative action plans to reach the bridge.

The dhri'll was now flying with the same speed as the *Nomad*, so when the outer bulkhead of the claustrophobic airlock parted in complete silence, Annataly saw the gray surface of the wrecker's hull. Exactly opposite her, sixty feet away, there was a rectangular hatch illuminated by a circle of light emanating from somewhere above her head.

Stepping out into the bottomless void wasn't as easy as it might seem. Especially when you realized that your destination was traveling with the speed of 0.05 standard light-speed. One mistake, one too strong push, one wrongly estimated grip, and— you disappeared into the blackness of space, becoming yet another frozen hunk that would hurtle ahead for billions of years to eventually burn in the atmosphere of a randomly encountered planet, or burst into myriads of fragments after collision with a similarly dead object.

Both visions made the navigator's blood run cold, for she'd never been in such a situation.

"Can't you get me closer?" she murmured pleadingly.

"It's the optimal distance to make a jump, Smiley," Morrisey assured her. "You'll be propelled to the hatch, but you won't hit it or bounce from it because you'll have more than enough time to react."

"I'd give anything to change places with you," she grumbled, still unconvinced.

"I wanted to go, remember?" the captain said. "But of course, you protested as if I meant to skin you alive, so please … shut the fuck up and jump. Ready … Steady …" he began the countdown.

Nothing happened even when he shouted, "Go!"

"I don't want to make you more nervous than you already are, Annataly," said Iarrey, who would have taken her place if only her helmet was a good fit for him, "but I must remind you that with every passing second our chances for survival weaken. The collapsar is already collecting up some bigger pieces of scrap from the L-point …"

Annataly was silent for a few seconds, and then—

"Fuck off and die!" she screamed, switching on the shoulder turbojets.

She got pushed out of the airlock thanks to just the right

amount of energy. The flight was horribly long, especially since adrenaline did its job too and time really slowed down. As Annataly glided toward the wrecker, it seemed to her the emptiness of space was thick as tar. She was lifting her hand so slowly that at some point, she began to wonder if it would grip the handle before she hit the ship's hull marked with hundreds of scars.

She managed to clutch the frozen piece of plasteel. The impact wasn't very strong, so she held on, announcing this to the whole world with a joyful howl.

She used not one, but two electromagnetic anchors to keep herself from falling off, and no one rebuked her, even though they all knew that this precaution would cost them another thirty seconds of delay. And every second was precious. On one of the Vimana screens, they could track the situation in the cluster. It was only a few minutes left to the tipping point.

Meanwhile, Annataly hung in front of the hatch, activating the system and waiting for it to warm up the mechanical parts of the lever. When a green light finally came on and the flap slid, revealing a small recess, everyone held their breath.

The first pull, and nothing happened; the lever didn't budge an inch. The navigator gave it another try, putting her feet on the hull, and this time she managed to move the lever and lower it all the way.

Ten seconds later the four-part hatch slid open noiselessly. The lights in the narrow airlock flickered on invitingly, but Annataly had to wait for the two anchors to shut off. Only when the electromagnets broke away from the plasteel could, she get into the wrecker, which she did in a few agile moves. There, it was enough to hit the emergency lock button with the palm of her hand and the hatch was hermetically closed again.

At that moment, they lost visuals. All they had left was audio.

"Talk to me, Smiley," Morrisey asked.

Nike noticed that the captain had gone soft on the navigator, watching her exploits.

He does have feelings toward her, Nike thought. *He just can't show his affection, used to hiding behind the mask of a troglodyte.*

"I'm in the changing room," she reported. "So far, no sign of a welcoming committee. I'll just grab a spare helmet for Iarrey and be back."

"No," Morrisey said. "We don't have time for this."

"The two of us will have a better chance of dealing with that clone-of-a-bitch!" she tried again.

"No, Annataly." The first officer backed up the captain. "Henrichard is right. If you come back for me, we won't manage to deactivate the collapsar."

"I could throw a helmet to your airlock," she offered. "Then you'll be able to join me."

"What if you miss? You'll lose even more time, and we'll gain nothing …"

"Move it, Smiley!" Morrisey interrupted their exchange. "The draft is already so strong that I'm afraid it'll tear my balls off."

"Oh. In that case, I think I'll wait a little longer—" she mocked, sure how he would react.

After he'd finished swearing, she added, "I'm in the side corridor now. Clear."

"What is this multilicensed clone-of-a-bitch up to?" Iarrey wondered.

"I've no idea, but he's not here," Annataly said. "I'm going to venture into the passage …"

There was a moment of silence. "Also clear. I'm on my way to the bridge," she added.

For a few seconds, all they could hear was her rapid breathing. Then there was a hiss and she spoke again, "I'm on the bridge. Clear."

"No way," Morrisey muttered. "He must be somewhere."

"I've locked the hatch," Annataly reported, ignoring the captain's last words. "I'm combing the area …" Rapid breathing again. "All side exits locked. There really is no one here."

"We'll look for him later," Morrisey decided. "Log in to the system and shut off the collapsar."

"I'm on it. Okay, I'm in. Switching to manual override mode ..." She went silent, and they held their breath. "How are your balls, Henrichard?" she asked suddenly.

"Don't play games with me, you—" He bit his tongue.

"He's holding them with his prosthesis, I bet!" Iarrey laughed. "Further delay won't put him at any risk."

"That's a shame," Annataly muttered, and louder she added, "I'm shutting it off."

Nike breathed a sigh of relief, realizing just now that he'd been keeping his fingers crossed until this moment.

"Well done, Smiley," he praised the navigator, earning the captain's angry look.

"I think I know where Pedroberto is," Annataly said, amused.

"Tell us!" Morrisey immediately forgot all about Stachursky.

"The clone-of-a-bitch went to sleep as soon as the cadets set the course for the jump zone."

"Wonderful!" Henrichard rubbed his hands. "Since we've already established beyond any doubt that gods don't exist and never have, our esteemed sponger priest is going to be the first man to attain eternal life."

"You don't mean to—" Iarrey began.

"Yes, I do. We'll flush this piece of shit into space right after we make the jump."

THIRTY-FIVE
THE ULIETTA SYSTEM, ZEBRA SECTOR

10/24/2354

As the shuttle bucked again, Nike snapped out of his reverie. His flight to orbit was over; they'd just docked to a cruiser.

A few seconds after the lights came on, the ramp lowered slowly, exposing a large, dim-lit hangar with a number of similar vessels in it. The evacuees were spilling out of all of them. Some soldiers in gray uniforms directed them to numerous exits.

A representative of the Fleet appeared by Nike's shuttle too. Standing at the far end of the ramp, a large man with boatswain's insignia on his sleeves read a brief message, peering at his holopad.

"Citizens of Delta. You are aboard the Federation's warship, which means that from now on, you are all subject to the regulations of the Fleet. You will be escorted to a designated section of the midship, in which you will stay until the end of the flight. We are unable to provide you with any comforts. If you have no food and water, you depend on your fellow travelers. That would be all." After a moment of silence, he added, "Any questions?"

"Just one," Nike volunteered. "How long is this flight going to take?"

"We'll get to this system's jump zone in four hours, then we'll spend ninety minutes in hyperspace, and finally, we'll need another five hours to reach the nearest transit station, where you'll be dropped off by our shuttles. To sum it up, the last evacuee will leave the *Djangonzalo Cervantes* in less than twelve hours. Anything else?"

The colonists had no questions. They were thankful to the fate and commanders of this ship for offering them a chance of survival.

"Second Lieutenant Statcherskee!"

Second Lieutenant ... Nike wouldn't have responded if the boatswain hadn't said his name. The wrong pronunciation didn't matter; Nike was used to it.

"I'm Stachursky."

"Follow me."

The started walking swiftly, weaving between the shuttles. Nike looked around him curiously, watching the uniformed people bustling about. Mostly, they were his age-mates.

If it weren't for the affair with Dredd's youngest daughter, I'd be one of them, he thought. *I might even be a full lieutenant by now.*

It took them nearly two minutes to reach the opposite end of the hangar, but only because they had to change direction several times to avoid the shuttles and patrollers being prepared for takeoff. Eventually, when they stopped next to the elevators, the boatswain told Nike to go to Section D on Deck 6.

"There'll be someone waiting for you, Statcherskee," he added before he said goodbye.

Only a fool would have got lost on this ship. All the corridors were well-lit and there were dozens of information boards and signposts on every wall. When Nike didn't know which way to turn at the last intersection, because for some reason, both arrows were marked with a letter D, he asked one of the few passers-by.

"Go left," he heard in reply.

So he turned left and after maybe fifty further steps, he found himself eyeball-to-eyeball with a black lieutenant, standing with his feet wide apart and hands clasped behind his back.

"My name's Stachursky—" Nike began, but stopped abruptly when he saw the short officer wince with revulsion.

"You mean, Lieutenant Stachursky?"

"Yes," Nike said, straightening his back. *Time for me to slide back to old ways,* he thought, *and saluted as per the Fleet's regulations.*

"I'm Lieutenant Mishkin. Come with me."

Nike didn't ask where they were going. He was sure some committee or other would ask him questions about the t'iru and the ma'lahn.

Recalling the events from four months back, he'd worked out his version of the story, knowing that the rest of the crew was dead and no one could tell truth from lies anymore. Besides, his new superiors would hear from him things so fantastic and unbelievable that there was no way it would occur to them not all the facts had been revealed by him.

He'd tell them everything that seemed important in the face of the war. And he'd duck the question of the collapsar, which they used to direct Murdermat's t'iru toward the New Rouen central star, thus saving him and ... starting the war.

If only I'd known then what I know now, he thought sadly. The truth was, no one could foresee what would happen, so laying the blame for the current situation at his door didn't make much sense.

He was going to put the blame on Morrisey because it was him who, as the commanding officer, decided to board the alien wreck. The clone-of-a-bitch had it coming, if only for his report, stating that the imprisoned crew member had been killed in action.

Stachursky wondered just how much he could and should reveal with regard to the true nature of the Aliens. Because saying that the alien flotilla belonged to something of a crime syndicate, and that the ma'lahn's aggression stemmed from the fact that they were desperately trying to eradicate the sentient "cattle" from the Milky Way since its creation threatened them with a galactic anathema—saying all of this was ...

It was so ridiculous that even Nike smiled under his breath. He doubted anyone in their right mind would believe in this part of the story. On the other hand, he knew the brass had to learn the whole truth; if he were caught hiding some of the facts, things would get very messy indeed.

Marching toward the hatch, guarded by two gendarmes, Stachursky made up his mind: He'd ignore everything that would show him in a bad light and confess the rest.

Yes, that's the way to do it, he thought, walking into the room with the members of the committee. *Let them worry ...*

THIRTY-SIX

DARSKI DROVE the rover to Ejector Three. The one which in the chief engineer's opinion was the weakest link. The reinforcement works continued. They weren't stopped even when yet another container with ore flew forty or fifty feet above the workers' heads.

Before Henryan got to the nearest pillar, a huge shadow fell over him.

"How does it look?" he asked, switching to the frequency used by the technician responsible for this work area. The bastard was in the control room. People like him never took unnecessary risks, but they took all the credit when it came to it.

"The structure seems to be stable now, but the braces aren't a permanent solution. They only delay the inevitable, they don't prevent it."

Having consulted the chief engineer, Henryan had suggested that the miners, apart from supporting the track with struts, should wrap the most damaged sections of the pillars with wide, thermoformable plasteel hoops, as was sometimes done with wrecks to hold fragmented hulls together.

"How much time do we have left?" Darski asked.

"Thirty minutes, no more," said the technician.

"Even if your people use more braces?"

"Look, this poro-concrete crumbles like chalk. With each launch, there are hundreds of new microcracks. It's a wonder that this ejector is still functioning."

"I see. Even though, don't give up. You must get the most out of it. Every load counts," Henryan reminded the technician.

Everyone, both the Board members and ordinary miners, knew perfectly well what the stakes were. Darski had explained it to them in a long, personal speech delivered a few hours ago. At this point, there was no one on the moon who hadn't consented to the punishing work. Even the technician hiding in the control room agreed to the conditions imposed by the officer in charge of the evacuation, although it was clear he wasn't going to risk his neck.

Darski glanced at the cliffs disappearing in the darkness; there, in a crater excavated billions of years ago, was the ore mined in this system. Plasteel structures of the force field emitters placed on the top of the cliffs protected it from space debris.

"Xavieric!" Henryan switched channels again to contact the director of the mine. A few hours ago, they started using their first names. Hard work brought people together even when they differed in a lot of ways.

"Yes?" Dupree answered almost instantly, although he must have had his hands full.

"I need a graviplane here at Ejector Three," the captain said.

"Is it very urgent? Can you wait a little?"

"How long?"

"Fifteen minutes. All our graviplanes are in the field now."

"Forget it!"

"If you need a ride, I can check who's going to fly near you—"

"I don't want to get back to the mine," Henryan said. "I want to have a better look at something. From on high."

"Talk to the guys on the site, they may have a gyroplatform."

"And what's that?"

"It's a contrivance used when some tall installations require maintenance. There should be one where you are now. They've x-rayed the upper parts of the pillars, haven't they? Wouldn't have done without a gyroplatform."

"How many people can it take?"

"Two, maximum three, but when overloaded, it's not fully operatable and certainly won't lift very high."

"What's its ceiling?"

"Under these conditions, no more than three hundred feet above firm surface."

Three hundred feet … Darski looked at almost vertical rocks; they were two hundred fifty, maybe even two hundred seventy feet tall.

"Does this thing move only up and down, or you can maneuver it too?"

"Thanks to gas thrusters, you can shift it horizontally, but only a couple of times due to the limited capacity of air tanks."

"That should do," Darski muttered. "Thanks, you helped me a lot," he added, and switched back to the general channel. "Guys, I need a gyroplatform, preferably with an operator."

He didn't have to wait long for a reply.

"What do you want me to do?"

Henryan winced when he heard the female contralto. Another *faux pas*.

"I'd like you to rise to the maximum ceiling just off the cliff, then shift horizontally over the rocks and make another climb, using the cliff as the firm surface. Can you do it?"

"It's possible," she said, a hint of hesitation in her voice. However, it might have been surprise at his unusual request.

"In that case, let's meet at the first pillar."

He jumped into the rover and headed for the exit of the tunnel. When he was directly under the electromagnetic rail-gun's rail, he heard the swoosh of a container being launched. He slammed on the brakes and looked up. Dust fell off both the pillars, one of the braces slid down a little. The technician was right.

All this will collapse any moment now, Henryan thought.

Nothing we do can prevent it. Not the struts supporting the track along its whole length, and certainly not the plasteel injections ...

The gyroplatform operator was waiting for him. The contraption, resembling a truncated cone, stood right next to her, on a trailer pulled behind a rover much bigger than Darski's vehicle.

"Are you sure it'll work?" he asked after they switched to a set frequency.

"Theoretically speaking, it shouldn't be a problem, but we've never tried such acrobatics before."

"There's a first time for everything, I suppose," he replied jokingly.

They got into a waist-high basket, and immediately fastened their safety belts. Then, the operator raised her thumb, but when Darski didn't react, she made another gesture—as if she was spurring him on. He figured out she was waiting for his response, so he raised his thumb too and the gyroplatform finally bestirred.

It moved upwards slowly as if it were a rocket equivalent of a snail. Also, it swayed incessantly, making Henryan grateful to the designers who hadn't forgotten about proper safety measures. When they reached the top of the cliff, the maneuvering jets were turned on.

The gyroplatform moved sideways equally slowly and hung above the jet-black rock.

"We're going to move upwards soon, after a short stopover," the operator explained.

Darski just nodded. It was her game; he wasn't going to interfere.

The gyroplatform began moving upwards again, as slowly as before. Twenty seconds later, Henryan saw what he wanted to see.

Inside the crater, there were many huge machines loading ore into containers and transporting them to the ejector's chamber. The electromagnetic railgun was the only fixed structure on the site, besides the towers on the ridge, generating the force field.

"We can go back now," Darski said before switching to the

director's channel. "Xavieric, listen to me carefully. We need a demolition team. You must have people here who can blow up anything?"

"What do you want to blow up?"

"The ejector's chamber and all the towers on the cliff. There must be no trace of human technology left in this crater. The machines, if they can't be moved, are also to be destroyed and covered with ore."

"Are you crazy?!" Dupree protested. "This might get me fired. It's corporate property—"

"The Aliens are going to blast it into bits anyway," Henryan said. "Besides, Etoile Blanc Corporation have left you here to die. If I were you, I wouldn't defend their equipment to the last breath."

"If the Aliens are going to destroy it anyway, why make it easier for them?" Xavieric asked reasonably.

"We'll do a controlled demolition," said the captain. "They'll blast the crater with kinetic rods, sending ore to low orbit. Your kids will be picking it manually for years to come before you raise a pile like this again."

"Okay," Dupree latched on. "That's a pretty good idea. Might even appease the CEOs. We're going to save trillions of credits, ri—"

"You're going to save trillions of credits, Xavieric. It's your idea, if anyone asks. Leave me out of it. If it was my suggestion, my superiors would have to ask your bosses before a decision was made, and we don't have time for that. By the way, I'll need that graviplane after all. I have to get in touch with the Admiralty if this plan is to hold water."

"Consider it done."

THIRTY-SEVEN

THE ANZIO SYSTEM, ZEBRA SECTOR

10/24/2354

"Are you out of your mind, Darski?" Rutta felt like he was having déjà vu.

Every conversation with the captain inevitably led to a point when this particular question was asked in one form or another.

"No, Colonel, on the contrary, I'm right in the head."

"Really?" Rutta sank back in his chair. "You've sent fifteen hundred civilians on board *Cervantes*, and you don't think it's insane? And what if the Admiralty tells you to fight?"

"Well ... then ... we'll fight."

The colonel knew it wasn't accidental stutter. "Huh?"

"I just can't be sure if I manage to get back on board in time," Henryan said.

This was a lie. He was one hundred percent sure that he wouldn't be on board the cruiser when it made a hyperspace jump. *Cervantes* was already heading for the jump zone, and he intended to stay on the moon for another two hours, until evacuation was complete. He just needed a good excuse, and might have gotten one.

"What?" the colonel erupted again. "On top of everything else, you're going to defect?"

"No way," Henryan shook his head. "But I've got a problem. With people. When I leave the moon, the workers will ditch the equipment, abandon their stations, and go about saving their own asses. And if they realize that we want to leave them behind, acts of sabotage may take place. Colonel, you don't want some kamikaze to flow their shuttle into our rod-ship's nozzles, do you?"

Rutta sent him a murderous look. He knew that this was exactly what was going to go in his protégé's report.

"One day you'll overplay your hand," he said tartly after he'd wiped sweat off his face. "And I won't defend you then, mark my words."

This was a lie too. The colonel didn't fully understand the Admiralty policy. According to his estimates, there were enough civilian vessels in the Inner Rim to successfully carry out the evacuation of all the endangered systems. However, the Council didn't seem eager to give the green light to such an operation. The requests, cyclically submitted by the metasector's staff, always met with a refusal, concise and quick, although much more important decisions required hours or even days to be made.

In fact, Rutta admired Darski's stubbornness and commitment. He didn't know all the details and didn't want to know them, but suspected that Ulietta's colony soon will be devoid of despairing people. And he liked the idea of it. He would be gutted if the Federation left tens of thousands of miners and their families to die. Not that he didn't have to stick to the official line.

"Colonel, here's something to pick your spirits up ... The director of the mine has come up with a brilliant idea."

"Yes?" Rutta said, a tone of resignation in his voice.

"As soon as the ejectors stop working ... and the first one's going to fall apart any moment now ... the demolition teams will start destroying the infrastructure."

"And to what end? The Aliens would do it more effecti—"

Suddenly, it dawned on him what the captain had just said. "He knows?!"

Rutta got blue in the face due to the sudden spike of blood pressure and immediately felt a sting in his wrist. His condition was so serious that the *en suite* auto-med unit dispensed a sedative. The colonel had been living under such extreme stress recently that he couldn't keep up with refilling the dispensers.

"Yes," Henryan nodded. "I had to let him in on what's going on, but don't worry, Xavieric won't say a word. He's well motivated."

"And how am I supposed to explain this to the Admiralty? Which part of the phrase 'strictly confidential' didn't you understand?"

"I'm a soldier, not a technician, Colonel. I wouldn't have been able to develop a plan to save the ore reposi—"

"So this was your idea after all!"

"It doesn't matter now. Dupree's going to take full credit and be set up for the rest of his life, and we don't have to go through the proper channels. Besides, if I'm not mistaken, the former Board of the colony had been informed about the situation a few days before the attack, so it's not me who should first swing for it."

The drug worked its way through the colonel's body really quickly, so the first symptoms of peace had been already overtaking Rutta, who suddenly became reasonable again and thanks to a low dose, didn't suffer any dulling effects of the medicine.

"I still don't understand what good it'll do to us?" he said much more calmly. "The Aliens destroy all targets, so they won't miss this one either, for sure."

"That's why we have to make the move first." Darski smiled in his characteristic way. "If there are no installations in the craters, there will be no attacks."

"So what?"

"With such low gravity, the impact of numerous kinetic rods is going to get the stacked ore blown all over the moon. Let's not forget that after we're gone, thirty or forty million metric tons will be left here."

Rutta laughed and then shook his finger at Henryan.

"Before Xiao has you shot for defection, you'll get a bucketful of medals from the Admiralty, and a letter of appreciation from Etoile Blanc," he said, amused. "Concoct a plan how to force the ma'lahn to back off, and I'll propose a motion to bury your remains on Earth. Free of charge."

Darski gave him a strange look, but didn't make any comment.

"Their attacks—" He paused, recalling the conversation with Fitz. "In my humble opinion, the Aliens choose targets, guided by the readings of spectral activity. And we're talking full spectrum here."

"Go on, Captain." Rutta clasped his fingers and rested his chin on them. "I'm listening."

It's not like him at all, Henryan thought.

"Their probes appear in successive systems for a few seconds, record all signals and then disappear. This way, the Aliens know the lay of the land … so to speak … not only in the visited system, but also in neighboring systems. This Bourne fellow, whom they 'absorbed,' was a weapon specialist, hence their extensive knowledge of the subject. Of course, he couldn't have known much about the Inner Rim's colonization progress. No one studies astronavigational atlases for pleasure. We only look at the systems we're sent to. Anyway … I think they select attack targets based on the amount of background noise."

He paused, surprised that he was the first one to have noticed this.

"It's not just about intra-system transmissions, but about signals coming from neighboring systems."

"This can be easily checked," the colonel said, typing a few commands on his computer. Before he got the results, he remembered one of the meetings in which they looked at this problem, but from a completely different angle. "You're a fucking genius, Darski," he muttered and disconnected without saying goodbye.

Henryan remained seated in the communications center of the colony's main dome, still protected by the force field cocoon. Never before had he seen his superior in such a state. The grand admiral must have had all the senior staff officers' health status monitored on a regular basis, but ... Darski had always considered Colonel Rutta mentally tough, even tougher than himself. Both were under tremendous pressure, however, and of the two, only he could use alcohol as a booster.

Henryan realized that in the last thirty-six hours he had drunk more than in the past month.

Yeah, because they serve sophisticated and expensive liquors here and Rutta is free of such temptations, he thought. Since the top brass is breathing down his neck, the stress of it must be killing him.

With that in mind, he reached for the keyboard to call Fitz.

"How is the situation?" he asked.

"The bad news is that there are only eleven thousand people willing to wait in the caves," the head of the scientific department said.

"And the good news?"

Olivernest smiled crookedly. "We had to turn away as many as three thousand volunteers."

"Really?" Darski shook his head.

"Don't you keep track of the reports?"

"Even my computer finds it difficult, and it has much bigger memory than me."

"You did it, Captain," said Fitz, genuine admiration in his voice. "Ninadine and I thought that eighty, perhaps one hundred thousand people would have to stay on Delta. You made us look like fools. But I don't mind. For the first time in my life, I'm glad that someone has proved me wrong."

"Thanks," Darski mumbled, quite flattered.

"No, we thank you, Captain."

"Is Ms. Truffaut going to stay?" Henryan asked, changing the subject.

"Unfortunately not. I suggested it to her, but you know what lawyers are like these days. Living in a cave, using clubs and striking fire, none of this appeals to them."

"In that case, will she leave on board one of the habitats?"

"No. She's going to travel on board a converted transporter, 460, which is already in orbit. By the way, Ninadine says hello."

Darski made a mental note to contact her at his earliest convenience. It was the least he could do in return for her hospitality and invaluable help. Without Ninadine, he wouldn't have done it.

"How's the situation in the caves?" Henryan asked, sticking to the matter at hand.

"We're going underground in an hour. From then on, it'll be complete blackout. All electronic gear is located seven hundred miles away. If it doesn't get destroyed, great. If we lose it, we'll depend only on you and your prompt return."

"I'll do everything I can so that you leave here as soon as the alien liners disappear from Ulietta."

"We can only pray that the Aliens won't smell out the reactor," sighed the head of the scientific department.

Performing a fast and full shutdown was yet another idea of his. At that point, whatever remained of the colony functioned only thanks to the emergency sources of energy which no one intended to shut off. They were supposed to further confuse the enemy, distracting the Aliens' attention from the tokamak hidden deep down beneath the sea.

"In light of our recent discoveries, I wouldn't recommend prayers," Darski said chirpily.

The news of so few colonists staying behind on Delta cheered him up, but only until he realized how great a risk those people were taking.

THIRTY-EIGHT

NINETY-SEVEN MINUTES past the zero hour.

The enemy still hadn't appeared on Ulietta, but it didn't matter. The operation was completed successfully. The last functioning ejector failed fifteen minutes before the scheduled time. One minute later it ceased to exist.

The Etoile Blanc's engineers could teach sappers in any military academy, Darski thought.

The damage in the ore repositories was impressive; not a single trace of the loading blocks or the electromagnetic railguns was left on the moon. With such weak gravity, the debris would continue to fall for an hour at least, covering a vast area and preventing the craters from being attacked.

Dozens of megabulldozers waited idly until they could bury the still smoking craters with mountains of ore, only to rest in the scrap heap which had been hastily created many miles away from the ore yards, but as close to the landing pad as possible.

In the meantime, the gigantic rod-ship left the orbit immediately after taking on the last bit of cargo. Darski had decided to take a chance and send the bulk carrier into a wormhole so that the ore would reach the Central Systems in the shortest time possible, for this option seemed to him real. Another thirty minutes and he'd be able to take credit for it too, unless, of course, the Aliens appeared on Ulietta before the rod-ship got to the jump zone.

The situation in the system was monitored by the *Cervantes'* officers of the watch. For the time being, van Vogt meters were silent, which meant that in the next few minutes no vessel, alien or otherwise, would appear on Ulietta. This was very good news because the two and a half thousand miners, who'd remained on the moon to mask the ore yards, were about to catch up with the rod-ship, traveling on board the last corporate transporter, converted with a view to evacuation. If the bulk carrier made the jump now, the people whom the Federation owed so much would be doomed to death.

Henryan's shuttle was intercepted by one of the destroyers in the squadron, brought to Delta's orbit specially for this purpose. Rutta insisted that the commander of the cruiser and the *spiritus movens* of the entire operation stayed close to the metasector's staff—especially during the final, decisive phase of the retreat, when everything could happen.

Minutes passed, and there still were no reports from the vessels guarding the jump point, informing about the detection of gravitational vibrations. Eventually, one hundred and seventeen minutes past the zero hour, Darski saw the holographic image of Commodore Hines. His co-commander was full of apprehension.

"The sensors have detected an impending transfer," Javiernesto said. "Six minutes until the jump."

Henryan looked at the simulator. The rod-ship's vector was bloodred, but it was the least of his concerns right now. He shifted his gaze and swore.

"The miners are nine minutes from the rod-ship," he announced, entering new data.

He wanted to check how much time he could save if he altered the course and slowed the bulk carrier down. The line joining the two vessels shortened, but didn't change its color. Darski made another correction, this time delaying the jump as much as possible. The vector in question flashed … and became green. That was reassuring.

Now, Henryan had to find out how close the two vessels would be to the enemy.

The rod-ship can moor for twelve seconds before it enters the field of fire, assuming that the alien liners wouldn't develop higher velocity than they had so far. Unfortunately, Nike didn't know anything about their maximum performance, although it was exactly the kind of information they needed at this point.

Henryan felt cold sweat at the back of his neck.

"What do we do?" Javiernesto asked nervously.

Darski hesitated. He'd considered various scenarios, but none with such a narrow margin of error. Twelve seconds is less than nothing, despite the fact that the Aliens would be still more than five and a half million clicks away from the automated bulk carrier when it made a subspace jump.

"Let's take this risk," he said with more confidence than he felt.

Hines didn't say anything. Both men were aware of the possible consequences of failure. Without the ore, the Federation wouldn't be able to stop the alien fleet. Along with the cargo, tens of thousands of colonists would be lost, and it didn't matter anymore that he'd tried to save them in the past two days, risking his own career, maybe even freedom. But at stake were the lives of two and a half thousand heroes. For he couldn't think of another name for the men and women who held the fort to the very end, regardless of everything.

"We'll do it your way," Hines said, "but please, think carefully about this."

Darski was adamant. "We mustn't leave them for dead."

"You're putting at stake the lives of millions, maybe even billions of people," Hines told him.

"I know."

All of a sudden, Henryan regretted that he'd given in to Rutta and changed his plans at the last moment. If he'd boarded the 407 transporter, he could order a jump in good conscience now. At worst, he'd die along with those he'd failed. That would be fairer and more equitable for all concerned.

"You can't put the decision off any longer," Javiernesto said.

"What do the readings say?"

"There are at least four objects getting ready to jump here."

Four alien liners.

The *Cervantes'* squadron wouldn't even be able to deal with one, but at least it could drag it away if only ... No, it could not. No one—not a clearheaded man, not a technologically advanced Alien—would take the bait and go after a dozen cheapjack goals, having a sitting duck right in front of them.

"Let's take this risk," he repeated gravely, entering the order and changing the course of the rod-ship.

"Are you sure?" Javiernesto looked as if he'd been told to shoot his loved ones.

"I'm in command of the operational division," Henryan reminded him. "And I'm going to take full responsibility if—"

"Wake up, man!" Hines erupted. "We'll all be sent to a penal colony if this cargo doesn't reach its destination."

He's right, Darski thought. *The Council will go bonkers. And the Admiralty, being under the Council's thumb, certainly won't hold back the fury of Chancellor Modo and her sidekicks. More likely, Xiao will pour oil on the flames, as the ancients used to say.*

"Trust me," he said.

"Henryan, listen to me ... I know it'll be hard for you to live the rest of your life knowing you abandoned these miners, but ask yourself a simple question: How will you feel when we lose the other eighty-nine thousand evacuees on top of it?"

"I'm not mad, Javiernesto," Darski said calmly. "I won't take unnecessary chances."

"Oh yeah? And what about delaying the jump? To me, it's pure madness. Those people knew what they were letting themselves in for," he said. "They'll understand our decision."

"No, they won't. They don't even know what's really going on. They think we are running away because of a supernova."

That shut Hines's mouth. He wasn't a fan of the Admiralty

either and he didn't like the way they'd tricked these people, but he very quickly realized that panic in the further belts would bring more harm than good. But these miners would soon find out what a whore the Fleet can be. Dying, they'd be cursing Darski and all soldiers.

"What are you going to do?" Javiernesto asked in hopes that he could persuade Darski to change his mind.

"We'll try to delay them. Move all the vessels as close to the jump zone as possible, go below the ecliptic plane, vector two hundred seventy degrees in relation to the current position of the rod-ship ..." Speaking, he entered data to the computer.

"Does it mean we stick to the original plan?" His co-commander asked.

"Yes, but with major modifications. We'll get closer. We'll be more aggressive. If we provoke them—"

Hines shook his head and finished for him, "—we'll lose even more ships."

"No! Look ..." Henryan sent the last bit of data.

Javiernesto smiled.

"You clever clone-of-a ..." he muttered.

Darski put all on the line, as the simulation clearly showed.

When the Aliens leave hyperspace, they'll see a charging squadron half a light-second away. The Federation's destroyers will start firing kinetic rods five seconds before the first t'iru appears in the system, to cause maximum chaos. The *Cervantes* will use up its entire missile supply, including ten nuclear torpedoes. Moreover, the cruiser with its escorts is going to fly right behind the barrage, straight at the alien fleet leaving the gravitational well. This maneuver should be so surprising, that it'll force the enemy to change course—and in this case, every second of delay will give the miners five times more time to pursue their goal. However, the Aliens will be in for the greatest surprise when the Federation's warships enter the field of fire and instead of evaporating ... will make a subspace jump.

"I have to hand it to you," Hines said after he'd run the simulation for the second time. "It's a long shot, but there's a good chance of success."

"You'd be fooled," Darski said with a broad smile on his face, "and I'd be fooled. That's a good omen."

"You'd better be right."

"You'd better be lucky."

They left it at that.

THIRTY-NINE

DARSKI TOOK a seat on the bridge of the *Chrisador Duncan*, the destroyer sent to pick him up from the moon. The commanding officer gave up his seat for Henryan without saying a word. He knew the stakes and was aware of the risk the entire squadron was taking. All of them kept their fingers crossed for the captain and his plan. And the battle with the—as yet undefeated—enemy was about to start.

"Six seconds to the emersion of the first object ..." the duty officer spoke in a dead tone. "The fire has been opened ..."

It was an age-old custom, a relic of the days when ships had been sailing the seas of Earth. Nowadays, of course, computers were faster and more accurate in relaying data, mainly thanks to quantum links, but no one was eager to change the rules, just as there weren't any daredevils willing to be ridden of other traditions of the Fleet, such as striking the hours.

"Three, two, one ..." Darski listened to the countdown without taking his eyes off the displays. "Engage."

A red icon appeared right before the swirl of vectors. Three decaseconds—the Aliens had that little time to react. But the blink of an eye was enough for their defense systems to zero in on the targets and open fire. The screens in front of Henryan were flooded with streams of data. The t'iru was fighting like crazy, but it didn't stand a chance against such an onslaught. The screens were ablaze with thousands of explosions, which instantly merged into dazzling glow.

Darski didn't know whether their success had been determined by the insufficient time the Aliens had for reaction, or maybe the t'iru defense systems were blinded by dozens of evaporating rods turning into plasma. What mattered was that the effect of human actions was seismic. For the first time in the history of this conflict, the shields protecting an alien liner were defeated, and it happened a fraction of a second before the t'iru was hit by the second barrage. The sensors went crazy, then everyone on board the *Duncan* started cheering. Not even one nuclear torpedo missed the unshielded target. The alien ship flew inertly through the rapidly dispersing spheres of atomic fire and began to slow down.

The captain didn't have time to whoop it up. The second t'iru had just appeared in normal space. It was met with the same welcome, although the attack was weaker this time. The third liner took a beating from the last salvo, faintest of all. The fourth one didn't even have to activate the defense systems.

But all of this was of little importance. The first alien ship dropped out of formation. Initial analyses showed that the outer armor was split open in several places, which in combination with radioactive contamination was enough to eliminate it. At least temporarily, because the ma'lahn in command was evidently still in control of his t'iru.

Darski enlarged the selected fragment of the battlefield and stared at the vectors of incoming alien vessels intensely. The second liner was just beginning to change course, thereby getting ready to fight with his squadron again. The third one followed suit. The fou …

"Galacticunt …" Henryan muttered under his breath. "What's this clone-of-a-bioprosthesis up to?"

The last liner, just as the first one, broke away from the formation, entering the *Cervantes'* squadron's intercept course.

The trick didn't work. The fact that three t'iru had been pulled away from the bulk carrier didn't matter. The lone wolf was going to destroy it nonetheless, since it had lost all its shields and armaments.

The whole operation gave us three extra seconds, which is nothing, Henryan thought.

The premonition of defeat dampened the joy that was being born deep inside him.

"The squadron made the jump," the duty officer announced a moment later, trying to outshout his cheering colleagues.

"Get me the commander of 407 transporter on the line now," Darski said, activating the personal force field.

When the director of the mine appeared on the screen in front of him, Henryan outlined the current situation frankly. That was all he could do.

White as chalk, Dupree listened to him saying, "The safety margin has increased to fifteen seconds. The velocity of the liner which is flying toward you hasn't exceeded our presuppositions, so there's still hope."

Xavieric licked his lips. His voice was muffled as he said, "For the time being, only I and the pilots know … I figured it would better this way."

"Yes."

Darski had a lot of admiration for this man.

If something goes wrong, he thought, *two and a half thousand miners, many of whom the director knows personally, will spend their last moments peacefully, happy that their impossible mission succeeded. Yes, Xavieric is right, they mustn't take it from them even in the name of truth.*

"You did what you could," Dupree added. "Now everything is in the hands of God."

The problem is that it's the Maker who intends to kill us all, Henryan thought, *but he didn't dare say these words aloud.*

"I'll try to buy you a bit more time," he said instead, getting a grip on himself.

"How?"

"We'll attack the liner."

The distance between the jump point and the *Duncan* was more or less the same as between the jump point and the rod-ship, with only a dozen degrees' difference. Maybe the Aliens would deviate off course a little to avenge their companion.

Remembering the eliminated t'iru, Darski looked at the readings. The probe relaying the quantum transmission from the battlefield was still working. The Aliens ignored it, going at the attacking warships first. After the squadron's unexpected disappearance, they changed course again and went after the rod-ship. But having lost over eight seconds, they weren't able to make it now. The damaged t'iru was loping along, falling behind more and more with every passing moment. This, however, didn't make the captain happy, though it should have.

He shifted his eyes to the rod-ship, which was to enter the effective firing range of the enemy in thirty-seven seconds. The transporter had been decreasing the speed for a while now, heading for one of the holds of the bulk carrier.

Henryan crossed his fingers.

"You can do it," he said, choking up.

Thirty-one seconds … He froze, and so did Dupree.

They both saw nothingness in place of the rod-ship.

"What the fuck …?!" The captain reached for the virtual keyboard. "Who dared change my orders?" he yelled, switching to the general channel. "Who?! Give them to me! I'll have them shot, and then I'll tear their corpse apart with my own hands!"

"Henryan …"

"Get me the Admiralty!" Darski was feverish. "Now!"

"Henryan!"

He looked up at the screen.

"I don't … My orders—"

"It's a corporate vessel," Xavieric explained. "Your orders couldn't override superordinate safety protocols."

"What protocols?!" Darski was storming.

"The Etoile Blanc's CEOs indemnified themselves for every occasion. The bulk carrier is fully automated. It's been programmed to leave Ulietta when danger rose above the permissible level. Apparently, the ultimate limit was thirty seconds. Our bosses never cared for people, only for profit."

"I'll bring them to trial!" Henryan didn't let it go. "They'll pay for their crime!"

"Calm down," Dupree said. "We have only a few seconds left. I want to tell you something before I'm gone."

Darski sat straight with his mouth agape. He had tears in his eyes.

"I failed you. All of you," he whispered. "It's all my fault. If I hadn't come up with the demolition plan—"

"You're wrong. Serving under your orders was an honor for us all. Don't forget what we accomplished together." The civilian saluted clumsily, like someone who'd never done it before. "Goodbye—"

The transmission was cut off, but Henryan didn't deactivate the force field.

"Make a jump," he ordered through clenched teeth.

EPILOGUE ONE

THE TRINITY 44 SYSTEM, ZEBRA SECTOR

10/27/2354

Ninadine walked over to a soldier standing by the hatch. When she put her hand on the scanner, her personal data appeared on the display immediately.

"Thank you, Ms. Truffaut." The soldier handed her a code card with the transfer documents. "Now go to Terminal 726."

The Trinity 44 system's transit station had received all the remaining refugees from Ulietta, but not everyone found a permanent place there, even though the station was gargantuan. The military had to bend over backward to solve this problem, and as quickly as possible. Soon, all kinds of the Fleet's vessels left the docks every couple of minutes, taking on board from several dozen to several hundred evacuees. Each such transport brought people to their new, temporary homes.

PA announcements, played without cessation, informed about the procedures, the location of registration points, and the lists of requisite documents. Ninadine was impressed by the efficient organization. There was no difference between Etoile Blanc Corporation and the army, which also seemed to be a reliable machine containing millions of perfectly matching cogs. The Fleet had been given a task of dispersing the evacuees and was going to do it in the shortest time possible, because in front of the station's docks, there was a long queue of vessels bringing in the refugees from other systems. At least, they were less numerous than those transported inside the cramped bowels of the pseudohabitats.

The soldiers helping with unloading watched the emptying containers with a mixture of awe and dismay. The army didn't offer any luxuries, but even they couldn't imagine traveling a distance of several light-years in such conditions.

It really is a miracle, Ninadine thought as she rode on a high-speed travolator heading to the other end of the miles-long arm where her terminal was, *that so few people lost their lives on this journey.*

Only three peopledied in her pseudohabitat. Two were killed in an accident involving a compressor, and the third one suffered a severe stroke. With no medical doctors on board, the miners could only watch their comrades' death throes. All in all, she'd heard of twenty-six victims of this cut and run, though these were just initial estimates. Ninadine would know the true number of fatalities when her wanderings were over.

For now, she was on her way to a newly built colony somewhere on the opposite end of the Inner Rim, near the border with the Inner Territories. There, she would wait for another transfer, this time to her final destination. She let her supervisors know of her whereabouts as soon as she got the assignment, in hopes that her bosses wouldn't leave her high and dry like they had on Delta. She couldn't be sure of anything, however, so subconsciously she was preparing herself for the longest vacation of her life.

I deserve a break, she realized, stepping off the travolator.

In the terminal, behind a see-through plasteel wall, she saw a group of more than one hundred people. Ninadine scrutinized their faces as she passed the checkpoint. No one of the raddled, dirty men and women looked familiar.

EPILOGUE TWO
EARTH, ALPHA SECTOR

10/27/2354

Chancellor Modo listened to the grand admiral's report. She didn't even bat an eyelid when Farland specified numbers and facts. After it had made a jump into the interstellar space, the rod-ship immediately put out a message. Two days later, it appeared on Trinity 44, from where it set off to the Central Systems after disjoining and leaving behind the pseudohabitats with almost ninety thousand rescued colonists.

"Do not worry. We have all necessary equipment at the ready. These people will be taken care of," Modo assured the Third Fleet's commander, suspiciously eyeing the officers who accompanied him.

Rutta looked exhausted, and Darski, who stood beside him, kept his head down.

"Also, we will put the colonel and the captain forward for promotion, recommending that the Admiralty countersign our motion as soon as possible. Furthermore, in recognition of your exemplary performance, the Council intends to decorate you with Gold Cross of Merit. Your contribution has been invaluable. Thank you, gentlemen."

Farland, Rutta, and Darski saluted and that was the end of the transmission.

Modo sat back with a soft sigh; keeping upright still caused her pain, especially since on special occasions such as this, she reduced the dosage of analgesic, not wanting her subjects—as she called the Federation's citizens—to notice her distraction.

"Fooling the Aliens with transmissions from uninhabited systems ... this idea seems brilliant in its simplicity," she said, feeling blissful numbness in her whole body after she'd been injected with a double dose of tronix.

Kaup was skeptical. "I don't quite understand how it's supposed to work."

"It's as obvious as the roundness of the moon, my friend," Benadetto rushed to explain. "If the operating principle behind alien probes is the same as behind ours ... and the reports clearly show that it's the case and that until now, the m'lahn have analyzed intensity of radio waves ... we can easily confuse them and direct them wherever we want, for example straight to the fake colonies. We'll record emissions in the most developed systems of other metasectors, and we'll broadcast them from the stations located several light-days behind Belts U and T. The Aliens, who listen for background noise, will go wherever there's most cackle in the ether."

"It remains to be seen." Kaup wasn't so easily convinced.

Benadetto laughed harshly. "I have no doubts that our soldier boys have come up with a good plan. Only one thing worries me: our modest contribution can be discovered too soon and ... misinterpreted."

Modo looked at him more closely. "What are you hinting at, Giancarlouis?" she asked.

"At our fallen hero," he replied waspishly.

"The clone-of-a-bitch knows too much," Kaup backed up the treasurer.

"Damiandreas will keep his mouth shut." The chancellor waved her hand dismissively. "He has too much to lose—"

"You're wrong," Benadetto interrupted her. "We humiliated

him, and people like him don't give up easily. I wouldn't worry about Stachursky. He's safe, but we ... There'll be buzz in the media. One or two crucial pieces of information, from an anonymous source, of course ... Maybe not now, but later, so that we have other, more up-to-date enemies in sight when it comes to planning revenge. This is what scares me, my dear."

"But the relocation was his idea!" Modo snapped.

"We won't be able to prove it without airing the recordings which incriminate us all," Benadetto countered.

"I think it's the best moment for our sorely missed friend to commit a spectacular suicide," Kaup suggested. "Something along the lines of: The old veteran couldn't take the heat and shot himself in the head. The sooner, the better ... if you ask me. At least, he won't have time for plotting."

When the Chancellor looked at Benadetto, he said, "I agree. The relocation of evacuated colonists is even worse than this Forge of his. If the truth ever comes to light, our heads will roll right under the feet of cheering plebs."

"Okay," Modo said. "We have come to a unanimous decision. Rubio should take care of everything."

Kaup reached for his private comlink and typed a short message. "You got it."

"Speaking of the evacuees, what are we going to do with these hundred thousand extra dummies?"

"What do you mean, what are we going to do with them?" Modo shrugged. "Rutta's transmissions will deal with the problem faster than you think. The Fleet have managed to build hundreds of colonies in places to which we want to direct the Aliens. Now, we must only populate them, so that no one sees through the scheme too soon."

"Aren't you afraid that something will go wrong?" Benadetto asked. "We're talking about a huge mass of people here."

"Would you rather let them go?" Modo sneered. "Do you want panic to break out in the Inner Territories? Who is going to believe in synchronous supernova? And revealing the truth about the alien invasion, which we are unable to stop for now, will lead to incalculable consequences. We will lose this war even before we stand to fight."

The chancellor paused and took a deep breath.

"People are bovine in many respects," she continued, "but at the moment we are their shepherds, and it is on us to save human civilization. The excess evacuees must disappear and, if so, let them at least be of some use. By sacrificing this handful, we will save dozens, if not hundreds, of inhabited systems. One life for a thousand, even for a million. This is more than acceptable. Future generations will appreciate our dedication, I am sure of it."

"Come on, it's time for dinner, and you're babbling about some people who, according to the reports, died a few days ago in Belt U." Kaup shrugged. "Darski did a great job for us, acting in strict secrecy from start to finish. Now, we don't withdraw the transit stations in time ..."

He smiled. "The Aliens will wipe all the evidence away more efficiently than we would, and there'll barely be a trace of the inhabited fake colonies left."

ACKNOWLEDGMENTS

I simply can't help myself and must thank several people who have made the impossible possible.

Dear Reader, you wouldn't be holding this book in your hands, and you wouldn't have an appetite for more (yes, there's more coming your way soon!) if it weren't for the great SF masters—Kevin J. Anderson, Jack Campbell, Nancy Kress, late lamented Mike Resnick, and David Weber—who all were kind enough to read *Easy to Be a God* (Book One in the series), made helpful comments and praised my work. Thank you, Kevin, Jack, Nancy, Mike, and David!

Also, I am immensely grateful to MaryJane Stricklin for her positive opinion on Book One and Book Two of the series, my three eagle-eyed proofreaders: Mia Kleve, Aysha Rehm, and Pat Olver, for an excellent job they've done, Marie Whittaker for her commitment throughout the whole book production process even though she's got better things to do having become Grandma recently (congratulations!), Michelle Corsillo for making it happen (again!), and Kevin J. Anderson for his favor and mentorship along the way. I'm sure Perci and Nicola had something to do with it too and I couldn't be more appreciative of their contribution. Last but not least, I'd like to thank Rebecca Moesta, the good spirit of WordFire Press.

Thank you, guys, for the one in a million chance. You've given Nike and Henryan a second life, which is more than I could hope for.

ABOUT THE AUTHOR

Renowned Polish author Robert J. Szmidt is a novelist, translator, and a former editor in chief of *Video Business, PlayStation Plus, Science Fiction,* and *Science Fiction, Fantasy & Horror* magazines. Szmidt's flagship novel series (a major bestseller in Poland) is a five-part space opera, The Fields of Long-Forgotten Battles.

He made his literary debut in the 1980s, and although his career path veered into other areas, he has never forgotten his roots. In the early 2000s, he went back to writing and has published more than twenty novels, a few novellas, and over twenty short stories.

A wiz at post-apocalyptic fiction, he is (not without grounds) called the Destroyer of Worlds. In *The Apocalypse According to Sir John,* first published in 2003, Szmidt foretold the Ukraine crisis and its likely consequences. His other post-apocalyptic fiction works include *Solitariness of the Angel of Doom,* and The Rats of Wroclaw series (*Chaos, Prison Bars,* and *Hospital*), which has been adapted into a thirteen-episode audio series and continues to enjoy popularity among audio lovers. *The Rats of Wroclaw: Chaos* is currently being translated to Korean and is going to be published in South Korea in late 2023.

Szmidt has traveled widely, crossed three oceans, and visited five continents. He is a prolific translator with a dozen video games, as well as almost one hundred books under his belt. He created two Polish science fiction awards and founded a website, fantastykapolska.pl, offering free access to the library counting nearly one thousand Polish SF novels, novellas, and short stories.

He is married and lives with his wife in the bucolic region of Poland called the Polish Jurassic Highland, where he can admire elegant ammonites in his back yard. He says, "When you commune with the past on a regular basis, you must have your mind on the future—for anyway, a hundred fifty million years is no more than the blink of an eye."

IF YOU LIKED ...

IF YOU LIKED *ESCAPE FROM PARADISE*, YOU MIGHT ALSO ENJOY:

Blindfold
by Kevin J. Anderson

The Silver Ship and the Sea
by Brenda Cooper

Noblesse Oblige
by Uri Kurlianchik

OTHER WORDFIRE PRESS TITLES BY ROBERT J. SZMIDT

Easy to Be a God, Book One

Edge of Extinction, Book Three
in The Long-Forgotten Battles series. Coming soon!

Our list of other WordFire Press authors and titles is always
growing. To find out more and to shop our selection of titles,
visit us at:
wordfirepress.com

facebook.com/WordfireIncWordfirePress

twitter.com/WordFirePress

instagram.com/WordFirePress

bookbub.com/profile/4109784512